"*The Dog Fighter* makes for an auspicious debut. . . . Bojanowski vividly conjures the voice of a strong, confused soul straining against desires and limitations he only half comprehends."
—*Washington Post Book World*

"This debut novel twists into a poetic justice that delves deeper than shocking bloodletting scenes." —*Chicago Tribune*

"A debut novel that delivers. . . . Marc Bojanowski makes hay of high expectations." —*Interview*

"*The Dog Fighter* is the most exciting debut I have read by an American writer since Jeffrey Eugenides' *The Virgin Suicides*. It is a relentless and remarkable achievement."
—Geoff Dyer, author of *Out of Sheer Rage* and *Paris Trance*

"A blood-sopped, sun-baked coming-of-age story. . . . Bojanowski doesn't settle for tilling an easy patch of soil, and this is partly what makes his novel so enjoyable. . . . Bojanowski's gambit pays off."
—*San Francisco Chronicle*

"Powerful. . . . What's remarkable is . . . how readily we become in thrall to the dog fighter's story. . . . There is much to admire in *The Dog Fighter*, not the least of which is Bojanowski's tenacious attention to physical detail." —*LA Weekly*

"The novel's idyllic setting, finely drawn with precise details, is evocative and unique—the perfect backdrop to underscore the villagers' barbarity." —*Portland Oregonian*

"Bojanowski's narrator has no name, but he is one of the most profoundly felt characters in recent fiction. Seeing his world, through his eyes, will change the way you look at ours."

—Dale Peck, author of
Now It's Time to Say Goodbye and *Martin and John*

"Bojanowski . . . has a gift for detail and a relentless dedication to his imaginative world. It's Hemingway for hipsters."

—*East Bay Express*

"Bojanowski's first novel is not for the faint-hearted. . . . But others will find a compelling plot and a strong new voice in this disturbing tale of destiny, corruption, and redemption."

—*San Jose Mercury News*

"An auspicious debut novel. . . . Bojanowski dispenses with most punctuation to produce a blank-verse, run-on effect. . . . It's a daring tactic, but Bojanowski pulls it off, drawing us into the narrator's mind and memory with a dreamlike transparency."

—*Seattle Weekly*

"Bojanowski's narrative is masterful. . . . He offers a sensitive interpretation of our expansionist history that manages to be remorseful but not simplistic, brave but not self-righteous. . . . The book is exceedingly readable and gripping."   —*Nashville Scene*

"A provocative debut. . . . Bojanowski is adept at charting the anxieties of a small city on the brink of expansion and the darkness of men's hearts."   —*Publishers Weekly*

"The riveting plot and passionate characters are as spellbinding as the horrific fight scenes. An exceptional story of human loneliness and passion that will haunt every reader."   —*Library Journal*

Marion Ettlinger

About the Author

MARC BOJANOWSKI graduated from the University of California at Berkeley and received his MFA in creative writing from the New School. His writing has appeared in *The Literary Review*. He lives in northern California.

THE DOG FIGHTER

Marc Bojanowski

Perennial

An Imprint of HarperCollinsPublishers

A hardcover edition of this book was published in 2004 by William Morrow, an imprint of HarperCollins Publishers.

FIRST PERENNIAL EDITION PUBLISHED 2005.

Designed by Renato Stanisic

Library of Congress Cataloging-in-Publication Data has been applied for.

ISBN 0-06-059758-5 (pbk.)

05 06 07 08 09 ❖/RRD 10 9 8 7 6 5 4 3 2 1

for deva,
to make good on an old promise

THE DOG
FIGHTER

ONE

In Mexico I fought dogs. I fought on a rooftop surrounded by bougainvillea and colorful shards of broken glass. Before the fighting I waited in a small room where bloodstained ragmen came hunchbacked from shadows to wrap my forearm in a heavy rug. Over my hand they placed a glove made to have metal claws. The leather of the glove softened with the blood and sweat of each fight and with each fight the claws were made more dull. When the ragmen finished wrapping the heavy rug they led me from the small room to a ring surrounded by yelling men. On these nights the sky of Canción darkened too slow for the eyes to see. The last of the sun always in the eyes and teeth of the dogs. Reflected into the ring from the broken glass buried in the walls. When the leashes were undone the yelling men stood shaking the metal fence of the ring. I crouched in silence and waited for the dogs to bark and show their necks. And then I tore at their necks with my claws. I let the dogs bite themselves onto the heavy rug so I could better put in their eyes with my thumb. Many times I snapped the bones of the small legs with my hands. I beat them in the heads with my fists. Once when a dog took me to the ground and went for my neck I caught her by the ears and dragged my teeth down between his eyes to the end of its nose.

I was a young man when I fought dogs in Mexico. There were many dog fighters then but none as great in size or as quiet. Then I was unsure of my words. But the fighting always was a language I spoke well. And the old men of Canción the men who have known fighting for as long as there have been dog fighters to admire placed upon me their most respect. These men spoke of my fights often and the stories they told of me then they still tell today. Of this I am sure.

———

As a boy in Veracruz my grandfather spoiled me with bedtime stories of men fighting beasts whose teeth were sharp as obsidian shards and whose eyes were lit by fire. The old man sat on a chair by my bed and the words of the old mans stories took the flames of candles and danced over the walls of my room shadows of men who wrestled sharks and wore the teeth of jaguars around their necks. He sat with his ruined hands wrapped in quilted cotton blankets laid between two charcoal braziers. Comfortable in my bed I studied the pinched wrinkles of his mouth until my eyelids closed. Lured by his whispering each night I followed my grandfather into violent dreams of glistening snarls and musky breaths. Dreams that were always the most beautiful and difficult thing to see. And each night in his whisper the desire to hear my own name in these stories of violent men grew strong within me.

Orozco went alone into the jungle with his dog and a one shot rifle and a miners candle lit on the brim of his hat. At noon into a jungle so choked with limbs the candle flame his only light. Orozcos dog went ahead following the scent of the beast. And when he heard his dog cry and ran to it curled with its soft belly torn open over the ground Orozco slit the dogs throat to save his bullet and knew the beast was very near and not afraid of him. But Orozco also was without fear. He knew that he would have to wait until the jaguar pounced from above from one of those wet black limbs and so he pressed on farther by licking his finger and thumb and putting out the flame and chose to rest his back against the trunk of a tree in that dark to wait.

And did the jaguar come then? I begged my grandfather.

You will have to wait until tomorrow. The old man teased. Then I will tell you what became of Orozco.

When I awoke the next morning he had placed in the palm of my hand a jaguar tooth. Dipped in silver and held by a leather strap.

Can you see Orozco waiting? My grandfather asked the following night. Looking to the shadows over the walls of my room whose shape I changed with the squinting of my eyes. My grandfathers whisper a warm hiss in my ear. The silver of the tooth cool against my chest. Can you hear him listening for the jaguars claws sinking into soft wood? Can you see him searching the dark for the light of the jaguars yellow eyes?

Yes.

Good. Now follow him to your dreams.

But my mother did not approve of these stories my grandfather told. And because of this he threatened always to take them from me if I ever shared our secrets with her.

I share my secrets with only you. My grandfather whispered. To everyone else I lie.

To everyone else my grandfather winked and smiled and shuffled from room to room of my fathers great house muttering to himself and scratching his head. When my mother asked for these stories I answered her only with silence. And for this my mother beat me while my father chose to read his books. But I did not care because I understood that her beating me only made my grandfather more proud and then as a boy my grandfathers stories meant more to me than my mothers happiness.

You cannot continue to deceive him. My mother yelled at her father. Our family has suffered enough.

But when my mother yelled at her father like this he only winked and smiled and shuffled from the room muttering to himself and scratching his head. And after she had beaten me always he came to my room and leaned over my bed and asked if I wanted a story. My answer a great smile in that candlelight. And before my grandfather kissed me on the forehead to say good night he reminded me each time.

Your blood is the blood of the men in these stories. This is a secret you and I share alone. Follow these men from the corners of your dreams and you will be them in the dreams of other boys to come.

My mother did not approve of the stories my grandfather told. When she was a young girl her brother fought a snake for money put on the bar between himself and another man.

The money to fight the snake was enough for only one drink. She told me.

But when I asked my grandfather for this story he hit me sharp on the ear.

Your blood is the blood of the men in the stories I give you. Do not listen to your mothers lies. He hissed. She believed that the mind of your doctor father would tame this blood in you. But I will not allow this. My grandfather leaned close to my face. And with the light of the candle flame dancing over the dark bronze of his wide flat nose he asked. Comprendes?

The snake struck your uncle on the face. My mother said. Come with me and I will tell you the story your grandfather does not want you to hear.

On this day my mother took my hand and led me from my fathers great house past the painted balconies and iron shutters along the side streets of our wealthy neighborhood. In the east over the Gulf of Mexico clouds the threatening gray of armor mounted the sky as my mother led me past wood walls built on stone ruins. She took me from my grandfather because it was a small game he and my mother played over me. Telling me their stories.

In Veracruz salt scarred gargoyles perch above foreign sailors who once called to my mothers beauty in words we did not under-

stand but understood the meaning of. She pinched my neck to keep
me from fighting men like these and hurried us on toward the zócalo
down hard packed dirt alleyways where a borracho stinking of
pulque urinated on blue and white glazed azulejos. His palm flat
against the tiles to brace himself. My mother led me past the large
square teeming with the destitute and starving dirt farmers in from
the country without work or food idle in the shade of cedar trees.
The days in Veracruz hot and muggy. Tram cars and American made
automobiles at the heart of the city honking their horns at mestizo
men hauling refuse carts sweet smelling from the rot of sugarcane
and goat and pig innards. Past the clanging cowbells of the ice men
who also sold milk in large tin cans slung across the backs of skinny
mules. She led me past the cemetery filled with only dead Spaniards
and past the cigar factory where my grandfather worked for years
rolling tobacco leaves. His fingers gnarled and difficult now to
move. Past a peeling customshouse and farther past iron and sheet
metal depósitos at the harbor and then down to the sandy beach
where dark skinned boys dove into green water from concrete
rompeolas built by hand by African slaves and mestizo and nativo
slaves to protect the trade ships anchored in the harbor from hurri-
cane waves. My mother sat in the sand and her soft pleadings were
quickly lost to the sound of the Gulf collapsing tired on the beach.

Your uncles cheeks went swollen over his eyes from the bite of
the snake. My mother told me. Her slender fingers dug a small hole
in the cool sand. Her eyes unable to look at me but at the clouds
threatening a warm rain. A dirty cargo ship staggered across the
horizon. Your uncle. She continued. Died surrounded by light in
some terrible unknown dark. Those once beautiful sad eyes in my
dreams nothing more now than knife slits in a swollen face. Promise
me that you will not grow to haunt my dreams like this?

Taking the leather strap she brought the jaguar tooth from
under my shirt and into her hand.

Please bury this here and promise me?

And because the jaguar tooth was not the secrets my grandfather and I shared. And because in this moment I was angered by her soft voice I said to her.

I promise.

I was twelve years old when my grandfather died in the night. His gnarled hands gone worse and worse until my mother had to feed him. But often even this he refused. In his last months I sat by his bed listening to the stories I knew already very well but now were told desperate with fever. I was terrified he would ask to see candle-light dance on the silver of the jaguar tooth one last time. But he did not remember. His mind was no longer his own but belonged to the fear of being forgotten.

You will not hear the lies your mother tells when I am gone.

I promise. I said to him.

Do not think that when I die I will not be able to hold you to our promise. His hiss that of a candle flame pinched.

The night my grandfather died from my room I woke hearing my mother run to him through the dark on bare feet after he yelled the name of my uncle from his fever and dreams. I listened to my mother cry as my grandfather cursed her. Cursing also my father who held me by the shoulders to prevent me from running to my grandfather when he yelled my name. My father the doctor who chose not to be with a dying patient but his only son.

When my grandfather was finally quiet my mother stood over him straightening the fingers of his hands and folding them across his chest finally able to touch her father but only now that he was dead. That night I cried listening for the hiss of his voice in the shadows of my room. I fought knowing that he did not approve of my weakness. Waiting for him to hit me sharp in the ear. But when I could not stop my crying I promised him.

If you forgive me I will never speak to her again. I will not speak to both of them again.

And only then did I sleep.

In the morning when I awoke my mother sat in my grandfathers wood chair by my bed with her fingers through my hair.

Those stories die with your grandfather. She pleaded in her soft voice. Can you hear me?

But I turned from her touch to face the shadows over the wall and from then was silent.

Still each night I searched for my grandfathers voice. Not knowing how it was growing strong within me. Other children soon laughed because of my silence and so I imposed upon them my great size. And when I fought and beat them slowly then did I hear his hissing whisper return some. And then one day sometime after his death when I threw a pillowcase full of kittens into the gulf and watching them tumble in the waves until they washed up on the beach drowned did I hear my grandfathers voice return completely. But now as my own. And in this silent voice again was the warmth of the candle shadows across the corners of my room. Of men who fought mountain lions armed with knives. Who charmed snakes with music. Now even more great than before.

But when my mother learned of the drowned kittens she pinched me by the neck and took me to my father sitting in his study. Behind him shelves heavy with books the damp heat of Veracruz ruined the ink of. My mother complained to my father about my behavior in a voice no longer soft but more similar to my grandfathers hiss. She held a length of sugarcane for my father to beat me with. Shaking it at him and yelling. But my father was a quiet man. Sure of the few words he spoke.

Do you believe that the decisions a man makes make him his own God? He asked me. My fathers light brown eyes serious over the top of his eyeglasses. These brave men of your grandfathers stories. Are the beasts they kill weak like kittens? I do not think so. He grinned. In fact I think your grandfather would be very disappointed in you today.

But my fathers questions were not enough for my mother and so she took me onto the stone patio of our house and told me to place my hands against the cool tiles of our fountain and there she beat me. But the pain was never as great as the shame that I felt from my fathers questions. Because of him I was terrified what my grandfather would hiss into my ear that night. I did not have the mind of my father then and my grandfathers stories were always more easy for a boy to understand.

In Veracruz my father stood taller than every other man. He was quiet but with great shoulders and large hands. A handsome light skinned Spaniard from Toledo where his fathers had made armor for conquistadors like those who first came to Veracruz with Cortés and his sixteen horses. Men the Aztecs believed grew from the spines of those horses. But from the stories his grandfather told him by the fires of those forges my father chose books and then medicine and then to return to Veracruz but carrying a different sword.

You were born in the first city of Nueva España. My father taught me. Each day a new lesson in the history of Mexico while I sat silent in his study. Moctezuma then was the emperor of the Mexican empire. To persuade Cortés to leave Mexico the emperor presented the conquistador with two disks. One of silver and one of gold. If not for these large coins history might have been much different.

I listened for hours each day watching dust spin in the sunlight coming down through the slats of the wood blinds. Listening to his stories of missionaries battle wealthy encomienda landowners for the hands and centavos of the Aztec and Zapotec and Maya and Tlaxcalteca.

The ancient peoples of this place where you were born were magicians. My father taught me. Olmec. They wore gigantic heads carved from wood and stone. Jaguar masks with thick lips and eyes of green serpentine and jade. These peoples disappeared south into the jungles of Chiapas and Campeche and Yucatán. Never to return.

History is the spread of power. From one place and people to over more places and people. Full of betrayal and murder. Victims forever having to prove themselves and conquistadors forever breaking the victims courage and will.

My father was a very knowledgeable man with a kind distracted smile. He spoke and read English and each day he sat with me patiently in his office teaching me mathematics and English and history. With noise of laborers working outside to put asphalt over cobble streets of our neighborhood my father was as patient with my silence as he was in waiting for my grandfather to die so that his son could be his own. His discípulo. But I was by then a boy more interested in fighting than my fathers books and learning. In breaking mirrors over the edges of wells and throwing rocks at stained glass windows of the cathedral.

Only when my father took me to visit his patients living in las ciudades perdidas the lost cities of Veracruz was I very interested in his learning. In the rubble of mud and straw jacales and canvas and palm thatch shacks he allowed me to put needles into the arms of wastes of men with no teeth smiling grateful for my fathers medicine. I unwrapped the wounds of slender knife fighters in the backs of cantinas. These dangerous young men I admired who only stopped themselves from hitting me when the stitches stuck to the bandages for fear of my fathers great size. On his patients my father showed me deep cuts red and swollen. Diseased skin. Children with measles. Faces scarred from smallpox. Eyeteeth and cleft lips. Showing me where disease lived invisible in blue sludge along gutters that still watered the most magnificent dahlias fuchsias magnolias and hibiscus. Once I met an old woman who was never sick but also had no family to eat the meals she cooked each day. Many of these people had nothing to pay my father. And he never asked them. They gave him food and small gifts of animals carved from limestone or dolls made of corn husks. They gave him glass bottles stopped with rags of home brewed pulque. He set these gifts on the shelves in his study with his books that he treasured.

And in each of these gifts is a history lesson as important as those in these books. He said to me. Why?

But I had no answer then. And my silence was much easier.

Some nights my father and I did not return until after my mother had gone to sleep. In the summer months when the heat was unbearable and everyone wandered to be out of their houses my father led me to the busy zócalo.

In this square they used to hang from gallows old pirates and sea adventurers. He taught me. Men with skin red like clay after so much time in the sun on long voyages.

In the zócalo we often sat at the cafés where patients came to speak to my father. To tell me what a kind man he was. But I enjoyed watching the boys my age throw rocks at terrible smelling buzzards perched on lanterns of the cathedral. I wanted to be with them and not my fathers lectures.

On nights when the men and women and children were swimming in the harbor to escape the mosquitoes and great heat of Veracruz my father led me down to the water. He had much to say on these walks. With time listening to my father I decided that he was not so much a quiet man as he was one who chose not only his words carefully but those he shared them with also.

These azulejos in this entrance. He taught me. In English the word for them is tiles. Blue and white tiles. The word azulejo is interesting because some of it is Spanish and some Arabic. Like the word arroz. Rice in English. And sugar for azúcar. Sugar. The word for los azulejos is similar to the entrance itself. A seven pointed horseshoe arch it is called. Some by design of the mestizo and nativo slaves who built it. Some by the design of the Spaniard who forced them to build it. And some from the Moors who designed it first. Remember that the Moors were in Spain for seven hundred years. And then the Spanish crown in Mexico for three hundred. This is how conquest also works. The language of the conqueror nestles into the language of the conquered. It is fascinating verdad? My father put his arm around me then but I turned away from him and he only laughed at this. With time you will understand mi hijo.

On these long walks we shared my father told me stories of how it was for him when he first arrived in Veracruz. For some time many of his patients did not trust him. They called him a peninsular because he was born in Spain but chose to live in Mexico. But with time word of my fathers quiet generosity spread and soon he was trusted and respected by many. I learned very much from my father during this time but still I did not speak. He spoke enough for the both of us.

When I am upset with your mother. He said once. Or confused by some idea in my head or something that I have read I enjoy walking. It is the best way for me to rest. I prefer it to sleep.

Once my father took me to visit a patient who had the flesh of his arm bunched and coming loose from the chemicals he worked with in a tannery. I vomited from the sweet smell of his flesh. My father told me to wait outside while he rubbed balm on the mans skin. On our way home he said to me.

They do not smell the filth and disease they live in. Just as we do not smell the soap and perfume of our own home.

Guilt is what makes your father weak. My grandfather once said. Great strength does not feel for anything but itself.

When my father was not visiting his patients he devoured books entire in afternoons alone. Reading in silence. The words his fever. My father was a quiet man who lived life quietly but felt much and for this and many other reasons my grandfather did not trust him. But still he encouraged my mother to marry my father for what his great strength and size would allow my grandfather in a grandson to shape.

I tell only you the truth of my secrets. My grandfather whispered to me many times. The candle flame wavering in the black of his eyes. His knotted fingers shaking some. My memory fantastic for the stories he called our secrets. I wanted for your mother to marry this quiet doctor from when I first met him. Be patient while I tell you why. You must trust me in our secrets. And I trusted my grandfathers voice even with his wink and his terrible smile.

———

While my grandfather was alive I never had this trust for my father. And when he was dead it was too late. My grandfather took me as a boy to swim against the waves of the Gulf. Waves the ships of the conquistadors had sailed into Veracruz on. And in this swimming I grew into my fathers great strength and size but for my grandfathers designs.

Your mother did not want to marry your father even for all of her love for him. My grandfather told me. She feared what her blood would do in the son of a man with those shoulders and hands. I did not like his talk of God but that doctor is lost in the maze of his own thinking. I held her hand and told her. Smiling. But he has come here to do good. I told her. And with time I convinced your mother any man who feels guilt like a woman is harmless. You are his son. My grandfather told me. But you are not so harmless. You are of his strength but my blood.

My father was sitting by the fire in his study reading when my mother brought me to him after I had drowned the kittens. She tried to give to him the length of sugarcane.

I will not do this. He folded his book across his knee and shook his head. I do not think your grandfather would be so proud of you today. He said to me.

But the blood of my grandfather was great in my mother. Her jaw clenched and high cheeks red. Her eyes lit by fire. When she beat me with the cane I could hear my grandfather whispering quiet over my mothers cries and with this I felt nothing for her. I felt only for the shadows of men standing over beasts in my dreams that my grandfather spoke of. And so when my grandfather came into the room afterward to kiss my forehead good night and saw this in my eyes his own dead eyes were much with pride.

Your mother did not want to marry your father. He had told me. Every day for a year your father asked her for her hand but she told him no. She was a beautiful young woman your mother. With a strong mind. But always with the fire in her blood. Your father read to her from books of poetry. He taught her some English. I did not approve of this English but I said nothing to prevent her from marrying him. What an intelligent husband he will make. I said. The fool and his books. His mind lost in the great strength of that body. Strong but harmless. Afraid of me. Allowing me to come and live with them when my hands went bad because he is so kind. How I prayed to God for what I could do with that strength in his son.

It was on their long walks that my father told my mother that he did not believe in God.

He said to me once that Jesus was the daydreamer of all great daydreamers.

Can you see him? Lying on the bank of the river Jordan in the sun. During when he was wandering all those years and no one knew where. Lazy on the bank in the tall grass staring off into the blue of those skies. His hands cradling his head. His ankles crossed out in front of him. Then uncrossed to itch without thinking at the top of his foot with his worn sandal where a fly had landed. A blade of grass in his teeth. The slender shadow of it passing the afternoon across his thinking face. Then there is a cool breeze. It moves the shade of a tree that has been sneaking toward him slow like the answer to a difficult question. Love your brother as you love yourself? He thinks. And then he says out loud smiling to himself. Fools that they are. They will believe that one.

I kept the beliefs of your father from your grandfather as long as I could. She told me sitting in the wood chair by my bed. I loved him but I was scared. Not even to God Himself in my prayers did I pray for your father for worrying of what God would do to him for these words he spoke. What God would do to me for loving a man who thought this way. But the excitement of these secrets your father and I shared was great. The excitement of sin. But still I feared for your father. And I believed then I could make him different than he is.

After my grandfathers death my mother sat in the wood chair by my bed telling stories of selfish boys buried in desolate roadside graves. Of men without mothers who are left to wander desert mountains chewing nopal to not die of thirst. I lay with my back to her and my teeth clenched. My father stood in the door of my room listening to these stories. Together they wanted to take the fever of my grandfathers whisper from me. But still I followed him. And still my dreams were the most beautiful and difficult things to see.

But much changed soon after the death of my grandfather. My mother became pregnant. She and my father both were very happy about this but still I spoke to no one.

After every day for a year of asking your mother to marry him. My grandfather told me. Your father told her he felt like some fool.

I told him of my dream of your uncle. My mother said. Of his knife slit eyes.

But I never saw the flames of those candles in the sad eyes of my mother. With my face to the wall I searched for the men of my grandfathers hiss in her soft voice.

From a window above a bench in the courtyard where your mother and father sat laughing and talking I listened to them then. To pauses in conversation when I knew they looked one another in the eyes.

Your uncle his head heavy with his face so swollen crawls across the floor of my room toward my bed at night. My mother continued. His tongue blue from his mouth. Laughing.

We do not have to have children. Your father told your mother. But she did not believe him. You forget that I am a doctor. He said to her. And that I love you. I sat above this in the window of the court-yard looking down on them knowing that what your father said was a great deception. That even the most great love could not prevent this. But I said nothing. I am the only one not to lie to you.

When my mother discovered that she was pregnant after my grandfathers death she went to my father. They sat me down in the kitchen and her eyes were with tears. She was smiling.

We will name him after your grandfather. She told me. But she said this only because they wanted for me to end my silence.

When your mother learned that she was pregnant with you there was much happiness. But your father asked her if she was sure.

Indudablemente. She laughed and hugged him around his great neck.

But not many days after my mother told me she was to have another child she caught me hanging a puppy from a tree. Other children watching this yelled my name while I wrapped hemp rope around the muzzle not to let it bark. I put the noose around the dogs neck and I raised and lowered it like a piñata. I lowered the dog until its back claws touched the ground enough so that it did not choke. And then I raised it and it swung dying until finally it was dead.

Again my mother begged my father to beat the violence from me but again he folded the book over his knee to not lose his place and he shook his head no. After this my mother woke us many times in the night crying my uncles name. Each time I woke I prayed to my grandfather for her death and the death of the child in her. I did many things to upset her after this. To make her beat me.

You need to be more calm. I heard my father say to her one night when they thought I was sleeping. For the child. He said.

Hearing this secret they had I only did more to trouble my mother. Between rows of corn in her garden I dug small holes for mice I found almost dead in their traps. With oil I filled the holes and threw into them matches. I stood over this with other children watching while my own eyes alone were narrow and dark and lit by fire. I stole from these children in their houses if I was invited into them. I beat girls. And when my mother learned of this even as she was more with child she beat me more and more until the strain was so great her jaw and cheeks reddened and I no more needed to pray for the child in her to die because I knew she was doing it herself.

Your blood is the blood of the men in these stories. My grandfather had said.

I was fourteen years old when my mother died. In this time while my grandfather was dead my mother was often the most happy I had ever known her. My parents like young lovers. For years I think she was able to end pregnancy in her without my fathers help. I do not think she would allow herself to be with him and for him to be with her and this was much that was difficult in their marriage. Even then I knew I had much to do with this. That the words of my grandfather in me ruined her. But my father was a quiet man. The words he chose were the ones that worked most powerfully.

He is dead. I heard my father say to my mother about my grandfather. This one will be our own.

But I prayed for the death of the child within my mother. I prayed to my grandfather. His hissing whisper my God. And the day my mother died a nurse led my father from their room with his face buried in his bloody hands. The room dark but for a candle like the one she had placed beside my grandfathers bed. The smell of blood clean in my memory as the smell of iron rust in cold snow. My mother curled on her side in a drift of white sheets. Her body still. A mess of blood to her side. The candle flame dancing shadows along the walls and up into the corners of the room. I stood in the doorway unable to cry.

Later that night my father sat in the kitchen by the fire of the stove staring down into his great hands. Dried blood still beneath his fingernails. I stayed to the shadows. At this time I was almost as great in size as my father. And this only at fourteen years of age. My father spoke to his hands as if they were my mother. Begging them to forgive him and hating them for not being strong enough to save her. To keep his words. My father had long despised my grandfather. But for all his strength my father was a weak man. Even in his mind. The stories of my grandfather had been too great. And when my father could not stand the pain of losing my mother and his only son to my grandfather because he did not use those hands he stood and buried them in the hot coals of the stove.

I did nothing. My father mumbled to the nurse when she wrapped his hands in aloe rags. This is the most strong I ever was.

I hated this weakness in my father. My grandfathers voice told me that to keep it from myself meant to kill him. But this was not so easy. For weeks after the death of my mother my father sat in his chair surrounded by his books. His hands wrapped in rags healing. Because my father was much respected as a doctor the rooms of our house had more than most. The openings at the tops of the stone walls between the oak beams allowed for the breeze of the Gulf to pass through bringing his crying from corners of all the rooms I listened to. I snuck at night like a murdering thief through the house holding knives in my hand and making hilarious smiles in the reflection of the blade lit by the moon. I studied our staircase to learn where the footsteps made the loudest creaks. I memorized the shadows to move in without being noticed.

I stood in the door of the room looking onto the empty bed pretending to cry for my mother. Wondering how it felt. The bed the nurse made was never again creased by my fathers weight. He slept sitting in a chair in his study. I stood for hours in the night or sat in a chair by the empty bed watching the moon slowly bring shadows to the room. I sat not asking my mother to forgive me for killing the child in her and herself but thinking of how I was to kill my father. My voice that of my grandfather telling me that he was to blame. How I would hide the blood on my own hands when I killed him. How my father was to blame for my own sins.

From the fire my fathers hands healed so smooth that he had much difficulty when turning the pages of his books. He sat for hours staring at the words unable to concentrate. He did not return to his work as a doctor. The careful words he had were almost gone now and he spoke only in mumbles. The nurse and some other women came to our house dressed in black shawls. They came with platters of rice and steaming dishes of beans pumpkin and squash. Eyes with much blame and hatred for me. These women they sat with my father in his study holding the beads of their rosary murmuring their prayers before my father silent. At night I crept through the hallways to stand over him where he slept in his chair with a knife blade in my hand held at his throat wondering what the cutting would feel like in the muscles of my forearm. Many times I heard him crying by the fire of the kitchen stove. Talking to my mother in his mumbles after the women had gone. His shoulders hunched. His greasy hair growing long and thin over his eyes. Many of those who knew and visited him believed he had given himself to drink. But we had no money for this. The food we had came from the nurse and the women who came to pray around my father. They sat with my father for some months before one day he stood suddenly with their eyes on him. He began laughing and showing them his scarred hands and his feet dancing before them.

If your hands cause you to stumble then you must cut them off. He yelled. The women became suddenly terrified of my father and hurried from the room. It is better your Savior said for you to enter life maimed than to have two hands and go to hell. My father chased them into the street yelling and singing. One woman dropped her rosary and my father twirled it around his finger like a toy and then wore it like a necklace yelling after them. Whoever blasphemes against the Holy Spirit can never have forgiveness but is guilty of an eternal sin. These are the words of your Lord!

After this my father began to wander from our house for days. He slept on the beach or in the sugarcane plantations outside Veracruz. He slept in the tall grass alongside muddy dirt roads where he begged for money from travelers and laughed at those who gave it to him. One time I saw him arguing with a man for stealing bananas from this mans stall in the market. The man pushed my father to the ground and for all his strength my father did nothing. I broke the jaw of a boy who said to me that he had seen my father stealing crumbs from the buzzards in the zócalo. Then I told myself that it was not because I cared about my father but because it was a chance to fight. It embarrassed me that my father was now a name followed by laughter and whispers. I refused to admit this but only told myself that my father knew I hated him and so he forgot me. He did not want to see the blame I placed on him with my eyes. The anger. His mind still alive some he learned how to forget who he was.

Because the nurse and the praying women no longer came to us I fought and stole for food. The old men of Veracruz arranged for me to fight for money boys that were older but not much stronger. I fought wild and lost many times at first. When I was fifteen I fought a man more than twice my age. We fought down by the water in an old warehouse whose blocks were made of crushed stones and sandy cement. The men stood us facing each other and we swung only one at a time and I beat him by receiving less of his punches to my face than his from mine. After this I could not see for two days. Several men carried me through the door of our house and left me on the cold tile floor of our kitchen. My head swollen and my ears hissing a high ring.

After the fights I lost my eyes were hot with tears from breaking my promise to my grandfather. Snot hung from my nose on my split lips bleeding. My chest breathing heavy fighting breaths. This was the only time I cried and I hated the feeling so much I promised my grandfather I would not lose anymore. But I did still. But not many more.

By losing you are learning how to win. My grandfather whispered to me and I believe this is true.

Soon the men of Veracruz came to know my name for something more than the begging of my father. I could not stop thinking of what they said about me. I began drinking some with sailors who told stories of men fighting bears in rings made of snow. Of tigers in distant jungles. I drank with the men I fought before until my eyes were blind with anger and fury and woke the next day with the knuckles of my fists torn and bloody and not remembering how.

Occasionally officers from the military with their sunglasses and mustaches came to watch me fight in the alleyways or in abandoned depósitos and they like the other men placed their bets. And then when I was caught stealing by the police they pretended to yell at me but only pushed me around a corner to brush me off and smile. Some even handed me money that I had won them.

One night after I had been drinking I came upon my father lying in the doorway of a house that was not our own. I had not seen him for some time and was very surprised. More than a year had passed since my mothers death. One of his eyes swollen shut. His ear bleeding from mange like a dogs. The edge of some book hidden uncomfortably behind him. I touched the cold metal of the switchblade knife I kept to his throat. When he felt the cold of the blade his eyes jumped open and I dropped the knife. Startled. But while the sound of it on the stones still rang in my ears he picked up the knife and returned it to my hand. He held it in my hand to his throat.

In this world there are men of books and men who know what is not in books. My grandfather had told me about my father when I was a boy. Fighting always is more than just words. It is the most beautiful and difficult thing.

But for all my fighting I had never killed a man. And then I could not do this. So I left my father lying in the dark of a door that opened into the house of someone else. I left Veracruz with his laughter following me. I walked that night over railroad ties beneath the stars until I was no longer in the lights of the city but in the shadow and dark beyond like walking from the light of some fire into an even brighter darkness.

———

For four years I traveled with work around northern Mexico and into the United States. Fighting and drinking and imposing my great size on others as I went. Hopping trains or by foot I traveled north through Zacatecas and Durango. Through country where the faint blue hills and mountains are honeycombed from so many abandoned mines. Unable to sleep in the rickety cold of a boxcar one night I passed under the full moon a small mountain city that shone blue with silver so much in the stones of its houses and buildings left from a time when reducing the ore did not remove all the precious metal. I remember sleeping by a long narrow lake and waking to the sounds of geese and ducks in the reeds. I once saw a mountain lion that did not see me come down an arroyo to drink from a fresh spring that I camped near. I witnessed half wild mustangs eating rich buffalo grass in the low country of the Bajío region. I rode trains past plowmen trenching dry sandy topsoil with wooden plows like those my father had taught me the Egyptians used.

When I was sixteen in the rock mountains of Sonora I found hard dusty work moving rock behind bulldozers and power shovels carving roads to link Mexico and the United States through the border towns of Nogales and Ciudad Juárez and El Paso. I watched great explosions take entire copper colored hillsides away momentarily coloring the sky orange. Below these explosions hundreds of shirtless men stood. Covering our ears as dust clouds settled on the sweat of our forearms like flecks of raining red gold. I watched graders scrape miles of shrubs and trees to expose dirt to use to level the roads over the desert of Chihuahua and Coahuila. We lived for weeks at a time in a land so desolate and dry we drank water warm from pouches with mold brought to us on the backs of burros. Over land so flat and barren small animals seemed great in size and where curious mirages consumed our imaginations. I worked to build roads for trucks to carry loads from the gypsum and silver mines into the United States. Gypsum and silver and copper and gold and iron and mica and marble and alabaster. These mines in Mexico but owned by American companies.

On the plains of Texas when I was seventeen I cut my hands on barbed wire stretching fences miles without end under that cornerless blue sky. Measuring days by the number of holes I dug and posts I set. At night setting fence posts in my sleep. Nightmares about bushes that if you touch them and then rub your eyes you will go blind. Death if you eat the leaves. Waking beside campfires doused in the mornings with orange piss from men who drink little water but much whiskey and tequila. Eating canned meat. I hid beside pickup trucks from great dust storms. Woke in the middle of the night by quiet wolves. Listened to men tell stories about work in the mines of Zacatecas. Of a worker lowered by rope into the smoking crater of Popocatépetl for sulfur.

By wide shallow sandy rivers ferried down by drowsy river men and by trains heavy with iron ore I traveled south to Ciudad México. When I was eighteen I hung from ropes tied around my waist dangling from the sides of concrete and glass buildings. Buildings built taller than those of the once great Tenochtitlán. Stories above the earth in black air braiding ropes to hold my great weight I coughed and spit black and green coins of snot near to those below. Daring men to fight me. My laugh muted in the roar of machines but my smile telling all.

And during all this work my hands only grew more strong each day. My shoulders more perfect for throwing my fists. The desire to put myself before other men more within me as my grandfather promised it was to be.

In 1945 during World War II in the north of California I worked in the Bracero Program as a laborer. For an entire year in the farm town of Burnridge I worked on a prune farm. In this small town I encountered the first woman I was with without having to give her money. This woman was the wife of a Mexican I worked for who also labored for the Americans but spoke English. Her name was Perla. I did not care for the husband but I believed then that I cared very much for his wife and so much that I would do anything for her. She worked as a waitress in a café for Mexicans. After work and late into the night I drank coffee instead of beer or whiskey just to watch her wipe counters with steaming white cloths. Her hands dry from washing dishes. Her fingers long and delicate. The other waitresses giggled behind the counter and smiled over their shoulders at me.

Once one of the other waitresses came to take my order but Perla hissed at this girl and then came to stand before me smiling as if nothing had passed between them. I spoke to no one but her. And then it was only.

Café por favor.

Nada más?

Por favor.

Late one night on my way to the café I stopped to comb my hair in the reflection of a front window of a hardware store. In the light of a streetlamp the windows of the other two story buildings and the redwood trees of the plaza were tall and dark in the window in front of me. The lights of the signs for the pharmacy and a clothing store dark around the plaza. A glowing white gazebo. Inside the hardware store a lamp shut off at the back. Then a young man came toward the front fixing his tie. He looked up to check himself in the reflection of the same window I was before but on the inside and there he found my eyes staring back at his. My hands making neat his blond hair. His hands at my neck. I startled him but then he smiled. We were two men preparing themselves to meet their women. At this time of my life I was working and earning money and I was taken with a woman. I thought little of Mexico and nothing of my father. If I spoke I chose not to speak in my grandfathers whisper. But still when this young blond man on his way to see his woman locked the door behind him he checked it twice. Then he nodded good night but said nothing. He did not look me in the eyes. Even as we had mistaken one for the other as the same. Both of us making ourselves handsome for the ones we wanted to impress. Later after walking Perla to her home I returned to that hardware store and threw a brick through the window. I have always enjoyed the sound of shattering glass.

It was some time before I was able to bring myself to speak to Perla about more than coffee. But when I finally did I made up stories about my family. My life. I told her things I had heard the men I worked with say to each other. I told her so much that was not true that when I told her my mother was dead this also felt like a lie.

At night after her work her husband did not come to walk her home to where they lived with many other Mexicans at a bend in the river to the east of the town. So I did. Perla and I walked slow and when I first kissed her we were below a railroad trestle. The light of the moon on the water and steel trusses. Some weeks later when I took her in my arms for the first time she kept her eyes closed from me. But I did not think this was important then.

She had led me to their small building. Her husband was gone north for the apples in Washington. We went in through the back and only after she believed everyone was sleeping. In the hallway with one light Perla searched for her keys in her purse and then placed her finger to her mouth and smiled. In the bed she shared with her husband she traced her fingers along my back as I lay with my face in her pillow awake but dreaming. She made jokes about how I did not fit into the bed. Later she spoke of how he hit her. Of putting makeup on her bruises. How smart he was never to hit her in the face. Of the other women he told her he loved more.

I do not love him. Perla said to me after we were together again that night.

This wife who in the sweet perfume of her bed one afternoon was to beg me to kill her husband. Pictures of them framed looking down on us from the walls. My eyes closed growing angry when I imagined him hitting her. Making love.

I want to be with no one but you. She said. Do you not believe me?

When her husband returned a month later Perla and I met down the Russian River on the bank of a creek that let into it. She washed his clothes and mine and while they hung from limbs or spread out to dry over bushes we were together on a quilt she laid over the sandy bank beneath some willow trees. Her husband playing cards somewhere or drinking someplace she said. A large bruise on her thigh she did not want me to see. The purple of the prunes we had picked in August and September. Yellow at the edges. Perla tilted her neck so that her face was to the sky. The clouds passing in the dark of her eyes she had opened now but not to look at me.

Why do you never look much at me? I asked her then. I kissed her ears so that she shivered. Soap bubbles reflecting clouds floated on the surface of the creek water emptying into the river.

I cannot think of anything but how much I hate still being with him even when I am with you. She told me.

You are still with him? I asked.

He forces himself on me.

Then we will leave. I said.

He will follow.

I am not afraid of your husband. I told her honestly.

I cannot be with you as long as he is alive.

Now you are.

But that is different. I am not as happy as I can be. Imagine how I will be able to look at you in the eyes and smile when he is gone.

I needed nothing more than to hear this from her.

Several nights later the bar for Mexicans in Burnridge was musky with the stink of workingmen who did not often wash. I had drunk there many times before I found Perla in the diner wiping down the tables. The music was loud and filled with cries in Spanish. I spoke to no one and the men in the bar pretended to ignore me. It was a game we played. This was sometime after midnight. When I knew that it was its most busy. The hands of the men in the bar cut and hard. Old mens faces gnarled as prunes after drying. Workingmen great distances from their families. Drinking.

At the back of this room the husband sat playing cards. I ordered a whiskey and after drinking it I took the small glass with me. Earlier in the evening I had waited under the railroad trestle by myself drinking whiskey and feeling how it was to be in the muscles of my forearm that night. In my hands. Close to the side of my leg I undid the switchblade of my knife. The husband smiling over his cards at the other men when I approached. Then the men at the table and many of those in the bar turned to the sound of shattering glass in the corner. I sank the knife into the husbands chest. When they turned to see him dead they leaped back as if the table were with flames. The husband remained sitting looking down at the handle. After the glass shattered only the husband and I heard the sound of the knife enter his chest. Warm blood came over the blade when I twisted the handle and soaked his shirt. He smelled of Perlas perfume. With his eyes looking into mine wondering who I was doing this I bent over and spit at his feet and whispered the last words he heard. Whispered them in my grandfathers hiss.

Tonight your wifes eyes are mine alone.

Cigarettes and spilled glasses covered the table the husband sat before dead. His fingers rested delicately like a womans on the handle of the knife. The other dangled at his side. His eyes had gone black as oil I had seen used to harden sand roads in the desert of Coahuila. I left excited. My hands shaking some I buried them in my pockets. The men in the bar stumbled into falling chairs and loud voices. Each others arms. The music continued to play and smoke escaped at the top of the door into the night. Outside two men shoved one another in the street. Another laughing on the ground drunk.

I spent that night along the creek under the willow tree where Perla and I had met in secret and planned her husbands death. Without a fire in the cold I slept little. I thought much of the husband dying in my hands. I said the words I had whispered to him over and over in my head like I had done before killing him. Then I whispered them aloud into the damp branch shadows moving closer to me soft in the wind. I began to think of what I was to say to my father now that I knew I could kill not only beasts but men.

For several days and nights I stayed by this creek. I ate around the mold of bread and kept cheese under a moss covered rock where I knew it stayed cool. I drank water from the creek and slept near fallen logs decaying with the sweet smell of insects and nesting mice. Perla and I had planned it in this way. But when I returned to the building by the bend in the river where she lived with her husband she was gone. I broke a window to get in and once in her bedroom I punched holes in the empty walls where the picture frames once hung. My hands bloody from breaking the window. When a neighbor came to her apartment I beat him until he did nothing more than groan lying on the floor. That night I went looking for the ghost of her husband. Yelling his name down brick alleyways and into the dark of windows that held my reflection.

One of the sheriffs deputies of Burnridge that arrested me was a short but strong young man with a blond mustache and serious blue eyes. I fought five deputies before he hit me in the back of the head with his revolver when I was not looking. He leaned against the bars of my cell picking at his teeth with the end of a key. I sat on the floor and held the knot in my head but I smiled at him and then he smiled back. His teeth straight and white and the most perfect in my memory.

I bet that smile will be the end of many men. He spit on the concrete floor at my feet. And then I bet it will be the end of you.

Because the man I killed was another Mexican the case was not looked into. For breaking into the empty apartment I forfeited the money I had and was only deported. On the train returning to Mexico I rubbed the palm of my hand with my thumb remembering how sweaty my hand slipped down the handle of the knife. I was surprised how easily the blade had entered the husbands chest. For three years I had spoken only a handful of words and most had been wasted on Perla. But in that time work turned a young mans body into a more terrible strength.

At the age of nineteen I returned to Veracruz. In Tijuana I bought a bus ticket and in the noise of the engines I said over and over in my mind.

You are a weak man. My voice once again that of my grandfathers whisper. Your wife and child died in your hands. And now you will die in mine.

Feeling the words deep in the muscles of my forearm to remind myself how easily a knife can end another mans life.

On the morning of the third day I found him. He wore tattered clothes and held a mud stained book tied with a leather strap close to his chest. For the entire day I followed him. Watched him argue with street vendors. A knife sharpener. Old religious women. Himself. His glasses were gone and he spent much of the day muttering or yelling and laughing and pointing at walls. The sky. He wore no shoes. At one time several boys less than half his size took the book from him and kept it. His words were not words when he yelled now but only yelling. They laughed wild and whistling. Swinging the book like some weapon above their heads. I chose to do nothing. They left him crying.

By night I followed him to where he was searching for food. He smelled of urine and the cuffs of his shirt were stained from digging through trash heaps. The flesh of his face ruddy like that of a workingman and not a doctor. I opened the blade of my new switchblade knife alongside my leg and he turned at the sound.

Anything. He begged.

But I gave him nothing. Not even his own death. I wanted my father to fear me but he did not recognize me when he turned with his scarred hands out in front of him. The burned out shadows of his eyes disappointed me. And there I left him for the last time.

TWO

From Veracruz I traveled north to Guadalajara and then more north and to the west to the sunlit city of Topolobampo on the eastern edge of the Sea of Cortés. In this city I learned of the need for workingmen to cross the sea to the small city of Canción to construct a large hotel there. In a dim room in Topolobampo a man with a pockmarked face sat behind a writing desk swatting at flies and promising me hard work on the hotel but good pay also and the chance for more work on the hotels and roads that were to follow.

First we need to fill the bones of this one. He spoke without looking in my eyes. Great things are happening in Baja. He said. You will tell your grandchildren one day that you were part of this.

In beautiful Topolobampo the night before I chose to take the ferry to Canción I witnessed an American fight a shark in a tank of water. I walked alone but with families toward the lights of a circus tent at the north of the city. The whites of the eyes of the children tainted beneath strung lights painted different colors. The paint curling on the bulbs above long eyelashes. At the entrance to the tent an organ grinder with one arm stood tall and thin with no emotion on his face. He wore a tattered blue coat with shiny brass buttons down the front. The cuff of the one sleeve pinned flat to his chest. He kept the organ pressed tight against his body to be able to crank the arm into its tune. Only I was tall enough to look down into his eyes.

Bienvenidos niños. He said flatly.

Ahead a man sat behind black painted wood dowels confined to some cell. After giving him my money I had only enough left for the ferry to Canción for the next morning. It was a foolish decision but I had seen posters of this blond American and the shark on the walls of Topolobampo and felt a great desire to see the fighting for myself. Into a cloth hallway I passed with the children and their parents. Framed paintings hanging from woven gold cord. The wood frames lightened by the sun carried on the backs of wagons traveling throughout Mexico. There was one of a blindfolded knife thrower. A man bound in chains underwater. The American with a knife clenched in his teeth. I stayed to the shadows at the back of the tent while the others found their seats. All of us excited by what was to come.

Soon the lights dimmed. Two young women walked into the center of the ring balancing on their tiptoes on heavy wood balls. Later there was much applause while a knife thrower threw his knives at one of these young women after the other had tied her to a wall and then placed the blindfold on the thrower to some music. In the bleachers children ate roasted peanuts their mothers helped crack from warm shells. Fathers yawned in the suffocating warmth of the tent.

After these acts two colorfully dressed young men and the organ grinder pushed a large glass tank to the center of the ring. Hazy water sloshed over the coping made of brass. At the sight of the shark the audience inhaled together. The organ grinder went to the shadows and soon the music from a dull needle set onto an uneven record played a scratchy waltz. The blond American came into the ring and circled the tank. He wore a robe of purple velvet. Walking slowly with the knife from the painting in his teeth for all to admire. The children in the audience looked to their mothers. The shark behind in its tank with its eyes dark pressed against the dirty glass.

The wind off the sea outside ran fingernails along the canvas tent like ghosts of poor children begging to come in.

We watched as the American climbed a short ladder the organ grinder brought from the shadows. At the top of the ladder the American handed the robe to the tall one armed man and then lowered himself into the tank behind the shark. Above this a string of blue light globes made the Americans skin more pale than he already was. His hair white.

Before the Americans head went under he took the knife from his teeth but his hand failed him then. He did not have the knife secured and it dropped to the bottom of the tank. Falling over itself the blade flashing blue light. The audience exhaled together as the American and the shark began circling each other. The American hit the shark in the nose with his fist while treading water and trying to dive for the knife but stopped when the shark was near and biting at him but missing. Children wiggled from their mothers fingers trying to cover their eyes. Several times the American dove for the knife only to come up for air. Hitting the shark to keep it distant.

When he finally beat the shark back enough to be able to have the knife in his hand the American stabbed the shark many times in the side. Blood filling the tank like smoke. The American and the shark were lost in an awkward dance with the sharks tail pressed against the glass wall at the bottom of the tank when it was killed. Finally the blond American came from the tank to the yelling. He put his fists in the air. The blood washing clean from him. I left the tent as the organ grinder and the two colorfully dressed young men pushed the tank back to the shadows to the applause of small children.

By dawn the circus had moved from Topolobampo over difficult roads to some other city. I woke with the first of the sun and wandered to the vacant lot were the tent had been. My stomach empty and the smell of still water nearby made me feel like I was to be sick. In the bright sunlight of that morning a haggard old woman went through trash left behind by the circus. Down near the water the shark lay in a curled heap. Dogs had torn into its sides during the night. Pushing it until its tail was in its own mouth. The teeth missing strangely.

He took them before the fight. The old woman said when she came to me standing over the shark. He drops the knife on purpose. She said. To make it more exciting.

I stood quiet for some time looking at the shark with its tail tucked into its useless jaws. Flies swarmed above the gums frayed like blood soaked rag ends. But when I turned to ask the old woman how the American removed the teeth while the shark was still alive she was already gone.

———

In early August of 1946 I was nineteen years old when I crossed the Sea of Cortés to work on the hotel in Canción. The ferry was heavy with workingmen. Wandering men dangerous and wanted but nervous when the land disappeared and there was only sea. On the rolling deck the workingmen sat in the warmth of the sun. Smoking cigarettes and tossing the ends into the painted blue water. They drank warm beer and handed each other tortillas wrapped around beans. Chunks of musky goat cheese if they had enough money. Tearing jerked meat with their teeth and dirty hands. Some to pass the eight hour journey more comfortably brought sombreros and straw hats over their eyes low and concentrated on the sound of the water against the ferry until they slept. Several men hunched over the railing admiring silver fish that leaped over the waves like skipping coins.

At first the women stayed below from the drinking violent men. A child came running up the stairs and across the deck laughing knowing what would occur if he were caught but then disappeared into the black door leading down again grinning. Husbands came above to talk of the hotel with soft faced young men wanting wives of their own but who were never settled and always traveling for work. Some of these men young husbands themselves disappointed after leaving behind wives and children.

When the shore of Topolobampo disappeared from sight a drunk stumbled to the railing and vomited many times into the clear water. One man handed this man wine so that he would have more than bile to vomit but the warm wine only made him more drunk and more sick and soon he was unconscious in the hot sun with his face pressed to the cool of the metal deck. I chose to watch as several men dragged this drunk by his ankles into the shade. On his back they dealt playing cards and laughed telling stories about this mans past as if he were not there.

After several hours when most of the workingmen slept drunk the women came to sit on the deck in circles with pretty young girls protected between them. Their faces sweaty from the heat below. The girls braided each others long dark hair. Whispered behind cupped hands when they noticed the workingmen staring at them. The mothers huddled in the shade of the cabin while the husbands played with the children scolding them to keep their voices down. To not wake these terrible men.

By noon the leaping fish had gone. Sunk like coins. Few on the deck besides children were awake to watch the passage. The sound of the water reminded me of the creek where I lay with Perla in my arms. But this air smelled only of salt. Not of wet trees and fallen logs and her perfume. We were some distance now from the smell of dirt and rocks. Of land. In the quiet of the journey I was quickly frustrated by my remembering Perla. I chose to ignore that she did not look me in the eyes when we were together intimately. I was a fool to think that she had cared for me. That I cared for her enough to kill a man that I honestly did not know if he should die. I never saw him hit her. Never heard him say a word against her honor. And to have her betray me. I had let myself be made the fool. My relationship with her while I was not drinking and imposing my size on others had been a time of peace in my young life. So much that I did not think killing her husband something violent but necessary. I decided this feeling of peace had been because of her. Now I was not sure.

I decided to end these thoughts by walking the deck of the ferry. I was a young man then thinking only of myself in ways I wanted others to fear me. To create and tell stories that held my name as my grandfather said they would. Soon I was drawn to laughter at the back of the ferry. A group of children crowded around a skinny toothless man who kept a pet scorpion in a mason jar. The face of the toothless man scarred by working in the sun. The gums of his mouth black but with shallow pink impressions where his teeth had once been. He held the mason jar at eye level for the children to admire the tiny yellow creature. They staggered back shrieking when the scorpion struck at their fingers touching the jar. At this the toothless man laughed delighted. Quickly I became jealous of his audience. Of how he possessed their attention.

When the mothers noticed me approaching they dragged the children by their small arms into the shade. Some husbands near a large box of hemp ropes and wrenches stood and crossed their arms. Some of the workers woke those who slept to witness the scene. The toothless man hurried to put the mason jar into his canvas bag but his dirty fingers struggled to untie a knot already undone. When the last child was gone I stood over the toothless man with my hand extended. My palm up.

Pendejo! A man hissed at the toothless man. Give it to him.

I held the jar to the sun. Turned it slowly. A drop of venom collected at the end of the scorpions stinger. Honey on a thorn. I had never before seen such a beautiful creature. It was something of my grandfathers dreams. My tongue tingled and if the workingmen had not been present I would have whispered to it.

She is beautiful verdad? The toothless man stammered his words. Holding out his grimy hand for the jar. I found her a year ago. I did not see her until she stung me. My arm went dead for a week. Before I kept her in a little box with some velvet. But in Pueblo I had to sell it to eat.

Knife tip sized holes were poked through the lid of the jar. I put my nose over these and the smell of the scorpion was a damp handful of black soil. In the reflection of the glass I enjoyed the audience that had gathered around me but some feet away. The toothless man looked nervously for help but those eyes he met only looked down. The older women crossed their hands over the chests of the children. Crossed themselves. Some decided to return to the heat below.

Her legs are not made for crawling over glass. The toothless man said but stopped when I unscrewed the lid slowly. I. He stammered. I.

To steal the toothless mans audience completely I handed him the jar and held out my hand. Children leaned forward. Eyes white and wide. They gasped when the scorpion staggered into my palm from the jar. My thighs shivered. This is when I felt most strong.

Fool. I heard a man say about the toothless man.

You would do the same. Said another.

The stinger at the end of the scorpions tail curled stiffly above its head. Almost to a vibration.

Count. I said then to the toothless man and the words were diamonds that cut the back of my throat having not spoken for a long time.

The toothless man gnashed his gums counting while I bent down to inspect the scorpion. My cheeks inches from its tail.

At the end of a full minute I moved my hand to carefully drop the scorpion into the open mouth of the mason jar the toothless man held. The scorpion slid along the glass walls to the bottom of the jar. I screwed the lid on tight. The toothless man began to breathe again. His shoulders dropping in toward his chest. I held the jar out for him to take but when he reached for it I tossed the jar over my shoulder into the sea. Three workingmen had to hold the toothless man back. He cursed at me. Spitting his words.

Let him be! A woman hissed. Her men looked to her and then to each other and then touched her arm to be calm.

I ignored the woman but smiled as the three men kept the toothless man held down. His eyes with tears. The muscles of his neck rose. Veins perfect for cutting. I knew they would not let him come to me.

Returning to the front of the ferry I slouched in the shade of the cabin and closed my eyelids to nap. I imagined the mason jar bobbing until the sun reflecting on its curved edge slipped beneath the surface leaving the light dull on the waves. Water poured in through the holes drowning the scorpion slowly. Its tiny floating body shoved against the lid. Clawing uselessly. The mist of waves broke over the nose of the ferry like glass shards cooling my cheeks. I held some trace of a smile still at the corners of my mouth for others to judge me by. For some time at the back of the ferry I heard the low sobbing of the toothless man.

Content now I dozed. In and out of the drone of the engine. The smacking waves. The constant sunlight and conversation muffled. The children had stopped trying to play marbles on the gritty surface of the ferry deck above the rolling waves and this led them to a game of tag. One boy strayed from the game. He came on tiptoes to my side. A piece of papaya in his small hand. I let the boy reach out to touch my forearm and then I caught him by the wrist. I felt his skin goose pimple when I narrowed my eyes and growled. The boys own eyes shook and in their reflection several men stood off to my side and rolled their shoulders. One man slid his hand into the pocket of his pants for the cool handle of a knife. In my own hand I opened my switchblade knife and at the sound of it the men straightened. I brought the end of the knife to the papaya and then I looked from his eyes to the tip of the blade. When the boy understood I let go of his wrist and smiled and ran my other hand through his hair. I was hungry and the papaya was delicious.

By evening the wind was strong. In the west mountains rose from the horizon small and insignificant at first but then high and

steep above the colorful buildings of the city of Canción nestled
before them. Soon two story rows of yellow and pink and blue and
white buildings came into view. The last of the sun glinted off iron
shutters that were to be closed over the windows to protect the glass
from rainstorms that come sudden over the sea in late summer and
early fall. Rainstorms with winds so strong they uproot palm trees.
Topple windmills and peel back roofs. But now the cool of the wind
brought some relief from the heat. From the shore came the smell
of coarse grasses and sweet flowering cacti across the salty water to
the ferry heavy with the stink of unwashed men. The women held
their faces to the low sun with eyelids closed. The wind noisy in the
folds of their serapes. Men held their sombreros palm flat against
their heads. In the distance coconut palms swayed along the
malecón. The stone walk stretching the length of a wide crescent
beach.

As the ferry came into the bay the water ribboned with many
small waves folding over themselves white in the wind. A rowboat
with a loud outboard motor piloted by a man with an unlit cigar
clenched in his teeth led the ferry through the narrow mouth that
opened from the sea into the Bay of Canción. Half naked boys
jumped from high rocks of the mouth calling to us. Dried by the
wind from when they left the water to climb back to from where
they jumped laughing nonsense words and curses. Some few masts
of fishing and old oyster boats wavered above the docks ahead. The
docks built of large sand colored stones quarried in the mountain
range beyond. I noticed the clay brick and stone towers of the massive cathedral rising above the center of the city. Only the mountains
then were more tall than the towers of the cathedral in Canción.

Workingmen lined the rails of the ferry as the women hurried
below for their possessions. One man pointed to the north end of
the wide bay and called through the wind for the men to look where
the hotel had already begun to take its great shape. The three stories
were without outside walls then but surrounded by wood scaffolding. Steel bars for reinforcement pierced the concrete and cinder

block sides. The empty hallways allowed the last of the days light and through these rose the wind moaning.

It looks like some monster. One man said.

Good. Answered another quick. Then I will not have to listen to you crying at night about how much you miss your wife.

Men without shirts scrambled up slender wood ladders of the scaffolding but stopped when they noticed the ferry. We stared back. Our eyes so distant from each other they did not meet but the postures we let our bodies take were still enough to tell that we were judging one another.

When the ferry docked the men that played cards on the back of the drunk rolled him into the water holding their laughter to not wake him. He came to the surface coughing. On the stone dock a short man with a muscular chest and a proud chin struggled to hold papers in that wind. He was well dressed and impatient looking. He cursed in front of the women without apologizing. This stocky foreman took the names of workers carrying their worn canvas sacks and baskets of woven maguey with handles coming undone. Those coming down the wood planks of the ferry held their hands in front of their eyes to shield sand blown by the wind. The workingmen stood in a line where I was a foot more tall than the man that was tallest. Meanwhile the short but confident foreman yelling at us to come to the hotel at dawn the next morning.

If work cannot be found for you. He yelled. You will not be paid for having made the journey. At this he smiled and turned to leave.

Most of the men from the ferry followed this foreman to a building near the hotel where cots were rented and the other workers slept. But with my sack over my shoulder I went to be on my own. Passing through the crowd with the wind I did not hear the toothless man sneaking behind me with his knife drawn. In the darting eyes of a pretty young girl before me I understood something to be wrong. I turned quickly and caught the toothless man by the wrist. The knife clattered on the stones. He fell to his knees holding his wrist above where his hand now dangled limp. The men left him crying on the ground hunched over himself. I smiled at the young girl and then walked on.

When the wind had died some and the sun had lowered behind the mountains to the west the last of the day was warm in the blue and green walls now dark as night settled upon the city completely. The wind had taken the heat of the day. The humidity was not like that of Veracruz but the warmth a dry heat from the surrounding desert. The mouth of the bay choked with shadows of fishing boats and the boys in their canoes tiny alongside. Down an alley a record played from a second story window. I could smell meat cooking. Oregano and chili. Behind wrought iron fencing of a balcony a young boy in cloth diapers played with a rag doll. His hand balancing himself dangerously as his dimpled knees held him up unsteadily. I walked through the streets of Canción content with where I was. Narrow streets led up from the water of the bay to the base of the steep mountains. These streets crossed by wide stone avenues that took the curve of the bay over the city like continuing ripples of water. Avenues lined with flickering electric lamps atop tall cordón log poles. Intersecting all these streets and avenues in an intricate maze were dim hard dirt alleys leading to tiny hidden squares with small cantinas and cafés where old men sat arguing. Around them mud walls crumbling to show bare the stones within them. And on these walls written in red paint the words.

Cantana a la chingada! Canción por los Cancioneros!

But these words meant nothing to me then.

As I continued to walk the moon rose and the spines of short round cacti in pots along the roof edges glowed in the dark. These same spines the Guaycurans used for fishing hooks and the large round bodies of them in the desert for ovens. Bougainvillea also grew but on trellises above alleys from rooftop to rooftop. Along electrical wires in the more wealthy neighborhoods. In beautiful glazed pots I saw white cuts healing in dark green bodies of nopal. The broad flat stems taken for meals. The red of hibiscus in that sweet smelling night the red of a bloodstained bedsheet in lamplight.

I walked alone those dark streets staying from the cantinas where the laughter of women and music welcomed workingmen each night. These cantinas where the women smiled and whispered while searching empty pockets before moving on to search for ones full. Instead that night I went down to the sand and ate salted papaya that I had stolen from a man in the market when his back was turned closing his stall. I cut it with my knife and enjoyed it with salt I kept folded in newspaper in my sack. Afterward I lay in the sand and picked at my teeth with my knife. I had not bathed in some time and so now I dove into the warm water naked. I swam until my feet no longer touched the earth and there I stopped to float on my back and admire the stars. I let my body be moved by the waves in all directions. My arms and legs dangled and my muscles relaxed and I realized then that I was very tired but with no place to sleep but the sand on the beach.

I enjoyed very much the warm salt water and the sound of the dark when I slipped beneath the surface with my eyelids closed. Underwater was the only time in my life that I allowed my body to be not my own but part of a drifting. My mind empty of voices. With my eyelids closed and the sound of the water in and out of my ears I was drunk. As a lonely young man that was the most easy way to be. I was floating for some time when I surprised myself and woke from a delicate sleep. Disappointed some that I woke I was so comfortable. The lights of Canción candles on the water around me. Little flames the size of coins swaying but without leaving their place on that gentle water.

A dozen men had come on the ferry to join more than one hundred others already working on the hotel. When we arrived that next morning the stocky foreman separated us into groups based on our skills or size if we had none. Immediately my strength

was noticed and working alone for two days I was chosen to reveal
with shovels and picks the roots of a coconut palm. The palm was
then uprooted using chains looped around the metal elbow of a
steam shovel. The salt air had peeled the paint and corroded the
joints of the steam shovel but still it lifted the palm entire and placed
it in a hole only twenty three feet away to create space for an open
air dance floor and concrete bandstand.

But what impressed me most was the scaffolding. Using warped
planks tied to sun bleached cordón logs with leather straps and wire
the workingmen had built an unsteady framework that rose just
above the third story of the hotel itself. As the cinder block and steel
walls of the hotel grew taller within the scaffolding the workers built
the scaffolding higher.

Do you think we could go on like this forever? I overheard one
man ask another.

You do not remember what God did the last time we tried.

At the base of the scaffolding diesel tractors struggled over light
colored rock and sand like slow moving animals put on the dry landscape to carve out terraces for shrubs and trees to be brought into.
Near the edge of the beach an area was saved for a large swimming
pool that was to have a bar made of cut palm trees and a thatched
palm roof. Down to this strong shouldered masons built stout rock
walls and beautiful arches intricately detailed with tiny azulejos over
stone paths to be lined with bougainvillea.

The work from dawn until just before dark was long and taxing
but never more than any other work we had done with our hands in
our lives. The faces of the workingmen raw from the sun. Noses
swollen from drink. In the mornings we put on our chapped lips animal fat that grew overnight in cast iron pots heavy with stew. When
the palms of the masons split from lye I watched them fill these splits
with wood sap or tobacco juice to stop the bleeding. Those men
working stories above the rest of us rubbed candle wax along the
handles of their hammers and trowels to prevent them from slipping

from their sweaty hands. We worked with our shirts wrapped around our heads. The men calling out vulgar jokes to one another over sunburned shoulders and backs.

Soon I was given the work of hoisting boards to the top levels of the scaffolding. I operated a crane using hemp ropes and an old pulley to lift as many boards and cinder blocks as was possible up to where two other men unloaded them for the scaffolding and inside walls. The men watched in awe of my great strength. Rumors of what had happened with the toothless man and the scorpion on the ferry took like fire among them. They feared me and preferred that I work alone.

During the day concrete dust fell through the light of the hallways as it had done through blinds of my fathers study. It settled around the base of the hotel for the feet of the men some bare to leave tracks in. Operating the crane at the center of all this working satisfied me greatly. I did not think of Veracruz or Perla much at all. The mens stares while I lifted great loads and the rumors they spread during lunch when I sat alone thrilled me. My own thoughts of others thinking of me was a great distraction. I spoke to no one to encourage the attention they gave me.

At the end of my first month on the hotel a worker returned drunk one afternoon staggering. Laughing to himself and pointing to the ground and sky. Some of the workers insisted he leave but the stocky foreman whose job it was to watch over the workers from a hammock he hung in the shade of two palms ordered the workingmen to let the drunk continue. Less than an hour later the drunk fell from the third floor of the scaffolding onto an uneven pile of cinder blocks below. His left leg bent out at an awkward angle from his hip. His neck broken. I did not witness this man fall but I did crowd around when several workers lifted him onto a cot to carry him away. This man went in and out of consciousness vomiting from the pain. But during the entire scene the foreman never rose from his hammock. Never uncradled the back of his head with his soft hands.

The name of this foreman was Eduardo. He would be the first to tell me of the fighting of dogs.

Until the scaffolding rose above the third story of the hotel for the construction of the fourth only the towers of the cathedral had stood taller than the two and three story buildings of Canción. But now the hotel was to have seven floors with more than one hundred rooms facing either the sea or the mountains beyond. A casino and restaurant were planned for the top floor where large glass windows would offer a tremendous view of the bay. After work at dusk I swam in the bay or relaxed underwater with my eyelids closed listening to the silence. I had not been drinking since my arrival in Canción. I slept most nights on the beach but also on the top floor of the hotel. I fell asleep to the most beautiful sky of stars and woke each morning to the most beautiful suns. Suns that were to be for American movie stars that would eat in the restaurant and lie by the pool and have their pictures taken to be sent back to the travel agencies to catch the attention of fishermen and tourists.

To check on the progress of the hotel the American investors came regularly to Canción. They stood with their backs to the city unable to see the towers of the cathedral. The beauty of old fig trees and date palms in the plaza. They drove north sometimes to the electrical station or to the depósitos along the harbor where oyster shells for decades had been heaped stinking but now sat empty and perfect for talk of new hotels. On the still water of the bay the investors landed in a small silver plane. Dozens of boys carrying steel harpoons went out in their canoes to greet them. For the boys the investors threw handfuls of nickels and dimes and pennies that fell shimmering through the clear water to the sand and coral below. While the Americans in their dark colored suits stood in the sand with the businessmen of Canción discussing the work on the hotel the boys dove after the coins as their fathers and brothers had done before but for pearls. The boys crawled over the silver plane or took turns sitting in the seat of the pilot while the pilot himself traded for pearls and mother of pearl that some of the boys kept in leather pouches tied around their necks. Rusted fishing boats came sluggishly in through the narrow channel leaving long trails of black smoke. The smoke washed over the silver plane and shirtless boys. Their skin darkened by the sun and scrubbed clean by the salt water.

When the investors were expected Eduardo told us to stay busy and not to waste time looking down on these men from where we were above working for them. The Americans draped their coats over their arms and dabbed at their pink foreheads with expensive handkerchiefs. No one man stood out in particular but all the men the investors and the businessmen alike took notes as if to report to someone more important.

One day when the investors were inspecting the progress of the hotel one worker pretended to sink the claw of his hammer into the backs of the Americans heads from where he stood on the scaffolding. The workingmen laughed at this gesture and those of the Mexican businessmen who witnessed it put their hands on the shoulders of the American investors and led them away. Later Eduardo was to have this man beaten.

But not so much so that he can no longer carry the blocks.

Satisfied with the progress the investors always left Canción before sunset.

Most days were uneventful though. The hot metal engines of the earthmoving tractors tinked cooling as the last trowels spreading mortar disappeared into the noisy wind of the evening. The men spoke in tired laughs as they stowed tools for the night. I had little money for food and none yet to be able to rent a room. And because I did not want to sleep with the men in the dormitory nearby I walked the streets until it was dark enough to return to the hotel to sleep on the concrete of the top floor without being noticed climbing the scaffolding.

But one night when I returned a man stood waiting for me. Calmly smoking a cigarette while admiring the lights of the city sprinkled over the bay. From the shadows his clothes took I knew that he was not a workingman but his frame was muscular still. His shoulders compact and strong. It was the foreman Eduardo who turned when he heard me step from the creak of the wood ladder.

Buenas noches. He smiled. Speaking in a normal voice but one I was not used to hearing at the top of the hotel after dark being quiet so as not to be caught. It is a beautiful view you have from here. He said when I did not answer.

Wondering if we were alone I looked over the top floor.

Do not worry. Eduardo smiled. There is nothing for you to fear.

When still I did not answer the stocky foreman understood that I was suspicious of him and he smiled more. He dropped his cigarette and put it out with the toe of his shiny black shoe reflecting the streetlights of the city below.

I need you for a small job. Eduardo said then in a serious voice as he reached into the pocket of his pants for a penknife. I had seen him use this knife many times when lying in the hammock to clean under his fingernails. Only for a small job. He continued. But something that pays better than this.

How much better? I asked.

Better. He answered.

I let my fists relax now that I understood why he had been waiting for me. That he knew where to find me told me that I had to think carefully about how to deal with this man.

You know they told me that you did not know how to talk. Eduardo said then. That you had no tongue.

Who? I asked.

Them. He gestured with his hand to mean the workingmen.

Tell me which one.

It is not important. But I like your attitude. Señor Cantana will like your attitude also. Eduardo took a step forward and the soles of his shoes made a hard noise on the concrete floor. It was unlike that of the workingmen in huaraches or bare feet. He kept his eyes on his nails until he asked if I knew of the Cantana he spoke of. When he asked this his eyes were staring into mine very seriously.

I have heard them talk. I answered.

Who? He asked.

Them. I gestured with my hand.

Bueno. Eduardo smiled. For a small man he was not afraid of me. He folded the knife and returned it to his pants pocket before continuing. Then you already know why you should take my offer for this small job?

I am not afraid of Cantana. I answered.

No reason to be. But understand you will fear the three dozen men armed with knives and guns and the dogs that lead them to you. Eduardo rubbed his nails clean on the front of his shirt and then held them to the moonlight. And do not be a fool and think that they will be the ones to end you. He warned. Take some time to think about this. But remember. He smiled. The money is better.

In the afternoons at the hotel the workingmen rested in what shade there was telling stories and making up lies. We spooned chipotle salsa over cold rice and beans and squeezed limón over fried eggs wrapped in tortillas that we warmed on rocks set around a cook fire built directly onto the concrete floor. The men passed around bottles of warm beer or damiana. Their hands stained from wood sap and grimy fingernails offering the bottles to even me but I refused. We urinated off the top floor of the hotel and went to the bathroom in buckets set in corners. After our meals we rolled cigarettes to relax and those who wore hats for the sun lowered them over their eyes for short naps. The strong evening winds came through the empty hallways moaning. Snapping shirts from nails where the men hung them. Carrying them out over the bay collapsing and changing shape like some strange bird before landing on the water and sinking. I mashed the food against the roof of my mouth so to be able to hear the words of the men clearly in my head. They spoke of their travels and work. Some told stories of women they loved or money they lost or won. Some like myself had greater secrets and spoke little or none at all.

But it was from these men that I first overheard the name of

Cantana after seeing it written more and more on the walls. I was jealous of this mans name. Wanting to have it be my own name the workingmen spoke of with fear and uncertainty. Of the power and mystery it held. The men said that Cantana was the wealthiest businessman in all of Baja California and some distance into northern Mexico. El Tapado many called him. The hidden one. The workingmen said that few of the politicians in Canción raised their voices when El Tapado made plans with the American investors for the hotel. And those who did now rest in unmarked graves in the desert.

During lunch one day an old storyteller with a thick flour white mustache shared with those of us new to Canción a well known and often repeated story about El Tapado.

I was born in this city long ago. He said. And for many years I made my living diving for pearls. I love Canción and refused to leave after the disease killed the oysters. I would rather be poor here than only a little less poor anywhere else.

But who is this Cantana whose name I see written on all the walls? A young man near to my age asked the storyteller.

For as much as many hate El Tapado. The old storyteller answered. You must understand that he is un hijo de Canción. A son of this city like myself. But because of his wealth and power his is an important story of this beautiful place. And this place is something we are all proud of regardless who it spawns. Let me have one of those cigarettes. The storyteller said. I cannot continue without one.

The father of Cantana was a difficult but fair judge in Canción for many years. As a child the judge had lost his sight from illness. But still the wealth of his family here allowed him to be educated in the law. The father was well known and widely respected for his decisions. Especially when many of those around him in the government and church were very corrupt.

One day when Cantana was a child he and some other boys were stealing in the market. Together they distracted a man and stole from him the money he made selling shoes belts and other beautiful items made from the skin of dead animals. This man chased the boys through the market but was only able to catch the fat boy Cantana.

Your son stole from me. This man said when he brought the boy before the blind father.

The judge asked his son if this was true but the son cried.

No.

The judge then told this man from the market that his son was not at fault. That a boy tells only the truth when a father asks.

Your son is lying! The man from the market yelled at the judge. And while the judge suspected this might be true he would never take the side of anyone but his family in front of others. The man from the market should have known this. This man should have known that he would receive mysteriously the money that was stolen. He should have known to stay quiet. But this man continued angrily at the judge. He is making a fool of you! I saw him with my own eyes.

These last words were a great insult to the judge. But more important they stopped Cantanas crying. Hatred filled the boy for this man from the market. Cantana was very ashamed of his fathers blindness. It is said that as a boy El Tapado fought often because he loved and hated his father but always he defended the judge before others because he understood that there is nothing worse than betraying family.

Some nights later the man in the market was attacked by a group of boys led by Cantana. The small boys climbed over the man like maggots in the stomach of a dead animal. They swarmed his legs and arms until he collapsed under their weight. The fat boy Cantana sat on the chest of the man making it difficult for him to breathe. Using a small knife Cantana then took the eyes of the man from his face.

Of course this man lived but he complained to no one. He is still in the market with his belts and shoes. He sits in a chair and feels for the different purses and bags. Runs his fingers over the designs in the belts to tell them from each other.

The people of Canción know this story of Cantana very well. The old storyteller told us that day.

This is one of many stories that los Cancioneros tell of the man who brought the hotels and roads to Canción. It is one they tell with some strange pride.

———

Some few evenings after Eduardo visited me on the top floor of the hotel I followed him to the house of a man who did business with Cantana. Using his penknife Eduardo opened the lock after some trying. It was not yet dark and this was very bold of him. An old woman had heard Eduardo cursing the lock and looked out her door. When she noticed Eduardos nice clothes and his confident smile she ducked back inside without a word. Eduardo worked for Cantana and by following him I did also. We were privileged men.

Inside the spacious house music played on a phonograph in a distant room. We heard the voice of a man singing. The white tiles of the floors were very clean and decorated with many colorful handmade rugs from Oaxaca. Hung on white plaster walls without smudges of soot were paintings of Zapotec women at looms. We followed the voice of the man singing. Eduardo ran his fingers along the walls. His fingernails trim and clean.

In the kitchen we found the singing man wearing the apron of his wife. He was bent over a metal pot of tomatoes and onions and cilantro boiling in some broth with a chicken carcass. I had not smelled food so rich in a long time. In a neat pile on a wood chopping block were cut guava pieces. Alongside this was a large knife. Eduardo and I stood in the door without the singing man noticing us. Eduardo waited for the music to end before speaking.

How does your wife feel about you wearing her apron? He said and the man dropped the wood spoon he held to the tiles.

It is our anniversary. The man answered.

The walls of the kitchen lined with shelves held many black

earthenware pots but more for display than cooking. Few had sooty bottoms from being set directly onto fire. Wood carved cooking utensils hung on hooks on the walls. A limestone metate sat at the center of a large wood dining table for decoration. Eduardo ran his fingers over vases made by artisans in Chiapas. A copper pan from Mexicali. The man undid the apron. He was embarrassed and scared. Eduardo looked at the ends of his fingers while listening to the husband say that he did not have the money Cantana demanded. While the husband spoke he did not take his eyes from me with fear and as a young man this is a tremendous feeling. Eduardo clucked his tongue and shook his head admiring a set of dishes in a wood cabinet glazed by old men in Jalisco.

I do not believe you. Eduardo said after the man finished. Especially after coming here to find you singing.

The man continued pleading with Eduardo when there came the sounds of the wife entering the home. Her voice reached us pleasantly through the hallways. Eduardo put his finger to his lips as the man was going to call to her. The wifes shoes were loud on the tiles now that the music had stopped. She entered the kitchen carrying a potted bougainvillea. She had been speaking to her husband as she walked but was silent immediately when she saw me. Then she looked to her husband who only looked down.

Señora. Eduardo bowed.

Get out of my home. She pointed. Her finger almost touching my chest. Leave now.

Señora your husband and I have business to discuss.

My husband has no business with you. She hissed.

Your husband owes Señor Cantana.

My husband owes no one.

Please. I would not call Señor Cantana no one señora. Eduardo clucked his tongue again. No. Your husband does owe. Otherwise I would not be here destroying your home.

Cómo? The wife asked. But Eduardo surprised her by stepping forward and hitting the husband in the stomach. The man crumpled to the floor but was able to catch his wife by her skirt when she charged toward Eduardo. I grabbed both the wife and her husband by the arms. The husband did not struggle but the wife clenched her jaw and spit at Eduardo while I held her.

This woman is fantastic! Eduardo said gesturing for her to come to him.

But I knew that Eduardo did not want me to let go of the wife. He walked from the room laughing to himself quietly and wiping the spit from his chin with a handkerchief. The wife looked at her husband sitting on the floor. She cursed at him and soon music came from the farther room. Eduardo returned. Beside the stove on the wood chopping block he picked up the knife and inspected the blade. He ate a piece of the guava and licked the ends of his fingers. His tongue was enormous.

Deliciosa. He winked at the wife. Very sweet.

Eduardo then set down the knife and moved to the shelves. He ran his finger along them collecting dust and clucking his tongue.

Señora why have such beautiful things if you do not take care of them?

Eduardo then threw the row of vases to the tile floor. Shards of clay scattering under the stove. The husband covered his eyes while Eduardo destroyed the hand painted dishes and cups. He broke a chair against the stout wood table and then turned over the chopping block where the guava was but lifting this plate as he did so not to spill the fruit. Then Eduardo kicked at the legs of the table like an angry little boy. His face red. His dark hair in his eyes. Cursing. Using the large kitchen knife Eduardo cut through one of the rugs in the hallway. When he passed us the wife kicked at him. The music came loudly from the distant room. Hard off the white walls. At Eduardo and then her husband the wife made bold curses frothing at the mouth. Her husband was almost as strong as Eduardo but nothing to me. Still I did not need to hold his arms he was so weak.

After destroying the house Eduardo ate some more of the guava and then came to stand inches from the face of the wife. He was enjoying the spit from her curses on his face. He ran his tongue over his lips moist from the guava.

This is your warning. Eduardo said calmly to the husband.

The wife tried to bite at the end of Eduardos nose when he came close to her but he only jumped back and laughed. Then he stepped forward and punched her in the stomach with his fist. I let her crumple to the tile floor. The husband did nothing. Catching her breath she still did not cry.

Just so you know. Eduardo bent over some and said to her as the husband tried to put his arms around his wife. Just so you know and do not have to have this happen again. He passed the back of his hand across the kitchen. His voice just above the music. This is your warning.

In the street Eduardo walked alongside me. We said nothing. He ran his fingers through his hair to make it neat again. Dabbed at the sweat on his forehead with his handkerchief. He was nervous some but now there was excitement in his eyes. A bounce in his step. A group of boys kicked a dried gourd back and forth down the stone street. Eduardo joined them for the moment that we passed. Laughing.

Then some streets later he said.

I should have said happy anniversary. That would have been better. I can never think of the perfect thing to say at moments like these.

When I was first in Canción and working on the hotel I took money many times from Eduardo for these small jobs. I never once questioned from where the money came and most of the times I only held the arms of men while Eduardo punched them in the stomachs or necks.

I never hit a man in the face. He told me once. I worry about breaking my fingers. Hurting my wrist.

One time I pulled Eduardo by the hair away from a man lying on the ground that he was kicking in the face.

Do not let me kill this one even though I want to. He said picking the lock of the door. Cantana does not always know what is best. But he is still Cantana. Be sure to stop me.

Eduardo leaned over the man curled on the floor gurgling soft cries. He wiped the blood of the man from the toes of his expensive shoes using the mans torn shirt. Eduardos face was flush with blood making the teeth of his grin very white. He stood over the man panting.

You are lucky I did not wear my good suit. He said. And then later he asked me. Do you think that was a good thing to say then?

After one of these small jobs one night in the dark of a cantina Eduardo spoke of holes the teeth of the dogs leave in the fleshy throats of men who bleed before an audience. He spoke of ragmen stinking of dog saliva and blood and mierda and of dogs whimpering and of the perfumed mistresses of the businessmen crying for the fighters. With Eduardos stories of the fighting of dogs the candles on the tables of the cantina danced beautifully in shadows along the walls of my memory.

The money is more than you have ever known. He clucked his tongue. If you are winning the men of Canción will carry you from the ring on their shoulders singing your name. And the women. He winked. They will lick your wounds.

The fighting of dogs in Canción occurred each full moon. It occurred on the rooftop of a stone depósito built by the United States to store weapons when for three months in 1847 during el Intervención de los Norteamericanos their army occupied Canción. But to escape the rains of the late summer months the first fight I witnessed was held in the sheet metal warehouse of an abandoned onyx mine tucked in the hills above the hidden city.

On that night rain fell sharply on the corrugated metal roof. The high steel trusses of the ceiling were lost to shadows. Thick tendrils of cigarette smoke escaped through small cracked or broken windows without screens. When I walked alone into the warehouse the crowd of yelling men surrounded a source of light that did not reach beyond the last man. I lingered in the shadows before pushing forward toward the twisted wood posts and metal fencing of the ring where bloodstained ragmen on their knees wiped furiously at the concrete floor. They wore no shoes and their tattered clothes were as dirty as the rags they used to clean the blood and mierda.

The yelling men argued and placed bets. They ignored the ragmen in the ring with their noses so close to the floor with the wiping that their tongues seemed to dart out now and then to lick the slab still warm from fighting. While the yelling men pushed one another to see the ring better the businessmen sat near this but alone and alongside their mistresses in a section of wood benches. These men controlled the fighting. They arranged the various bets and supported the fighters they favored most. Their mistresses perfume sweetened the smoky warehouse. Painted lips glistened in the light and their moist eyes shone brilliantly. I recognized some of the yelling men from the work on the hotel. These men staring at the mistresses so that it made the women uncomfortable but the businessmen did not care because above all they enjoy most the jealousy of other men.

Within the crowd several young men carried pencil stubs and pieces of paper and handfuls of paper pesos taking the bets of the yelling men. But only one young man dressed better than the others took the bets of the businessmen. As he crouched before the businessmen scribbling their bets he had the sleeves of his shirt rolled to show that he was honest. Dabbing the pencil on the end of his tongue as they put money now and then in his shirt pocket while he wrote. Nodding to them before moving onto the next. But the businessmen gave him no money for their bets. They operated the fighting and did not want to encourage the yelling men to run at them as a mob. The yelling men knew this and accepted it as a game the businessmen played with them sitting there on the smooth wood benches with their beautiful mistresses. This balance was delicate. One they never challenged out of fear and an overwhelming feeling of impossibility. The rings on the fingers of the businessmen gleamed where they were placed on the thighs of the mistresses. Gold necklaces and pearl earrings glimmered when the women brought their long dark hair from their slender necks. But all of the faces of the men at the fighting were greasy and red. During the fighting all the eyelids of the crowd opened wide like those who choke on their tongues. But still the yelling men were separated from the businessmen. And of all the businessmen only Cantana wore sunglasses. And only rarely did Cantana stand.

That night I did not have to be told which of the businessmen was El Tapado that the storyteller had spoken of. I knew the moment the well dressed young man knelt before him. The businessman was of medium height with broad shoulders and chest. His skin light in color but his hair shoe polish black. With a glove over his right hand he smoked a thin black cigarillo. The smoke of this white in front of the lenses of sunglasses. Silver like mirrors. While the yelling men called out their bets and waved their money Cantana leaned toward the well dressed young man and whispered his.

When this well dressed young man finished taking Cantanas bet he stood and walked through the yelling men toward where I stood with my arms crossed. Two businessmen not far from me argued loudly. The well dressed young man walked past them and as he did I watched his hand dart into the pocket of one of the men and then quickly into his own. The well dressed young man looked then directly into my eyes after he did this and when he knew I saw what he had done he just smiled. I chose to do nothing.

When I looked back to Cantana a man who had stood at the door of the warehouse when I entered leaned over the businessmans shoulder and whispered into his ear. Cantana nodded as the crowd began to yell and applaud. I followed the businessmans eyes to the ring where a tall handsome young man entered jumping lightly from foot to foot. In a far corner a ragman began to wrap his arm in the heavy rug stained with saliva and blood and put on his hand the glove fitted with metal claws.

This is his first fight. Eduardo yelled then standing suddenly next to me. His name is Ramón. Put your money on the dog. The foreman smiled. He has chosen one of Mendozas.

Light from the one large electric lamp dangling above the ring from a steel rafter reflected sharply from the claws of the glove the dog fighter wore. As the ragmen finished tying the heavy rug to Ramóns arm a dog trainer pulled back the fence for his dog to enter through at the end of a frayed leash. The leash was one rope looped over the collar of the dog that the trainer held both ends of through the fencing. One end in each hand.

Mendoza. Eduardo yelled. He is famous for taking a file to the teeth of his dogs. You can bet on the fighter or the dog. The odds pay better if the dog wins. You can bet who bleeds first. If the fighter gives in before he dies. If the trainer stops the fight. You can bet on almost anything here. But listen to me. If you are ever to put money on a dog you always put it on one belonging to Mendoza. The old men will tell you that it is wrong for Mendoza to sharpen the teeth. But they are fools and try to hide this by acting with pride when they lose betting against his dogs. Tradición. They say. Eduardo said shaking his head. They die for tradición.

Across the ring from Ramón a ragman teased the dog with a bloody cloth. The dog fighter leaned his head from side to side stretching the muscles of his neck.

Mira. Eduardo pointed and laughed a short hard laugh. His knees are shaking. He is too handsome to fight dogs.

The dog snarled and barked at the cloth the ragman held before it. Studying this Ramón suddenly collapsed in half and vomited in his corner of the ring. Two of the three ragmen fell on it immediately and a wave of new bets rustled through the crowd. Ramón stood and wiped his mouth along his forearm and when the hunchbacked ragmen stood the area where the dog fighter was sick came up clean. Across from this but outside the ring Mendoza held the leash smiling.

He must have seen the teeth. Eduardo yelled at me. If Mendoza was not the friend of Cantana that he is the older businessmen would not allow him to sharpen the teeth. It is good to be the friend of Cantana. Remember that.

Ramón straightened himself. His knees shook while the ragman continued to tease the dog. Then Mendoza yelled.

Bastante!

Pulling one end of the rope leash quickly so that it slipped free of the dogs collar and slithered from the ring through the fence. The ragmen fell back to the shadows grinning.

The yelling men stood on the toes of their feet as Ramón fended off the sharpened teeth of the dog using the rug tied around his forearm.

Mendoza trains his dogs to ignore the rug. Eduardo yelled. No one knows how he does this but his dogs are the most successful.

The dog drove Ramón back stepping against the cold of the metal fence where a drunk stood laughing hot spittle into his ear. Ramón slipped and fell to the floor bringing a roar from the men that came down hard on my ears from the metal roof as the dog gaping went for the neck of the dog fighter. A stir of excitement fluttered through my groin. Down along my thighs and up into my abdomen.

La lucha de los perros! Eduardo shouted. This is the fighting of dogs hombre!

Ramón hurried to his feet. Pushing the dog from him. The eyes of the drunk behind bloodshot and mad. He rattled the fence of the ring as if he wanted to be the one on the inside. Fear twitched in the slender muscles around Ramóns mouth and eyes.

As the yelling men cried for more Ramón swung wildly at the dog. Stopping only when he had fooled it into locking its jaws around the rug. Mendoza shook his head. But with the dog hanging from his arm Ramón shook the rug as if it were on fire. His eyes showing pain from the teeth. The dog hung limply with its eyes rolled back into its skull. Eyelids fluttering over pearls. Soon from under the rug a line of blood came to show on the back of the dog fighters hand. The sharpened teeth had gone through. When the blood lashed onto the concrete floor with each swing of Ramóns arm the ragmen stepped closer to the light from shadows wetting their lips. The dog weighed heavily from the dog fighters arm. He tried to make a fist of his gloved hand but ended up slapping the dog repeatedly on the head.

Pendejo! Use the claws! Eduardo yelled. He fights like a woman.

Trying feverishly to break from the dogs locked jaws Ramón stepped back and slipped on his own blood. The men cheered when he had fallen to the ground. Some of the businessmen stood in anticipation.

Now the dog has him! Eduardo clasped my arm.

Those businessmen who sat patiently watched the mistresses carefully from the corners of their eyes. Cantana seemed to not be watching the fighting at all. He brought his left hand from his pocket to light a fresh cigarillo. I did not understand then why he wore only the one glove. When Cantana finished lighting the cigarillo with great concentration he took his sunglasses down from his face and while keeping his eyelids closed cleaned the lenses of the glasses with a fine cloth from the inside pocket of his coat.

The yelling men returned my attention to the ring. Embracing on the ground the claws of the dogs hind legs dug into the skin above Ramóns knee. The yelling men laughed and cheered. Ramón screamed in pain. The mistresses hid their eyes from the bone showing white through the loose skin. But those mistresses who had seen the bone began to cry. The businessmen wrapped their arms around the womens shoulders and over their sweet smelling hair they made eyes at each other.

This was a small game the businessmen played. Waiting to see which of the women cried first and which would cry last because to put money only on the fighting of dogs was never enough for them.

The teeth of the dog went deeper into Ramóns forearm. The

muscles in his handsome face had tightened into a knotted bunch. But something passed over his eyes still. For as much pain as there was he was aware. The pain does this I would learn. Strengthens your concentration.

The yelling men cheered as Ramón put his free hand under the dog and swiped at its neck. Stabbing it with the short metal claws. The dog snarled until Ramón tore free a fistful of throat. Then a loud gurgle came from within the dog as it unlocked its jaws and began to claw at the floor. Ramón dragged himself to the fence. His hands holding his bleeding knee. Across from Ramón the dog lay shivering. Blood came from its mouth deep from within its throat. Its nails scraping the concrete floor could not be heard with the men yelling who had bet on Ramón to win.

Behind the fence Mendoza shook his head. While watching the fight he had coiled the rope leash around his palm and elbow. He then turned from the ring as his dog searched with shocked eyes for air to breathe. Some men yelled because they had won and some laughed because they had lost. The warehouse shuddered.

Using the fence Ramón pulled himself to his feet. He raised his gloved fist above his head and the men began to chant his name.

Ramón! Ramón! Ramón!

Cantana put his glasses on and smiled. His eyes closed during the fight. Some of the mistresses peeked thinking the fight was done. Their mascara streaming black tears down powdered cheeks. Ramón hobbled over to the dog and then he jumped onto the head of the dog to crush its skull. Twice he did this with his face knotted in pain. Once after the dog was already dead. Slipping in its blood and waving his arms comically to keep his balance. The mistresses witnessed the moment clearly and it broke them in tears.

There were several more fights that night. All very bloody and real. When the last fight was done I walked behind the yelling men down the hill from the mine into the dark streets of Canción. Eduardo had gone with Cantana and some of the other businessmen and their mistresses to a cantina.

You should come with us. He said to me afterward. Find yourself a whore.

But I chose to be alone with the yelling men. The rain had passed for the night to the north and the air smelled clean of wet flowering cacti and the yellow petals of the herb damiana glowing under the full moon. The men talked of the fighting as I followed them along an uneven dirt road. Our footprints black in damp earth already dusty though in the warm air of Baja. The talk was mostly of Ramón. Praising his strength and the return he made from death when the dog was locked on his arm. Those who did not have money to bet did not talk of what was won or lost but spoke of the skill of the dogs and the fighters who killed them. They spoke of the fighters that had been seriously injured. Of one fighter who pulled the head of a dog free from a bite it had into his leg by burying his fingers in the ears of the dog and pulling against the inside of its skull. When this dogs jaws came away a tooth had broken off into the muscle of the fighters leg. The men laughed about this. Shivering. But that night all the fighters had won. The ragmen were left with the blood and mierda of dogs alone.

As we entered the city the lights of Canción were gold coins scattered over black stones rinsed of the sandy dust. Soon the businessmen passed in sturdy black American made automobiles. The mistresses fixing their makeup in blue mirrors. Their glowing teeth passing in the dark. I walked alone among the men as they made their way to the large plaza to drink in the cantinas. It was late in the night but the music was made stronger by our voices arriving. A single rain cloud passed overhead lightly sprinkling. The lights from the cantinas shone warmly on the undersides of the fig trees lining the large square.

I decided to drink one beer. I sat at a table by myself listening to one man tell another of the fighting. This man reenacted the fight with his entire body while other men interrupted from time to time to build on the action. The men who had not been at the fighting listened carefully to every word. While they spoke I expected Ramón to walk into the plaza with his arm hurt and his leg in bandages but his appearance clean and proud. The men repeated his name in his absence. They would have bought him cups of mescal or damiana or rum even and patted him on the back I imagined.

But Ramón did not come to the plaza. I realized that he did not need to. The men took him from the fighting with their words. They carried him on the shoulders of their stories. Sitting there alone I realized that it was myself I wanted to see come into the large square that night. To be the one the men praised for such great strength and ability. Soon I was drunk on their talk. I heard my own name in their words and voices. My victories were very great. My fights all very dangerous. The dogs all very intelligent and valeroso. The men in the cantinas and cafés went on and on talking about my fighting and the stories they told of me then they still tell today.

THREE

I would have to wait until the next full moon before I could stand across from the teeth as Ramón had done. In this time of anticipation my grandfathers voice was never so strong in me. I passed the days dreaming of how I was to kill the dogs. Of how the crowds would sing my name and carry my story to the plaza mayor. During the workday now I expected the other men to recognize who it was that passed among them.

He is the best of them. I imagined. No one is stronger or better skilled.

At this time I was a very lonely young man. And thoughts like these are fine company. They kept me from remembering that I was nothing more than a murderer and a bully. Quiet or not.

Still I did not know how to prepare for the fighting of dogs. Working at the hotel I improved my strength by increasing the loads I lifted. Once I won some money on a bet after I raised a skinny young man from Matamoros to the top floor sitting on a pallet of blocks. Each evening after work I swam with my canvas bag filled with rocks tied to my back. And in the mornings to the smell of dawn stove fires I searched for the dogs of Canción. I stalked them in the dim streets while lamps came on in kitchen windows. When the air was so still that sheet metal blades of the windmills moved backward. But more and more on these morning walks thoughts of my greatness were interrupted by words painted in red on the walls.

Canción por los Cancioneros! Cantana a la chingada!

I despised this mans name more than the man himself because I desired the fear he possessed in others. The attention he commanded from many.

After your first fight. I told myself. Your name will be known to all. You will no longer have to construct his hotel.

I spoke in this way to myself constantly. Only when I floated on my back in the calm water lost to the drifting did I allow myself to think.

Or maybe you will die by the teeth.

When I did encounter the dogs of Canción I studied how they fought one another. They were thin and wild and hungry and this made them very fierce. Children threw stones at their pinched sides. Their eyes dark and sunken. When they fought they snapped at each other from the shade of fallen walls where they rested weak with hunger. They tore into one another fighting in sandy lots littered with sharp coral and broken glass under their soft paws. Where paper trash had been made worn like paper money by the constant sun. Down by the docks over decaying mounds of fish innards I watched how they bent in half and showed their teeth. Growled and leaped. Twisted and snarled or whimpered and bled. In all the fights their movements the same and only for each was the death unique.

One morning early I allowed one dog to kill another where a fisherman had thrown the stomach of a dorado onto some warm dusty stones. The two dogs fought until one began to bleed from the corner of its eye. Other dogs seeing that one was injured and the other was exhausted came together against the exhausted one knowing that the injured one would retreat. Again and again they fought over the stomach. I watched as they tangled and the injured fell back. Snarling with the last of their panting breaths. I did not stop them but waited with the fisherman to see finally the one that was last to be seriously injured and therefore left alone to eat.

The dogs were all very fast and vicious. But when I walked alone searching for them my name was in the sound of my steps on those stones. Over and over with each step on the voices of many. Only then was I not alone. I desired more and more the mistresses crying on my shoulder. To feel through expensive cotton shirts the cool weight of the businessmens rings patting me on the back. To have my name said in the same breath but before Cantanas.

As the fight neared I no longer slept easily under the stars. I was very excited about the fighting but I woke often from difficult dreams of my grandfathers voice leading me toward the sharpened teeth. I woke feverish to the hotel still and quiet around me. A cool breeze passing over metal tools warm from the hands of the workingmen. The wires of the scaffolding shrinking in the cool dark after the full sun of the day. Often when I woke from these dreams unable to sleep I sat with my legs dangling over the edge of the scaffolding. On certain streetlamps I fixed my eyes until their halos squared in a recession and came or went from me spinning. In the center of these squares of light I chose what was real and what could be with a focusing of my eyes. I was tired and this was an easy way to think that I could affect the world by moving my tiniest muscles.

I tried to empty my mind in this way before returning to my bedroll. But most times my thoughts would not let me rest. Before I drank to shut down my mind but I knew that if I began drinking again I would become weak and slow and lose. And so I never left the hotel for the cantinas but sat dangerously close to the edge of the scaffolding thinking for hours. Eventually my thoughts led to my father. Wondering if he was still alive in Veracruz. It was easier for me to blame him for my mothers death than to consider what my grandfathers stories had made me into. I refused to follow thoughts of my mother. It was easier to imagine my victories than think of my faults.

The moon grew slowly more full. One night there was a lightning storm in the east. The surface of the sea in that distance glowed with electricity. I thought of how thoughts come. If they are born within us new as we grow or born with us forever limiting our growth. Other nights I studied how shadows in the buildings of the small city changed with the days and weeks of the changing moons. I looked over the buildings that were nothing more than walled rooms and wondered how many men slept with their backs turned to their loves. I was shamed by my memory of Perla and how I had allowed her to mislead me. When I closed my eyes I saw the photographs of her and her husband on the walls of their room. Remembered them vividly at the corner of my eye. Her hair draped over my face and neck. Her forehead pressed to mine. Kissing the thin flesh along the insides of her forearms after she collapsed onto me. The small room was warm from our breaths before I left into the foggy mornings for work in the prune orchards. At night on the top floor of the hotel I no longer experienced dreams. I had confined them to my days. To forget her I thought of the dogs. And even though I was very tired after nights like these I lifted more and more with the crane to exhaust my mind. Dreading the sleeplessness that was to come.

Much changed late one night. Listening to the tiny waves wash onto the beach unremarkably I stirred from a half sleep to the sound of feet shuffling over the sandy concrete floor below. The breeze carried that faint sound to where I raised my head from my pants rolled as a pillow. I recognized the creaking of the scaffold when someone was climbing on it but then the wind died suddenly and I heard nothing. Some moments later the shuffling of feet returned. That and whispering.

Niños. I thought to myself and lay back down.

I rested my head on the pants again and listened for the waves. Some few minutes passed like this before an explosion of fire came up the stairwell. The sky blossomed white. Ridges of the citys rooftops were bleached bones of some skeleton disorganized by wind. The streetlamps a shade darker than that pale burst of light. I scrambled from my bedroll as the darkness returned some. Yellow and red flames burned along the top of the scaffolding at the wall to the north. My ears rang from the explosion. I had little understanding of direction. With my balance undone I struggled to put my pants on. I fell to my knee and saw that cracks had coursed through the floor. I heard chunks of concrete and metal falling beneath me and then the northwest corner of the hotel began to sink. The scaffolding at this end bending and collapsing onto itself until a cloud of concrete dust surrounded the hotel traveling through the empty rooms and hallways thick and sweet smelling from smoke. In the confusion I heard several voices cheering. I was in shock. Angry from being startled by the sudden explosion.

The collapsing corner settled. From the ground I watched the fire climb along the wooden beams and posts like skinny ghosts made of flames. Some mans shirt burned along the sleeve toward where the collar was hooked on a nail. I stood watching this when a group of men arrived shouting and carrying buckets. Soon we were filling the buckets with bay water and throwing it on the collapsed scaffolding before it spread to that which was still standing. When more men and women arrived we formed lines from the water to the fire. The water sloshing over the tops of the buckets and soaking our pants from the knees down. Yelling and hurrying the buckets along. Our fingers aching from the thin metal handles. I carried three or four at a time until there were enough men and women to take them from me. Boys ran along these lines smiling chased by dogs barking excited by being so near to something so dangerous. Something los Cancioneros would tell stories about in the years to come. Childrens eyes already remembering flames dancing on the surface of the sloshing black water.

At some point a stir of yells came just before the crashing of the last of scaffolding along the north side of the building. Fire and embers sifted down around us like hot snowflakes dying black. A man danced out from his burning shirt as boys pointed and laughed. Women thinking to wet the childrens hair. The scaffolding that had fallen was left to smolder on the ground when it all came to settle. Tiny fires were left to burn themselves out on the concrete floors and piles of slender iron reinforcement bars. A solitary palm down by the water burned like some enormous candle. The children watched this amazed. Wondering how the flames had reached it. Men and women wiped soot dampened by sweat from their noses and foreheads. Looked down at their hands. We stood judging the slouched corner of the hotel when two young boys came calling for us to follow them to a wall where written in fresh red paint were the words.

Cantana es un muneco de los gringos!

Putting out the fire had been instinctive. But now there was some shame in the eyes of many who read these words. Rumors spread of brave young men dressed in black throwing paint on the buildings owned by the businessmen. On the banks and storehouses. There were several other fires in Canción that night. A businessmans American made automobile was destroyed. Men and women whispered to one another of these young men carrying bags filled with explosives laughing high laughs like demons as they went through the city striking at Cantana and the other businessmen from the shadows.

At dawn looped wires glowed orange beneath the gray ash and charcoal. Workingmen who were not already down at the hotel from the dormitory arrived and we shoveled sand onto the smoldering remains of the scaffolding. We set aside those cordón logs and posts that could be used again. Architects and engineers arrived soon after with a number of the businessmen. The sun came above the mouth of the bay as it had each morning bright and full and without clouds. We shoveled and watched as the engineers inspected the walls. One workingman who coughed and spat dark blood on the concrete deck after years of working in gypsum mines in the north of Baja without thinking reached into the ash for the burned handle of a hammer. We laughed as he danced hunched over his fist. Flesh left on the handle of the hammer. The smell like spiced meat. The businessmen paused when they heard his cry but then returned to running their fingers over the cracks in the floors.

Just before noon a dusty 1932 black limousine came down a cobblestone street to the hotel. I had heard of this car often and of how it was brought to Canción on a boat from the United States some years before there were any automobiles in Canción. How three dozen men and sets of pulleys and fishing boat masts buried in the sand with concrete were needed to lift it from the deck of the boat. Cantana emerged from this limousine. His left hand in his pocket and his gloved right holding a thin black cigarillo to his lips. His sunglasses reflecting the scene before him. The businessmen and architects and engineers led Cantana around the base of the hotel and then up into it. In the stairwell coated in soot from the flames that had rushed up through it they took him to the top floor. He said nothing but listened closely to what they had to tell him. His face was without expression and his shoulders without tension.

A high corner of the lobby ceiling sagged some. Cantana ran his gloved finger through the soot where brass railings were to run alongside the wide staircase where a mural of the bay was to be painted. He came to stand looking over the edge of the sagging corner. Eduardo was with him. I could see that he was smoking nervously at the businessmans side. The other businessmen also very nervous. Noticing this Cantana put his cigarillo in his mouth and then with both of his hands he pretended to push against a column as if to push over the entire hotel from within. When he made this gesture several of the men placed their hands on him to stop. He smiled and laughed and patted them on the backs and pointed at them to let them know he had made some joke and then the men laughed but not easily.

Look how he plays his games when all the work we have done is destroyed. One workingman said.

Destroyed? Another asked. This is just more work they will have to pay us for.

Destroyed or not. They said. Cantana will find some way to profit from this in the end.

Before Cantana left the hotel in his limousine that morning he listened carefully to Eduardo while nodding his head. Then he followed the stocky foreman and several others down the street to where the painted words had dried on the wall. Cantana stood before the words just as an old man prepared to paint over them.

No. No. Cantana said in a soft voice to the old man. Let me. Cantana put his hand on the shoulder of the man. He stepped on the end of his cigarillo after dropping it to the hard dirt and then with the brush held carefully so as not to drip onto his glove Cantana said to the old man.

There is an accent over the n in muñeco.

The businessman smiled. And then the others around him laughed and he laughed and the old man laughed also. Everyone knew that the old man was to leave the words in this way but only until the limousine was gone.

In the excitement of what I felt for what the fighting of dogs would give me I had given little thought to how the people of Canción felt about the construction of the hotel. For me it was only work. And I was there to be paid for doing it and then when it was done there would be more or I was to leave to some other place to be paid to do work there. This is what workingmen do. If there was talk against the hotel before the explosion I had not heard it. The words I saw painted on the walls of the city did not refer to the hotel so much as the name of Cantana. A name I despised for being more known than my own. As a young man I listened mostly to conversations within myself about the victories I had not yet won. I put my own name on those walls but knew nothing of the struggle they spoke of.

The engineers and architects had decided that the building was still strong enough to continue. Eduardo went about the hotel yelling at the men to work harder. It was decided that only the north side was to be rebuilt and then not rebuilt but shored with more steel and concrete. I did not see Eduardo do it but I heard that he hurried to take down the hammock before Cantana arrived the morning of the explosion. But other businessmen had seen and now even he rolled up the sleeves of his shirt to yell at us to sift through the ash and charcoal for that which we could use again.

After this attack a dozen or so of the workingmen left the work on the hotel in Canción. But others soon arrived to replace them. When these men came into the bay they lined the railings of the ferry and we stopped our work rebuilding the scaffolding to judge them and laughed because the sooty concrete monster that they saw they had not expected.

Cantana had some of the police and his own paid guards posted with rifles throughout the day and night and a metal fence like that around the ring of the fighting of dogs put up around the perimeter of the hotel and its future grounds. Because of this I was no longer able to sleep on the top floor but on the beach again in the lights of the stone malecón and those cantinas whose music and laughter called to me each night. I was very tempted to drink. But I did not have enough money and the fighting was only days ahead when the attack had occurred and then I would have plenty of money or I would be dead.

The rooftop of the depósito where we fought dogs was in the south of the city in an area that had once been busy with the pearl industry but was now old and run down. In their war against Mexico American soldiers had used the people of Canción to construct the stone warehouse. Then they used it as a place to store their weapons but also to defend the city with cannons aimed over the bay. Los Cancioneros did not mind the Americans very much. It was not as bad for them as it was in other parts of Mexico. My grandfather told me stories of how when the American army captured Veracruz he and many other men were forced to clean the streets. That the Americans spit on him and other men working with brooms and called them pigs.

All that cleaning when the Americans occupied Veracruz was the best thing that came from el Intervención. My father said to me. And as soon as they were gone the filth returned.

But when I told my grandfather that my father had said this he whispered to me.

Your father knows nothing of war. Of difficulty and hardship. Look at his hands. So soft and clean at the nails. Remember. You can never trust the words of a man whose body is not a little ruined.

The Americans had the rooftop of this two story depósito made strong enough to support the weight of soldiers who slept and kept watch there. The walls around this came to the chests of the men standing before them and were lined with colorful shards of broken glass and several openings constructed to shoot the cannons from. In one corner a small room had been built to shade the officers. This is where we waited before the fighting. We came up into this room by a metal spiral staircase from a back door made of thick metal planks and heavy iron hinges. At this door when the fighting was held stood a man with a revolver. His name was Elías. The story I heard of him was that his brother was the toughest man in Canción but that he was always beating on the younger Elías and this only made Elías even tougher than his brother. When I once asked Elías why he did not fight dogs he said.

Because when I die I do not want to mess my pants in front of dozens of men with some dog hanging on my neck. Besides. He continued. Señor Cantana pays me enough not to.

On this first night I approached Elías standing before the thick door and told him that I was there to fight dogs. That Eduardo had instructed me to come there and introduce myself.

We have been expecting you. He said. Across the alley a group of ragged boys sat on wood boxes waiting at the entrance for the dog fighters. I could feel their eyes on me. Elías took a toothpick from his mouth and stared me directly in the eyes. He rested his hand comfortably on his belt near the revolver that was between us. But before I tell Señor Cantana that you are here I must ask you if you are loyal to Eduardo?

No. I answered him.

Seguro?

Yes. I answered and this was the truth.

Bueno. Elías smiled at me. Because Eduardo is dead. Wait here a moment.

Elías tossed the toothpick to the cobblestones and disappeared into the dark of the door he guarded. He was careful to secure it behind him.

Across the alley I noticed that one of the ragged boys held a box of matches. When I faced them they seemed suddenly unable to move. The voices of men on the rooftop talking loudly came down to us. I looked to the boy with the matches. I held out my hand and after a moment he came over to me but reluctantly. Checking over his shoulder at the other boys he gave me the matches. I turned the box over in my hands before taking one out and then closing it. As the boy stood at my side I struck the match and in the same motion threw it in the air. I had not thrown lit matches since I was a boy. The boys eyes watched it arc and die and then I handed the box back for the one boy to try. Several times the sulfur did not start or he threw the match too quickly and it went out in the air immediately. I took his tiny hand in my own.

Mira. I said. Like this.

When the boy learned it correctly the others swarmed around him grabbing for the box but he kept them back by threatening to throw fire at them. Señor Cantana knows who you are. Elías said when he returned. That you are good worker and that you are interested in the fighting. He told me to tell you he is very pleased that you are not loyal to Eduardo. And that he looks forward to your first fight. Buena suerte.

The other fighters were sitting quietly in the dim room when I came up through the floor on the spiral staircase. Lined by a thin and fading light of the full moon the only door of this small room opened onto the roof. Beyond it I could hear the barking of the dogs. I smelled the cigarette smoke and the perfume of the mistresses. I studied the light around the door.

On a chair in a corner Ramón sat rubbing a balm smelling of eucalyptus where the dog had cut his leg above the knee. The scar was still very pink. The two other fighters in the room also wore scars from the fighting of dogs. One fighter was a Tlaxcaltec from Ciudad México. His blood of those who joined Cortés to fight the Aztec my father had taught me. The other a fugitive named Vargas. Immediately I recognized them as the men from the stories that my grandfather had told. They had scars from beasts and their narrow eyes were lit by fire. We all bore scars from fighting other men. When I climbed to the top of the stairs I looked the men in the eyes. On my way up I had decided to do this. To make them fear me instantly. But the dog fighters were very tranquil. They said nothing. The heavy musk from the balm Ramón put on his leg filled the room. He sat quietly in his chair while the other two jumped in place or stretched. Vargas sharpened his toenails with a file. Then he put tape around his toes. The Tlaxcaltec watched him carefully do this and then asked him why he needed the tape.

The nails tear off when I claw at their skin. Vargas smiled. This is easier than having to wait to grow new ones.

That night the Tlaxcaltec fought first. He fought two dogs. One on a leash that was released at the moment the first dog was seriously injured. He killed both dogs but only after the second had torn some muscle from the calf of his leg. The room filled with light and smoke when the ragmen carried him in with his arms around their shoulders. He did not scream but his breathing was a hiss through his lips pulled tightly over his teeth. He grimaced when they sat him down and pressed his hands against the blood soaked rags around his leg. Cursing the dog. He narrowed his eyes at us. Ramón continued to rub his leg and the fugitive did push ups to strengthen his arms. His toenails scraping against the floor.

I want the teeth of that dog. The Tlaxcaltec hissed at one of the ragmen.

Mendoza? Ramón asked.

No. He smiled a wicked smile. They are saving him for you.

The Tlaxcaltec dug his nails into the chair when the ragmen took the cloths from around his leg for the inspection by a short bald doctor. The fighters knuckles went white. The doctor sweated through the arms and back of his shirt. A bloody flap of muscle fell to the floor still held to the Tlaxcaltecs leg. None of us in the room looked easily from this however much we tried to impress each other. Before coming up the staircase we had all drawn sticks from a velvet bag Elías held hiding their painted ends. The painted ends told us which dog we were to fight that night. If we were to fight only one dog or two. Our fate left to chance we thought. We did not know whose dogs we were to fight until they entered the ring.

No fighter wanted a dog belonging to Mendoza. We all feared the sharpened teeth. If a dog of Mendozas bit into you the teeth went to the bone. The pain went through your skeleton like electricity. Other trainers did not take files to the teeth of their dogs because as Eduardo had told me the men of Canción had been fighting dogs for many generations and they thought this wrong.

It does not stop Mendoza though. Eduardo had told me. They fear Cantana. Many of us young men of Canción bet on the dogs of Mendoza. We laugh at the old men and their tradición. It is a small game we play.

Vargas fought next. The fugitive ran the metal claws along the walls of the room as he left. Whistling as if it was nothing. The yelling of the men came through the edges of the door. The light was more electric than moon. Alone together Ramón and I said nothing at first. The ragmen had taken the Tlaxcaltec from the room with the bald doctor. The doctor had decided that the muscle would have to be cut away.

The calf is ruined. He said. If we do not take it off you will die from infection.

I am sure you will find a way. The fighter smiled his wicked smile.

You are forgetting. The doctor smiled back. Who it is that pays me to help you amigo.

The Tlaxcaltec spit at the doctors feet.

We will blame that on your pain. The doctor said.

When the fugitive returned to the small room after his victory Ramón also asked him if his dog had been one belonging to Mendoza.

No. Vargas said. Wiping the sweat and blood of the dog from his face and body. The Tlaxcaltec was right. After your last fight they have decided to save him for you. They want you to continue to impress them.

While the ragmen cleaned the ring from the fugitives fight the crowd began to chant Ramóns name in anticipation. He studied the painted end of his stick.

Maybe I have Mendoza. I said to him then.

No. He smiled a small smile without taking his eyes from his stick.

Why are you so certain? I asked him.

The teeth are in my dreams.

During Ramóns fight I was left alone in the small room. I wiped the sweat from my face and could taste the blood of the Tlaxcaltec still in the room at the back of my throat. I did not know what to anticipate. The dogs had been trained to kill. I knew only the fighting of men and labor. A small moment of doubt almost took me before I heard the yelling men outside.

Ramón! They chanted. Ramón! Ramón!

The door swung open and I could see the brilliant light globes strung above the ring as they had been at the circus. Low in the sky beyond this the full moon a glowing white orb. The cigarette smoke thick but still a faint scent of the mistresses perfume reached me. Ramón stood at the center of many men patting him on the shoulders. Their hands came away with blood. His face was flush. His eyes bone white. Still very handsome. Behind Ramón the dog lay dead in a pool of its own blood and voided bowels. Its tongue lolling in this with the dirt of the floor.

My eyes fell upon her.

Suddenly and unexpected. She came from the shadows on the arm of Cantana. Her skin the color of the earth after the first rain ends a long drought. Eyes a brilliant shade of jade. A dark red dress of silk. Her hair hanging lightly down the curve of her back black as charcoal but with glints of silver.

The ragmen wrapped my forearm into the heavy rug. She did not see me but I saw no one else. My ears rang hot as my eyes fixed upon her gentle face. Her high strong cheeks. Her painted lips. When finally our eyes met I felt her putting mine instantly into her own. She opened herself to me as much as I was open to her.

I came from this dream when a drunk grabbed my arm through the fencing. Clamped between his teeth a corn husk cigarette burned inches from my face. His eyes rattled behind a pair of glasses. He yelled at me over the yelling men.

Are you ready to die for us!

As he spoke the crowd swelled around this man. His shoulders hunched as he crumpled into himself laughing. None of the men owned the expressions their faces took. She was lost to me in the crowd of men. Searching among their teeth and noses and eyes for her I did not notice the ragmen leave. I did not hear the leash end slip through the fence. I only looked down at the dog that biting onto the rug took me to the ground. Specks of white fire danced across my vision. I smelled the sour warmth of the ragmen. The strength of the dogs jaws tearing at the rug. In the blur of fury I fell before her. Hot claws singed the flesh of my chest. My mind had not come away from the greasy faces. The laughing drunk. The wealth of her beauty. Finally I was there and there were no shadows traipsing across the corners of the bedroom of my memory. Only myself on the ground at its center losing. The fear of having my eyes taken from her tremendous.

Without thinking I threw the dog to the side. My grandfathers voice had been in me too long for there to be any other reaction. The eyes of the men widened unblinking. Several of the mistresses already crying when the dog sprang again. Instinctively I put the rug before it. As the dog tore at the rug snarling I grabbed a hind leg with my hands and broke it. The men yelled for more. But I turned from the dog to look for her. The men cheered. They mistook my searching for part of the show. It was as if I had dropped the knife just as I was lowering myself into the tank of water. The dog came at me again but weakly and again with my hands I snapped another of its legs. The dog limped to a corner of the ring where it toppled over like a broken chair.

Hot from the fighting and angry that I could not find her in the crowd of ugly faces I kicked the dog in the soft of its stomach. I refused to believe that she was a dream. The dog snapped pitifully at my feet. Then with the men yelling and mistresses on the arms of the businessmen watching I clenched the wire fence with my fingers and jumped with both feet down onto the ribs of the dog. Blood came from its mouth and mierda rushed onto the floor from behind. I stood in the pooling mess desperate to prove her existence when a loud roar came from the hollows of my chest over the growing sound of men chanting my name. I did not hear the men I was so lost for her in myself then. I did not feel the dream within me pass from sleep into what surrounded me continuously.

The drunk had wedged himself against the fencing of the ring again. His glasses crooked on his face. We looked into each others eyes for a moment before he was again trampled to the floor by the yelling men storming the ring. But before he disappeared he smiled and showed me his teeth. His gums were purple and those few teeth he had were black.

Inside the ring the ragmen fell to their work. I had imagined her.

The mens hands were cold on my flesh. Unremarkable. One ragman dragged the dog by its legs that were not broken to a split in the fence. He dragged what I had done. The result of my grandfathers hiss. I was ashamed of myself. But this ragman led me to her again. She stood next to Cantana. Her right palm cupped over his right forearm. Her face free of black tears. Her green eyes lovely and calm. My legs tingled and the blood from the cuts in my chest ran cool down my legs. There was no judgment in her eyes when her painted lips blossomed into the tiniest of smiles. She took her hand from Cantanas arm and lowered it to her side. It was a handsome gesture.

Our eyes remained fixed as the ragmen tugged at the maguey ties holding the rug around my arm. Removing the claws. Then Cantana stepped to where she had been facing me. He stood between us so that I could see myself in the mirror of his sunglasses. I could not feel the yelling men with their hands on my arms and shoulders and back surrounding me. But the sight of myself in the businessmans sunglasses with blood on my neck and chest filled me with shame. Cantanas eyes lurked behind my reflection in those glasses. Hot and satisfied. He had seen us together. Her and me. I suddenly heard the sound of the men around me chanting my name and it was disappointing. I dropped my eyes weak in the stare of Cantana showing me to myself then. Of what my mother had fought my grandfather for me not to become. Of the choices I had made to place myself there for his pleasure and games. I was not scared of Cantana but of what this beautiful woman at his side thought of me now that I had suddenly seen myself. Cantana stepped aside and placed his hand in the small of her back just beneath the line of her dark hair. She bit into her lower lip. Shied from his touch.

Cantana also won that night. She was the only mistress not to have cried. It was rare for mistresses not to cry and it meant that she would return to the fighting until she did.

I did not walk with the men or go to the plaza to hear my name in their stories that night. Hot flashes of humiliation coursed through my body each time I remembered jumping onto the stomach of the dog. Of myself roaring like some beast. I had felt the tiny ribs splintering beneath my feet and piercing through the skin. But mostly I thought only of how I wanted to see her again.

That night fire overcame the thatched roofs of a small village in the mountains beyond Canción. Amber firelight and the twinkle of stars through rising smoke. The people of Canción stood in the streets looking to the west. The glow of flames taking over the dark of their eyes.

When the fights on the rooftop had begun the last of that days sunlight wedged through the cracks around the small door. But after the bald doctor had sewn the cuts in my chest and I left the depósito the stars shone silver and bright in the sky. Coins falling to the bottom of some bottomless well. I knew that the cantinas and cafés on the plaza were busy with men from the fights. Suffocated by thoughts of her I walked unnoticed among those admiring the fire in the mountains. My shirt sticking to the cuts in my chest. I went down to the sea. The cigarette smoke from the fighting thick in my clothes. The breath of the drunk and his awful teeth. The tide was out and the fire in the hills reflected small but vividly on the black mirror of the bay. The hotel stood ominously to the north. Its rooms exposed. The small cook fires of the lonely guards.

Leaving my clothes crumpled on the beach I eased my fevered body into the cool water. The salt stinging my wounds. Naked I swam out until I could no longer touch the cold sand of the earth with my bare toes. The backs of small waves carried the wavering lights of Canción. Shimmering flecks of gold. I tried to relax. I let my arms slack. My shoulders loosen. I slipped beneath the surface of the water and swam with my eyelids closed until I came to the surface and to her again.

I spoke to her in whispers. Then I yelled for her under the water. Above the water I whispered for her again and her answer was that of the waves lapping against my neck. I was lost to the drifting. Floating on my back I matched my breaths with those of the passing waves. Her dark hair spilled over the cuts in my chest like a soothing balm. The straps of her red dress fell about her dark shoulders. Her cool breath along my neck. Our lips moist from kissing. Difficult breathing when kissing again after not having kissed for so long. She washed over my body as the stars fell onto the water around us and we were together there as she sang in a voice reserved for me alone. And in this voice she forgave me for the fighting of dogs.

FOUR

With the money I won from my first fight I quit the work on the hotel and rented a room on the third floor of a three story compound several blocks south of the plaza mayor. The compound was owned by a dentist named Jorge who lived on the middle floor across the courtyard from me with his blind mother. Jorge was a slender man handsome in his sixties. His hair a messy gray but thick black eyebrows.

The dentist sat his patients in a chair on the bottom floor of the compound in front of a large window that opened onto the street. He left the window open during the day to allow the breeze from the sea to pass through to the tiled courtyard where his mother spent her days in a chair with a thin cotton blanket over her lap napping. Children gathered on the cracked and broken sidewalk in front of this window where Jorge worked. The dentist gave them candy to enjoy while they played waiting to watch him drill and pull teeth from the mouths of his patients.

They find it very entertaining to watch my patients dig their fingernails into the leather arms of the chair. Jorge said to me once. Their knuckles turn white and the children make faces as if they are in pain with them. Often I get very distracted because the children are so amusing.

The dentist was always something of a showman. He was known to spring back from the mouth of some man or woman with a bloody tooth raised above his head bowing to the childrens applause.

This is not good señor. Jorge said to very nervous patients sitting in the chair. He sucked the tip of his tongue down sharp from the top of his teeth. I think we are going to have to extract.

The ears of the children were trained to these words. They dropped their iron hoops and marbles at the sound of them. Every now and then for effect Jorge ran a razor he never used along a worn strop to produce the grisly sound of it sharpening.

I don't like the looks of this one. He smiled to the children over the patients shoulder. We might have to amputate.

Applause was not uncommon when the dentist was at his finest. Once he confided in me that he frequently dreamt of being showered in roses.

But when not passing out candy to the children or leaning over his patients Jorge spent his days comfortably in the cool of a large room at the back of the courtyard. With the doorway shaded by flowering palms the dentist relaxed with his records. This compound was a very pleasant place to live. Along the south wall there grew a red bougainvillea the owner before Jorge had planted some years before when his wife died. After swimming in the morning I would return to my room and lie on my bed listening to the records Jorge played while staring out at the beautiful little red flowers on the vines. Daydreaming of how I was to be with her someday.

Most afternoons and evenings however the dentist took time from his work to visit in the back room with a group of young men that often stayed very late into the night. The young men made selections from Jorges records to play on his Victrola. They spread out over the cushions of couches smoking cigarettes and talking in soft but serious voices I strained to understand the meaning of. Many times I heard them laugh over the music. Drinking cola Jorge bought especially for these visits. In the young mens company the dentist was careless with his gestures. The muscles in his face eased.

In his work with the windows opened to the street Jorge was like a fine actor but one who is always onstage. Only in the back room was he himself.

My own room at the dentists compound was large enough for only a small bed and a wood chair. I hung my clothes from the chair at night and placed my huaraches under this. A window with iron shutters opened over a garden the dentist had made for his blind mother on the roof that went around the courtyard below. For many years Jorge had worked to train the bougainvillea to creep along the low inside walls of the rooftop. In pots along the walls there were other bougainvillea and these he trained to hide shards of glass buried in the walls to keep others out. Sitting in my wood chair on the rooftop I focused my eyes many times to see these vines grow over the city like thin paint strokes on a moving canvas. The bright red flowers and brown vines decorated the colorful buildings and swaying palms of Canción. Delicate succulents and flowering cacti filled dozens of other but smaller terra cotta pots. For his mother Jorge painted tiles with blue and red and yellow designs of waves and suns and more flowers. I sat for hours in this garden thinking of this young woman I had witnessed at the fighting. Now and then distracted by the tall mountains to the west and to the east the shining Sea of Cortés.

Each night after the sun set but there was still some light the dentist gently guided his mother by the arm from pot to pot through the garden. The young men played record after record below as he described to her the flowers and cacti.

The pink bougainvillea is doing well. He said to her.

How many blooms? She asked him.

More than four dozen.

And the color of our little weak one?

More red each day. Like the sunset after a fire in the hills.

A week from now it will be the color of velvet.

I think so too.

Jorge rubbed waxy hibiscus blooms in the small of her palm.

Once I saw him delicately place her fingertip to the sharp spine of a cactus and it brought a smile to her face. Watching Jorge with his mother often made me very sad. She was old and frail and he was very good to her. She wore the same flimsy dress every day to keep her cool in the constant sun and heat of Baja. When she was not napping in the courtyard she spent her time with a woman Jorge hired to cook and to clean the compound. This woman washed clothes and stretched them over a line below my window to drip over the soil of the terra cotta pots to give them water. Jorge rich-ened the soil of his garden with eggshells and guava rinds and limón halves. The dentist was a smart man. He wasted little.

I woke in the mornings to the sound of the woman sweeping the courtyard. Mopping the tiles. For the first time since leaving my father I was not working every day but also I was not drinking or fighting. The frustration I felt from the energy I did not exhaust when working usually had turned into violence. But I did not feel this living in my room at the compound. After encountering her at the fight there was some peace now in my life. I exhausted the frus-tration there was not being able to be with her by walking for hours. Swimming in the early mornings and late at night. I was feverish only with thoughts of her. I thought nothing of myself and was the most content I had ever been.

But still I had to fight dogs to be near to her. Some nights I was unable to sleep my mind was so busy imaging her. Without the work on the crane to gain strength I did sit ups and push ups in the dark of my room. I jogged in place. During the day after the woman hung the clothes on the line to drip I snuck onto the roof garden and twisted the wet towels and shirts dry over the pots until the muscles in my forearms felt like fire with strength.

One night not long after I moved into the small room I heard a gentle knock on the door of the compound. Immediately I con-vinced myself that it was her. That she had found me. I hurried to the window only to witness the shadow of the slender dentist cross beneath the palm fronds of the courtyard with another shadow I did not recognize. I was very disappointed that it was not her. Minutes later I heard music from the back room. This knocking came regularly. Late in the night. After the mother of the dentist had gone to sleep and after the young men were gone. The young man who came to visit the dentist always dressed in black and his movements across the courtyard were secretive. Then I suspected nothing.

At the compound I lived listening closely for her in the common noises of others living in the buildings around me. The muffled arguments. The bedtime conversations. The sounds of the dentist waking up in the middle of the night to piss. As I lay in my bed the compound shifted around me in the calm of night. I memorized its songs as I had done in my fathers home. The winds came through the cracks in the shutters. The clothes on the lines tapped flatly against the stucco walls. The mother of the dentist coughing on the other side of the courtyard a floor below. Beneath my window the young men as they left trying not to wake the mother. It had been four years since I had lived in a house with others.

Desperate to find her I began to walk the streets of Canción at night. Often I returned to the hotel to convince the guards to allow me to sit on the top floor. Word of my fight had passed through the city in the way that fire consumes dry grass. My name was finally in the voices of many men. It was what I had dreamed of but now I preferred people not to know me. Still the view from the top of the hotel had changed none. Little work had been done to continue building more floors. The workers instead concentrated on fixing the damaged north corner. The destroyed scaffolding had been rebuilt. The windows of the city below were lit for her. All were for her to stand and comb her hair in at night. Looking out for me as I searched for her.

I slept only a few hours each morning before going out and walking more. I began to pray to God for the chance to encounter her on the street. I did not care that it was begging or that I had never asked Him for anything before and that I never prayed to Him in thanks. As a young man I did not think in this way.

I walked the mercado on Saturdays. I bought vegetables from women with wrinkled faces and from women surrounded by cilantro whose bodies I remember being shaped like teardrops from sitting on pallets all day long. Women who sold tomatoes and peppers brought over on the ferry. Others sorted through heaping baskets of beans with fingers gnarled by years of this work. The market smelled of leather. Raw meat and raw fish. The aisles busy with children screaming and laughing and chasing each other or chickens and pigs.

On Saturdays the market was particularly busy. I enjoyed being among the women who at first did not know who I was. They argued yelling at each other over and across the stalls and aisles. But one day when I passed they were suspiciously quiet. I decided then that they had learned I was a dog fighter and feared how I would act toward the children. None of the women looked me in the eyes or encouraged me to buy from them. One woman known for her outrages wore a sly smile that showed awkwardly in the lines of her stubborn face. In my suspicion I did not notice a boy following me from stall to stall. I did not see him hiding among the goods that hung in the aisles.

At one stall I asked a woman to choose some of her best onions for me. I was still learning how to use my voice again and often I had to repeat myself I was so quiet. While the woman chose the onions I turned from her to look at the other women. In a nearby stall filled with typewriters sat an old man. There were very few men working in the mercado and this man particularly stood out. He wore eyeglasses. A full white mustache stained yellow beneath his nostrils from smoking cigarettes. He held a newspaper before him. As the woman weighed the onions this man lowered the newspaper then and looked me in the eyes over the tops of his eyeglasses. He looked at me very purposefully but I did not understand why. Confused by the old mans look I did not feel the boy brush against me. When I went to pay for the onions my money was gone. The woman held the bag out for me to take and it shook with her giggling. Then all the women nearby were laughing at me loudly while I searched my pockets. I looked up to see the old man shake his head.

A small pickpocket took your money. He said folding the paper. I tried warning you.

The old man set down the newspaper before him. From one of several ashtrays in the stall he lit a fresh cigarette using the end of one he was already smoking.

I thought you meant something different. I said to him.

You thought?

I thought.

You thought wrong my friend. The women laughed when he said this. I am a poet of women.

The women in the market around this laughed even more. But the poet only smiled and said a vulgar phrase to them in English. His teeth stained and crooked. Smoke rose before his face. Between his glasses and his dark eyes. The women did not understand what he said but they understood the teeth of his smile and cursed at him for his words.

No one writes poems for ugly women. He responded to their curses. Waving the back of his hand over the whole of the market.

And only men without women write poems. Said the woman whose stubborn face looked awkward when she smiled.

You should have warned me. I interrupted.

Why? The poet asked.

Because I. I stammered but stopped. And when I did not answer the poet understood immediately how poor I was with my words.

I see this little pickpocket every day. His voice rising. But this is the first time I have seen you. It is not my fault that you are a fool and did not understand my warning. The poet picked up his newspaper again. Now leave me alone.

Leave me alone. A woman mocked the poet in a deep voice.

I left the market like a boy scolded by his father. That night in my room the typewriters surrounding the poet haunted my restless sleep like the books that had lined the walls of my fathers study. Just as it was when my father asked me questions as a boy I had been unable to mouth an answer.

The next day I returned to the poets stall and stood before him. He smoked as if I were not present.

I want to learn English. I said.

Why? He asked without looking me in the eyes.

So I can say things without people understanding what they mean.

That is a stupid reason.

My father spoke English. I admitted then. It has always been something I have wanted to learn.

I make money typing letters for people who cannot write their own names in Spanish. The poet answered.

You look busy. I responded quickly and the poet smiled at this. His gums were purple. The teeth he had black. He dabbed out his cigarette in an ashtray and lit another.

I do not want your money. He said.

Then I will buy you cigarettes.

I smoke very expensive cigarettes. He lied.

I can afford them.

What do you do for work to be able to afford expensive ciga-rettes? He asked.

I fight dogs.

After saying this I felt ashamed of myself. I had fought only one dog. The poet said nothing in response but licked his thumb and peeled a sheet of paper from a stack in a box nearby and fed it into a typewriter at his side.

Your first lesson. He spoke while beginning to type. Is to copy a poem of mine. You can write verdad?

Yes.

Where did you learn to write?

My father.

What does this father of yours do for work?

The poet lashing his long fingers over the keys with the cigarette smoke rising in his face. Forcing him to squint.

He was a doctor. I answered.

Was?

Yes.

What happened?

He is dead to me.

The poet laughed a short laugh.

You are a very serious young man dog fighter. Well. He said taking the paper from the typewriter with a wave of his hand. If your father were still alive to you he might have enjoyed this poem of mine very much. It is about the body. A little something I wrote for fun some years ago.

I copied the lines of the poem that night dozens of times. I sat on my bed and when the paper was gone I wrote on the bottom of the seat of my chair. Picking out the words I recognized and repeating them aloud in a quiet voice so the dentist and young men conspiring in the back room below would not hear me. It had been many years since I heard the words in English that my father had taught me. I had forgotten most of them but some returned beautifully over the page as I sounded them carefully with my clumsy tongue.

There once was a man from Nantucket

I wrote it again and again. Sounding each letter as best I could. Savoring them like pieces of fruit. Reducing them to nothing in my mouth like hard candy. Exhausted I slept easily that night and for years now whenever I have trouble sleeping I copy old poems by lamplight. Pretending the words are my own. Pretending that I am composing them for the world for the first time.

In my time in Canción I came to know many people. But the old poet was the one I spent the most time with. We spent many hours at his stall in the market where he typed letters for those who could not read or write. But mostly he drank beer and made eyes at the young women and girls walking with their mothers and grandmothers through the mercado. He spoke vulgar phrases to them in English without caring if they understood or not. But always his terrible smile told everything. One time I watched the poet spit at the feet of a young woman when she laughed at him for smiling at her with his small black teeth. Many women and mothers in the market yelled at the poet and many men wanted to fight him for the disrespect he gave to their women.

He is worse now that you are here. One of the old women of the market told me. He knows you will defend him.

Like my father the poet was a very intelligent man. Always he was teaching me of the history of Canción as my father had done with Veracruz.

Cortés himself landed on the beach here. The poet said. Even in the sixteenth century we were famous for our pearls. Some made it into the crown jewels of Spain. But even the great conquistador could not establish a settlement here and for centuries Baja was considered a desolate land. Only since the end of the First World War have we become much in the minds of anyone. American investors in particular. And that is because Díaz encouraged this.

I learned from the poet that during El Porfiriato American surveyors discovered veins of iron ore and entire mountainsides rich in gypsum graphite mercury nickel and sulfur.

Suddenly Baja was a land not so desolate after all. The poet said.

But Canción was always famous for its pearls. For its calm bay and neighboring islands that sheltered great oyster beds. Quickly the city became the main port of the peninsula. Busy with trade of pearls and later precious metals. But just before World War II disease ruined the oyster beds along the peninsula. Without the pearls to dive for many Cancioneros were forced to return to the mainland or venture there for the first time. The city although still very beautiful was now very poor.

We became happily forgotten. The poet said. But this was not to be for very long. American investors and their Mexican puppets were soon warming their hands over other possibilities for Canción.

When I arrived in the forgotten city men drank beer or damiana in the shade of cantina awnings talking of the war that had taken place in Europe and Africa and the Pacific. Of what we won with the Americans victory. Of what we would lose.

Much will change with the construction of this hotel. The poet told me. In war there is always a winner. And the winner will always want a place in the sun to relax.

Although the poet spit at the feet of young women who did not return his smiles he was more good than he let people know. Many in the market told me often of what a horrible man he was. How he looked at and treated women. About the way he spoke to them. They said that the old poet had never known love and that he never would. But I was the one killing dogs then and of me they spoke only with praise.

Often. The poet said. For these men who work on the hotel. Or the businessmen. Or people I do not like the look of. I type vulgar things in English when they are paying me to write letters to their mothers. But sometimes I write poems. People ask me to write about how poor they are. About the death of a sister or father. They want me to write to others for money. But these people they write to are as poor as they are. So I write a poem instead. I think receiving a poem without expecting a poem is something of a poem itself verdad?

The poet was always talking this way. Always he was reciting to me some of his own poems.

That love is all there is. Is all we know of love. It is enough the freight should be. Proportioned to the groove. You like that? He asked. Smiling sheepishly when I nodded speechless at such beautiful and difficult words. It is nothing really. Only a little something I came up with the other day.

If the poet was not speaking of poetry then he was speaking of women. Once when I was quietly writing out my lessons at his stall in the market he interrupted to ask me which part of a woman I prefer the best.

Which part? I asked. Thinking out loud.

Which is your right hand! He yelled at me then. There! He slapped. If you need to have time to think then you do not know women!

I have known many women. I said.

The old poet leaned toward me with his eyes narrow behind the thick glasses.

Do not ever lie to me.

The poet sat back. This was true. Perla was the only woman I had known more than once and without having to pay.

Which part of the woman do you prefer? I asked to take his attention from me.

The smell. He said.

The smell? I tried to laugh.

Yes. That smell too. He smiled. But I mean the smell of a woman you love.

But that is not part of a woman. I argued.

The poet removed his glasses to clean them with a rag he used to oil his typewriters. He lowered his voice so that the women around us did not hear.

You have much to learn young man. The smell of a woman is the most beautiful poem. Unwritable. A woman may leave you for another man and take her face from you but you cannot know the face of a woman like you can remember her smell. She may leave you forever. She may die. But her smell will haunt you when she is gone. Like a blossom opening she comes. The time when you kissed her neck in the shade of a flowering tree. The smell of her soap. Of a perfume you bought for her. Sweat on your own body together. The taste of her left on your upper lip the morning after you make love. You can never touch the hand or the face of a woman after she is gone. But if you love a woman you discover the smell of her in many things. And in those things she surprises you forever. The poet came to the edge of his seat with his cigarette at the corner of his mouth. His eyelids closed and his hands wiping the glasses with the rag. Young man when you find a woman that you love do many things with that woman so that when she is gone from you you will have memories of her to surprise you in your every day.

I was quiet then. Because of how vulgar the poet often spoke of women in the market I did not tell him of her. I was afraid even with all of his talk of poetry and beauty that he would not understand.

After the smell. The poet said then putting on his glasses and smiling at me. I prefer the ass.

The market closed just after dark each night. In those first weeks without knowing anyone else the poet and I did much walking together. He spoke often of friends of his who spent their time play- ing billiards in the evenings. Of old men who knew me as a fighter and young men who appreciated the fighting and also wanted to meet me.

I would prefer not to. I told him. I prefer the calm of our walks. Of practicing English together.

You act like some young fool in love. The poet said but I was quiet.

In lamplight of small squares after dark I walked with the poet listening to his stories of Canción.

There was a poor man who lived in this building here. He once said about a stone wall destroyed by time. The door still stood but it was easy to walk around. This man loved his wife. The poet contin- ued. He bought her cheap jewelry. Whatever he could afford. She knew how hard her husband worked. But one day she was bitten by a spider. Her entire leg went swollen. He wanted to take her to the doctor but she knew they did not have the money. I am fine she said. It will go away. But it did not. And finally when the husband did take his wife to the doctor the doctor had to cut her leg off.

Is that a true story? I asked him.

Yes. He said. I do not lie to you.

On our walks we passed old women bent over water pumps who

whispered my name. Men chewing on toothpicks or standing in doorways recognized me by raising their chins. There were times when I suspected that the poet did not enjoy being alongside me for all the attention I won.

You must be careful now that they know you. He said. People will want things from you or nothing but to have their name said with yours. Some will want to be with you when you walk these streets only for the hope of having others recognize them with you.

What about you? I asked him.

Me?

Yes. You.

You are lucky to have me as your friend dog fighter.

Late at night when I was awake copying the poets poems in English the knocking came on the heavy wood door to the compound. I could not help but hope that it was her. But always it was the shadow of the dentist and someone I could not discern. The music from the back room that always followed this knock made me restless. As my second fight approached I was more and more anxious to encounter her again. The knocking only made me want to search the city at night even when I knew I was not to find her.

Along the malecón on these nights I passed a young couple kissing. Holding hands on the beach in the light of the cantinas with the laughter and music. One night I decided to walk toward the electrical station because it was a mile south from the outskirts of the city and I had not been there. I passed the depósito where we fought the dogs. It was dark with the windows boarded. Someone had thrown feed for chickens in the vacant lot where the businessmen had parked their American made automobiles. Not far down the street from this I walked into the light of an open window through the sheer curtains of which I could see a man in his undershirt sitting at the kitchen table while his wife worked at the stove. The radio was turned to a station from Ensenada. Neither spoke as the wife set a plate of eggs and flour tortillas in front of the man. She sat across from him at the table while he ate in silence. I stood in the shadows of a doorjamb across the narrow street from this watching them in their home. The man was bald but for some few hairs just above his forehead. When he was near to finishing his meal the wife rose and brought from the stove hot coffee. She set this in front of him while she sat and then he reached out with his free hand and set his hand on top of hers resting on the table. They sat like this for some time. Tired. The man finishing his eggs with his hand massaging the wifes hand.

At the outskirts of the small city the neighborhoods were very poor. The jacales were of mud and straw or some of wood planks and the worst of canvas. Women threw dirty water into the uneven alleyways. From behind a canvas tent I could hear a man or a woman coughing from deep within their chest. For as beautiful and peaceful as it was in Canción the city was not without its troubles. Near the electrical station there was a man in shadows bending over and standing up collecting his belongings from the ground. Then a woman came from the door of the building and threw more of this mans belongings onto the hard packed dirt. She cursed at the man as he gathered his clothes in his arms. I did not want to walk through this intimacy. I decided to return to my room at the compound in hope that the music was no longer playing softly.

For all my walking I never learned the names of the streets in Canción. I came to know them by memorizing the crumbling walls or holes in sidewalks. Or if there were sidewalks at all. I knew the windows covered with iron shutters or where there were cacti along the windowsills. The creaks certain windmills made during the evening winds. I followed memories of signs advertising cigarettes or cola or the names of cantinas and cafés and restaurants. I walked repeating the names of things in English that I knew. Wall. Pared. Window. Ventana. Door. Puerta. Door. In this way I navigated myself around Canción.

One night late when I was returning to the dentists compound I recognized Ramón and Vargas walking some distance ahead of me. I thought about calling to them but the two dog fighters were with

Elías the doorman and a handsome young businessman whose name I came to know as Rodríguez. The four men were drunk and from how they walked I knew somehow they were not on their way home. I slowed wondering if they knew where I lived. Wondering if they were walking to the compound for me. But then not even the poet knew where I lived. I was nervous some. Although I was not working I was swimming every morning and evening and doing sit ups and push ups to stay strong. But still I did not want to fight. The anger for this was leaving my body. I had spent much time thinking of her or practicing my English. I was relieved when they passed the compound door and continued on toward the large square. I decided to follow them.

The four young men walked north through the plaza empty at this late hour but decorated some with tissue for Christmas. At the center of the square under a palm frond roof was a miniature Nativity scene. The plaster figures painted each year and each year more paint chipped from their faces. A finger missing on the hand of one of the wise men. Baby Jesus a pale childrens doll wrapped in a light blue blanket. The cantinas and cafés were closed for the night. The tables and chairs stacked. The moon almost full. The light of this on the dark stones silver blue. Dressed in black laughing high laughs like demons the young men passed through shadows and light. Rodríguez knocked over a plaster mule. Elías kicked up some of the palm fronds onto the crib. The four of them laughing at this.

They continued down from the plaza. In the streetlight I could see that their hair was shiny with grease. Their shoes made noise on the stones unlike my huaraches. They turned west. Some ways down the block they stopped at a gate in a metal fence that surrounded an abandoned church. Narrow rectangular openings lined the long tall stone walls. The four men stopped before the gate and then it opened some and they disappeared in the shadows. I did not follow farther.

On the Sunday before my second fight the poet and I relaxed on a shaded knoll across the open square from the cathedral. The poet rolled cigarettes with papers I had bought him while studying the old women dressed in black. Admiring their walks from behind. The women huddled in small groups in the middle of the square or holding each other by the arms they climbed the steps to hear mass in the cool of the cathedral. Laughter chased children playing a game of tag. They circled a group of men with combed hair and mustaches waxed. When the small bells tolled from high above the massive wood doors pigeons in the cupolas and alcoves tore over the plaza in a wash of flapping wings. Their wide shadow flickering over the sand colored stones. The poet lit his cigarette. The plaza emptied for mass.

There is much praying in Mexico. I said to the poet.

I hope you do not fight dogs like you think. He answered me. I will miss having you around to appreciate my stories.

Whenever there was something on my mind and I told the poet of it he was always quick to laugh. But he was also very good at making me think with his questions. He could be very patient with me in this. I never lied to the poet or pretended to know more than I did. Nothing escaped his eyes. And with his talking my mind came alive in ways only my grandfather had accomplished. But this was much different. And better.

Do you read the Bible much? I asked the poet then.

Only the parts I needed to to know that it was not for me.

Which parts were those?

Most of them. But I do enjoy all the contradictions. I think they are a good way to understand God.

The plaza was still and empty but full of sun. I heard the men and women in the cathedral singing.

Do you pray?

I come here each Sunday. The poet answered. To be with Him but not to ask for anything.

Is that why we did not go in?

The poet lit his cigarette from the end of one he had been smoking.

I like for God to know that I am here. Entiendes? But I do not believe in the forgiveness that they ask for inside. I know my sins and I can admit them without going in there. Out here is where I make my sins and out here is where I live with them. God does not need to forgive me for my sins. We forgive each other. You and me. The poet picked a fleck of tobacco from his lower lip. Listen carefully. He said. God is indeed a jealous God. He cannot bear to see. That we had rather not with Him. But with each other play.

That is one of my better poems. The poet reached under his arm and removed a pebble that had been uncomfortable where he was lying on his side. God is nothing but an excuse to them. He waved his hand over the plaza. This sun. This knoll with some shade and the smell of the salt from the sea. This is more than any priest can tell me about God. This is what I answer to.

I told the poet then that I disagreed. That I did not think that it was wrong for people to need a place to pray together. That not everyone was able to think as he did.

No. You are right dog fighter. But this is a small game I play with God. I am always wanting Him to walk out and He is wanting me to walk in.

Early that evening the poet and I walked into the hills near the abandoned mine where the view of Canción was very impressive. In the mountains beyond this place the road that was under construction at this time was a light colored brushstroke on the dark hillsides. The road from Canción went west before heading north to where we could not see it the mountains were so steep. On Sundays the men were not working and the great machines used for grading and cutting into those rocky hillsides were still like sleeping metal beasts. During the weekdays in Canción now and then I heard blasting in the hills. Men who came to work on the hotel but were turned away for one reason or another went to work on this road.

El fin de Canción. The poet called the roads. The end of this forgotten city.

I worked on the roads in Chihuahua. I said then. From Chihuahua to Ciudad Juárez.

For the mines?

Yes.

During the war I read about these roads. The poet said. The Americans wanting a new one each day it seemed.

I wanted to tell him then of how I had stood by as the faces of mountains were destroyed. Witnessed entire villages told to move because some men with some instruments said to move. Thousands of sunburned ears gone deaf from the blasting of boulders into pebbles. But I did not have the words then and the poet was always an imposing figure.

Roads in Baja will be very slow to stretch the length of this peninsula. He said. Before a man went from spring to spring. In this way from Tijuana to Guerrero Negro. Ciudad Constitución to El Arco at Cabo San Lucas.

I learned from the poet that during the war access to the copper and gypsum mines in Baja was greatly desired by the United States. A road was paved as far south as San Quentin. But along this bandidos struck with machetes and rifles whose ends were filed to cut like knives. This upset the American investors very much. The Mexican businessmen also. But for many Mexicans it was something of a quiet and often not so quiet pride.

But here. In the south. The poet continued. A truck with a flat tire or one stuck in the sand will leave a man to die of thirst before he comes to any water but that of the salt of the sea or the ocean. You leave Canción and you find bones in the middle of these roads delicate as chalk in a landscape watered by the sun. Shaded only by vulture wings. This road they are working on. It will not connect us to anywhere for many years to come.

How will Cantana bring the tourists? I asked.

Airplane. The poet said softly. He threw his cigarette to the ground and looked quietly where it lay smoldering.

The uneven roads were good footpaths for the poet. But as the sun set he had some difficulty walking with his eyes not the best from years of reading in shadows. His vulgar talk and nasty smile made me forget sometimes that he was just more than sixty years old. His mind so young and alive. We passed the abandoned mine the metal roof of which was light in that coming dark. The poet did not speak to save his breath for his smoking as we walked. Many times I lent him my arm.

Did I ever tell you about my time in el Bajío? The poet said. I worked on the railroads there just before la Revolución. I met a girl whose father I worked for. Melones hasta aquí. And she had pretty eyes. When I looked into them. The poet laughed. This girl. Her father was a drunk. He left out pliers and wrenches and hammers on the kitchen table whenever I came to take her on a walk. I had no place to sleep and I washed in a river. But I was a hard worker and he respected this. But he was right to have those tools out to intimidate me. When he fell asleep drunk and after her mother went to sleep this girl would sneak out of her window to meet me. I talked her into doing this on those walks we took. Late at night I waited behind a low mud wall throwing stones at trees. Fence posts. Cats. This girl had the most beautiful neck. I would kiss it for hours. For so long because it was the only thing she would allow me to do to her. I would make those pretty eyes roll back like pearls in that moonlight.

But the old poet never shared stories of his family. The women he mentioned all were in stories like this. In his talk I knew the poet was very lonely. Much more than me.

I am convinced that the hillsides are the most beautiful poems. The poet said when we were resting on several large stones the men working on the road had pushed to the side. These mountains here have seen almost as much change as a square of dirt during a rainstorm. He sighed smoke. Rolling a cigarette with one already between his lips. I read poems every night. They compare women to a flower. To a breeze. I cannot tolerate these poems. We have done much to these hills. And only more will be done in the future. Our landscape is not of trees and forests and deserts but hotels and tourists and their cameras and airplanes. We are as far west as this part of the world can be you know. And instead of it ending it just rolls back on itself. It refuses to stay old even when old is just fine. Look at me. He laughed lighting the fresh cigarette. I am a perfect example of how wonderful old things can be. Baja has never been Mexico and it is not the United States. It is becoming a bastard child of both and no longer its own. The businessmen want the tourists to spend their money. And those of us who are not the businessmen allow this. Maybe I am just jealous that none of the money ends up in my pockets.

He laughed then but I knew that he was testing me. From the hills the work on the hotel seemed insignificant. But the sight of it growing taller than the buildings below higher even than the cathedral upset the poet. I understood that when he spoke in this way it was best not to interrupt him.

And I am not even Catholic! He yelled pointing to the towers of the cathedral. But so few complain about the height of this hotel. What this means to their religion. Not when the businessmen promise them money. Only the priests maybe are more corrupt. For centuries they have answered only to wealth. Bleeding the poor they have fooled.

For all the time I was friends with the poet we never spoke of my work on the hotel. It was a difficult struggle. The work it brought to Canción. The money it might bring to those who lived farther and farther from the plaza mayor in canvas tents and mud jacales. The poet knew I was ashamed to speak of why I had come to Canción now that he and I were friends. Most of the time talk of the hotel dissolved the poets words into grunts and gestures. And for a poet I think this is the most beautiful and difficult thing.

Dark was coming and I had not yet swum to ready myself for the fighting the next night. I rubbed my hands on my cotton pant legs thinking the poet would recognize that I was ready to move on.

Do you pray dog fighter? He asked me then.

Sometimes.

You understand that God is not for sometimes?

He is also not for everyone. I answered.

Bueno. The poet smiled at me but not so that his teeth showed. Then taking his cigarette to his mouth he said. But remember that there is a time when everyone will turn to God. And it is wrong to do this if you have said wrong things of Him. Especially saying that He does not exist. Because He does. God is a beautiful thing. The best poem we have. You do not want to say bad things about Him. This way when your time comes to turn to Him you will not look like some fool. The old poet paused. And do not lie. He said. Lies exhaust me.

We came down from the hills and into the hard packed streets. Then onto the cart and hoof polished stones nearing the large square. Here we passed a small girl struggling beneath an accordion. With her arms wrapped awkwardly around the instrument her tiny fingers pressed the worn keys as she began to sing. A boy skipped from person to person accepting coins that plinked at the bottom of a tin can above the music sharply. Wind came through dusty palm leaves softening the sound of the poets raspy breathing. Our shadows intertwined against the drawn shutters of the buildings we passed. The boy moved quickly to those walking toward the plaza. When he turned from the poet he bumped into my leg and fell onto the ground. The coins clattered over the stones. The sister collapsed the accordion. I offered my hand to the small boy but he jumped to his feet and hurried after the coins. A band of poor children that had been lurking in the shadows dove into the street but the sister snapped them back with hard vulgar words. The poet laughed smoke. The eyes of the boy shone white in fear of my size.

You have a good heart dog fighter. The poet said as we left. But people only notice your shoulders and hands.

That night I stood at the window of my room looking over the garden on the rooftop. The cleaning woman had hung the clothes on the line earlier in the day and the smell of the cacti in the wet soil of their clay pots was comforting. The long walk with the poet had been good. The day had been dry and warm. Not too hot. I concentrated on the towers of the cathedral across the rooftops. The streetlamps cast thin lines of glaring light along the windmill blades. In the shadows of the windows I kept my questions. Stared into them standing in the dark of my room feeling the contours of my fists. I thought then of the dogs. Of my father. I feared somehow he was going to be at the fighting. Hunched with ragmen wrapping my arm. Or at the fence with red eyes like the drunk. I feared him standing among the yelling men. That he would whisper.

I put money on the dog.

A lamp turned on in the room of the dentists mother across the courtyard. Spilling into shadows and making other shadows. The dentist undressed his mother from her dress while she sat on the bed. Wrinkled skin the color of thin paper the poet used in his stall at the market. While he folded her dress she felt for the nightstand and then the pillow as she lowered herself to rest. Jorge pulled a thin blanket from the foot of her bed neatly to her chin. He spoke to her soft words I was not able to hear. He brought his ear to her mouth when she spoke. Then the door to the back room opened below and music from the Victrola seeped into the courtyard. One of the young men called for the dentist but Jorge kept his ear to his mothers whispers. Then the door to the back room closed and in the quiet Jorge turned off the lamp by his mothers bed and the shadows were dark again with time. I heard the dentist on the creaking stairs. The young men laughing in the back room. Then the sound of another door closing to me. Another light turned off.

In the quiet of the dark I stood at my window and listened for her in the music of the sea and the breeze and the laughing and the lights in the distant windows flickering votive candles. I thought about the fighting and my grandfather and the old poet and I was very nervous and scared even when I tried now to hear the yelling men calling my name.

I sat on my bed in the dark holding my own hands.

I n the small room on the rooftop using a small knife Ramón worked at dismantling a skinny leg from a wood chair. He tried sawing through the leg at its narrow ends but the knife was not for sawing and when this became too difficult he cursed the knife and broke the chair against the metal railing of the spiral staircase.

Where do you hide yourself? Ramón asked me while trying to saw the leg. People in the cantinas are always asking where you are. Wondering why you never come out with us.

I saw you the other night. I told him then. You and some others.

Where?

Near the abandoned church.

You should have stopped us. We are always out late. Walking the streets. Causing trouble.

Maybe next time.

There is going to be a Christmas party next week. At the house of a friend of ours. Plenty of beautiful women. You should come.

When he had broken the chair over the railing he picked one of the legs off the floor and held it in his hand admiring it in the golden light. A wicked smile eased into the corners of his mouth.

I should have done that in the beginning. He said.

In the month since my first fight the cuts on my chest had healed. Ramón sat in a different chair rubbing the eucalyptus balm over the scar above his knee. Now it was nothing but a long pink slash of thick skin. To be fresh for more scars we stretched and did push ups and sit ups listening to the fighting on the rooftop. I could tell that something distracted Ramón. He looked to the stairs with much anticipation in his eyes. Listening to the sounds of voices two floors below where Elías the doorman stood guard. The yelling men on the rooftop cheered for the first two fighters but waited for Ramón and myself. For Ramón because he had beaten two of the dogs of Mendoza. And for myself because my great size is rare in Mexico.

When Vargas footsteps came heavily up the metal stairs Ramón walked quietly on his toes to a far corner of the room where the person climbing the stairs would have his back to him. When the fugitive reached the top of the spiral staircase he looked to me and smiled. His eyes scanned the room for Ramón but then across his face he realized where Ramón was and this was when Ramón hit him with the leg of the chair in the back of the head just above his thick neck. Vargas fell to the floor unconscious. A welt rose along his neck and below his ear instantly. Ramón giggled. He bent over and took from the fugitives hand the painted stick he had chosen below. Ramón replaced this stick with his own.

Let Mendoza be for someone else tonight. He said.

With the loud thud of the fugitive falling to the floor Elías came running up the staircase with his revolver drawn. He put the revolver back in his pants and he and Ramón stood over Vargas laughing.

One bottle or two? Elías asked while shaking the dog fighters hand.

No. Ramón answered. María.

María?

De los ojos grandes.

Muy bien.

When the door opened and Ramón went out to fight two ragmen helped the fugitive to sit in a chair. His eyes were glassy. They threw water in his face to wake him. I had not moved from where I sat.

You are going to have to kill him now. I said to Vargas as he shook his head to stir himself awake. He did not realize that Ramón had switched the painted sticks.

Why? He asked without looking me in the eyes. So Cantana can have me killed?

Ramón is friends with El Tapado?

They drink together in all the cantinas. Share women. Steal other mens women.

I sat quietly. Before I had not thought of Ramón as the way for me to meet her. I suspected the dog fighters spent time with all the businessmen except Cantana. Ramón was handsome though. And colorful in his fighting and this made him very popular.

Why do you think I spend time with him? Vargas said a moment later.

Cantana?

No. Ramón.

No sé.

I like the women he brings. I am not a handsome man like he is. I do not have the money or power Cantana has. But I do not mind their scraps. Their scraps are very tasty.

This was over a woman? I held my hand to the side of my neck where his welt was. María?

Some whore. He winked. I bet Ramón that he could not knock me unconscious. Vargas laughed a short laugh after saying this. It was a bet. Nothing more. The fugitive lowered his face and shook his head slightly to stir himself. I will get him though. You wait. The golden boy will get what he deserves.

But then came the yelling men.

Ramón! They chanted. Ramón! Ramón!

Cabrón! The fugitive chanted. Cabrón! Cabrón! He looked at me and smiled but I knew that he was disappointed.

I was next to fight. While the ragmen prepared my arm with the heavy rug I searched for her in the crowd of businessmen and yelling men busy placing their bets. The well dressed young man went among them but I did not see him stop in front of Cantana. I could not find Cantana.

It was not until I caught the back legs of the second dog I had to fight and swung its head against a metal pole of the ring that I saw her. Each time I did this the dog came back and flashing its teeth snapped uselessly at me until the skull was crushed and blood spilled from its ears onto the floor of the ring. Under the light of that full moon the businessmen stood around her yelling my name. Again and again while the mistresses of the businessmen cried and the businessmen themselves clapped their hands. When I found her alongside Cantana her eyes sunk like teeth into my skin. I was panting. Standing in the blood of the dogs I had just killed. And still I could think only of kissing her neck. Of rubbing the back of her soft hand against my cheek. Burying my face in the fragrance of her long black hair.

While Vargas killed his dog I stood among the men looking through the fence across the ring into her eyes. I did not care that Cantana could see this. The fighting had been between the three of us. Furious and violent between our eyes. She sat next to Cantana but never taking her eyes from me. Her high cheeks red from the warmth of the lights above the ring. The corners of her mouth turned down some but only enough to push up gently the plush of her lower lip. Her eyelashes long and dark and beautiful when she blinked. My mind went empty like the dark water surrounding us when we made love in the bay. The quiet of her eyes like stars falling onto my chest. Her singing to me in a voice she shared with no one else. Her smile a slight pinch at the corner of her eyes. But plenty.

I felt strong but of some different strength. I felt good. It was better than any number of men yelling my name. I felt myself a great man above the fury between us. I told her that I was for her alone. That my days were spent imagining us talking in the kitchen of our home. Kissing in the quiet of our small room. Our children asleep. She looked into me without judgment. And together we were alone surrounded by yelling men before the fighting of dogs.

After Vargas had killed his dog Cantana put his gloved hand on her arm. I awoke from her to find the businessman staring at me. His eyes hot coals behind his sunglasses. But a smile on his face because he recognized our love. He nodded at me then as he stood to leave. I knew that he enjoyed allowing this love. That this was the power of

Cantana. It was this way when I stood in rooms knowing how scared others were of not what I did with my arms and hands and chest but what I could do. Cantana and I understood one another very well.

That night once more though he took her from me into the shadows beyond the light of the ring. We had stared into one another and admitted our love. But to do that without words was also to admit Cantanas hold over us both.

FIVE

The Christmas party the following week was held at the house of the young businessman Rodríguez. He was the fourth man that I had followed walking through the plaza mayor with Elías and Vargas and Ramón. He lived alone in a neighborhood at the north of Canción where in the hills the roads were of stone and the houses not built alongside one another but with fences around them containing landscaped yards. Tall palm trees lined the path to the front of the house and on the side wall I noticed a bougainvillea as old and beautiful as the one at the dentists. Music from a mariachi band came from the back of the house. Inside I heard women laughing and through some windows saw the twirl of their skirts dancing.

Earlier in the week to impress her I had bought a suit of cotton that the tailor was forced to fit especially for me. My feet were uncomfortable in the new dress shoes over the stone path. The shirt tight at my neck. I was nervous. When I came into the entry of the house Ramón was coming down the stairs with a beautiful woman. Rodríguez hurried behind them trying to get Ramóns attention.

Que chingón! Ramón yelled ignoring Rodríguez. Many turned to look. Who is this?

I handed a bottle of expensive tequila to Rodríguez.

At least one of you dog fighters has some courtesy.

Ramón shrugged and said.

I invited the women. It is not my fault you do not enjoy the company of women.

Ramón laughed more and squeezed the girl toward him while Rodríguez blushed trying to think of a response. Ramón recognized this and laughed more at the young businessman.

I am joking hombre. Everyone here knows that you love women. Ugly ones. But still.

There were many people in the house. It was very well built and similar to no other house I had seen in Canción. The floors were of stained hardwood with intricate designs around the doors and hallways. The walls were of stone but inside lath and plaster. On these walls someone had hung many paintings of the sea. There were also several portraits of one man who I guessed to be Rodríguez but older. Young men and women well dressed went from room to room carrying drinks or eating from plates of food. Several businessmen I recognized from the fighting sat on a large couch in the corner before a large stained glass window of the malecón and the Bay of Canción. These businessmen sat by themselves but with their mistresses constantly at their sides. One of the mistresses wore a close fitting green dress. She was a little drunk and begging one of the businessmen to dance with her but he wagged a stubby finger between them and shook his head no. His face very serious. Holding her hand tight like some treasure. Ramón and the young woman he was with had gone outside where I saw him through a window near the fountain making a group laugh. The women in this group stared at him with fixed eyes. The young woman he came down the stairs with continued to put her hand on his arm but it fell to the side ignored when he spoke with his great gestures. I turned from the window to the paintings.

I have a nephew with one eye and a clubfoot who rubs his snot on the furniture and it looks better than this. Vargas said suddenly standing next to me. He was dressed in black but wearing old comfortable huaraches. Nice shoes. He smiled.

Who is the man in these paintings?

The father. The mother died when Rodríguez was young. Or maybe she is still in Spain. I do not remember. I was drunk when he told the story.

And the father.

Dead. Vargas said sipping from a green bottle without a label. But not after making plenty of money in oil to leave to our friend here.

I think so. I said.

Do you? Vargas asked.

Cómo? I was confused by this answer from the fugitive. I was accustomed to speaking with the poet who when I said things such as this it was usually just to let him know that I was listening to his rambling. But now I did not agree with the tone of voice Vargas spoke in.

Nothing. He drank from the bottle.

What is that? I asked him.

Mescal. Homemade by some old man Rodríguez is friends with. Later we are going to drain the gasoline and see if Cantanas limousine will run on this. He held up the bottle for me to try. You want some?

I shook my head. Looked over the crowd. I was disappointed not to find Cantana. Not to see her. But I did not risk mentioning her or the businessman to Vargas.

I am surprised you came tonight. He said to me.

Why?

You do not seem like the type for parties.

The fugitive made me uncomfortable. I already felt very uncomfortable in my suit and without a glass of something in my hand I did not know whether to have my hands in my pockets or to cross my arms.

No sé. I said to say something.

You do not know what? The fugitive asked.

What do you mean?

He laughed more. Drank from the bottle and wiped his mouth on the back of his hand. His eyes were already glassy and his breath sharp from the alcohol.

Well. Vargas said then. I am going to go and find a lady for the night. And if not then I am going to find someone to beat and take their money so I can buy myself a whore later.

I was happy to be alone again. I walked through the house admiring the paintings of Rodríguezs father. The detailed wood-work. In construction I was always doing much of the heavy labor. None of the careful work. But this always fascinated me. The details. How the joints of molding fit together neat around the doors. The cuts made and sanded in the railing and banister. The doorknobs were of brass. The doors stained dark red.

Soon I came to the back of the house. Outside lights had been strung and more chairs were set near a small stone fountain. The musicians in their sombreros with silver threads and silver buttons along their trousers. The horn sounding nicely with the strum of the guitar. The faces of the party becoming more and more flush from the alcohol as the night went on. One young man hunched over alone in the far shadow of the backyard vomiting. A friend went up to him and put his hand on his back and whispered something to him and then turned to those by the fountain and pointed down at the back of the young man heaving. They all pointed and laughed. There was much laughter and talking and at some point in the night there was a fight in the backyard between two young men over an idea but really over a woman.

The businessmen left before it was too late. The headlights of their cars showing through the uneven stained glass windows at the front of the house. I sat on the couch and listened to one young woman talking jealously to another about the gifts one of the businessmen had bought for one of the mistresses who had left. Most of those who remained at the party lingered outside smoking around the fountain or sitting in the chairs. Ramón came into the living room then. Tall and broad shouldered and handsome in his suit. He held a glass of red wine. The young women stopped talking when he entered. They noticed that he was alone. When he sat in a chair across from me he leaned toward me so that his forearms were on his knees. The light of a tall shaded lamp softened his face. His skin almost golden. The one girl with her back to me on the couch sat back so that the two of them faced Ramón.

Are you enjoying yourself in here with these two? He asked smiling at me only with his white teeth but also for the girls.

It is a wonderful party. I answered.

It is. He agreed. You should try enjoying it some.

I smiled with my lips closed.

There is a woman here asking about you. He said.

Who? I asked.

I do not remember. Ramón said. Then he turned to one of the young women sitting on the couch. What is your name?

Diana. She smiled. Holding out her hand but Ramón did not take it. Instead he turned to me and said.

Diana.

On the second floor of the house there was some yelling then. A mans voice laughing. Then heavy steps coming down the stairs. Rodríguez. He was drunk and with his pants unbuttoned. His face red and combed hair messy. He came down the stairs to Ramón and took the glass of wine from the dog fighters hand. He finished the wine in the glass in one long drink and then he smiled. His teeth stained red.

What was it you said the other night? He asked. Ramóns eyes judging him carefully. What is a woman like?

I do not remember. He answered plainly. He looked at the knots in the hardwood floor.

Women. You said. Are like a fine glass of wine.

Maybe that was it then. Ramón said without lifting his eyes. He was very embarrassed by the young businessman.

But I disagree. Rodríguez said. He stood unsteadily before Ramón. I prefer the women.

Later I walked with Ramón from the young businessmans house back toward the plaza mayor.

How old are you? He asked me then.

Nineteen. And you?

Twenty-two.

How old is Rodríguez?

Twenty.

Young for a businessman. I said.

His father died.

Vargas told me.

Vargas. Ramón laughed to himself. Shaking his head slightly.

We walked with our hands in our pockets at a slow pace. I enjoyed Ramóns company in the way I enjoyed the company of the old poet. But with Ramón I did not feel the need to be so careful with my words.

He is going to get himself into some trouble one of these days. Ramón said after a moment.

Vargas?

No. Rodríguez. He wants to fight dogs but the businessmen will not let him. This is why he is always taking us out and buying us drinks. He figures if he cannot be a dog fighter then at least he should be friends with them. I should probably not tease him so much.

Maybe. I said when it was my turn to speak.

We entered a neighborhood where the run down houses had been built almost on top of each other. The streets no longer stone but hard dirt. It was quiet and the light we had was that of the many stars now that the moon was new. The air pleasant and cool.

You do not talk much do you. Ramón said.

Why will they not let Rodríguez fight? I asked so that we would not have to talk about me.

He would be killed. Ramón answered. He does not have the mind for it. The heart maybe. But not the mind.

What mind? I asked him.

The one we have I guess.

The iron shutters of many of the windows were closed. We passed a skinny dog baring its teeth at us as he snuck up in the shadow of a wall toward some hens escaped from their pens. Ramón made as if to kick the dog but the dog lowered its ears and cowered against the wall. We went on. I was surprised that Ramón had left without a woman and I told him so.

I had to. He said. The girl I came with does not interest me anymore. Besides. He checked an expensive watch he kept tucked inside his coat. I have plans to meet that girl from the couch in an hour or so.

Diana? I asked.

Was that her name? He smiled.

From the beginning my intentions toward Ramón were dishonest. I decided he was to be my way to her. That I would use him somehow to be introduced to Cantana and by him to her.

I returned to the dentists late that night. Always I came and went from my room at the dentists only when it was dark or very early in the morning when I was certain no one noticed me. The compound was peaceful. As hidden in the world as I believed Canción was then. Because of how my life had been before I very often worried that I could be responsible for upsetting the calm of the compound. Ruin it somehow by my presence alone. That it was as if what troubled me most could follow me there and was not buried within. But was something I was.

One evening just after dark while I waited to leave for my evening swim I heard the voices of Jorge and the young men below. The courtyard was empty and the lights off but for the light of a dim lamp in the back room. Then carrying the end of a string of red light globes already lit Jorge stepped from the shadows bathed in red light. Two young men assisted the dentist by holding lengths of the looped and sagging cord while a third brought the ladder to stand on to hang the lights along the walls around the courtyard. Their faces glowing in that lit progression. Their eyes small and dark. Hooded by shadows. Music from the Victrola a melody beneath their barely intelligible voices.

Once the lights were hung Jorge led his mother into the center of the courtyard. The three young men stood off to the side close to one another but quiet. Jorge took his mother along the walls and where the strung lights drooped some he placed his thumb carefully in the palm of her hand and raised her arm so that her fingers could sense the warmth of the globe. The young men turned quietly toward the back room while Jorge led his mother whispering from light to light.

Later that night I sat in my chair with my forearm resting on the windowsill admiring the red hue of the empty courtyard. Palm frond shadows cast over the tiles. I had been sitting there for some time reciting the poems in English of the poets that I knew when the knocking came softly through the compound. The dentist crossed the sandy courtyard from the back room in his slippers. His steps quick but measured. Moments later he returned with the shadowy figure I had witnessed him with several times before. But with the strung red lights now I was able to distinguish more of this figure than before. He was a young man. The same height as the dentist but wiry. He wore all black clothes and his footsteps made no sound. Then something occurred that surprised me very much. Jorge tenderly wrapped his arm around the waist of this young man and rested his head on his shoulder. When they were in the full of the red light at the center of the courtyard the young man leaned forward as they walked and kissed Jorge on the lips.

I knew very little of the dentist then. We had spoken only a handful of times and never about more than the weather or of what I was cooking in the kitchen. Once he had asked me in passing to help him trim a stray bougainvillea vine that was out of his reach. For all of the attention the dentist craved when the window was open to the street for all to see him work I knew that he was a very private man. Sitting at the windowsill I watched him and the shadowy figure disappear into the back room where they could be alone.

This behavior disgusted me. The calm of the compound had been broken.

———

In Canción sand collects against the bottoms of unused doors blown each evening by the heavy winds. The buildings are colorful but dusty low along the walls and only when the rains come is the mierda of burros and dogs in the gutters and depressions dissolved some. In tiny squares throughout the city goats stand tied with rope to limbs of date trees while chickens peck at the ground for seeds that are not there. In the outskirts of the city children play in oil drums. Laughing and squealing. Walking each day I felt very much a part of the city. I believe now that lonely young men in love do much walking.

A young man with thoughts needs no other company. The poet once said to me.

At this time my mind was very open to the poet. I practiced copying out his poems in my room or at his stall. In the corners of my mind swimming in the bay I pronounced the sweet words over and over. In the streets where people noticed and would have pointed laughing if not for my size. I was fascinated as a boy with how my father had shaped these same words with his own mouth but differently. His clean fingers around my jaw. Once he held my tongue and I bit him.

Never hit a man in the head when you have your hand in his mouth. He said playfully. His riddling words between us a fathers game.

At night the black water is still warm from the sun of the day but cool where I kicked down beneath the surface. I tried not to think of my father much though. More and more often I followed my thoughts like waking dreams to those of my mother lying dead. The heart of the deep bloodstain next to her black. Exhausted.

During the days I swam with the ragged groups of boys in their canoes made of cordón logs. Racing them over the ribboned water. The waves slapped against the hulls regular as laughter. Treading water among them to work on the strength of my legs I kept the time by telling my own stories.

In Northern California there are trees packed into fields until the limbs grow into one another they are planted so close. And the grass around these trees is lush as this bay but a deep green beneath the charcoal colored limbs. When spring comes the orchards are filled with blossoms. But winter lingers some and a cold wind knocks the early petals from the trees. They fall like snowflakes.

Snowflakes? One boy asked another.

Snow.

What are the girls like there? One boy asked.

Nothing but trouble. I smiled. Now race me back to the beach. See if you can keep up this time.

I had listened to the stories of my grandfather carelessly. Greed and anger were his truths.

They have been for all time. He had whispered.

But they did not have to be mine.

Long iron harpoons lay at the bottom of the boys canoes. They carried them like walking sticks into the city with twine or thin rope tied to the ends. The barbed ends sharpened and made with a cord to open inside the fish once it had pierced the skin and the fish went to escape. The boys jumped from the steep rocks at the mouth of the bay. Turning and twisting in the air to show off yelling before the ferry and fishing boats.

One afternoon I sat on the docks with them watching as two boys stole the skiff of a drunk fisherman while he slept. The skiff weighed down some by an engine that leaked gasoline into the bay. They ran the skiff in tight circles churning water behind them. Steering back into it. They chased their friends in the canoes chasing them to get on the skiff. An endless game. On the dock some of us sat laughing while the drunk went from fisherman to fisherman and even the women repairing the nets pleading with them for help.

When the skiff finally ran out of gas at the middle of the bay the boys left it floating. They disappeared among the others. All their smiles the same.

Canción is a poem. The old poet liked to say when things like this happened. We like to think we are hidden and unique to the world.

I sat with the poet in the market but some days I also went to chase the children and buy them brown sugar cakes. Panocha. The women argued in hard voices over vegetables with other women. Women sent to the market by other women. Some of the stalls displayed colorful bonito and other skinny mackerel lying over beds of dirty ice. Men sank scarred hands in tanks of salt water after fast pink crabs that changed color when you took them struggling for air from the water. Sea turtle shells gutted and scraped clean with shiny dull blades hung to dry. The faces and legs of the men who sold carbon for fires were sooty and black. The fingers of the basket weavers old but nimble and quick weaving coarse reeds. The children hid behind all this or one another holding their laughter as I stalked them through the aisles growling like some horrible monster with one eye closed and my hands searching the air for tiny arms and smiling lips glistening with sugar. When I caught the children I lifted them above my head or swung them above the ground close to my chest. They loved being caught. The market was a maze I came to know very well.

When I visited the hotel after the workingmen had gone for the day the heat was nothing more than a pleasant breeze for the guards to smoke their cigarettes in while the sun went down. I climbed to the top floor where work on another story had begun since the scaffolding had been rebuilt. Below mangy dogs followed refuse carts pulled by burros leaving the plaza mayor. In the small squares throughout the city hunchbacked women gathered their wares after leaning daylong over creaking looms. The warehouse of the abandoned mine a glint of silver in the distance. A building covering a hand dug shaft that drove toward the center of the earth. The mountains dry red. At twilight gold. The metal of the tractors working on the road glimmered like glass on a beach. From the top floor of the hotel I watched the canoe boys throw their harpoons at black cormorants from the raised malecón now that the tide was high. Somewhere she was reading a book by some window. Napping on a couch with her fine dark hair splayed over some pillow. I enjoyed the view the hotel allowed me. The comfort it afforded. It was as if it was from the overlook above the mine but more because it was closer to the city. A part of it. I wanted for the poet to share in all of this. To be able to see what the hotel allowed for all his talk of not wanting it in Canción. I wanted Cantana to build the hotel if only to allow the poet to see Canción the way the workingmen saw it within it. But the poet never thought of it in this way.

It is easier to see things from a distance. He had said to me.

Think of the man who has lived here his entire life. The poet said sitting at his stall in the market cleaning sand from the oiled underside of one of his typewriters. Think of the woman who wakes up each day with the sun over the bay coming through her windows. Reflecting in the mirror she puts her hair up in. Wait until this hotel is finished. The poet said to me. When the money comes to build taller ones there will be no view for this woman. Less light for her mirror. This man will see only the back of these monsters where the tourists wake up with his view. They pay for it. Yes. But we pay more. This hotel is only the beginning. He said to me. After this we will be even more lost to this world. We will be servants to it.

Many times I did not know what to feel for Canción. But for the canoe boys and the children of the women in the market I cared very much. I never spoke to them in my grandfathers hiss. I never told the stories he buried in me. Instead for them I bought great bags of hard candy. Honey drops and sugar cubes. I bought metal toy cars for the boys and paper dolls for the girls. For the poet I bought expensive cigarillos like the ones Cantana smoked.

A dog fighter who plays Santa Claus. He laughed at me.

In the market the children came to me snarling like dogs with

snot dripping from their noses into their smiles. I held my giant fists
before them and they ran shrieking with laughter. The meat hung in
the aisles of the market touching the ground where the women
threw their dirty water at night. The smell heavy with cilantro and
smoke from a beautiful young woman who stood over a grill serving
food to men who sat at her counter. The air thick with limón and
dirty water where the children and I played for hours. And in their
laughter I heard echoes of my ferry journey to Canción. Of the
laughs the toothless man with the scorpion gave them and the
delight he felt. I enjoyed this attention.

There is little in this world better than the attention of children.
The poet told me once. It is a simple and generous thing.

The children ran from me with candy spilling from their pockets
and sticky hands. Stopping only when their mothers caught them by
their arms and held them squirming. When playing with the children in the market I did not feel so alone. I thought nothing of
myself.

One evening some weeks after Christmas during a game of hide
and seek an American and his wife wandered down the aisles of the
mercado. Tourists at this time were not rare in Canción but they
were not many either. In their limited Spanish the Americans asked
one of the old women for a photograph with the children. The old
woman would not touch the camera. The poet approached the
Americans in a humble voice pretending that the English he spoke
was not much. He called to the small pickpocket who had stolen my
money and stood him next to the man. I watched from the poets stall
as he gathered other children around the Americans and their white
smiles. Then the poet stood back with the camera and winked. The
wife told the American to give the poet some pesos for this help but
the poet refused.

Bienvenidos a Canción. He smiled his terrible smile. The wife
shuddered when she noticed his teeth.

After the Americans were gone the small pickpocket came to the
poet with the wallet of the American. That afternoon the children all

had candy and the poet drank cold beer and grilled steak with grilled onions from the young womans counter.

To small victories. The poet raised his bottle of beer.

The small pickpocket and I had made friends soon after I became friends with the poet. This boy was very brave. Never afraid of me. One day as a present I gave him my switchblade. I told him not to tell the other children.

Only with you do I share this secret. I said.

He held it in both hands watching the light gleam off the blade when it flicked open immediately.

But when the American returned looking for his wallet I was teaching the small pickpocket where to place his thumb when he made a fist and where are the best places to punch a man in the neck so not to break a bone in the hand or hurt the wrist when hitting the face. The small pickpocket practiced into my hands before him.

You have stolen from me! The American yelled slowly at the poet who only shrugged and said.

Yo no comprendo inglés.

The women and I laughed. I kept the small pickpocket next to me. But when the American cursed at the poet pointing his finger near to the chest of my friend I stood and the American was quiet then and left looking behind to see if I followed.

Often after the poet closed his stall in the evenings he asked me to play billiards with him and his old friends he called them.

What do you do with yourself all night dog fighter so that you are too busy to come and meet some old friends of mine who I tell so much about you?

I copy your poems. I said. I walk.

I think. He smiled and stepped closer. You have a woman that you are not telling me about.

No. I blushed.

The old poet put his hand on my shoulder.

You can lie to yourself my friend but you cannot lie to me.

Still I wandered the streets of Canción looking for signs of her.

Memorizing the buildings of the streets. Admiring their design. Naming the doors and windows and roofs and pots in English quietly to myself. The words my fathers voice in my head.

In January my twentieth birthday passed without my telling anyone but her. On this night after being together with her in the water I went home and dreamed of Cantana. He stood at the foot of my bed as a fat little boy smoking with his sunglasses on. Toying with the knife he had used to take the eyes of the man from the market. In our bed I turned to her sleeping next to me as he watched. Only when she awoke and put her lips to my eyelids did the businessman disappear.

———

I lay one night late listening to the sounds of the city beyond my window. To a cart rolling over stones. Two men discussing war. The smell of the garden pleasantly woven into a cool breeze that came over me. I had finished earlier in the night copying out a new poem the dentist had given me. I was reciting the words in a whisper when a loud knocking came on the door. I leaped from the bed to the window in time to see the dentist hurry across the courtyard. Almost tripping in the worn slippers he only walked slowly in. I dressed quickly. The violence of the knocking made me realize that it was for me. Hurrying down the stairwell I heard muffled yells coming from the entrance to the compound. My hands clenched into fists. My eyelids pulled back. I awoke then and lowered my head into my neck to ready myself for a fight.

It was Ramón. The dentist sprawled on the ground before him. His hands before his face. When the dog fighter saw me he threw his own hands above his head.

Amigo! He yelled. I have come to take you to a party.

I offered Jorge my hand but he did not accept.

How did you know where I live? I asked Ramón then.

Shhh! The dentist hissed.

Shhh! Ramón mocked him.

Take him away from here. Now!

Ahorita! Ramón hissed mocking the dentist again. But then he asked in a loud voice. Why are we whispering? Are the other maricones asleep?

Do not call him that. I said. Drunk Ramón looked directly into my eyes and only smiled. He was not afraid.

Come with me! He yelled. All the beautiful women will be there. Unless you prefer the company here.

Please leave now. The dentist hissed at me.

Let me get my money. I said to Ramón.

You do not need money. Ramón said. This is what the businessmen are for.

I followed Ramón north of the plaza mayor toward the abandoned church. As we walked he spoke of the women we were to meet that night and the drinks the businessmen would buy us. I could not listen to him. I did not know why I had defended the dentist from Ramón. The kiss Jorge shared with the mysterious young man had disgusted me. But watching them walk arm in arm to the soft music of the back room had made me jealous. And the jealousy I felt slowly replace my disgust then only made me more anxious to fight the dogs. To be near to her even if Cantana stood between us.

At the abandoned church we came to the gate I had seen Ramón and the other men enter some weeks before. The tall stone walls of the old church rose to meet boarded windows. On a stool behind the gate a man sat smoking a cigarette.

Qué pasa? Ramón asked the man as he stood and opened the gate for us.

Nada. He answered. Y tú?

Nothing good.

Both men laughed at this and shook hands with great familiarity.

Through a side door of the church I followed Ramón down some worn stone steps into an unlit hallway cool and mossy smelling. Ahead there was soft electric light and music and laughter.

A couple passed us holding hands and giggling. Through a bright door at the end of the hallway we came to stand on a landing that overlooked an enormous room below hazy with cigarette smoke. Dozens of well dressed men and women sat at rectangular tables drinking. Some stood at a bar to the back of the room. To the music Ramón tapped a ring he wore against the wood railing at the top of some stairs that led down to this. To where men and women were dancing in an open space before a band. Cigarettes cluttered ashtrays and the wet rings from glass bottoms glistened in that light. All the tables were very crowded.

Remember this place. Ramón said to me over the music. This is the best church I know of.

The stone staircase led down to where women spun dancing in colorful dresses. As we walked I searched among them for her. The musicians in light suits played on a stage at the far end of the high ceilinged cantina. The floor moved like dozens of colored pinwheels to the music. Swollen businessmen in wood chairs around rectangular tables whispered into the ears of their skinny mistresses. Two women had paired off and were dancing together. Slicing cleanly through those less graceful. Dancing as if they were alone. Some of the businessmen watched them hungrily. Bringing expensive cigarettes or cigarillos to their wet mouths while nodding to the rhythm.

When the musicians came to the end of their song they held their instruments against their bodies. Accepting the applause with smiles. A small man with a thin black mustache wearing a blue suit stepped onto the stage. He faced the musicians and then the guitar player strummed a soft chord followed by another before the dancers applauded and came together again. The small man in the blue suit began to sing in a low voice about the Bay of Canción.

The sun was setting. He was walking on the beach. As a boy he dove for pearls in the bay. He had had many friends.

Short round candles held to the tables by wax that dripped down their edges. Some set in crags in the crumbling walls. Ramón introduced me to a group of businessmen sitting at one rectangular table and then to a group sitting at another. We went from table to table with our large hands consuming those of the businessmen. The furrowed brows and sunken eyes in shadow from the flickering candles before them. Without the work on the hotel my hands had gone as soft as their own. But still mine were scarred from fighting. Ramón patted the businessmens shoulders and kissed those hands of the mistresses that were offered him.

The small man in the blue suit sang of how disease had killed the pearls. Many of his friends left Canción. The beautiful city became very poor.

The businessman spoke excitedly to Ramón and me about our fights. All of them asked us to sit with them. Offered to buy us drinks. I said thank you and one man laughed.

No hay de qué. He said. You just keep killing dogs.

Finally we came to a table where Vargas sat with the young businessman Rodríguez.

Ramón! Rodríguez said jumping up to find us extra chairs.

Cabrón! Vargas said bringing his drink to his lips.

The man on stage sang of the beauty of the sunset. On the beach he watched the waves gently dying. He knew he would never see his friends again. Only the sunsets are certain.

I was very disappointed that she was not there. For this and because I knew then that after what had occurred with Ramón the dentist would not allow me to return to my small room at the compound. As the last of the notes came to a slow death the man in the blue suit stepped down from the stage. The two women dancing came together as if to kiss but broke apart with the hard strumming of the next song. But in that lull before the new song the other dancers held each other a moment longer comfortably not having to think that anyone watched them.

At our table the businessmen drank damiana. Mescal and rum and beer. The teeth of some of the mistresses stained from wine. Without the man in the blue suit singing the yelling and laughter soon blended with the music. Rodríguez sat next to me asking about the fighting of dogs.

With the gloves. He said. You are assured a victory.

You think so? Vargas asked him. Leaning back in his chair so only two of the legs touched the floor. Ramón sat across from us listening to a beautiful young woman who whispered something very important to him into his ear but with her head turned to the side so that she did not see the eyes of the woman that Ramón was smiling at across the table. This woman herself with her hand on the hand of a businessman on her thigh. And this man watching the two women twirling through the crowd of less graceful dancers.

Of course. Rodríguez answered with a straight face. Believing what he said because the fugitive did not disagree.

Maybe the businessmen should let you fight. Vargas said.

You see! Rodríguez said to Ramón. We need to convince them. I would be great.

You would piss yourself. Ramón said and those at the table laughed. Rodríguez sat back in his chair.

It was then that I felt a hand rest on my shoulder. A mistress from another table.

Buenas noches. She whispered into my ear. Her breath warm on my neck. May I sit with you?

Ramón smiled at me. The other mistresses looked over this young woman. The businessmen smiled as she came around and sat on my lap. Her black silk dress tight against her thighs when she crossed her ankles. Her fingernails tracing the back of my neck as she put her arm around my shoulder. I leaned back some shivering as she did this. I had not been touched by a woman in some time. Ramón raised his glass and the others at the table did the same except for one businessman who poured rum into a cup in front of me.

Canción. Ramón raised his own glass.

The alcohol settled warmly in my stomach.

I do not know how much I drank that night. I drank to enjoy this woman in my lap. To stop thinking about her whose name I did not know and who I never encountered for all of my walking and searching. The woman in my lap was very beautiful. When I was not holding my glass or bringing it to my lips I rested my hand on her thigh. Slowly passing my fingers over her dress. Adding some pressure now and then to which she responded by pressing back against me. I lit her cigarettes for her. Leaned some to smell the fragrance of her hair. Her perfume. Her nails were painted red. Her eyes smiling dark and large and beautiful. Leaning to speak so close to me I felt her lips brush my ear.

Throughout the night Rodríguez continued to bother Ramón and Vargas about the fighting of dogs. Once he faced me and drunk he asked.

Do you enjoy the fighting?

No. I answered and Vargas heard this and smiled.

The businessmen at the table now leaned in to hear through the music.

Why do you fight then? Rodríguez asked.

But I did not want to give them my answer. I was drunk. I no longer fought to hear my name on their voices. Or to see myself in the stories my grandfather told. I wanted to tell them the truth. That it was to be near to her. But that was our secret. Instead I answered.

Because it is what I am best at.

Vargas raised his glass to this and drank on his own.

I would be good at it. Rodríguez said with a straight face. I would be better than the rest of you.

Ramón raised his glass and we all drank. When I sat my glass down on the table for the woman in my lap to fill across the room the small man in the blue suit came through a side door followed by Cantana with her holding his arm. This man led Cantana and her to a small round table near the stage. She sat facing me. I found her eyes in the blur of all the alcohol I had drunk and arms and bodies of those dancing and passing between us. When I smiled surprised to see her it made her laugh a small laugh over which she covered her mouth with her hand. Cantana looked over his shoulder at our table but Ramón was already on his way to the businessmans and this kept me hidden from El Tapado. As Ramón crossed the room I realized the mistress remained sitting in my lap. I felt feverish then thinking she would not know of my longing for her with this other woman between us. My smile was gone but hers was not. She looked down to the table and then back to me. She was beautiful. Her eyes a brilliant green even in that smoke and candlelight. Her hair in tendrils just beyond the dark skin of her bare shoulders.

May I have your attention please. The small man in the blue suit had stepped onto the stage as the song ended. His sweaty forehead glistening under the lights. Looking for us all in that light directly in his eyes. Tonight we have a very special guest of Señor Cantana who is going to sing for us. A young woman with a fine voice.

I sat forward to applaud as the man in the blue suit welcomed her to the stage and the mistress sitting in my lap almost fell to the floor. She removed her arm from my shoulder and took a step from our table when Vargas grabbed her hand and led her to his own lap.

Me recuerdas? I heard him say.

Por supuesto. She smiled.

When she stood before us all on the stage one of the musicians stepped forward to whisper into her ear something that made her laugh. I was very jealous of this man. He stepped back and just as he strummed his guitar there came the distinct sound of glass shattering at the back of the room. Yells around men fighting. I had not noticed Rodríguez stand from the table and stumble to the bar. The man in the blue suit encouraged the musicians to play something different. Everyone in the bar stood. Over their heads I could see her step from the stage. I could see Ramón push toward us through the crowd on his way to Rodríguez fighting some man at the bar. The musicians began playing. A woman cried out. I turned and there stood Rodríguez holding a knife. Blood over his hand. The other man fell back against the bar clutching his stomach. I turned to see Cantana take her by the arm and lead her back through the door through which they had entered. When she looked over her shoulder at me she smiled. Dumb I raised my hand and waved.

Vargas and Ramón were fighting friends of the young man Rodríguez had stabbed. The young businessman was looking at his hands. I shoved my way through the shoving and grabbed one man by his shoulders and held him while Ramón punched him in the face once. The man slumped to the ground. Then I stepped forward and took Rodríguez by the arm. The bartender climbed onto the bar holding a heavy stick. Swinging at whoever came near. I dragged Rodríguez through the crowd and up the stairs. Ramón and Vargas fighting behind us. Their backs to the stairs back stepping. Vargas fighting two men at once.

When the man at the gate saw the blood on Rodríguezs shirt and hands he shut the gate behind us.

Let no one in or out. He said before he turned to run down the steps into the abandoned church.

It was quiet outside. The air cool and easy to breathe. The smell of smoke and alcohol thick still in my nostrils. Rodríguez was panting. Soon Ramón and Vargas came up the stairs passing the man at the gate. Rodríguez wiped the blood from his hands onto a silk handkerchief. Staining it. As I let Ramón and Vargas through the gate Ramón yelled at the young businessman.

What happened in there?

No sé. Rodríguez mumbled.

We need to leave. Vargas said softly. Inspecting his knuckles.

Where did you get the knife? Ramón continued to yell at Rodríguez.

I do not remember! Rodríguez yelled.

We need to leave. Vargas repeated. They are coming.

Vargas then grabbed Rodríguez by the arm and began to walk in the direction opposite of the plaza mayor.

Where are you going to take this maricón? Ramón asked Vargas.

Someplace else. The fugitive smiled. I am still thirsty and his wallet is still full.

The three of them began to jog but I did not move. I suddenly felt the alcohol very much.

Hombre. Ramón called back to me. This way.

But I stood where I was.

Leave him! Rodríguez hissed.

Ramón jogged over to where I stood. He put his hands on my face and smiled.

We will do this again sometime. He patted me on the shoulder. I told you we would have a good time.

I am going to call you Ferocious. I heard Vargas laugh to Rodríguez over Ramóns shoulder.

Go home. Okay? Ramón said to me.

I nodded.

Little Ferocious. Vargas said and tousled his hair. This gesture produced a short proud laugh from Rodríguez. Ramón turned and they all ran from the shadows of the abandoned church.

I walked in the opposite direction. Toward the smell of a bakery down the street at the end of the block. The smell warm and sweet and made me feel sick some. I had not been drunk in many months. My legs were not steady. My eyes red from the smoke. I walked one block and then turned down from the mountains toward the cathedral. From there I would take the back alleys to the plaza and then on to the dentists. Not thinking about whether or not Jorge would try to stop me from climbing the stairs to my small room.

Blocks ahead I heard the laugh of a young woman ring clear as she and her lover stumbled over the uneven stones. Arm in arm. I could no longer sleep on the beach. I had gotten used to my bed. The thought of the hotel impossible now that there were guards and I was so drunk. In a narrow alley just north of the cathedral I stopped to be sick in a doorway. I bent over holding my stomach with one hand and wiping the vomit from around my mouth with the other when there was the sound of bricks moving above me. Confused I looked up to see a young man with a bag over his shoulder hanging down from a balcony. A light came on in the room above. The sound of a woman screaming and her husband yelling. The young man dangled a story above. When the wife came out onto the balcony she stepped on the young mans fingers. Cursing and yelling. Letting down his arm to avoid her stomping feet his bag fell to the ground. A glass broke inside. A silver candlestick clattered on the stones. Suddenly the young man landed at my feet. He cursed. Grabbing at his ankle.

Hold him! The wife yelled down at me. Do not let him run away!

Drunk I grabbed the young man by the shirt where he sat on the ground. He looked up at me with round dark eyes. Then a smile came across his mouth.

I know you. He said. From Jorges.

Jorge? I asked.

The dentist. You live with Jorge. I come later. He explained. After the others have gone.

The husband unlocked the door from the inside.

The young man cursed again. He tried to stand but his ankle was injured. In my confusion over what he said I had let go of his shirt. The wife was yelling at me from above as the thief hurried to put the candlestick back into the bag. When the husband opened the door he stepped in where I had been sick. He stepped forward to look at his bare feet in the light and then at the thief on the ground hurrying with his bag. The husband stood with his back to me. He aimed a rifle he held at the young mans chest. Over this mans shoulder the thief looked into my eyes and shrugged. Smiling.

When I hit the man in the back of the head with my fist he fell to the ground. The rifle fired. Splitting a flowerpot hanging by the head of his wife. Some dirt went on her face. She cursed this swatting at her fat cheeks. She cursed her husband. I cursed the husband. His head hurt my hand very much.

We need to run now amigo. The young thief laughed. Help me to my feet.

We hurried down the street leaving the husband lying facedown. The rifle by his side. His wife on the balcony cursing us all.

SIX

The young thiefs name was Javier. When Jorge opened the door of the compound to the soft knock he looked at Javier and then at me and hurried us inside without question. In the kitchen that morning we sat holding wet cloths against our injuries while the dentist cooked eggs standing at the stove in his pajamas. Invisible morning birds weighed the slender limbs of the date palm in the courtyard.

I know you have something more for the pain than this old man. Javier smiled playfully. His eyes on the cigarette he rolled with long quick fingers.

Jorge said nothing but reached into the stove for a skinny stick of wood. He turned with a small flame at the end and lit the cigarette for the thief.

Not even a little something? Javier begged playfully.

The medication I have for pain is for my patients Javier. The dentist said over his shoulder.

Perfect. Javier pointed at me and then to himself. Here you have two patients.

Enough. The dentist said. Or I will ruin your breakfast on purpose.

When the eggs were cooked the dentist set them on large plates on the table in front of Javier and myself. Next he poured hot cups of strong black coffee for each of us. Then from the oven he brought a basket of tortillas bundled in warm towels. The crackle of the stove fire early in the morning was pleasant. Javier and I ate hungrily. The dentist sat in an empty chair. He delicately lifted Javiers ankle and rested it in his own lap. I ate without taking my eyes from my plate.

After what happened last night. Jorge began to scold me but Javier interrupted.

Jorge. The young thief said in a tender voice.

And you. The dentist redirected his attention. His voice very upset. You know how I feel about this. Pointing to the bag with the stolen items he searched for the words. This stealing.

Javier cupped his palm around the unshaven chin of the dentist. After a moment the dentist calmed some. Then turned to me and said in a serious tone.

So you know our secret now dog fighter?

Still I had not lifted my eyes from my plate.

Do not play stupid with me young man.

Jorge. Javier interrupted again. We are tired. He carried me all the way here to you. If not for him I would be in jail now.

Or dead.

Jorge. The thief pleaded. Placing his hand on the cheek of the dentists face again.

In my life before Canción I had beaten men like this for my own satisfaction or for the satisfaction of having others around to encourage me. I split their lips with my knuckles. Kicked them in the soft of their stomachs when they went to catch their breath. I did not care to understand their love. I believed that it was a great sin before God. Both my grandfather and my mother had taught me this. But now watching Javier calm the dentist with such subtle gestures I understood that there existed between the two men a great love. This is what I desired for myself. I had been very envious of the quiet laughs and slow dancing they shared. The shadow of them crossing the courtyard had frustrated me many times but that morning I felt good sitting with them. Peaceful even though my hand was swollen and the knuckles bruised.

To prevent the dentist from scolding either of us anymore Javier began telling the story of what had occurred in the house that night.

You should have seen this man. The young thief laughed. Head like a cinder block. A stomach out to here. And when I saw how ugly the wife was. She is what scared me out of there. My screaming woke them. Not my clumsiness. I am not a clumsy man.

Thief. Jorge interrupted.

I am not ashamed of what I do. Javier said to the dentist. But if you call me this then I will tell you what I did not want to have to tell you. This hag of a wife? She snored worse than you mi corazón. I never thought it possible.

Carefully raising my eyes from my plate I laughed at this interaction. Immediately Javier joined me.

Bueno. The dentist said. Smiling some. I allow you criminals into my home in the middle of the night. Make you breakfast. And this is how you thank me?

Although the dentist did not approve of what his young lover did for work he found much humor in the stories of the thief. When our laughter ended we sat quietly in the kitchen together. Jorge gently raised Javiers swollen ankle to rearrange the cool damp cloths. I looked through the doorway and into the sunny courtyard. I felt tired.

It was good of you to help me. Javier said then. This dog fighter has a kind heart Jorge.

The dentist leaned toward me careful not to put pressure on Javiers leg.

Let me see your hand again. He said.

What does a dentist know about broken bones? Javier joked. Smoke escaping from his smile.

More than a thief. Jorge responded.

One of my knuckles hurt very much. The pain in my wrist was sharp along my forearm.

I thought a dog fighter would know how to throw his fists so as not to get himself hurt. The dentist said holding my hand in his own.

It will heal before my next fight.

I am not so certain. Jorge said. I think you have broken a knuckle.

I am fine. I took my hand from him uncomfortable with his touch. Javier is much worse. I said.

This one is always making things worse for himself. The dentist sat back shaking his head. I am through trying to look after him.

I scooped the last of the eggs on my plate with a folded tortilla. Sipped the hot coffee. My head hurt some from the drinking but I felt better after having been sick. It felt good to be eating and laughing and listening to Javier and the dentist chide one another. When Javier yawned I stood and wiped the plates clean with a towel and stacked them in the cupboard.

Last night. I said to Jorge before I was to leave for my room. I am sorry.

How did he know where you live? Jorge asked me of Ramón.

Ramón works for Cantana. Javier spoke up. Blowing on the lit end of his cigarette. El Tapado knows everything in this city.

Not everything. Jorge patted the thief on the leg resting in his lap.

No Jorge. Todos.

The two men were quiet.

Let me sleep some and then I will find someplace this afternoon. I said.

No no. Jorge clucked his tongue. You will continue to live here with us.

Someone will need to keep me company during the day. Javier said. Do not go anywhere. It will be fun. I can teach you how to pick pockets.

This is when I remembered Javier from the fighting. As the well dressed young man kneeling alongside Cantana to take bets. Accepting money in his shirt pocket from the other businessmen.

I have seen you at the fights. I said.

Yes. Javier smiled. You are very talented. But I can tell you do not enjoy it as much as the others do.

I was tired. I could feel both of their eyes on me. I shook my head.

Thank you for the food and the conversation. I said to the dentist and Javier then. It is exactly what I needed after all of this.

Javier passed the next few weeks with us at the compound. He spent his days in the cool of the back room playing records. The evenings with the other young men laughing. There was more music in the compound during that week than there was during my entire stay with the dentist. Many times in the evenings while I copied out the poems the poet had given me I heard the dentist scolding Javier for dancing with the other young men. For not respecting his ankle. But how Javier and the dentist scolded one another only revealed how much they cared.

Gordito. Javier called the skinny dentist affectionately. Or a whispered. Mi corazón.

One night when the dentist was undressing his mother for bed Javier stood in the doorway of the back room and called for the dentist.

You must come and dance if you want us to stay old man. His voice magnified by the courtyard.

But the dentist did not lift his ear from his mothers lips.

I do not think Javier would have called if he knew Jorge was with his mother. Javier respected the mother of the dentist very much. Loved Jorge for the attention he dedicated to his mother. There was much passion between them. One night I passed the back room returning upstairs and from the shadows I witnessed Javier wrap his arms around the dentists waist.

I am the only one left to dance with you gordito. He kissed the dentist on the mouth.

I think you dance better with a swollen ankle. The dentist teased the thief. It lends you a grace that you did not have before.

When the young men would leave for the night I heard from my room Javier and the dentist laughing the quiet laughs of lovers before they retired to the privacy of themselves. It was enough to send me out into the night grinding my teeth with jealousy.

But in the warmth of the kitchen over the simple food the dentist had cooked for us that morning I realized what was wrong with having wanted to hear my name called on many voices. I awoke then knowing that what I desired most was what those two men had together. The mature love of another. How their names came from each others mouths alone. It thrilled me to think that love is not possible when it comes on the voices of many. But only on one who even in the company of others can change the tone of your name for it to mean a thousand different things but understood only by the two of you alone. I longed for the intimacy of giving myself to another completely. Even if it was a false intimacy.

There is much deception in love. The poet had said to me once.

But there was no deception in the sound of the dentists slippers on the sandy floor of the back room while he and the thief continued to dance even after the music had ended.

I am pleased by the number of men who claim to understand the words of God without questioning Him. The poet had also said to me once. It makes me feel like less of an idiot than I already am.

But even the poet with his questions of God would not understand the love of the dentist and the thief. And this remains something I do not understand.

———

After the night in the cantina beneath the abandoned church I did not see the poet for several days. On my return to the market I noticed Ramón sitting at a table at one of the cafés with a young woman I had not seen before. She was very beautiful and dressed very expensively. The old women in the plaza mayor who went from table to table begging for money gave her mean eyes but sitting with Ramón she did not care. She kept her eyes on Ramón while he spoke looking over the large square. Sipping his coffee. When Ramón noticed me from afar he shot his hand into the air and waved me over. But I was already walking toward him.

How did you know where I lived? I said before he could speak.

Good afternoon. Ramón smiled. Relaxed in his chair. Nice to see you too.

The young woman ran her fingers through her hair. She seemed suddenly nervous. Ramón reached into his pocket and brought out some paper pesos.

Muñeca. He said sweetly. Remember that dress you liked so much the other day? Give my friend and me a moment here. I will meet you soon enough.

But I am not finished with my coffee. She complained.

I will finish it for you.

The young woman blushed. Ramón said nothing but continued looking me in the eyes as she gathered her things and left. I sat in her seat where her perfume smelled strongly around us still at the table facing the square.

Cantana was having you followed. Ramón said then. His voice serious.

Was?

You are fine. He knows you are not a threat. Things now with the hotel are very uncertain for him. A man in his position cannot take risks.

What do you do for Cantana to know him so well? I asked.

You remember the small jobs you did for your friend Eduardo? Something like this.

Eduardo was not my friend. I said. And Eduardo is dead.

He is. Ramón lifted the cup to his lips and delicately sipped. And the differences between Eduardo and myself do not end there.

What does Cantana want with me?

He finds you very interesting hombre. For what he will not say. Apparently you walk often.

And this is interesting?

And how quiet you are. It is not good to be so quiet. People suspect.

I am not quiet now.

Maybe it is too late.

I looked Ramón carefully in the eyes. A young child came up to our table selling cheap cigarillos and Ramón bought one from him paying much more than the cost the boy asked for. Several other boys saw this and came to Ramón but he waved them away. They chased after the small boy.

You do not have to worry. Ramón said. Cantana does not care about where you live. You and those who live there are fine.

It is none of his business.

Ramón laughed at this.

Everything in Canción is Cantanas business amigo. Or are you deaf and blind as well as mute?

An old woman sat on one of the wood benches of the plaza near to us throwing bread crumbs to the pigeons. At one point a mouse scurried out for the crumbs scattering the birds. The old woman laughed. It was brave of Ramón to speak to me in this way. I could have easily killed him. But he fought the teeth and he was not afraid.

We are friends. He continued. Do not let this be a problem between us.

Ramón smiled with his eyes. He was very handsome and he knew this. I did not hate him. But I did not care to tell him that I was not his friend because there was the chance Ramón could introduce me to her.

Did Cantana ask you to bring me to the cantina that night? I asked then.

Yes.

Why?

He wanted to meet you. He thinks you will be a valuable asset.

How do you know that he does not want to kill me?

Cantana does not kill anyone. Ramón smiled sipping from his cup.

It would take you and Vargas and Elías and all of Mendozas dogs.

If that is what it would take then Cantana would see that it was done. But this is foolish talk. Ramón shifted in his seat. There are no problems between you and me. I respect you.

I was being foolish. Only making it more difficult to be with her.

How is Rodríguez? I asked him then to make the conversation easy between us.

Fine. He gave the man some pesos. Vargas and I went and threatened to kill the man if he did not accept it. It was generous. For as much of an idiot as Rodríguez is he does have a kind heart.

The dogs would kill him.

He will not hear it though.

We were quiet. The pigeons had returned. Now an old man who was in the large square each day sweeping the stones came and swept the bread crumbs from in front of the woman. She sat patiently while he did this. She did not argue. Once the old man was done and the pigeons returned again looking for more she threw them more when the old mans back was turned. The tension between Ramón and me had eased.

I will see you at the next fight? He said.

In two days. I stood. He looked at my hand.

What happened?

Nothing.

You need to be good to your girlfriend there hombre.

I am on my way to buy her a dress now. I smiled thinking I was clever.

The poets stall in the market was closed. Heavy cloth drapes brought down over the typewriters. I found the small thief when one of the women chased him from behind her stall where she was selling fruit. I bought him a panocha.

Where is the poet? I asked him.

The hotel. The boy answered with his mouth full of the sweet. He told me to stay here.

And you listened to him? I smiled.

He said he would break off my arm and beat me over the head with the bloody stump.

And you believed him?

He showed me his teeth.

You keep eating all this sugar and you will have teeth just like him.

You bought it for me.

A large crowd of men and women had gathered in the street leading down to the hotel. The workers climbed the scaffolding ahead and I could hear their hammers echoing over the rooftops. The space between the two palms where Eduardo had once napped in his hammock was empty. Another floor had been built since I left the work there. This fifth one taller now than the towers of the cathedral. There would be two more built onto this. Two men worked on the crane pulling down the hemp ropes to raise the boards and posts for the scaffolding. Cinder blocks for the walls. None of the workingmen stopped to look over the crowd for fear of the guards with their rifles. As I came to the edge of the crowd I overheard a woman say.

The birds will eat his eyes.

From a rope tied to the scaffolding hung a naked young man. He dangled two stories above the earth. His skin dark but for where his underclothes had been. His crotch in the evening light already a black shadow. Painted on his chest and back were the words.

Viva Canción!

Vultures perched on the scaffolding above him. A man next to me crossed himself. When I found the poet in the crowd I learned that it was the body of a young man native to Canción and not one of the workers. His chin rested on his chest. His toes aiming at the ground as he swayed from side to side. Already men and women were shielding their eyes from sand blown by the evening wind.

They found him with a bag of explosives. The poet told me.

That is the rumor. Responded a man standing next to the poet in a voice that made his disgust known.

Both the poet and this man did not take their eyes from the body. The rest of the crowd looked at the naked young man but also at each other. A group of women were consoling one woman who cried uncontrollably. Her loud cries broken only by the short silences of gathering what was left in her chest to cry.

The mother? I asked the poet.

No sé. He said quietly. I noticed then that the man standing next to him stood with a cane but also with a hand on the poets arm for support.

I need a drink. This other man said.

We will let the dog fighter treat us. The poet smiled.

The name of this man with the cane was Guillermo. He and the poet were the oldest of friends. They had come together to Canción in 1912 after losing faith in la Revolución. Guillermo owned a shop where young men worked on fishing boat engines and on the few cars that were in Canción at the time. At the shop they also worked on tools and machines for the construction of the road and the hotel. The poet argued very much with Guillermo for providing this type of work to the businessmen. But Guillermo argued that he kept the young men of Canción employed.

I am teaching them a trade. He once said.

A trade that benefits the businessmen.

And who does poetry benefit? Guillermo asked the poet.

This is my best student. The poet said of me.

How has poetry benefited you?

I thought for a moment before answering.

No sé.

Well put. Guillermo leaned close to my face. His index finger raised between us. I think the two of you have more going on than you want me to know.

Guillermo was successful enough in this shop of his so that some years after he had been in Canción he was able to buy down the street a salon where he put a half dozen billiard tables and charged the men of Canción to play. He could not play himself because his knee that was injured in la Revolución would not let him stand for long without paining him very much if he did. But the veteran as the young men called him enjoyed watching. Often Guillermo placed bets on the outcomes of the games. Shouting encouragement. In the afternoons young men came to drink beer at the salon and play billiards. Most were dangerous young men who slept late into the day choosing to spend their time in the dark. Some of those with lighter skin were almost white from so little sun. These young men had much respect for Guillermo and the poet. They called the old men abuelo or señor. Many times I saw Guillermo sit alone with one or two at a time talking intensely. As if his relationship with each of them was as strong as what I had with the poet. Soon I learned he was a maestro to them all.

On our way to the salon we walked slowly with Guillermo and his cane. When we were beyond the crowd at the hotel the poet introduced us.

You fight well. Guillermo said. His eyes staring directly into mine.

Gracias. I said and he smiled and I felt foolish never knowing how to respond to this praise.

At the back of Guillermos salon the three of us sat at a small round table. That day Guillermo spoke more than the poet did. He drank more than the poet also. The time I spent with them I began to think that all old men do is talk of their past and drink. Now that I am an old man I know this to be true. There builds in you a great desire to share what you are. What you have done and seen of the world. It is not so much to tell others how to be but to show that you were busy in life. The stories the poet and Guillermo told they repeated again and again but for the first time forgetting they had told them. The stories they told were often funny but sometimes very sad. Stories of women they had known and friends they had lost with time.

On this first day I met Guillermo sitting in the back of the salon both he and the poet became very drunk on damiana. Seeing the young man dangle from the crane had affected them very much.

At the beginning of la Revolución I was a vaquero Guillermo said. Like Francisco Villa.

Nin madres. The poet chided. You worked in the mines.

I never slaved in those mines. Guillermo snatched the bottle from the poet.

Only a few of the young men bent over the tables in the salon. None were near to where we sat and if it were not for the sounds of the games I would have thought we were alone.

I was a little older than you in 1910 when I was separated from my compañeros. Guillermo continued. Men from my village. We were armed with only a few rifles and homemade bombs then. Knives mostly. One man had a pitchfork. Of course he was the first to die but we kept the pitchfork. Passed from hand to hand the handle stained with our blood. Of those we killed. Guillermo took a sip from the bottle and rested it on his thigh with his forearm over the mouth. Several days after I was separated I was found by the Federales.

You fight for us or we will cut your eyes out. They said to me. Most of their soldiers were prisoners released on the condition that they fight. Pelados. Ragged men. I agreed to join but only until they were not looking and then I could escape. So many times we did not know for what we fought but fought only to stay alive. The veteran laid his cane across his lap like some weapon. The bottle in his hand. Luckily I was shot in the knee. I knew this was my chance to escape. I did not know where I was. But then you never knew where you were until you came to a village and asked. But many times there was no one to ask and even if there was you did not know if what they said was the truth because they lied hoping you would move on. Every Mexican knew that whoever won would be as bad as what we had in the past. In the Federales if you did not raise your weapon they raised one at you. Why I never raised my own rifle at them? No sé.

We were young. The poet said. Scared.

You must understand dog fighter that I am not proud of the several days I fought for the Federales. When I was shot in the knee the pelados left me behind to die. I knew that I could convince the rebels that I was not a Federale. It was the truth and the truth does not need convincing.

Should.

What?

Truth should not need convincing. The poet said.

Palabras. Guillermo waved the back of his hand away from him carelessly before continuing. When the rebels found me the poet was leading them. He asked questions about the Federales and for my answers he gave me the last of the water in his canteen. The others wanted to slit my throat to save bullets. But the poet would not let them. My lieutenant had been captured alive. Prove to us that you are not loyal to this man. One said. Handing me a knife. And so I did. But over this gift of water the poet and I became friends.

For several days a dozen haggard but better armed Federales chased the poet and Guillermo and the small band of men over the rocky landscape. Guillermos knee was very bad. The poet should have left him.

The smell of his wound was terrible. The poet smiled. Rotting afterbirth from the womb of a whore.

We raced the Federales to the mountains. Guillermo continued. We came to a narrow canyon we defended from behind boulders until nightfall. Then we found the caves.

Two or three of them to a hole. Turning their backs when the other had to defecate. Living with each others smells.

The poet and I had one rifle between us.

Maybe fifty bullets.

At night we bet pebbles playing cards by the moonlight. We spoke like boys of kisses we had stolen from beautiful women. Told lies about women we had known. From our cave we communicated with our compañeros in their caves by whistling. What the birds in those hills must have thought of us.

They stayed in these caves for two nights. Fighting some in the day but using their bullets carefully. Shooting every now and then to keep the Federales pinned down at the mouth of the canyon. But then the Federales stopped.

We did not know why they did not attack. We figured they thought they could wait for us to starve and surrender. When they came up the canyon we would lower our fury onto them. That is how the poet said it. Guillermo said. All this for land.

The word alone empties your chest. The poet said.

During my time in Canción I came to know this story very well. We respected the old men very much after hearing it for the first time. We did not question these old men but felt privileged to hear the telling of it.

For three days we lived in the desert on nothing. Trying to chew water from dry roots. On the second night some of our own men deserted. They stole some of our water. Guillermo said. We would have shot them ourselves if we had known.

If we had the bullets.

The next morning we learned why the Federales had stopped. A dust cloud came storming across the desert. Three dozen pelados on horseback. I will tell you this now. Guillermo said with a change in his voice. Because I know the old poet is a good friend to me and he would not tell you himself to save me the embarrassment.

I would tell him.

Then I want to beat you to it. I am not ashamed dog fighter. I was a young man then and I thought much of my own life. I had many dreams that I felt were more important than others of this world. But when I saw that cloud of dust I was so scared I shit in my pants. When I saw this great dust cloud of soldiers I knew I was to die that day and the only thing my body could move to do was this.

The smell was worse than his leg. The poet laughed. We had been eating mice.

But that day. The veteran came to the edge of his seat. His drunk red eyes inches from mine. His breath smelling of fire. We killed them all. Close to four dozen men.

Psssh! The poets lips wet from the alcohol. Five.

They never saw us. From where we were in the caves along the canyon they could not have beaten us. We shot until the canyon was filled with bodies.

Choked.

Palabras. Guillermo waved his hand at the poet before sitting back to continue. And in the evening I went looking for a new pair of pants. To steal a pair of pants from a man that was not yet dead because the dead ones had done what I had done alive.

They ate the Federales food and drank their water. They slaughtered several horses for stew. During the night from the warmth of their fires they listened to the injured cry for water.

In the middle of the night someone woke up and slit the throats of the dying. Guillermo said.

Knelt by each one and spoke in the soft whisper of a priest before he cut their throats and went to the next.

Some of us considered staying there because it was a valuable canyon. Guillermo continued. One easy to defend. We had more ammunition. Food and water. But at that point in la Revolución you did not know where you were fighting or who. We did not know what it was behind us that we were defending or what was in front of us to be conquered. There were groups of men running around the desert looking to kill each other dressed in the clothes of their enemy. Shot by their own from afar.

And your leg? I asked him politely. You found help?

The poet laughed at this.

Do not let this old fool get you down. He did this so we will offer him the chairs with legroom and the best view of the women passing.

Some friend you are. The veteran said sipping from the bottle. Sharing our secrets.

I said nothing about the pants.

You would have.

Maybe.

This bickering is how the old men enjoyed each others company. When the story was finished and the laughter died down a quiet mood settled over us. Then I did not know what to believe of their story. But in the telling I felt more friendly toward them both. They had shared with me some intimacies of their friendship and for this I was grateful.

We moved to a table on the street. I drank some beer from a bottle they now shared. The poet slurped hot chicken broth. Some children kicked a wad of unsoiled butcher paper in the street.

That was something awful today. Guillermo said after he took a sip of the beer.

A bold move by Cantana.

Where did they catch him with these explosives? I asked.

He had no explosives. The poet said.

What do you mean? I asked.

That boy is not one of those who are fighting Cantana. Guillermo answered. Cantana made an example of him.

Probably someone who owed Cantana money.

How do you know? I asked.

We have been around long enough to know how Cantana works.

He should have done it right after the attack on the hotel. The veteran said. It would have been more effective.

In the company of Guillermo I looked at my friend the poet much differently. He had never spoken to me of his involvement in the Revolution. Of his time in the cave. I sat like a boy among these two men learning much.

By dark Guillermo was already very drunk. Without saying anything he stood and hobbled down the street to his shop leaning heavily on his cane.

He sleeps in the back room. The poet told me. Walk with me over toward the hotel to see if they have taken down the young mans body.

They will not leave it hanging through the night?

Cantana knows to take it down before dark. He wants to threaten los Cancioneros. Not anger us.

We walked along the malecón watching the water of the bay unfold onto the beach in tiny waves. The tide was out and the hotel loomed to the north. Between the end of the malecón and the hotel there was a rock outcropping where feral cats with scarred noses lived in the shadows and crags. The starving cats came salivating to the cathedral bells that rang at sunset. They hissed and meowed rolling over one another when the old men and women of Canción approached with food. Without this food the cats ate fish that washed ashore. When I was in Canción there was a story of one old man who came after dark and left beans mixed with poison. Dozens of bloated cats floating on the foamy waves. Floating with paper and tin cans and corks.

On this evening a small group of men and women gathered at the edge of these rocks. Beyond them at the hotel I could see two men untying the knots that suspended the skinny shadow of the young mans body. The poet was correct about Cantanas decision to take the body down. As we approached the crowd came undone with loud cries. Seven cats had cornered a baby rattlesnake in the rocks.

The poet cursed the hotel. Shook his head. Since the first months of the construction on the hotel the malecón had begun to slither at night with snakes. They came to warm their bellies on the stones now that their favorite rocks had been moved. Mice scurried in the moonlight past barefoot lovers and those like myself who slept on the beach.

Surrounding the baby rattlesnake the hissing cats tested the air between themselves and the snake with their claws. The rattlesnake coiled into a small crack in the rocks. Striking out at the cats but then recoiling as instantly as it had shot out. Some of those in the crowd laughed nervously. Five or six of the men brought out money to place bets. One young boy wiggled free of his mothers hands cupped over his eyes.

They will wait. The poet said about the cats. Look at the marks on their noses. The missing fur. These cats know that the baby rattlesnake cannot control its venom. They know that after it has killed one of their own they can easily tear through its scales with their claws without being harmed. The baby rattlesnake is too eager. Look.

I do not want to watch this. I told him and turned away.

When the poet came back alongside me farther down the malecón he said.

Some dog fighter you are.

We had not taken many steps when the loud cries sounded again. From the crowd a young man fell back hunched over and holding his stomach with both hands. His face in pain. He fell to the stone sidewalk laughing.

I am afraid to die fighting the dogs. I said then. I am afraid I will go to hell for the things I have done.

There is no hell. The poet said confidently.

For me maybe there is.

And what makes you so special?

There are many things I have not told you.

And many things you do not know about me.

I have killed a man. I said.

Did you not hear the story Guillermo told you today? We laugh about it now. Two old men. But on that day. And on others like it. I shot at many men and I do not know how many I killed.

But that was in war.

Each day is war.

It was quiet then. Uncomfortable with the silence I felt compelled to speak. I told him about my father and the death of my mother. Of sleeping alongside the creek in Northern California after having killed the husband. I spoke with fever almost.

Who am I to judge you my friend? The poet asked after I had finished.

That is not why I told you.

Then why?

I do not know. I do not want there to be any lies between us as friends. You have done much for me.

What have I done?

The English. The talking. The time in the market. Many things.

You buy me expensive cigarettes.

I just want to thank you.

When did you become such a woman? He laughed. I looked away. No. I am joking. The poet continued. No hay de qué. We are friends. But I have to tell you dog fighter. The poet studied the end of his cigarette grinning to himself. I think I enjoyed your company more when you did not talk so much.

We laughed together at this. I was comfortable with the poet. But still I was not ready to tell him of her. I had lied to him. She was my only weakness. And this I was not willing to share with anyone yet.

———

On the night of my third fight my hand was not healed completely but the money I had was not much. Jorge offered to wait some before I paid him but my pride would not allow this.

You can return to work on the hotel. He said.

I would not be able to make a fist around the hemp ropes of the crane I told him. And if I returned to construct the hotel I would not be able to face the poet. I did not want to admit how anxious I was to encounter her. I would have fought dogs to be near to her even if I had no hands.

From the small room on the rooftop I heard squealing children chasing one another down the narrow street below the storehouse. The light around the door darkened slowly with the moon full but clouds gathered some and the men earlier in the day had spoken of rain. Ramón and Vargas sat drinking coffee to sober themselves. They had been drinking until late in the night before.

We went with Cantana and the other businessmen to church.

Ramón said. You should have been there. One of the mistresses punched Vargas in the mouth.

It was nothing. Vargas smiled. One of the front teeth missing from his mouth.

What happened? I asked. Only Ramón and I were stretching before the fight. Vargas sat in a new wood chair with a small bruise at the corner of his mouth.

I asked her to dance. Vargas said. His voice a bit sad even maybe. I asked if she would like to dance with me. We had been making eyes at each other during the night.

She was looking over your shoulder at me. Ramón smiled at the fugitive.

Then she hit you? I asked Vargas.

No no. She said. You say another word to me and I will hit you in the face. So I said. Another word.

It was a good punch also. Ramón gestured.

She was standing too close. Vargas argued.

Close enough to knock out your tooth.

That one was loose before she hit me.

I do not understand. I said to them both.

Neither do I. Said Vargas. Rubbing the bruise. His tongue inspecting the dark space between his teeth. His brow wrinkled.

Ramón and Vargas went on about the night before. Discussing which mistresses lips were the fullest and most beautiful. Who had the roundest eyes. Ramón made jokes about hitting the fugitive in the head with the leg of the chair again when Vargas mentioned an ugly mistress Ramón had danced with.

Cantana. I asked carefully. Did he dance?

No. He sat smoking. Vargas said. Watching us all. Smiling. You wonder if he even likes the women sometimes.

Ask him? Ramón joked. But before you do be sure to leave behind some nice words about yourself so I will have something to say at your funeral.

Later Ramón told me that after they left the cantina Vargas was still upset about losing his tooth to a woman. When they were leaving the abandoned church the sun had barely risen. Vargas stopped a young man in a suit walking to the cantina. The young man had two women on his arms. Vargas asked him for a cigarette. Ramón spoke with the women smiling. When the young man lit the cigarette for Vargas he accidentally brought the flame from the match too close to the fugitives hand. Vargas beat the young man down to the stones. Ramón helped by keeping the young man pinned with the toe of his shoe placed on the young mans shoulder. The women cried for the dog fighters to stop but Ramón only continued to talk at them in his smiling voice.

I was drunk. He shook his head when telling me this. It was a blur.

Later when I would look on the dead body of Vargas I would see that even in death his face showed that he thought nothing of his decision to beat this young man. It was nothing to him. All the men he had beaten occurred in the blur Ramón spoke of. The dogs the same for all of us I think. I can remember how it was to be this way as a young man of great strength. You think nothing of it at all. It does not bother you like a sliver beneath your fingernail or a mosquito you hear in the dark. It has nothing to do with your body or mind. This is when men are the most dangerous I think.

My fight was difficult that night because of my hand. I told the ragmen to wrap the rug on my right arm and the claws this time on my left. This felt much different. As if my body were not my own. I swung wildly. Weak swings. To better use my left hand with the claws I positioned my body in a stance I was unused to. My fight went longer than it should have. I was angry with myself for this because it was time away from her. But when the dog sat back to snarl I broke its jaw with a kick to its muzzle and then sank the claws awkwardly into the soft skin of its belly. I did this stabbing until the dog its jaw hanging limp from its face was dead.

After the fight I sat on the benches with the businessmen. I sat off to the side and behind her several rows. I stared at the gentle curve of her neck beneath her hair. I memorized the three tiny black moles along the straps of her dress on her dark shoulders. I followed the blue veins beneath her skin like words of a poem. I read her hair down to the small of her back where Cantanas palm rested. With his gloved hand he smoked watching the fight. His other hand on her. From where I sat behind him I tried to look into his eyes in the reflection of the inside of his sunglasses. But I only saw through the dark lenses. The world before him easier on the eyes.

When I witnessed his hand move in an intimate caress I refused to believe he had known her. I considered standing and placing my hands on his warm ears and breaking his neck. But I was not ready to die without knowing her. It was easier to think that he had never known her. I convinced myself of this to prevent myself from attacking Cantana and being killed after I did. The poet had taught me if anything to be smarter. To be patient for my time. So when he touched her like this she sat erect under his touch and it thrilled me to see that she was uncomfortable. She was beneath his hand but away from him also. She could feel my eyes on her and this was a game she played sliding from him to let me know that she loved me. And when his fingers would move to adjust to the pressure of her moving from him he would follow her. Knowing I think why she moved from him. The fighting happened in the ring in front of us but I only watched his hand placed in the small of her back and her moving from him. And in all this all my hatred for Cantana and all my love for her lived.

It was during the fugitives fight that the yelling men turned their backs on the ring. Over the rooftops of Canción black smoke rose from the direction of the hotel. There were several fires. The yelling men pushed toward the edge of the rooftop but careful not to cut their hands on the shards of glass along the tops of the walls hidden some by the bougainvillea vines. The black smoke of the fires captivated us all. Fighting his dog while no one was watching Vargas looked strange in the ring when I turned to him. He was alone. I realized then that the fighting of dogs does not exist without an audience. The fire at the hotel the same.

Many of the businessmen clenched their teeth in anger when they saw the smoke. Pointed in the direction of the fire and waved their hands. The businessmen took the mistresses by the arm roughly as if they were threatened but responsible for the fire somehow also. One of the women refused to be pulled in this way and she slapped at one of the businessmen. I wondered if this was the one who had punched Vargas. The businessman hit this woman in the face then. His hand closed. She went to the ground holding her eye. Several of the yelling men stepped toward this but Elías was there between the yelling men and the businessman with his revolver.

My eyes went to find her. Also to see the reaction of Cantana. But they were gone from the rooftop. Ramón gone with them. Vargas was alone in the ring and only the ragmen witnessed him kill the dog and they now were bent over the blood on the floor with their backs to us all mopping hungrily.

After I dressed quickly I went to the hotel to see what the fires were from. The throats of two guards had been slit and their rifles stolen. The tractors used for moving the earth to make the swimming pool and terraces for sunbathers had been set on fire. A woman came down from her window across the way and was speaking quietly to a man next to me of what she had witnessed.

They climbed onto the backs of the machines and attacked the wires to the engines with the claws of hammers. She said. Then they poured something on machines and threw matches onto this. They ran laughing.

You should tell the businessmen what you saw. The man said to her.

Why? She asked. So they can torture me when I tell them the truth. That I do not know who the young men were? That I saw only shadows in this moonlight.

Down the crowded street the men and women had come carrying buckets of water. Some men encouraged them to stop and set the buckets down. The reflection of flames danced in our eyes. The buckets made it no farther. Children used the water to splash the dogs snarling and barking at the machines. The light of the fire from the burning tractors cast the shadows of the boys watching from their canoes tall and lean across the black bay. I looked for the poet and Guillermo.

Businessmen who came from the fight were ordering a group of workingmen to throw the water on the machines. One of the businessmen put his hands on the neck of one man who was not running. While choking this workingman the businessmans suit jacket tore. A crease of narrow lightning down his spine.

Throw the water! He cursed.

But the man could not stand. Police wrestled back men crowding the businessman with his hands around the one mans neck. Other businessmen watched this. Their hands empty. The hands of the one businessman with the torn jacket grew from the neck of the man whose body was trying to stand from his knees where he was choked down to.

Off to the side of this commotion the bodies of the guards were covered by a woman with canvas sacks I once used to carry sand for the cinder blocks. The dead mens skin had paled some in the moonlight. But more from the dark slits in their throats. Like when a fish is brought from water. Not far from this painted on a concrete column at the corner of the hotel in red paint were the dripping words.

Viva Canción!

Words that burn slowly around the wood of a door up its walls and into the roof before the building collapses into itself and as the last flames exhaust themselves slowly. Looking at the words in the light of the burning tractors I remembered seeing them painted on the body of the young man to mock him more already naked hanging from the scaffolding. I had been blind to so much of Canción then I was so taken with images in my mind only of myself and her. For all of its peace and beauty Canción was at war. The businessmen constructing their dreams in the daylight they shared with los Cancioneros also dreaming but different dreams.

First it will overshadow the cathedral. The poet had said. Soon enough the city itself.

That night on more and more walls the dripping words appeared. On many of these walls those who owned them or lived behind them refused to paint over them. Stories of young men striking from shadows only to disappear.

These young men they speak of are stronger than us all. The poet would say to me. We are blind to think we have no place in this war. Foolish to believe that we are an audience.

Lightning cracked above. Thunder collapsing over the bay. The man next to me looked to the sky and said to the woman who spoke quietly.

If it rains then God does prefer Cantana.

But it did not rain then. The tractors burned until late in the night. Smoldering until late in the morning of the next day.

I was eager to hear what Guillermo and the poet had to say about the newest attack on the hotel. But Guillermo was busy at the back of the salon talking in whispers with the crying mother of the young man that had been hanged from the hotel scaffolding. The poet took my arm and we walked in silence to the knoll across from the cathedral. There I asked the poet if this was the mother but he answered no. I did not believe him but I did not think the poet lied to me and so I did not ask him.

The plaza was empty and in our silence I listened for the voices of those singing inside.

I am going in there one day. I said finally to the poet.

Good for you. He answered.

You have never been in there?

A long time ago. When Guillermo and I first came to Canción we slept in the pews at night until the priest found us. He told us to leave. Told us to sleep on the beach. We were lucky he only found us sleeping.

What do you mean?

We stole coins from the feet of the statues. Or from the box where people pay to buy candles. We had nothing. The poet took a long drag from his cigarette. His eyes far off. Then he laughed remembering something. You should have seen how fat this priest was. He barely fit in the pews.

My father said to me once that if he was to go to church with my mother he would go only to a church where the priest was skinny.

Your father was a wise man.

You two would have had much to talk about I think.

Maybe.

The voices in the church came to us then from across the sunny plaza. Soft and beautiful. The words indistinct.

My father used to tell me that Jesus was the greatest daydreamer. I told the poet then. That what He taught was beautiful but difficult also. He said Jesus deep in His heart wanted to be the most famous man that will ever live. That He sat on the bank of some river thinking to Himself how He could put His name not in the voices of many but in the voices of all. God. He thought. My father said to me. Tell them you are the son of God. Who is more known than God?

Ninguno. The poet answered.

Yes. That is what my father said. No one.

There is a mosaic of Him in there. The poet said when the singing ended. I used to sit in the pews at night studying it while Guillermos snoring kept me awake. Thinking about what I knew then of the Bible. What I had seen in the Revolution.

Did you think much of the killing?

Constantemente. But I did not ask him to forgive me. I would have to ask those who are dead. The poet kept his eyes on the cathedral.

I was toying with small stones while the old man spoke. Throwing them and watching them skip over the stones of the plaza and come to rest in the light. Their own shadows stark as themselves.

In Veracruz. I said. There was a politician who was murdered when I was a boy. He was walking with his own son down the street. The son was some feet ahead. The men came up behind this man when he was watching his son look into a shop window. Thinking nothing probably. And then they stabbed him in the throat. The son saw this. My mother was very sad for this boy. But my father said over and over that the politician was a bad person. One who deserves to die. That his son would grow up in a better place. A place Jesus would have wanted him to. My mother was very upset with my father for saying this. Yelling at him about God and Jesus and my grandfather just laughing and scratching his head and playing dumb. But my father was very calm. He explained to my mother that Jesus was a selfish man maybe.

Your father said maybe? The poet asked me.

No.

Go on.

He said that Jesus was a selfish man for wanting all of us to believe in His ideas alone. To live in the way that He wanted while beautiful but difficult. That innocent people die for the better of us all.

But the politician was not so innocent.

No.

Then I do not understand what you mean. Maybe your father did not call the politician innocent.

The poet looked at me carefully. I had been talking much and was very excited to have him listening but I could not remember where the story was or why I was telling it. The poets eyes were very intense. He bit his cigarillo with his teeth and smiled at me.

Is that it? He said then.

I cannot remember.

I think maybe you have more thinking to do on this one.

I nodded. He stood and wiped the dirt from the back of his cotton pants. He stretched and yawned.

Let us go and see if the old drunk is good for a laugh today.

The poet had become more and more patient with me. I went on with stories like these more and more if only to hear myself think. Often he led me to believe he thought one thing about one thing and the next moment something else. Laughing at me for agreeing when then I was only disagreeing with myself. It was an engaging confusion.

You have a good heart dog fighter. He said more and more. And strong shoulders and good hands. But your mind is behind your body some.

I knew he was right. I was learning from the poems he gave me. I would tell him how much I enjoyed them and then he would tell me he did not like them very much at all.

But why did you give them to me then? I asked.

I thought it was important for you to learn them. If they were good for you then it does not matter that they are not ones I like.

I do not understand. I said.

Most of the time neither do I. He laughed. But it does not stop me from having my ideas though.

Guillermo was much different than the poet. What Guillermo said he believed in entirely. He would not hear others. If you disagreed he interrupted you and went on with what he had to say. Only the poet seemed to have some influence on the veteran. But how much I did not know then. The poet and Guillermo sat for hours in the back of the salon talking with themselves while the young men and myself played billiards.

Only the poet disagrees with Guillermo. One young man said to me. The rest of us listen to him in the way people listen to a priest.

When I spoke with the young men in the salon or the shop many times their arguments were only repeating what the veteran had said. They would laugh at me for stumbling on my words. Confusing my arguments. Most of these young men had never left Canción. Knew its streets only by name. I do not mean to say that by arguing with them I spoke often because I did not. But I listened more than they did. I went out and walked some before making my judgments. All these weeks with the young men and the poet and Guillermo I did not realize what I was coming into. What was for all of us. How my confusion and quiet would play into their games.

The only thing I was sure of was that I would not be able to survive long on these brief glimpses of her. That I needed a way to get to her. Something I could offer of myself or do that would take her from Cantana. But I was not smart enough yet to see what was happening in front of my eyes. I knew that I would have to be more patient than I had ever been but my body was caught with fever for her. Each fight while I was thankful for them because of how close they brought me to her only made my desire for her greater and more painful. I was convinced that with her I was to be sure of my words. My ideas.

On my walks at times I despised the beauty of Canción. The colorful walls under electric lamplight. Vacant alleys and streets where my steps sounded loudly. Sounding as if I were not alone and turning to look but realizing then it was myself that was making those walking sounds. It was myself desperate not to be alone but to be with her who would finally understand everything. But after the fight when I sat watching Cantana with his hand in the small of her back even the daydreams I entertained of happiness no longer suited me. I worried that no matter how skilled I was or praised by the yelling men I could still fall before the dogs. That even with God much in this world seems left to chance. Unlike my father I believed that chance was decided by Him. I could not think my way out of this. I only thought that Cantanas will prevented us from being together and that had to be ended. I thought of ways to destroy Cantanas will. But I have never been a very clever man and nothing came to my mind through my anger and frustration.

It was not until one afternoon when Javier came limping to the salon carrying the bag full of items he had stolen the night I helped him that I began to know more about how I was to be with her finally.

Guillermo stood from one of the seats at a table where he and the poet and I sat in front of the salon.

Look at this! Guillermo yelled to the young men in the salon. He turned to the street with his cane hooked over his forearm and his arms opened wide to receive the limping thief. The poet stood to steady the veteran. You look good my young friend!

Watching Javier approach I was reminded of Ramón. Both men were handsome and full of pride. But with Javier there was a feeling of generosity. Of being allowed near to him for reasons other than his own needs being satisfied by you. With Ramón you served some purpose. When Javier came near and noticed me his look changed some but not enough for the others to notice.

In the arms of which beautiful woman have you been hiding out amigo? The poet clapped Javier on the back.

What makes you think I stayed to just one? Javier smiled and the men roared. Pinching his sides and patting his shoulders to welcome him.

Guillermo introduced me to Javier and I stepped forward so he did not have to. We shook hands.

Look at the size of this mans hands! Javier said loudly. The old poet here must be jealous of this ones fingers alone.

The young men in the salon laughed as the poet blushed.

Guillermo would tell me later what I already knew from our evenings at the dentists together. That Javier had been a pickpocket in the market as a boy. But that now he was a very accomplished thief.

Watch out for this young man. Guillermo said while Javier spoke with the other young men. This thief will steal your woman just as easy as your watch.

When he is not busy falling out of windows. The poet laughed.

Guillermo took the poet by the arm. Resting his weight upon him. Come now my young friend. He said to Javier. Show me what you have brought.

The poet helped Guillermo through a door at the back of the salon. Javier shook many hands as he limped by the other young men at the tables. After some minutes the poet returned to the table in the front where I sat alone.

What is in the bag? I asked the poet nodding toward the door. I was nervous and I knew the best way to distract the poet from guessing that I knew Javier was to make him talk.

Guillermo is a very busy man. The poet said. He knows that in this city of ours there are many talented young men looking for work on something besides the road and the hotel. More than picking the pockets of the poor in the markets. He knows where many of the most wealthy homes are. He has boys in the city find out for him. They sit on corners or they ask the girls who work in the houses of the businessmen. Cleaning and cooking in their kitchens. Then the young men you see here they go and take what Guillermo can send on the ferries to Topolobampo. Mazatlán. Acapulco.

Javier knows the city well then?

He does.

And he is a talented thief?

He once stole gold from the mouth of a man sleeping.

And these young men do not run out of work?

They do other things as well.

What?

When did you become so curious?

It is your fault.

Mine? The poet asked. How?

Not to discover weakness is. I recited to the poet. The mystery of strength. Impregnability inheres. As much through consciousness. Of faith of others in itself. As elemental nerve.

Dog fighter! Guillermo interrupted from the door at the back of the salon. Tell your deaf friend there to come here a minute. Javier was limping toward us folding money and putting it in his shirt pocket. The poet stood and smiled at me. He shook his head as he took a few steps before Javier stopped him. The thief took from the bag a small gift wrapped in newspaper.

I was enjoying this in the comfort of their living room when the old man got up to piss. He said. I thought you might enjoy it.

The poet unwrapped the paper and held a slim book with leather binding and gold lettering in English down the spine. He admired its delicate pages.

This is very generous of you Javi. I appreciate it very much.

The poet clapped the thief on the shoulder and hugged the young man before walking on. When the door closed at the back of the room Javier sat down in an empty chair at the round table I sat at. He rolled a cigarette in silence. I looked over the street as if there were nothing important to be spoken of between us.

Do you want a cola? I asked.

That sounds good. He said.

I walked to a cooler at the back of the room. When I sat down at the table he took a long drink before setting the bottle between us.

Gracias. He said after a moment.

De nada.

Most of the young men at the salon kept hours similar to Javier. They slept late through the sunny days to come in the afternoons to drink beer and play billiards. They kept their working hours to the cool of the night. Some also working at the fights or for gambling that businessmen did for the other men of the city but in secret. But the salon was a good place for the young men. They shared secrets of their work. Spoke of troublesome locks and the houses that had nothing of interest. Behind which doors and over which walls slept the most vicious dogs. When they spoke of the hotel they all spoke in the same voice. About Cantana and the changing of Canción it was the same. Their voice the voice of Guillermo. Occasionally also in the voice of the poet that I knew so well and even spoke in myself now and then. None of us said much of our own. The two old men at the back of the salon sat quiet during the day enjoying the sound of their echoes.

In the evenings the young men practiced picking pockets in the aisles between the tables. Guillermo gave them a game to play where one wallet was the wallet they were all after. Keeping it in their pocket as they went about their games pretending not to go after it.

It will teach you how to be quick and good with your hands. How to make it seem like you are not after something. Always to be on guard of what you have. The veteran told them.

Guillermo huddled with them in the back room over drawings of houses they made on their walks through the city at night. Deciding the best entrances. Telling them what to steal. Paintings. Jewelry. Silverware. What customers on the mainland wanted. He always spoke of Mexico as if Baja were not a part of it. He knew that the young men loved the small city but like all young men they were eager to move on.

The thieves were hungry. Anxious to pursue the connections Guillermo promised them in Ciudad México or in the United States even. Guillermo convinced them that they made the decision at first to steal for the money. And then the excitement took them and he no longer had to convince them. Their eyes were constantly restless but their bodies calm in the afternoons searching each others pockets for the one wallet. Eager for the veterans drunk praise.

This is a different life you have chosen. I heard him tell one young man. There are serious consequences. But it is a life with more adventure than building roads. Than ruining your back and hands working on the hotel. Do not let me decide for you what you do with your life. But I can help if you want. I know people in Tijuana. Los Angeles and San Diego. You have to be a very good thief to live in these cities. But I will teach you.

Javier smiled and laughed when we heard this. He shook his head and said to me. When Guillermo told me this story it was New York. He had a cousin there.

After being introduced to Javier at the salon I went there many times to meet with him while the poet was in the market at his stall. We sat at a table or played billiards while Guillermo settled disputes between the thieves. He listened carefully and judged fairly. Thinking for hours with his chin denting the back of the veins in his hands folded over his cane. If one of the thieves thought the decision unfair and believed that he had been wronged then the veteran always gave him something extra the next time he came to the salon with items to sell.

Sitting with Javier I listened to the thieves stories of sneaking and stealing and from this I knew how much they enjoyed the chance of being caught. In this they thought nothing of how their stealing affected others. The items for them merely shone with wealth or had gone dull with age that might promise wealth also. I thought the stealing wrong.

People should not put their memories in things. The poet said to me when I mentioned this. Most of the people that these boys steal from own these things to impress others. They own them not to admire and cherish for themselves but to remind others of what they do not have. These things cost nothing to people like this.

I spoke nothing of these feelings to Javier. Because he was my friend I did not consider him one of these other young thieves. Besides I was similar to them before the fighting of dogs. I was not affected by the pain I had brought on others. I even maybe felt more alive then. I know that if I had not found her or the poet or the dentist and Javier I would have been like these young thieves until I died in prison or with a knife in my chest sitting at an empty table in a bar. I am grateful for these others. For Canción.

At the salon I spent more and more time with the poet and Guillermo also. We bet on games the young men played and sometimes I was there to break up fights. There was always the threat of the young men dancing in the aisles flashing knives. But more and more often the poet and Guillermo spent their time in the back room talking. Or pacing back and forth from the salon to the shop down the street to be alone. The veteran with his hand on the poets arm. The cane dangling between them unused. Their heads bent together. Once in a while the police visited and went into the back room with Guillermo. Later he shuffled out of the back room pouring them cups of damiana while calling me over to be introduced to them and shake their hands.

The best dog fighter there is. Guillermo placed his hand on my arm for support. Everyone says so.

Thank you my young friend. Is what he said to me after they were gone.

But there was much that happened at the salon without my knowing. I could not help but wonder how the conversation between the poet and me would have finished if Javier had not interrupted to give him the book. Every time I saw the words painted on the walls I thought to check the young mens hands when they played pool.

I knew before I would admit to myself that I knew.

Still I was walking much at night alone. It was very strange for me to think that I was now in the words and stories of others after for so long being nothing in the words of anyone. All for the killing of a dog. But in a horrible way that earned me much respect. I preferred the shadows and light of the growing moon at night. When I asked once what the poet thought of the fighting he answered.

The fighting of dogs is something that the men of Canción have enjoyed for many years. You should feel proud to be of this tradition.

But shame also I think.

Still I searched the city streets for her. Spoke of her to no one. The poet sat in his stall in the market with the women. The workingmen continued construction on the hotel while around it the burned tractors sat. The road in the hills above Canción crept down toward the abandoned mine and then into Canción. No one mentioned the fire in the village in the mountains from the night of my first fight. No one spoke of those who lived there. I was too busy in my search for her to think of them. Every day I found her at the end of a street. Turning a corner to disappear. She taunted me with brief encounters. Led me down empty streets that ended leaving me in a maze that changed each time. I visited and revisited places I had imagined seeing her. Created her out of memories we never had together. Once when a little girl discovered me talking to myself she laughed and ran. Wandering like this through Canción I was only passing time until the next fight when I knew I would see her again. The streets light with the sun and softened by dust because there was so little rain in this part of Baja. The buildings beehives with people behind walls. Now and then there was the distant sound of blasting in the hills. The hammers at the hotel. But never anything of her.

I floated on my back in the bay at night with the tiny waves splashing into my ears and I whispered to her again and again.

Te quiero mi amor. Te quiero.

I said this again and again until the words became unfamiliar. Until their sound lost meaning. But knowing that this confusion when words lost their meaning was also a dream. That I only had to stop and take my ears from the water and concentrate again on the words alone and not their repetition and I would come to the surface of this dream and understand the words completely again and then know why it was that I was telling them to my love. I shared them with her because for us they had meaning. They were something we understood together. Each of us may have understood them differently. But for as much as I felt for her these words held that feeling. And for as much as she loved me the words held that feeling for her she told me. Holding one another we understood the words belonging to each other that we shared.

I imagined how it would be to tell the poet of her. I walked in the hills by myself before going to his stall in the market. The men working on the road above looked at me with hate in their eyes for being able to be out for a lazy walk. Working to feed their children and wives and themselves while I fought dogs. I waited until I was beyond the sound of the bulldozers to speak. Forgetting the little girl who laughed at me. Not caring.

I feel ashamed to tell you this. I told the imaginary poet. But I will not be able to live without her.

He would smile. Light a cigarette after sliding his typewriter to the side. Ink stained cigarette papers.

Young men in love are fools. He would say. This is nothing to be ashamed of.

But my stomach is in my chest when I think about her. All the time I feel sick. I wonder what she is doing with her day. If she is sleeping. If she is sleeping I wonder what is she dreaming of. I put myself in her dreams. The way I put her in mine. The other day I saw her in the market. Then in the plaza. Along the malecón. Each time when I ran to catch up with her she was gone or she was some other woman. When I fight dogs there is nothing in this world for me but her. If to fight dogs means to be near her then I will kill them gladly.

The poet would be quiet. He would study the end of his cigarette.

I enjoyed your company more when you did not talk so much. He had said to me. Smiling his terrible smile.

After the dentists mother slept one night Javier hobbled into the courtyard to sit and rest and admire the stars. The stars in Canción were like no others then. There were not many lights in the city to ruin the sky. And so we sat in wood chairs looking up through the dark palm fronds. The moon was almost full. My knuckle had not been broken the night I helped Javier but still it hurt me very much. The dentist sat with us drinking red wine until the wine made him sleepy. Then he yawned and stood and stretched a moment longer than he needed to hoping that Javier would join him. When he did not Jorge smiled disappointed but kissed Javier on top of the head.

He cries himself to sleep. The thief joked when Jorge was gone.

How is the ankle? I asked.

I will be fine soon enough. And this being injured is not such a bad life. I enjoy the attention.

Javier took a long drag from his cigarette. The smoke came in bursts from his mouth when he spoke.

Do you miss your home? He asked me then.

Some.

Your family?

I have no more family. I said.

No wife? A girlfriend?

No. But I am in love with a woman.

I had said it carelessly. We had never spoken about love. But I knew afterward that I had been wanting to say this to the thief for some time. That we were becoming friends and this was the last thing between us.

What is her name?

I searched for the exact words to explain.

No sé. I admitted finally.

How can you not know the name of your lover? He laughed. Where does she live?

No sé.

You do not know where she lives. You do not know her name? My friend we need to fix your hand fast so you can return to your imaginary love.

No. I stumbled for the words to explain. She is real. I said when he laughed more. I know that she lives in Canción.

Who is she to you?

My love. I said not understanding his question.

Who is she to others?

I hesitated.

She is the mistress of Cantana.

The thief whistled a long shrill whistle into clucking his tongue against his teeth. This is a very dangerous woman to love hombre.

I understand.

I do not think that you do. Cantana is a wicked man. I do not care how strong you think you are. He is stronger. Cantana is the only businessman in this city that I have never stolen from.

I sighed. Javier put his hand on my arm.

But I have always wanted to. He smiled. I will tell you something dog fighter. Because you have helped me I will help you search for her. I know the houses of this city better than anyone. I know all of its people. I will find out for you if she lives with Cantana. Or if she does not I will find out where she does live. But. He grinned. When you knock on that door all the boys and I are going to be standing there behind you for a good laugh.

———

The day before my fourth fight tiny birds took flight from the shade of the trees of the plaza across from the cathedral and into the comfortable February sky. It had been some time since I had gone into the hills on a Sunday walk with the poet. Guillermo came with us. Once or twice we stopped on the side of the road to rest on our way to the overlook above the abandoned mine. I offered Guillermo my arm.

It might be easier if you just carried me. The veteran teased.

You should be paying him not to drop you. The poet responded.

The city shimmered below us.

How long have you been helping the young men? I asked Guillermo once we came to the overlook and he settled on a rock with a nice seat worn into it by the weather.

For some years now.

Were you ever a thief?

Guillermo turned to the poet. I do not remember him always asking this many questions.

I think the dogs have knocked something loose. The poet answered.

Are you looking for a new line of work? The veteran smiled at me.

I do not think he would fit through the windows. The poet said.

No. I answered them both. I am just curious.

The dentist had brought a bottle of mescal and some oranges and salt mixed with powdered chili. We took sips and sprinkled the salt and chili on the sweet orange. Below in the center of the bay the plane of the American investors had landed earlier in the day. They had come to see the destroyed tractors. Men in the streets were talking about their arrival for days. Of how brave the young men who wrote on the walls had been. The silver plane was difficult on our eyes with the sun lowering slowly over the mountains above and behind us. It caught the sun as a coin does.

Have you been in an airplane before? I asked them to change the conversation.

No. Guillermo said.

And you? I asked the poet.

Neither of us. Guillermo responded for him.

I would like to someday. I went on. To see all this differently.

The old men passed the bottle between them taking small sips. The poet rolled his cigarettes. They did not seem much in the mood for talking. When I sipped from the bottle the mescal burned my stomach some. I often forgot to eat in those days I thought of her so much. I coughed when I swallowed the alcohol again and the old men smiled to themselves. No one spoke. I felt comfortable in the shadows of the mountains creeping up on us from behind as we faced Canción. The boys in the canoes circled the plane on the bay.

We should stay up here long enough to watch the plane take off. I suggested and the old men nodded.

Below tiny dark burros pulled carts making their way to the plaza mayor. At the hotel I squinted to see the men. I searched the rooftops for her. I wondered what was blurred and what was not blurred for the old mens eyes. Concentrating on the hotel I pretended to hear the taps of their hammers on the backs of their chisels into stone. From the alcoves of the cathedral I listened for the rush of pigeon wings. I searched for the compound in all those colorful buildings and the poorer ones also. The market was busy. I looked for the street where Guillermo had his salon and shop. I wondered where she lived. In the light of which windows. Behind which wall Javier would find her for me. I wondered where he was down in the red and brown metal roofs beneath the windmills.

Where Ramón slept in the arms of some businessmans mistress. Where Cantana lurked. The glass bottle clinked against the boulder when the old veteran lowered his arm by his side.

We were not there long when several men came jogging down the road from working on the other side of the mountains on the road. A man had been injured they said. Some rocks came down on top of him. They said that they were sent for an extra burro to bring him down to a doctor.

You do not have a burro do you? One man joked.

Only this one. Guillermo pointed to me and we laughed. But he is my crutch so you cannot have him. I do not care whose leg is broken.

Do you have any water? The other man asked.

The poet held up the bottle of mescal.

Both the men took great drinks from the bottle and wiped their wet lips on the backs of sunburned hands leaving dust caked to their faces. Then they began running again. Barefoot over sharp rocks.

I bet one of them vomits before they make it to the edge of the city. The poet said.

I was bored waiting for the plane. We had been sitting for more than an hour and my legs were stiff. My side ached. I had to go to the bathroom. I suggested we return to the salon but neither of the men wanted to leave just yet.

We should wait for the sunset. The poet suggested. When was the last time you and I enjoyed a sunset together?

This might be the last time I ever make it up here. Guillermo answered.

I will be right back. I said.

Where are you going? Guillermo snapped at me. When he drank his anger was very great. But his voice still surprised me.

I began to undo my pants and the poet laughed.

You want me to do it right here in front of you? I asked.

Get away from here you pig. Guillermo laughed and threw pebbles at me as I jogged up and around a short bend in the road and squatted near a flowering plant with a few leaves. When I returned I was surprised to find Javier sitting with the old men. The walk difficult on his ankle. His face sweaty.

Good to see you. I offered my hand. We still had not let on to the old men that we knew each other.

How are you? He asked me.

Javier was just on a walk of his own. Guillermo said before I could answer.

I like it up here. Javier smiled. The view is very good.

The old veteran looked to his watch. He seemed impatient now. Down below on the bay the boys in their canoes had gone from the plane. I squinted to see the pilot sitting on the pontoons. He probably had taken off his shoes and put his feet in the water. The sound of the explosion came to us not long after the plane burst into a bloom of fire. A cloud of black smoke rose into the sky. Then more smoke lay along the water of the bay where the diesel burned. I stood with my arms flat along my sides. Stunned as the explosion faded in those mountains. People ran along the streets to the malecón. I looked down to the poet. Then to Javier. Both were inspecting the city below us. When I looked to the old veteran I was surprised to see him pointing a small revolver at me.

Sit down. He said.

The poet nodded.

Everything is fine. Javier nodded also. His smile genuine. Sit.

SEVEN

They want him dead. Javier told me later that night when we sat in the courtyard. The old men learned somehow that Cantana is interested in you. They believe this is their best way against him.

How long have you known they wanted me for this?

The thief had not looked me in the eyes since I had looked to him from the revolver Guillermo held. His voice soft. Ashamed even.

Not long.

Have you told them you know me?

No. That would put Jorge at risk.

Do you trust them?

Yes. I do. And no. I do not. They care for Canción enough to risk themselves for it. I feel the same way. This fight of ours against Cantana has been coming for some time. They see you as a way to help end it.

I thought the poet was my friend. I said then.

He is. But his love for this city.

His hatred for Cantana. I interrupted.

Is more important to him than your friendship. Javier delicately picked a piece of tobacco from his lip. You need to understand that these old men come from a time much different than ours. What they fought for. What they fought against in la Revolución is the same thing that came into power. Javier sat forward in his chair. The dentist had gone to sleep. The thief had a difficult time keeping his voice down he was so excited. It is hard for them. He continued. Such a defeat is very great. They believe that Canción is much different though. That it is worth protecting.

And you agree?

I do.

The poet has betrayed me.

Javier looked at the end of his cigarette.

I do not know what to say to you about that.

The chair scratched on the tile when I stood to leave.

I will kill you if you mention her to them. I said then.

I have told them nothing. I would not do that. Know that I am with you in this my friend. That I will not betray you after what you have done for me.

You are a thief. I said to him. What have you given me to trust you that is different from what the poet or Guillermo has given me to trust them?

My word.

That night in my small room I debated leaving Canción. Taking the money I had won fighting dogs and finding work someplace new. I would have if not for her.

Imagine if the sun was to become weightless. I had told Javier some nights before. The planets would all lose their way. This is how my soul would be without her.

I was very hurt that the poet had deceived me. He and Guillermo were very clever men. And while my life had calmed in the peace of Canción I knew enough then of fire to know that if I remained in the small city I would die. But the old men had been honest in their deception somehow. Listening to the poet on the overlook that day I had believed that what he and Guillermo and the young men at the salon were fighting for was good for Canción. I also did not like Cantana. But for my own reasons.

You are no stranger to killing. Guillermo said to me. This will not be difficult for you.

The boys in the canoes hurried to the smoking plane to be among the pieces of metal that floated burning with diesel before sinking to the coral below. I learned some days after that Javier had given the bomb to one of the older boys. A young thief. He hid the bomb on the plane while the pilot traded with the boys.

If I do not accept? I asked the old men.

You will die right here.

What if I say yes but only to betray you later?

Then you will die later. The veteran said confident in his words.

Imagine how they will say your name. The poet said to me then. Thinking I might still be susceptible to this for all the conversations we had had.

The poet had not observed my change. He did not know that I no longer needed the voices calling my name. Not now that I had her own. But because I had shared the secret of my love with Javier I worried he knew of that which owned me. That owned my thoughts. That they would use this somehow against me. I did not know if I could trust Javier yet. That if what he told me had been a lie.

Lying on the blankets of my small bed that night I listened to a man on the street below pushing his cart. His whistling in the quiet of that troublesome night. I knew the city well by this time. I enjoyed its song. I kept time by the voices of mothers calling their children. The radios left on. The tired men cursing their burros. The sound of her dress sweeping over stones when she came to me after the city slept. I thought then that Guillermo and the poet were right. That Canción might stay like this forever if I were to murder Cantana. The poet was right to remind me of the voices. I could hear my name faintly on them again. Long after I was no longer of this world. A hero for what I had done for the hidden city. But still they were not as strong or beautiful as her own.

Other businessmen will take his place. I told the old men as we came back down the road into Canción slowly. I let Javier hold the veterans arm to help him walk because to live that day I agreed to kill Cantana. Cantanas death will not end construction on the hotel. I said to them. Greed does not die. I said to the poet because he had said this to me many times.

The poet did not answer. He knew I was correct. And I think that he was ashamed of himself for betraying me. He had been drinking more of the mescal than I had or Guillermo. But this was something he was convinced of. That Cantana had to be killed.

You are wrong dog fighter. Guillermo said once we had returned to the salon. Night had settled completely. Under the flickering electric light the wrinkles of his old face reminded me of the cracks in the concrete floor of the hotel. The flames. Cantanas death will put the fear of God in the hearts of the other businessmen. His death alone will be enough to stop them. The hotel will stand forever as a skeleton. As a warning of what will come to those should they try again.

They will not ruin this city. The poet said softly in that light. But still he would not look me in the eyes.

I have not told them I know where you live. Javier said to me in the courtyard in a voice eager to keep my friendship.

For Jorge. I responded.

Yes. But.

Have you thought of what they will be asking you to do when you are standing before the end of their revolver? I asked.

The thief looked ashamed when I said this to him. He was trying to convince me that he was more loyal to me than he was to them. He feared I would betray his love for Jorge to the old men.

Keep him thinking you are his friend Javier. I imagined Guillermo telling the thief. Make sure he does not go to Cantana.

He will not go to Cantana. The poet saying.

What makes you so positive?

He is not smart enough.

I did not know who to trust but her. And when I asked her lying in my small bed that night she took my face in her hands and kissed my forehead.

I will not leave without you. I said to her.

Come to us after this next fight. Guillermo had said before I left him and the poet at the salon. We want you to kill him sometime after this. But first we need to know when the American investors will be here. There is one in particular we want dead.

Will the Americans come now? I asked. After this attack it will be too dangerous.

They will come to prove that we are nothing to them. Guillermo said.

Flies on the ass of a horse. The poet said.

They will come to prove to Canción that our efforts are unimportant and that nothing will stop the hotel from being built. And this is when we will prove them wrong.

What if I die fighting the dogs? I asked.

You will not. The veteran said. Everyone knows this. This is why we have chosen you.

How am I supposed to get near to Cantana?

You have access to him that we do not. We know that he wants you to work for him. He values your strength.

Your popularity. The poet said.

Approach him about this. Let us know what he knows.

And when you hear of the Americans let us know. The poet said.

I turned to leave.

And dog fighter. The veteran said. Do not think to give us over to Cantana. I will kill you myself.

———

The night of the dog fighting Ramón and Vargas came to the storehouse smelling of alcohol and smoke. I heard them down the circular staircase talking with Elías and Rodríguez. There were the voices of women also. Much laughing.

They still let you choose? Vargas asked Ramón about the

painted sticks as they climbed the stairs. I thought you and Mendoza were wedded.

They keep expecting me to die. Ramón answered. Besides. You may have chosen the teeth tonight.

I do not think so. Mendoza is for you alone.

There was a new fighter in the small room that night. A short man from Monterrey with a large chest and electric blue eyes. Ramón and Vargas made jokes between themselves to scare him. Talking about deaths they had witnessed. Clucking their tongues and shaking their heads but with their eyes on him to see his reaction. But in the small room this man was very calm. I remembered how I was before my first fight and I was very impressed by him. His confidence genuine.

That night I killed my dog easily. Just as Guillermo said I would.

After Ramóns fight he returned to the crowd of yelling men from the small room to stand next to me at the edge of the wood benches where the businessmen sat.

I have the worst luck. He said. I knew that he was sobered some by his fight. He had chosen a dog of Mendozas once again. His fifth in a row. Across from us this trainer sat next to Cantana. Ramón stared at Mendoza and this made the trainer smile with his toothpick in his mouth. I am not sure if Ramón noticed me staring at her sitting on the other side of Cantana because his eyes never came from Mendoza. And Mendozas eyes never moved from him. It was a small game they played.

During this the fighter from Monterrey came into the ring. He was still very calm. Vargas would fight last that night. The young men from the salon took the bets from the yelling men while Javier went from businessman to businessman. Jotting down notes quickly with his sleeves rolled to make them think he was honest. Jumping back and forth but skillfully to the snap of their fingers. Most of the yelling men bet on the dog because it was this fighters first fight. But if he heard them taunting him it did not affect him any. His eyelids did not blink. But for as calm as he was he would never be able to control the ring in which he fought. I knew this. And each time Ramón drew a painted stick he knew this to be true also. The businessmen owned the ring. Chance.

When the leash was undone he proved to be a skilled fighter. He lured and then avoided the dog with great ease. Slashing its side with the claws on several different passes. Eluding the dog in the manner of a matador. He even smiled at one point which gained great favor from the yelling men and brought Ramóns attention from the trainer to the fighting. Ramón at this time was the most colorful of the fighters. Vargas and myself the strength. Other fighters were there merely for the men to wait through until we came into the ring. But this man was better than us all. The dog did not touch him until he slipped on a spot of blood missed by the ragmen. He fell to the ground on his back and his head hit hard on the concrete. He was not awake when the dog locked its jaw around the soft of his neck and tore away the flesh of his throat. Its ears perked. The trainer ran to the dog to pull it off the dead fighter but the dog turned on this man and bit him on the arm. Ragmen tried to distract the dog with blood soaked cloths. Mendoza walked calmly into the crowd. He held a revolver. The yelling men woke suddenly to the sharp gunshot. The ragmen fell back. Mendoza had shot the dog in the head. No one believed that the skill of this fighter was broken by a spot of blood on the floor. The shot had come over us all hard in the ears. Echoes slipping between the blades of the windmills above the rooftops before dying over the bay. I looked back to her. Only when the fighter fell to the ground had our eyes broken apart. And this to see the man die horribly. But now her eyes looked back to mine and I smiled. With all that before us I smiled. And she smiled a tiny smile back.

I went to the cantina beneath the abandoned church that night with Ramón and Vargas. Elías the doorman and the young businessman Rodríguez went with us also. I hoped to encounter Cantana there. Coming down the stone stairs I looked for her on the dance floor among the swirling dresses. I searched for the gleam of Cantanas sunglasses in the crowd. But nothing. Neither of them.

That night Ramón drank very much and talked much of himself. I suspect the dreams of the dogs with sharpened teeth never left him. His eyes at times were very wild and the smiles he gave to the mistresses were more and more sinister. Vargas chided him constantly in his ear about the dogs of Mendoza.

How do you think he sharpens the teeth Ramón? Vargas asked. How do you think he gets them to sit still?

I could tell you but there are ladies at the table. Ramón smiled to no one.

No. Vargas went on. Do they cry when he takes the files to their teeth? Do you think he does it when they are puppies?

I do not care. Ramón forced a laugh.

I hear he is going to begin dripping metal over the teeth and then sharpening the metal. Vargas said taking a sip of his drink to conceal his smile. Several of the businessmen at the rectangular table smiled also. They enjoyed this between the two dog fighters.

I will kill you. Ramón said. But the fugitive only laughed more.

Then Rodríguez went to say something more but Ramón and Vargas both were silent.

You fool. One of the businessmen said when the two dog fighters were not at the table. What do you know of fighting dogs?

I would be the best. Rodríguez answered. At this the businessman only laughed.

Ramón and Vargas always played games with each other in this way. Games that made Rodríguez the fool. The young businessman needed the company of the two dog fighters. And they did not mind so much when Rodríguez bought them drinks and introduced them to new mistresses.

Watching all of this take place in the cantina beneath the church I realized that Vargas was very jealous of the women who loved

Ramón. And that Ramón enjoyed the attention he stole from the
strength of the fugitive. They worked well together. Businessmen
other than Rodríguez bought them many drinks. Everyone wanted
to be sitting at the rectangular tables with them. All the most beautiful mistresses were there. Their eyes always on Ramón.

The golden boy. Vargas called him.

But there was something sad about Ramón also. A mysterious
quiet. The death of the man from Monterrey I thought maybe made
him like this. The sharpened teeth maybe. After some time Vargas
clapped him on the back and said.

Chingón. What is bothering you?

The mistresses wondered the same.

Nothing. Ramón said. Shaking his head slightly.

Seguro? Vargas asked.

Ramóns eyes staring far off at the wet glass rings on the table. I
was thinking of my mother. He said simply.

Me too. Vargas laughed.

No. I was. Ramón said. Ignoring the fugitives insult. Those at
the table noticed the serious tone of Ramóns voice and were quiet
then to listen. When I was a boy my father spent much of his time
drinking. Ramóns voice light as if he were going to make a joke of
something that was not funny and by doing this try to convince us all
that what was bothering him was great indeed but not so great as the
troubles we all knew and therefore could understand well ourselves.
In fact I never remember my father working. I only remember him
working at hitting my mother.

Several businessmen smiled to themselves at this. The mistresses
concentrating on the dog fighter.

My mother. Ramón continued. She was a very beautiful woman.
My father beat her with his fists or if he was feeling lazy his words.
Whore. He called her and spit in her face. But she did nothing. She
did not cry. I get my strength from my mother. Your words cut me
like glass. She said when my father finished. Like glass. He would
mock her.

Ramón then looked at those who listened in the eyes to measure their response before deciding to continue.

Sometimes. He said pouring rum into his glass. I think my father got bored with hitting her so often. And so he got a job. But soon he was bored with this job and went back to hitting her. Ramón shrugged and there was a polite laugh. When my father was bored with hitting her one day he decided to hit me. You are old enough now. He said to me. But he had never hit me before. My mother had never let him. But this one day he came home drunk and she was gone and he said. You are not my son. You are the son of this whore. And then he beat me until he was tired.

Ramón massaged the back of his neck until one of the mistresses began to do it for him. Vargas shifted in his chair but silently to not disrupt the telling.

My mother loved me very much. But when she saw the bruises on my face she did not yell at my father. She did not say anything that would only get her beaten. Instead the next morning she took a small glass bottle outside and wrapped it in a towel. I heard her breaking it over a rock into fine shards while my father snored. I went to see why there was this sound. Go back to sleep. She said to me. But I stood barefoot in the kitchen while she patted out tortillas. Humming to herself softly. Beans boiling on the stove for my father to take to work that day. I sat at the table alone for some time until my father came for this food to take with him to work. He kissed me on the forehead where I sat at the table. His hand on my head. His breath warm from sleep. I am sorry. He said to me. I looked up and his face was tired. Hungover. But I said nothing and my mother she kissed him at the door. When he was gone I checked the towel in the kitchen and it was empty of the glass.

All of the mistresses were wiping their eyes. Ramón sat back and finished his drink looking at no one. When the last of the mistresses excused herself to fix her mascara Vargas waited a moment before clapping softly. And then the businessmen at the table were laughing and trading money from the bets.

Well done. The fugitive laughed.

When you said your words cut like glass. Rodríguez laughed. Counting the money he had won. I think that is what did it.

You do not think that part was too much? Ramón asked.

No. No. The others reassured him.

I was worried. He smiled.

Well done cabrón. Vargas raised his glass. I did not think it would work this time.

Ramóns eyes were alive. Watery from the smoke in the room and glassy from the drinking. They were fragile. Beautiful eyes. I knew that night that Ramón did not have long to live in Canción.

I began visiting the cantina beneath the abandoned church almost every night with the other dog fighters and businessmen. Rodríguez was with us always begging to teach him how to fight and Elías was often there to laugh at him with us. But there was much that was serious also. There was much talk about the attacks. The plane explosion. The businessmen were very worried about the construction of the hotel. Cantana had more men placed there to guard it. A week after the plane was destroyed in the bay two young men were laid out dead on a canvas in the middle of the plaza mayor as a warning. I did not recognize them from the salon. But still word spread that these were the men responsible for the bombing. And this was to be the fate others would find if the attacks continued.

But what disappointed and frustrated me most was that because of the attacks Cantana did not come as often to the cantina.

He is afraid. Rodríguez said.

Smart. Vargas corrected the young businessman.

There was much talk of the attacks among the businessmen in the cantinas. They discussed the hotel and future of Canción. Of the money that was to be made and the best ways to lure tourists. They laughed at the people of Canción. Of how they would have to be trained to serve like the Americans expected. Taught to fold bed-sheets and wait for propinas. When the businessmen spoke of Cantana though it was with strained respect. With jealousy in their tone.

One very drunk businessman questioned the others wondering if they would ever receive the money they had given Cantana for the construction. The other businessmen hushed this man not wanting him to speak in this way around Ramón. But Ramón was always distracted by the eyes of one of their mistresses. One businessman silenced this drunk by mentioning to him the story of the man in the market with no eyes. The mistresses begged for the story until the quiet of the businessmen made them stop. The drunk blushed with embarrassment. Vargas laughed at all of them.

To the day when roads reach to the end of Baja. One businessman raised his glass.

To the money. Another cried.

To roads that lead to the wallet of Cantana. The drunk slurred. He finished his drink and stood unsteadily. Struggled to put on his jacket.

Be grateful hombre. Someone said to him. You will have your taste too.

Who are you to tell me what? The drunk argued. His chair clattered against the floor. La madre de El Tapado. He slurred grabbing himself. Many in the cantina staring at him now. I am not scared of some story. When he looked at the dancers on the floor he lost focus of his eyes and collapsed. With a mistress sitting on his lap Ramón threw his head back with laughter. The other businessmen joined him. They left the drunk where he lay.

In the conversation of the businessmen I listened for word of the American investors but there was nothing. But more I listened for talk of her whenever they spoke of Cantana. Desperately I listened for a name that would suit her beauty. The thought of these men sharing rooms with her made me angry and jealous. I knew that they sat at tables with her drinking wine and maybe even had admired her dancing. Knew her voice.

Through them. I convinced myself. Through them you will hear her sing.

Rodríguez introduced us to many different mistresses. Ramón

was a favorite among them all. The women laughed with his stories.
They yielded to his charm. Ramón was not as violent as the fugitive
or myself even. Vargas was respectful of most of the businessmen.
He knew when to turn his advances toward their women into a
laugh. They feared him the most of us all. It was a game the fugitive
played with them.

Late at night in the cantina I listened to the stories the businessmen told of the many great fights in the past. Fights between the
dog fighters and the dogs and between the dog fighters themselves.
The businessmen understood very well that dog fighters were not
always finished fighting and the best thing to watch after the fighting
of dogs was the dog fighters fighting each other. I drank with them
all but never enough to be very drunk. Vargas often joked about
fighting me but I only smiled at him quietly. The businessmen loved
this. Ramón only shook his head and threatened to have Rodríguez
fight Vargas. At this the businessmen laughed. In the voices of the
businessmen trying to get Ramón and Vargas and me to beat one
another I heard my grandfathers whisper. But now it did not have
power over me.

One night a skinny businessman with pockmarks in his face
leaned toward me and said.

There are always women to be impressed. You should destroy
your handsome friend there in front of them. Win them from him.

I looked this man up and down. Some of the other businessmen
heard him say this and waited for my reaction. Everyone knew me to
be quiet.

Or. I said calmly. I could destroy you and save them from your
breath.

The businessmen broke into laughter. One draped an arm over
my shoulder. The weight of his rings on my back made me uncomfortable. He held his drink up before me and the others who heard
me did the same. I was angry that I had not seen her after spending
so much time with these men and I did not enjoy their company so I

took the cup before me and emptied it to their applause. Ramón laughed. Vargas grinned.

But Ramón was not respectful of certain businessmen. He took advantage of his friendship with Cantana often. Late one night when he was very drunk Ramón left the cantina beneath the abandoned church with a favorite mistress of one of these businessmen. The businessman struggled with a small knife wanting to stab Ramón but Vargas and I held his arms easily stopping him.

We watched as Ramón climbed the stairs. Helping the mistress while also kissing her neck and looking back at the angry man. The shadows of Ramón and this woman flickered like flames upon the rock wall.

You will only fight the dogs of Mendoza! The businessman called after him.

Because I am the best! Ramón turned back and yelled.

The cantina beneath the church was quiet for a moment. Then the laugh of the mistress in the dark hallway leaving broke the businessman even more.

I left the cantina not long after this. Just before the sun lightened the dark of the blue sea. The air I walked into was cool. The man at the gate said.

Buenos días.

I looked to the sky. Disappointed.

It was more difficult than I thought encountering Cantana. I began to worry that the old men would not believe me. I went regularly to Guillermo at the salon to report what I learned. But this was nothing.

There is talk of an airstrip to be able to fly in the tourists on airplanes. I said.

Yes. The veteran answered. We know.

And there is more construction to be done to the electrical station.

Yes. Guillermo ran his hands through his gray hair. We know this also.

When the poet was at the salon I said nothing to him. I never went to see him at his stall in the market anymore. The lessons I practiced in English were ones that I had done many times before. But even then I did not want to practice much because it only reminded me of the old poet and the friendship I thought I had had with him.

At the salon the young thieves leaned against the walls or sat on the edges of the billiard tables looking suspicious of me. We no longer offered our hands or jokes to one another. They were loyal to the old men and they suspected that I was not. That I was in a position where if I did not do what the old men ordered me to do then they were to kill me. This was a respect we gave each other. But many of the young thieves were not able to look me in the eyes.

One day I sat with Guillermo and the poet for a short time in the back of the salon. I was drinking late into the night before at the cantina but still had nothing new to tell them.

Cantana never comes to the cantinas and we never go to him. I said. Ramón and Vargas say nothing about him.

But the other businessmen? The poet asked.

I looked him in the eyes for a moment before answering.

They complain about Cantana in the same voice that you do. I said.

We have him scared maybe? Guillermo said to the poet.

No. The poet disagreed. El Tapado is too smart for that. He knows that to stay to the shadows only creates more mystery about him. It only makes him more powerful in the eyes of the people of Canción. He wants them to believe he cannot be bothered by us.

Those men in the plaza. I asked. The ones lying on the canvas. Were they with us?

No. Guillermo shook his head. I do not know who they were.

Maybe I should ask Ramón to introduce me? I suggested.

No. The poet said. He will suspect you. We must be patient. This is a game he is playing. But one we can play also.

Several days after this in the middle of the night there was a great explosion in the mountains above Canción. An entire hillside settled over the road the men had been constructing for the businessmen. Small fires on the tractors could be seen from the streets of Canción. They burned throughout the night. A dozen sleeping workers died in the explosion. When I met with Guillermo and the poet after this I asked them nothing of the attack. The young men in the salon were in high spirits. But this lasted only until word came that three more young men were on display in the plaza. Naked and dead. Their mothers crying over the bodies. The fathers vowing revenge not on Cantana but on those responsible for the increasing attacks.

They have said nothing of the Americans? Guillermo asked me growing impatient.

No.

He cursed. We are losing time.

One day down on the malecón a large crowd gathered to watch as two new large tractors were unloaded from a boat to replace those that had been destroyed two months earlier. I stood in this crowd listening to the men and women tell stories about how the police had come to their homes in the night searching for their sons. Fathers and grandfathers were beaten for information that led nowhere. No one knew anything. In one of the stories I heard of the men who stormed into homes and destroyed belongings the man described was Vargas. Of this I am almost positive. I wondered if this is what I was to do for Cantana if I was to be asked to work for him. I could not.

At the compound with Jorge and Javier was the only time I ever felt at peace and even then I did not yet know what to think of Javiers relationship to the old men. Jorge knew nothing of his young lovers involvement in the attacks. And just as Javier had this over me with her and the old men I had this knowledge over him with the dentist.

During Javiers time at the compound when he was injured Jorge would sit for hours when there was no one in his chair to pull teeth from. Reading with Javiers ankle in his lap. I thought back upon these times often. Javier would let his fingers coil the dentists hair as the dentist focused on his reading. Occasionally reading to us both aloud. Or I listened to the stories from my room while I did sit ups on the floor. I lay on my bed and lifted the light chair over my chest with my injured hand. The words of a poem the poet had given me scrawled across the bottom and legs.

Crumbling is not an instants act. A fundamental pause. Dilapidations processes. Are organized decays.

Much had changed between us all.

One night late I remember sitting with Javier and the dentist in the back room. Jorge had been reading to us from the newspaper. Javier had fallen asleep with his head in the lap of the dentist. I sat in one of the couches listening to the stories Jorge read. Some gentle music played on the Victrola. The light golden on the dull horn. The curtains the color of dark red wine. With all that surrounded the dentist. With all that was asleep in his lap. I mumbled to him interrupting his reading.

You are a very lucky man señor. He set down the newspaper to his side. Looked at me over the rims of his eyeglasses. You have many good things in your life here.

I do. He said. But it has taken me a long time to recognize this. Javier has taught me much.

Your mother is very special to you as well.

Of course. She is my life.

But you keep Javier from her?

She would not understand.

I understand. I said.

Do you?

I think so.

Forgive me for saying this my friend. But I do not think that you understand.

Without looking in his eyes I nodded.

May I ask you something? I said after a moment.

Please.

Is Javier your only love?

The poet looked down to see if the young thief was sleeping. Javiers eyelashes flickered with dreams.

No. The dentist answered in a quiet voice. When I was your age I was engaged to be married to a beautiful young woman.

Really?

Yes. The dentist smiled. My mother arranged this. My father had died when I was very young. His family was very wealthy and so my mother did not have to marry again. I was afforded a very good education. I was very fortunate.

This was in Canción?

No. Michoacán. My mother brought me to Canción after this young woman died.

I am sorry.

No reason to be sorry. I was not in love with her. Her father was a wealthy landowner. Our families were more to be married than we were. She and I would sit for hours in my mothers garden when we were young. I spent many hours listening to her talk. She was very intelligent. Very beautiful. Strong temper. But still I felt nothing for her. Are you not going to try to kiss me? She asked me many times. Disappointed by my lack of interest. Questioning her own beauty. Still I did not try to kiss her. I could not tell her that I did not love her. She had many men who wanted her hand. But none that would keep themselves from her as I did. And so she loved me. Not men better educated or with more money than me. Not men who would confess a love for her. Is that not what we all want? For others to love us regardless of whether or not we love them?

I do not think so. I answered.

I used to think it is this way. But now I have known a unique love. A complete one. Now I do not know what to believe. And I am fine with that.

The dentist rested his hands on Javiers shoulders. He toyed with the ends of the sleeping thiefs fingers.

How did she die? I asked.

Jorges voice quieted some as he continued.

This young woman had an older brother. He and I became good friends. When I was not spending my time with him my mother made me spend time with his sister in the garden. You are to be married to this beauty. My mother scolded me. Convince her that you love her. I did not know this then but the money my mother had was not much at this time. The marriage was to benefit our side of the family by opening our land to her father for his cattle. The brother and I rode horses for hours and hours over the lands that would soon be joined. We hunted together and swam naked together in the mountain streams icy even then in summer. It was easy to fall in love with this young man. I fell in love with the voice he used to fill the silence between us. One day we lay naked on the warm rocks in the sun. We had been swimming. My eyes were closed. I felt his fingers lightly across my stomach. It was the most gentle touch and yet it moved me greatly. There were a thousand soft lips at the ends of his fingers. We made love then for the first time there. My lips met the lips of a lover that day for the first time in my life. We returned to those rocks often. But never once spoke of what happened anyplace but there. We did not try to stop ourselves for all the talk we heard about sin. We were too hungry for one another. Too hungry to discover ourselves in this way in each other.

This was not long before I was to marry his sister. She became very jealous of the friendship I had with her brother. One of the suitors who most needed the land that came with her marriage had suspected our love and told her of it. When she confronted me one afternoon in the garden I denied my love for him. Foolishly I tried to deceive her into believing that she was my love. She said nothing.

Not long after this she disappeared. For several days we searched the countryside for her. He and I searched together. But we never thought to search our place by the stream because it was our place. We thought it was a secret. But we could not keep ourselves from touching one another even in this time of great sorrow. We returned to the rocks on the stream. Her hair was beautiful on the surface of the water. Moved by the smallest movements of the wind. Her chest wedged against a rock. Turtles scooted off her back and slipped beneath the surface of the water. When I dove in to pull her out even though she had been dead for several days I thought I could save her. Even when her body was heavy with death. I touched her arm and her skin seemed to come from it loose. Like tissue paper left in the rain. We brought her onto the rocks and closed her sharp green eyes. Her brother crossed her hands over her stomach. He cried very hard. This is Gods way of punishing us. He said. We can never be together again.

I loved this young man and would have done anything to keep him. But I was not the one that lost a sister. He and I buried her in those mountains not far from the stream. We put heavy rocks over her body where no one ever found her. We did this so no one would know of our love.

But what about this other suitor? Did he not tell anyone?

He did not have the chance to. My love killed him. He slit his throat with a hunting knife. He left the knife in this mans chest so everyone would know who did it. And so they would suspect it was because this other young man had wronged his sister and this was his familys revenge. And after that he hanged himself. Believing that he had to join his sister in hell.

We both sat listening to the silence. To Javiers breathing.

Do you believe in God? The dentist asked me then.

I am not sure. I answered and then it was the truth.

The one who says that if you are as Javier and I are then there is no place in heaven for you? The one that says that if you die as my first love died then you will never see heaven?

I am not sure.

Let me tell you that this is a horrible thing. Think of this carefully dog fighter. This is a horrible thing to believe in. But I am lucky. Because each evening when those young men come to visit me. When we sit in the back room together unashamed of how we are listening to those records and dancing together I know heaven. I refuse to leave here just to go to hell.

You do not think you will ever die? I smiled at him.

No. I will not. He said this without smiling back. I am too strong and too old and too angry for death. If I die it will be only because my mother dies. I will leave with her. And there in heaven I will watch her give God hell.

I wanted to tell the dentist about my love. But Javier stirred.

I had a wonderful dream. He grinned. Rubbing his eyes with the knuckles of his fists. You were both in it.

The dentist smacked Javier on the knee.

Do not be dirty in front of our guest Javi.

———

In my room I imagined her standing at her own window. Lying in her bed with the cool of the breeze up from the bay closing her eyes. The fragrant smells of some garden similar to the beauty of the dentists. Her breathing the same as mine. Our air and thoughts the same. I lay on my bed and closed my eyes and when I awoke I remembered that it was not all a dream but a lie. I knew nothing of her for all my love.

Nightmares of the dogs came to me. I woke before the sun rose and walked down to the bay to swim angry with myself for making up these lies. She was the mistress of Cantana. I had been careless with my imagination. As a young man this was an easy way to be. She went with him at night to the cantinas and parties but only when he decided that it would be so for her. Cantana was not worth deciding such things. But neither was I with my imagination of her. Even for all my love. When I swam in the bay as the sun rose over the perfect blue water I swam past the mouth and into the Sea of Cortés. Past the coral and where the water cooled some and the waves grew. I decided to swim until I would be too exhausted to swim back. It will be easy this way. I will not have to kill Cantana. I will not betray the old poet as he has betrayed me. I will leave them to their war. When my arms were finished I let myself float raised and lowered by the waves. I let my feet fall from the warm surface to the cool beneath and then my entire body sank some until my head was under and everything was silent. I decided to swim down with my eyes shut and my hands reaching out for anything and the more I went the water was much cooler and the pressure on my ears tremendous. I did not have enough breath to return to the surface. But I did not mind because I was so determined to reach the bottom of the sea. But there was no bottom and no sound. I opened my eyes and they burned in that dark. I put my arms to my side. I was desperate for breath but calm. I would float to the surface by the speed of my own rising weight and if I made it in time it was because God wanted this.

I was like a child in this way so miserable for her. At night I let myself be satisfied with the imaginations of us together. But the mornings were very bad. In the small bed I was alone and only when I woke in the dark and went to the bay to swim into the mouth of the sea did I encounter some comfort. I was on the sand with my legs in the water and then diving into the waves enjoying that first touch of the sea around me. It was like sleep. I swam until my arms could no longer move cursing Cantana with one stroke and myself with another for allowing him the power he held over me and then swimming for the bottom of the sea. Then I began to challenge God. To give up and to see if He would come to me. Always I returned to the surface for that breath. Then to the beach and the small hidden city once again. In cheating death I was more alive. Born again into imaginations of her.

It was on one of these mornings that I came onto the malecón still wet but drying in the warm morning sunlight when the poet was there on the stone walk waiting for me. A corn husk cigarette in his mouth. One hand in the pocket of his pants. Thin and tired looking.

You should be careful. He said. It is dangerous to be that far out.

What do you care? I asked.

Do not be a child. He smiled at me. You are too old for that.

What do you want?

I have not seen you in a while. He said. How is your English?

What do you want?

What have you learned about our friend?

Cantana?

The poet said nothing.

Cantana. I laughed. Raising my voice. Nothing. I said then in English. Nada.

Do not be so careless with your voice dog fighter. It does not suit your silence.

What do you care?

I am your friend.

You are lucky I have not broken your neck.

I began to walk along the malecón away from the poet but he followed.

I am too damn old to have my neck broken! He raised his voice now startling me. Do you believe I wanted to betray you? That I did not appreciate and enjoy your friendship?

What stopped you?

Do you enjoy it here? These long swims you take? This is gone! He said and his yell was a desperate whisper. All of this. That building there is the end. A year from now you will come out of the water and pick up a rake and rake this sand for some tourist to lie out on this beach. But the businessmen will not have you on this beach. Your strength will be used to carry suitcases. They will put you in some neat little suit. The English I have taught you will scrve you well. But it does not have to be this way. Entiendes? He lit another cigarette. Smoking inexpensive ones now that I no longer bought them for him. I did not betray you dog fighter. I brought you into the war. I would have betrayed you if I let Cantana get you on the wrong side.

What makes you think you are so right for Canción?

I will kill you right here if you say to me in an honest voice that you think Cantana is better.

You are as selfish as Jesus. I smiled but the old man did not smile back. The thieves at the salon. I asked then. Are they tired of your constant talk old man? Is that why you are here? So I can listen to you ramble on and on about women you never knew?

Those thieves. The poet smiled some. They are pawns. Necessary. But pawns. You my friend are a knight. Besides. All the women loved Jesus verdad?

I looked to the sand on my feet. Swiped my toes clean along the stones.

Let me buy you a coffee. He said to me then.

I am not thirsty for coffee.

Something stronger then? He grinned.

I did not trust the poet. But it was not bad for me to let him think that I did. I knew how to measure my words around him now. I understood how to measure his own. I did not swim out beyond the mouth of the bay each morning searching for the bottom of the sea just to be tricked once more by some old fool.

———

It was good to visit the poet in the market again. He sat at his stall stabbing out cigarette ends while focusing on a folded newspaper. The many typewriters quiet around him. When the children saw me they wrapped themselves around my legs so I walked like some monster down the narrow aisles. Banging my arms on purses and signs while the squealing children clawed at my sides and arms and chest asking to be thrown into the air or begging for treats. When I went to buy candy for the children the woman refused to take my money. She only smiled as the children took handfuls. When she was not looking I left the money for her. We began the lessons in English again and again the poet was grateful to be smoking expensive cigarettes.

This is really why you want to be friends with me. I smiled.

This and the men are too afraid of you to say anything to me when I say things about the young women that pass.

We laughed. But not as easily as before.

What do you know of the mistresses of the businessmen in Canción? I asked.

Whores. He said. All of them. But very beautiful just the same.

They are not all whores. I said.

You see how they are with the women at the fights. It is all some game to them. Much of what the businessmen do is for them. The love they think the mistresses have for them. It is a great desire in men to be desired by that which they would not have if they did not have money and power. This desire to be desired entirely. It is a great deception. The greatest maybe.

I did not agree with the poet but he expected this of me. By calling her a whore I knew for certain that Javier had said nothing of my love to the old men. That the thief had kept his word. My silence in the past when the poet spoke was serving me well now.

Early one evening after the poet closed his stall he and I were walking into the plaza mayor when I noticed Ramón sitting at a table at one of the cafés. Cantana and several young women sat with him. I had not seen the businessman in many weeks. It made me nervous that I was with the poet.

Tranquilo. He said. Pretend you do not see them.

When Ramón noticed me he waved for us to join them.

Do not walk over there. The poet whispered. I cannot go with you.

But it was too late. Ramón pushed away from the table and jogged over to us. Behind him Cantana said something to make the beautiful women laugh.

I am not going over there. The poet whispered.

Qué pasa chingón? Ramón smiled at me when he was upon us.

Nada. Y tú?

Nothing good. Ramón grinned. Come sit with us.

We are on a walk. I said.

To hell with your walk.

Maybe some other time. I said.

Over Ramóns shoulder a man in rags approached Cantanas table and began to strum a weathered guitar and to sing. His voice rose evenly over the bustle of the plaza but fell unnoticed by those he was not bothering for money. Cantana waved the man away with the back of his hand.

My friend. Ramón said looking me carefully in the eyes. Come and sit. You understand who it is I am with?

We do not have time. The poet broke in.

Ramón smiled. He took a step back from the poet and straightened his posture. Held out his hand.

My name is Ramón.

I know who you are. The poet said without taking his eyes from Cantana. Without offering his hand to Ramón.

Where did you find this old man? Ramón laughed.

We met in the market. The poet answered for me. The dog fighter had no friends.

Ramón smiled at this. Behind him an unlit cigarillo dangled from the corner of Cantanas mouth. He wore a white button down shirt. The frames of his sunglasses gleamed. His hair combed back carefully.

Come over. Ramón insisted. It will be very disrespectful of you if you do not.

He is right. The poet said. But I cannot stay. I will only come over and say hello.

Good. Ramón smiled. You have met Cantana before? He asked me as we approached.

No. I said.

Are you feeling well? He asked me then.

Do not mind him. The poet said. He has been acting funny all afternoon.

Cantana did not stand when Ramón introduced us. It was

strange to see him shake hands with the poet. His gloved hand felt awkward in mine.

I am a great admirer of yours. Cantana said to me. It is a great pleasure to finally meet you.

A group of children I knew from the market came running to the table. Cantana reached into his pockets for some coins. The women sitting at the table lifted their arms and bunched their shoulders to not have to touch the children with their dirty clothes and faces.

I gave the children money for candy and Ramón did the same. But the poet gave them each cigarettes.

You should not give them those. Cantana said as he put the rest of his coins back in his pocket.

It was all I had. The poet shrugged. The women looked away. Cantana smiled. You will have to excuse me. The poet said then. I have someplace to be.

Interesting friend that you have there dog fighter. Cantana said as we watched the poet cross the large square.

He is a poet. I answered. A very intelligent man.

The intelligent men I know do not give children cigarettes.

They will sell them. I said. He does this often.

Ramón laughed. Cantana rested his hand on the thigh of the young woman he sat next to.

How are you enjoying Canción? The businessman asked me then.

I like it very much here. It is very beautiful.

Have you been here long?

No. I came for the work on the hotel.

Really? Cantana said sounding surprised.

Yes.

He also used to work with Eduardo. Ramón said.

Eduardo? Cantana asked.

He is no longer with us. Ramón answered.

Oh yes. Eduardo.

The businessman seemed to be very distracted by his thoughts.

Since he had his sunglasses on I did not know what he was looking at. And for all the eyes he and I made in the past at the fights over her he did not seem to remember me or think me very important then. We sat like this for some time. Ramón told stories and made the women laugh while Cantana smoked his cigarillos and smiled amused. Cantana and I were both silent. He studied over my shoulder the busy plaza while sipping from his coffee now and then.

When Elías arrived I stood and shook the doormans hand. Ramón quickly finished his coffee as Elías and the businessman spoke.

Everything is ready. Elías said.

You have the dog? Cantana asked.

Vargas has it. Ramón answered reaching into his pocket for coins to pay for his coffee.

Ramón. Cantana smiled at this gesture. Please.

Thank you. Ramón bowed slightly. But Cantana only waved the back of his hand.

He is at his home? Cantana questioned Elías.

Vargas?

No. Cantana smiled. Our friend.

Sorry. Elías answered. Yes. Yes he is.

You should go with them. Cantana said to me then. You will enjoy this.

Come with us. Ramón urged me.

Where? I asked.

Rodríguez is going to fight the dog. Cantana answered for him. You should go.

Will you be fine here? Elías asked Cantana.

Oh yes. Cantana smiled. I have the company of these beautiful young women to enjoy. You boys go and play.

We had taken several steps from the businessman when he called to Ramón and waved him back. Ramón bent over so the businessman could whisper into his ear. The fighter nodding. I felt uneasy watching Cantanas hand rest on Ramóns shoulder. His face concealed. His words silent. Then Ramón stood and jogged back to Elías and me and said.

Ándale.

On the walk to the house of the young businessman Elías and Ramón were almost jogging they were so excited.

Is it one that has been trained? I asked.

No. Ramón answered. We want to scare him. Not murder him.

In his home Rodríguez stood at the top of the stairs leading down to the basement when we entered. He was more excited than I had ever seen him. He and Vargas had been drinking. The young businessmans face was red with fever and alcohol. I wondered if my own did this before the fighting. Barking came up the stairs from the dark below.

Vargas is down there teasing the dog with some rags I gave him. Rodríguez told us.

If you mess yourself when we let go of the leash. Ramón said. None of us are going to clean up after you.

Elías and Rodríguez laughed.

Did you bring the claws? Rodríguez asked the doorman.

Yes.

Then I am not afraid.

The basement was a small space with a concrete floor and posts supporting the cordón log joists that the planks of the kitchen floor crossed above. Rodríguez had pushed aside dusty furniture and more paintings of the bay and sea like those that hung on the walls throughout the expensive house. Empty jars lined a row of bookshelves.

Whose paintings are these? I asked Rodríguez.

My mothers.

They are beautiful. I said. Very well done.

They are the only things she ever painted. The bay and my father.

Vargas held a bottle in one hand and a cloth in the other just above the reach of the leaping dog tied to one of the posts. The five of us stood just beyond its reach.

He looks like a good one. Ramón said.

He is. Vargas responded. Good enough for little Ferocious here.

Rodríguez smiled at this. He enjoyed the name.

Help me with the rug. The young businessman ordered Elías and myself.

But first. Ramón said producing a pencil and piece of paper that he had brought down to the basement from the kitchen. A little ceremony. Ramón stepped toward the young businessman. Before every fight we write down a number between one and ten.

Why? Rodríguez asked.

Well. Ramón looked to me and then to Elías but we stayed quiet because we did not understand and thought it was another of Ramóns jokes.

This is just something we do. Vargas answered immediately. We will tell you when it is over.

When you are a dog fighter. Ramón smiled.

Rodríguez took the pencil. He chose a number in his mind and wrote it down on the paper.

But you cannot tell us. Ramón said. That will break the tradition.

When Rodríguez was finished he went to hand the folded paper to Vargas but Ramón took it instead. Smiling he put it in his pocket. Then Elías tied the rope around the heavy rug that I held tight around the young businessmans forearm.

Is that too much? I asked him.

No. He answered. It is perfect.

Elías then put on Rodríguezs hand the glove fitted with stubby metal claws. Vargas and Ramón took turns teasing the dog snarling at them. Rodríguez took his eyes from the teeth of the dog to inspect the sharp metal. His eyes wide and watery. His legs shook some.

Do not be scared. Elías said in an encouraging voice. You are a fighter of dogs.

We should have gotten you one also. Rodríguez said to Elías.

No no. The doorman shook his head. I am not the man that you are.

Ramón undid the leash from the post but Vargas kept the dog from charging the handsome dog fighter with the end of a long pole he found standing in a corner.

Give him some room. Ramón laughed.

Rodríguez positioned himself across from the dog. He hunched as he had seen us do in the ring. The dog lunged at him but the taut leash kept it back.

He is hungry. Vargas laughed.

But Rodríguez did not flinch. I was surprised that they had let this progress so far. I did not think we would allow him to fight the dog. For as untrained as the dog was he was sure to kill Rodríguez.

Tell us when you are ready. Ramón said.

Vargas stood back with the pole in his hands. Rodríguez drew a deep breath.

Now. He said.

Vargas swung the pole and hit Rodríguez in the back of the head knocking him to the concrete floor. Dazed the young businessman was on all fours reaching up to touch the back of his head when Elías stepped forward and shot him with his revolver in the back of the head. The force of the bullet flipped him over onto his side.

Jesus Christ! Ramón laughed a short nervous laugh.

I did not move. I could not if I wanted to. The dog whimpered and went to a corner. The leash trailing him when Ramón let go. The three men stepped forward. Vargas pushed the body flat on its back with his foot and then spit on the dead businessmans body. Ramón and Elías undressed Rodríguez until he was completely naked.

Tie the dog to the back post. Ramón said to Vargas without looking up from the work. When they find the body they will think the dog did it. Ramón joked.

When Vargas came back to where the other men were undressing the body he asked. Why did you have him choose a number?

Ramón stood and took the folded piece of paper from his pocket careful to not unfold it yet. The naked body at our feet. Blood pooling in an awkward circle following the slope of the concrete floor.

Cantana wants us to cut it off and put it in his mouth.

What! Vargas laughed. Smiling uncertainly. I am not touching it.

Neither am I. Elías said.

No one had said anything to me until Vargas pointed.

He can do it. It is his first time with us.

No. Cantana said this was his introduction. This one is still ours. And I am always the one who is left undressing them and I do not want to be the one to cut it off and put it in his mouth.

I am not touching it. Vargas repeated. Never.

Pick a number between one and ten. Ramón said to Vargas.

No.

Vargas.

There was a great amount of tension between the two fighters. I still did not believe or understand what was taking place between us. Ramón then spoke in a patient explaining tone.

Cantana said to have him pick a number between one and ten. Then when it was done we would do the same and the closest one to it will cut it off and put it in his mouth.

What if it is a tie? Elías asked.

Then we do it together. Ramón answered. One holds it and the other one cuts.

Who puts it in the mouth? Elías asked.

Whoever is holding it.

I think it should be the other way.

I will not do this. Vargas repeated. Staring at the body.

Ramón took the revolver from Elías. He pulled back the hammer and aimed it at the fugitives face.

Jesus. Elías said softly as he stepped back.

A number between one and ten Vargas. Cantanas orders.

Vargas spit at Ramóns feet.

Then you die also. The handsome dog fighter answered confidently.

Vargas! Elías yelled. Do not be stupid.

He is the one who raped the girl! Vargas yelled. Pointing at Rodríguezs body.

And if she had murdered him when he forced himself on her then none of us would be here. But she did not. And so now we are here.

Vargas leveled his eyes at Ramón. There was much hatred in them both.

I will not forget this Ramón.

The men picked their numbers. It was as if I were not even there standing in the basement with them. No one looked to me for anything. They expected me to understand.

Ramón Elías and I waited in the kitchen. Afterward when Vargas stood at the top of the stairs I noticed that he had vomited on himself. We left the dog tied to the pole in the basement. None of us spoke. Vargas did not walk with us back into the city but alone and toward the sea.

I thought of the night of the Christmas party. Some more than two months before when Rodríguez held the railing of the stairs coming down to us drunk with his pants undone to prove his strength. His face flushed. Then I thought this was from excitement but now I thought it was red with embarrassment for what he had done to prove himself to us all. I do not know if it happened that night or some other. But it had been done.

There is no doubt in my mind that the young businessman deserved to die. And strangely in the killing I thought little of Rodríguez and more and more of Cantana. Though he did not kill the young businessman himself it was a decision of his and one for which I held much respect for him. Elías and the other two dog fighters all feared Cantana. But they respected him also. He wanted me to be there to witness his decision. Then I did not know why.

I learned later Ramón Elías and Vargas had been deceiving Rodríguez for some time. That Cantana knew that the young businessman had committed a great crime but there was the matter of being certain.

Cantana is not one to make mistakes. Ramón said to me before I left him and Elías that night. He is a patient man.

And in this time although Rodríguez knew nothing about it the businessman was giving him a chance.

One night in the cantina we worked from Rodríguez a confession. Ramón said to me. We lied to him saying that we had done the same thing plenty of times and asked him what man had not?

For all of their contradictions there was much honesty in Ramón and Elías and Vargas. Much that I admired. I knew they had never deceived me. And in this I could not help but think that much of this came from the time they spent in the company of Cantana. My opinion of the businessman had come from the time I spent with the poet. Not the businessman himself. The thinking of these three young men was not similar to that of the poet. Their passion not like Guillermos. Still there were many contradictions in their behavior. The killing of the innocent men for there to be bodies to be laid out in the large square naked in revenge for the attacks on the hotel. In the basement at Rodríguezs house when Ramón and Elías undressed the young businessman I understood that these three men were responsible for these deaths. For the young man dangling from the scaffolding at the hotel. But they had not deceived me. They worked for Cantana and I did not. I did not know if the poet and Guillermo had lied to me about the innocence of these dead young men. I did not know if Cantana would kill them just for display or if they were guilty. I did not know who to believe but her. I did not question her loyalty.

———

I slept even less after the death of the young businessman. As my fifth fight approached my body was more and more tired. So much so that I did not hear Javier come up the stairs to knock on my door early one morning his steps were so light.

Get dressed. He whispered. We do not have much dark left.

The smell of baking bread was fresh and warm behind the soot stained walls when we passed a panadería in the neighborhood of the dentist. Javiers strides were so long and quick that even I had some difficulty following. We stepped over a man sleeping drunk in a doorway. He held a hibiscus blossom in his dirty hand. In a second story window above him behind thin green curtains the light from a lamp set on a table shone.

When we crossed the plaza mayor Javier slowed his pace to not be suspicious. We walked side by side. The chairs still stacked for the night. The tables pushed against the walls beneath the awnings rolled back. The thief walked without noise to his steps. Heel first and then to the outside of his foot up off the front of his toes.

Quick and silent. He had said to Jorge and me once in the court-yard to prove his ankle was healing. A thiefs walk. He called it.

Leaving the large plaza I sweated some already we walked so quickly. I followed Javier staying close to the walls. Hidden in the shadows. We slowed again to walk through a small square north of the plaza mayor. Empty but for some mangy dogs scratching themselves against the stones of a well. I had come this way many times on my walks to the salon.

If we are going to the old men tell me now. I warned the thief.

Do not worry. He whispered.

I worry for you.

Javier looked back at me and smiled. In the light of an electric bulb above a door he appeared as if he had not slept in several days. His smile genuine but his eyes drooping and tired.

We passed the salon and the veterans shop. Turned east down an alley that if we had followed the entire length to the bay we would be in front of the hotel. But soon we turned north again and then came into another small square where a line of date palms shaded a row of wood benches. In my late walks I had passed through this square many times. There was a small dry fountain at the center of the square. Stray palm fronds and sand. Cigarette ends. Javier slowed. He walked to one of the middle benches and sat. He gestured for me to do the same. I stood before him as he crossed his legs and stretched out his arms comfortably.

Who are we waiting for?

Sit. He said. And I will tell you.

I clenched my jaw and looked him carefully in the eyes.

She lives there. He said when I did not sit. Pointing across the square behind me to a narrow building with two tall windows above wrought iron balconies on the second floor. She wakes early. The thief smiled. The lamp will come on in that window to the left.

I do not believe you.

I have been following Cantana for some time now for the old men. But last night was the first night I saw him here with her. Then Javier stopped himself. His eyes went to the stones by his feet. She lives here my friend. That is all you need to know.

How did Cantana not see you?

Javier laughed. Smiled as if I had insulted him.

Look at me. I am the best thief this city has ever known. I stayed on the roof over there. Cantana had a man guarding the door all night. He smoked more cigarettes than the poet. Go look on the ground over there if you do not believe me.

Maybe you put them there.

Maybe I am trying to earn your trust.

Javier was correct. He had not told the poet and Guillermo about my love for her. I was almost positive of this.

How do I get onto the roof?

Sit in the café behind us. Javier answered. There are some chairs in the front where you can sit and watch without being seen. No one will suspect you.

Cantana was here last night? I asked but the tone of my voice told Javier what I was asking.

Be grateful for what I have given you dog fighter. Do you understand me?

Yes. I said.

Good. He stood then. It has been a long night. He said. I need sleep.

I sat on the bench until a lamp turned on in the window just as the sun was rising. Just as Javier had promised. I waited for the café to open and then I sat at the table Javier suggested. I ordered rice and beans and hard boiled eggs with tortillas and hot black coffee. For lunch I ate the same. I bought a newspaper and pretended to read it. At some point in the morning the lamp was turned off behind the curtains. I did not see who it was that did this. Later the curtains were pulled back but again I did not see by who. My neck hurt from looking in the direction of her window for so long. My legs grew tired from sitting. Anxious. The owner of the café was a small man whose wife stayed in the back making fresh tortillas and soup from dorado and onions and tomatoes. At lunch some others came into the café but for most of the time it was only the three of us.

But after lunch an old woman with small steps and white hair crossed the square from the door of the building Javier told me was hers. The old woman entered the café and looked me in the eyes as if she knew why I was there. But she did not.

Señora. The old man stood from his seat at the counter where he was reading his newspaper. Buenas tardes. He bowed to her.

Good afternoon. She said.

The mans wife came from the back carrying a towel wrapped around several warm flaky pastries covered with sugar.

How is the señorita? The old man asked.

Singing. The old woman smiled. Always singing.

Then she turned and was gone.

Javier had not betrayed me. I left the café after this. My head filled with thoughts of her beautiful voice.

When I returned to the dentists there was a note for me saying that Cantana wanted to meet in the plaza for breakfast the next morning.

The man who brought this was carrying a gun. Jorge said.

Elías? I asked.

He did not leave his name.

Did he threaten you?

No.

Later sitting on the edge of my bed I listened to the dentist climbing the stairs to my room and I knew that it would mean nothing good.

I respect you dog fighter. He said. And I like you as a friend. But I worry for my mother. For myself and Javier.

I nodded in silence.

Javier will not tell me what is wrong. He has begged me not to send you away. Understand that he also values your friendship.

I will not be here long Jorge. I said without thinking whether or not this was true.

I worry for my mother. He explained.

I understand.

After the dentist left my room I sat on the bed holding the note. I was exhausted but I knew I would not be able to sleep that night.

Then meet with him tomorrow. Guillermo said when I went to the salon that evening with the note. The veteran sat in front of his shop while the young men worked at the workbenches behind him. The poet not with us but working at his stall in the market. Wait until night before coming back here to tell us what occurred. Guillermo continued. If he offers you work. You take it. No matter what he tells you to do.

I awoke the next morning surprised that I had slept some. Still I did not feel rested. The raspy sound of the woman sweeping the courtyard did not wake me but the commotion of many voices. Trumpets and guitars on the street. I followed these musicians to the plaza mayor where women decorated the large square with green and white and red tissue paper. Small children stood below the trees watching some of the boys from the canoes climb out on the limbs with the paper. One boy pretended to lose his balance and his mother yelled at him and the children laughed knowing that he was pretending and then laughed at him for the scolding he received. The lampposts around the gazebo woven in twirls of these colors.

White for religion. My father had taught me. Green for our independence. Red for the blood of the Europeans mixed with your own.

Little girls in bleached white dresses chased one another over the stones barefoot. Hawks and Xantus hummingbirds embroidered into the hems of their skirts and blouses. A boy came up to the girls holding a lizard by its tail. The lizard dangled between them until it came free of its tail and fell to the stones and scurried off. The boy held the writhing tail with two fingers between himself and the screaming girls. At a rectangular table behind this Cantana sat raising a match to his cigarillo with his gloved hand. We looked each other in the eyes his behind his sunglasses and he nodded for me to join him.

You look as if you had a long night my friend. He gestured with his hand for me to sit.

I did not know what to say. A waiter brought two small cups of coffee to our table. On his tray was a tall skinny bottle from which he poured some liqueur into Cantanas cup. I refused. Cantana smiled.

Ramón told me you were not one for the alcohol. The businessman stirred his coffee with a tiny spoon. His tiny finger out. Still I did not know how to answer so I only looked at my coffee and sipped. He also told me how quiet you can be.

Yes. I said while trying to smell her perfume on him.

After this we sat in silence for several minutes looking over the plaza. Cantana did not seem uncomfortable with my quiet. We watched children run with handfuls of candy. Old men positioned themselves on the empty benches early in the day. Our waiter leaned against the column of the building checking on us now and then. Drowsy.

What do you like the best about Canción? Cantana asked me then.

I looked at my hands.

The food? The view from the malecón at sunrise? Swimming in the water of the sea? Our beautiful women? He laughed. There must be something. I know that you are not like these other dog fighters we have here. It is easy to know what they like. But you. I see something different in you.

He was quiet then. I looked for his eyes behind the sunglasses. He took his cigarillo down from his lips and the smoke came evenly from his mouth when he exhaled.

Come with me. He said then very suddenly. I want to show you something.

Parked down the street from the plaza was the black limousine. The small pickpocket from the market sat on a box nearby with his little arms crossed and his face looking very serious. Other children from the market watched him from an open door. Cantana gave the small pickpocket a handful of different coins and he smiled gratefully. As it was with Javier I knew to pretend that I did not know the boy and he did the same with me.

Have you ever driven one of these? Cantana asked.

No. I answered

He threw me the keys over the top of the shiny black roof.

I am lazy. He smiled. And I have been drinking some. Take us for a drive. I insist.

Cantana opened the back door of the limousine and waved for the children to climb into the backseat. They did this laughing and jumping. Cantana invited the small pickpocket to sit with us in the front. He sat on his heels to be able see over the dashboard. With some little directions from Cantana I brought the car into the middle of the street. I had driven some in Northern California but I was out of practice and the ride was jerky. Cantana and the children laughed at this. I could not help but smile also. Cantana laughed more than any of us when I accidentally ran the front tire of the passenger side up onto the sidewalk and then down over a melon in the gutter.

Soon though we had driven from the busy streets around the plaza filled with people coming down for the festival and headed out to the road that curved around the bay along the malecón. The children ate candy in the backseat that Cantana had me stop for. The pickpocket sat quietly between us. His eyes darting back and forth over all that we passed. His nose dripping. I enjoyed driving the limousine. At one time I had the window down and was steering with only one hand. I did not drive very fast and now and then I let the small pickpocket honk the horn at a burro or an old woman who cursed at us because the noise had startled her. Cantana tipped an imaginary cap in her direction. His cigarillo dangling at the corner of his thin smile.

I love this city. He said to me then. When I was young I went away for several years. Not that I am old now but when I left I was very young. Very stubborn. I wanted to see what else there was of this world. Do you understand?

Yes. I answered.

I did not respect my home much then. He continued. I wanted what most young men want. To get a taste of the world. The places and people. The women. So I went to the north. Tijuana. Mexicali. This was when there was much to be made for bringing alcohol into the United States. I worked for un contrabandista. Bootlegger en inglés. But I was smarter than he was and soon I had his business. Cantana paused. His eyes on me. The small pickpocket looked at me also. Do you think I killed this man? Cantana asked me then.

I looked at Cantana for a moment. I was not driving very fast.

No. I answered.

It does not matter that I did not. People will say what they will say and stories are meant to grow. We say men are demons without ever knowing them. I said this about the men of Canción when I returned with my money and I know this is what the young men who make these attacks on the hotel say of me now.

I did not look in Cantanas direction when he said this even though I no longer felt his eyes on me. As we drove north toward the hotel slowly along the malecón Cantana suggested the small pickpocket sit in my lap and steer. The boy was very careful. Very focused as Cantana directed him on how to steer. At one point Cantana leaned back some to where the boy could not see him and indicated with his gloved hand that I speed up. But the small pickpocket was not scared. He bit his lower lip in concentration. The streets going from the hotel became very narrow and bumpy. The children in the backseat were laughing. The small pickpocket was fearless. I regretted giving him my switchblade. When I slowed the limousine he sat on his heels between us again. If I failed the old men this boy would grow to fight Cantana one day.

Muy bien. Cantana tousled his hair. Muy bien.

It was afternoon by this time. When we went out toward the hills I had walked so many times with the poet several of the children were asleep in the backseat. Cantana said nothing but seemed to be enjoying the sharp rocks that were delicate along the hills looking as if they were ready to fall. Soon we passed the last of the peasants trickling down from the hills dressed in their best clothes. Children riding burros.

Slow to keep the dust down. Cantana told me to do and I did.

On our way back into the city the sun lowered over the bay. The small pickpocket had fallen asleep with his head against the businessmans shoulder.

You told me that you worked on the hotel. Cantana said when we neared the plaza.

Yes.

What did you do?

I worked the crane. Lifting the beams and posts for the scaffolding. Cinder blocks for the inside walls.

You did this by yourself?

Yes.

Then you are as strong as they say.

I remained silent.

Do you understand why Rodríguez was killed?

Yes. I answered.

Do you understand why I wanted you to accompany Ramón and Vargas that day?

Yes. I answered but the businessman continued.

I cannot have men like that working for me. I do not want men like that in this city.

I brought the limousine to a stop in the same place where we left just down the street from the plaza. All the children were asleep in the car with us. Cantana lit another cigarillo as he spoke.

I said earlier that I love Canción. He continued. When I came back from Mexicali with the money I had earned I convinced others in this city that we needed an electrical station. It took us two years to build but we built it. And it is a good power station. One that will not need to be replaced for years. The streets are more safe with the light. Then we built better wells and a better sewer system. One that would one day be able to support the hotel. I had a vision you see? After this we helped to pave some of the streets. To make it easier to get vegetables and meat to the markets. And all this? All this was work for the men and women of Canción. You have seen some of Mexico?

I nodded.

Do we have the poverty here of other cities our size? No. Cantana answered himself. We are fortunate to be a hidden city. But this work cannot last long. There is only so much we can do to improve the city without being paid back. Returned our money to invest it in new ways in Canción. The hotel will turn this city into what I know it can be. The tourists will bring their money to help us build our schools. To get all the children and not just the children of the businessmen in schools. We will build a better hospital. There is much we can do. But others want to destroy this. He paused for a moment while a group of colorfully dressed young men with instruments passed onto the large square. They want for this city to stay untouched. To remain as it is. For as much as they complain they do not want to end this division between the businessmen and the poor. They do not want to make the sacrifices that have to be made. They put my name on the walls. Curse my mother. They write Viva Canción! Canción por los Cancioneros. They call me un muñeco. Say I am a puppet to the American investors. But I say we can use our rich neighbors to the north. We can allow them to come down here and fish in our waters. Sleep in our hotels. And with the money we will make this city better. We will educate our children and they will provide better educations for their children and with time my friend after you and I are dead Mexico will come into its own. Cantana lowered his voice then. Tell me something dog fighter. Have you ever met a skinny priest?

These were the poets words exactly.

In Mexico we have God and money. Both are very powerful. Many have one but only a few have both. My dream is not for every person to be rich. Not for every person to be able to buy their way to heaven. But for every person of Canción to live in a home. And yes to work at the hotel if that is necessary to have it. Look around. This is heaven. And yes. I am trying to sell it. We are a hidden city and with this we have limited resources. Remember we are in the desert here. A desolate peninsula. But we have great beauty also. And it is our beauty that we will use to the advantage of our people. Canción will be por los Cancioneros. We will be the model for the rest of Mexico.

When I left Cantana I went to Guillermo and the poet and repeated what the businessman had told me.

Cantana is pimp. Guillermo hissed. Our children will be not his whores.

On the night of my fifth fight Cantana nodded to me as the trainer brought the dog into the ring. Sitting next to him she looked to me with wonder in her eyes at how it was that the businessman and I now knew each other. I smiled at her while the ragmen wrapped my arms and fitted my hand with the metal glove and she trusted me and smiled back. Then I believed so much in myself that I believed love to be this easy.

Once again Ramón drew the stick of Mendoza. The yelling men spoke of how rare this was for him to fight the sharpened teeth six times.

In the ring he does not have the luck that he has with women. One said.

But he is still alive. One man argued.

In the end though he will die by the teeth.

But it was Vargas that night who was the unlucky one. During his fight an argument in the crowd between two workers from the hotel became a knife fight. Another ring developed outside our ring. A ring of men. Once more Vargas was left to kill his dog while the men had their backs to him. When his fight was done and he did not hear the yelling but saw that the men were distracted watching one man stab at another he left the ring with his head down. His chest sprinkled with dogs blood.

After the fight I went down to the water instead of the cantina beneath the abandoned church. I swam out to the mouth of the bay to a place where I stood on the coral with the water crashing against my chest. I stood there and yelled back over the bay for her laughing and singing of my love. The moon full and the sky the color of the water. She was there with me in love. The two of us in me alone. I floated on my back and with the tiny waves splashing into my ears I whispered to her.

Te quiero mi amor. Again and again. Te quiero.

When I came up from the beach to the malecón the streets leading toward the mountains were empty. Dimly lit by the few buzzing streetlamps along the curve of the bay. Lonely benches beneath them. I stood for a moment deciding which street to follow to my room at the dentists. I had walked them so many times by then that often I stood in one place wondering which way to take. Wondering what might be new along each. While I walked the night breeze dried the salt water dripping from my hair onto my forehead. My pants wet after being naked in the water. Over the stones I made squeaking noises in my huaraches. I enjoyed the sound. I made it on purpose as loud as I could and it made me feel like a child. The simple distraction took from my mind thoughts of Javier and the dentist and the soft music of their back room I knew I was to return to. I did not want that loneliness after being so near to her.

The stones of the street were uneven but smooth from sand blown by years of the evening winds wearing them down. Ahead several men staggered from a lit door. A woman stood in the light of a doorway. Her face a hideous mask as she cursed the men. She held the folds of her skirt in one hand and a handful of paper pesos in the other. A strap of her dress fell from her shoulder. The men laughed and like boys pretended to run from the woman. Their gestures absurd. Their laughing bringing only more anger from her. I slowed my steps but the woman was still in the door yelling as I approached. But then another woman gently took her by the arm back into the house. When the door closed the street was dark again. The men were gone and I was alone.

I passed farther into the city. The streets became more dark where some of the electric lamps and their glass coverings had been broken by boys throwing rocks. The shards crunched beneath my steps. The slender poles held the shattered bulbs like long stemmed glass flowers. Sharp dark petals. The salt water had dried on my face in a sandy grain. I stopped before a wall where the paint of the words Cantana a la chingada! was still wet to the touch. The young men had been busy. Not far from this I threw a pebble at the ratty hide of a dog sniffing at a drunk sleeping drunk against a wall. The bottoms of the mans feet black and hard and splitting at the skin in the heel in even darker crevices. I wiped the paint from my fingers onto his pant leg and then realizing what I could have done to the man I rubbed the pants together until it thinned away. He did not stir.

The streets grew more and more narrow the farther I walked from the plaza mayor heading south the long way to the dentists. I had not slept in what felt like nights but I was never tired after the fights. There were fewer stones but more of the hard packed dirt of the streets with ruts from refuse carts and old dried mud prints of burros and pigs. Thousands of tiny chicken scratches. I walked up a small knoll and then down into a small square where night birds sang in the trees. At the end of the square under the electric light of a cantina door I saw Vargas. A fugitive from what none of us ever learned. His chin on his chest he leaned toward the wall with the palm of his hand flat against it to support him while the other was holding himself as he urinated. He whistled but the notes came unevenly from his lips. Wet from drinking and glistening in the faint light. He shuddered when he finished.

Hombre. I called out to him. Your mother would be very disappointed in you for behaving in this way.

Chinga tu madre. He answered without looking over his shoulder at me.

I smiled because I expected this type of answer from the fugitive. But to joke with him I said.

Say that again my friend and I will take your tongue from your mouth and feed it to the dogs.

Come try. He laughed. I offered him my hand and he clasped it like an old friend. Is it raining? He leaned back to check the sky and lost his balance before catching himself against the wall.

I have been swimming. I said.

Why did you not come to the cantina tonight? Cantana asked about you.

He was with you?

I wanted to ask the fugitive if she had been with Cantana but I could not think of a way to do this without revealing my love. I never asked about the women the businessmen kept or those that the other dog fighters were with. To do this now I knew I would only provide Vargas with information I did not want him to have about me. Fortunately he did not wait for my answer.

Let me ask you something. He smiled. How come you never leave for home with any of the women? Everyone is always wondering this. How come he never leaves with one or two of the women on those big arms? We know he is shy. And quiet. But everyone suspects that you are a maricón. Are you a maricón dog fighter?

The fugitives breath was heavy with the smell of alcohol. His hair and face greasy and shining from the smoke of the cantina. When he smiled his missing tooth made him appear a little sad. He was unshaven and the round of his chin was raised back and to the side so that he had to look at me from the bottoms of his eyes when he said this. It had been a long while since I had taken offense to a man standing across from me looking at me in this manner. Few had done it and those who did did not do it for long. But at that moment in time I was just up from swimming in the bay. From losing myself in the warm salt water until I lost myself in her. Still though Vargas laughed until his laugh was false and only intended to provoke me. But I did not give in to this. I knew that she would not want me to. I had promised her that this time of my life ended when I first glanced upon her. And I thought that if anything here was Vargas standing across from me as myself testing me. My shadow was over him although our light the same.

Maybe I take other women home? I tried to smile. Maybe yours wait for you to pass out and then they come to me for the satisfaction you cannot give them?

But the fugitive only laughed again. He knew that what I said was not true. He laughed until I knew that he was making noise only to provoke me and to wake those around us. The thrill of fighting shivered through my arms. I found myself warming to it.

You are a liar. Vargas said suddenly. And I think you are a maricón. But you are a good dog fighter. And tonight for that I will let you live.

Thank you my friend. I showed him my teeth by stretching my lips back in a hideous smile. You are very kind.

Now help me home. He said.

I took the arm of the fugitive over my shoulder and we began to walk. He smelled of something I could not place then. He was not as heavy as I thought he would be. Vargas was almost as tall and as broad in the shoulders as myself but I was stronger. More of my weight was muscle. And in my fights the men of Canción agreed that I was faster and with more intelligence while Vargas was pure furor.

It was a good night tonight. He said as we stumbled. Damiana mescal vino. And the women. Dios mío. You would not have appreciated it maricón but the women tonight. He whistled. To silence him I considered mentioning his killing the dog without an audience but I chose not to provoke him further. The mistresses sat in our laps wiggling. Letting us smell at their necks. Y El Tapado. He brought his favorite mistress.

I stopped walking.

But I played a good trick on her. Vargas continued. When Cantana got up from his chair to piss I leaned to her ear and licked it. Everyone had a great laugh when she slapped me. And then laughed more when I took her by the wrist and called her a whore and spit at her feet.

I dropped the arm of the fugitive and stepped back.

Which woman was this? I asked him. My voice calm. My hands clenching into fists without my having to will them to.

The one that does not cry. Vargas smiled. The one whose lips are perfect for.

My knuckle split his bottom lip over his teeth. Immediately blood spilled down his chest soaking into his shirt. He staggered back against the wall but remained standing. The punch sobered him some. I saw this in the way his eyes opened. He shook the hit from his brain and without bothering to touch his lip to check for the blood he stepped toward me. But I had already stepped toward him. Our arms locked. I pushed him back to the wall when suddenly a flash of light erupted before my eyes. I could feel blood from my nose spill over my lips. Down the back of my throat. I fell to one knee on the ground. I remember that he kicked me then. I heard my ribs crack and I then had some difficulty breathing after this. But still I gained my feet and quickly threw my fists into his face and arms and neck. He did the same.

We fought blindly. In a dream where our arms moved impossibly slow. I concentrated on his horrible face. The world around this spun empty. We felt in the dark for each other. A corner of his lip had come free from his face. I felt the need to vomit but did not. We locked arms more and his breath came hot into my ears when we went to the ground. Holding one another fierce as lovers even. He smelled of lovemaking. That was the smell. And this infuriated me more. We pulled on one another to be above the other. He bit into my arm and I crumpled in toward the hot pain before leaping back. When I felt his hands around my neck slip on the blood from my nose I wrapped my own hands around his. I had never found it so difficult to fight. But then I was straddling him and banging his head against the stones of the street listening to the sound of his choking.

With my thumbs I felt his throat caving. His hands wrapped around my forearms to try to pull them apart but then he gave up and pounded on my chest and cheeks and chin. Between his punches I saw his eyes become large and glassy. I had choked men before and knew that this was when to stop but thought only that he had licked her. Had shared time with her. He had heard her voice and felt her touch when she slapped him. And then to call her a whore. To spit at the feet of my love. I refused to believe that she had known anyone but me. The two of us were together even just that night. We swam and made love in the bay. Rough waves of the sea made gentle by the coral break. The muscles relaxed in Vargas neck and I knew that he was almost dead so I released him. When he hit me in the cheek with the full of his fist I did not think but hit him square in the face. His head swung loosely on his neck. He fell back and cracked his skull on a stone and was dead. I fell over with my chest pressed to his face. Smothering the fugitive as I heaved for breath crying.

———

For two weeks after this night I did not leave my room at the dentists. Because I had not slept well for some time before this fight I fell ill. In my small bed I wandered through feverish visions as the room spun around me. When I breathed sharp splinters of broken ribs seemed to pierce my lungs. I gagged on snot at the back of my throat and coughed blood.

The dentist and Javier took turns sitting beside me in the wood chair. Speaking in soft voices. Candle shadows flickering across the walls of the room. But when the dentist and Javier were not in the room my grandfather pulled the chair screeching closer to lean over and whisper his hot breath into my ear.

You were made by me for this. I felt his lips pressed against my ear turn into a smile. You can never bleed my blood from you.

The dentist held a bucket for me to vomit in. Javier pressing a wet cloth to my brow.

Jorge.

No.

We need to call for someone.

He will recover.

Javier Guillermo and the poet stood at the end of my bed passing something to each other secretly behind their backs. I held out my palm flat. The fat boy Cantana with his knife lurked in the corners hiding absurdly behind the skinny limbs of the wood chair. Ramón set a handful of sharpened teeth into the palm of my hand. Then he looked into the palm of his own hand and his face was powdered white by giggling mistresses.

Words are words. The poet said to me in English locking the door to my room as he left. And sometimes they are worse.

I smelled the sea. My bed was on the top floor of the hotel. Mangroves stinking like rotten eggs. The first lover of the dentist sat in the chair with the wind of the sea in his dark hair. Armor colored clouds behind him. The sound of the waves crashing from his open mouth. I could hear the toothless man climbing the scaffolding but I could not see him yet. Perla and her husband with the knife handle protruding from his chest danced with the young men from the back room. She wore a red dress and black shoes. The yellow scorpion beneath my quilt. The claws cool as tiny nails crawling toward my neck over my naked chest. My skin hot. The venom drips cool. The one armed organ grinder brought the water tank filled with the American investors swimming in their suits naked and pale. Waiting to have their teeth sharpened by Mendoza. The blond American stood above the tank stirring the water with his knife. Pretending to drop it. Circus music.

You should have given me my death. My father said to me then. I read to your mother from books of poetry. But the poems. And she did not know this. They were my own. I loved your mother more than you can ever know. As much as you love her.

She sat in the chair at the end of my bed while my mother ran a mother of pearl comb through her long dark hair.

Your love is not unique. My mother said to me. It is just your own.

The teeth of my mothers smile the white of a full moon. I reached for the hand of my bride and she took mine. Our fingers locked. My callused hands in her delicate own. I looked from our hands to her eyes but there was the swollen face of my uncle. My grandfather stood behind him with his hands on his shoulders as if posing for a portrait. The images of men killing beasts dancing across the walls of my small room behind them.

I woke from my fever screaming. With Javier holding me down with his palms flat on my shoulders. The dentist placing cool cloths on my forehead that I shook off. My breaths sharp pains. I slept.

Some friends of Javier found you. The dentist told me.

Facedown like some drunk. Javier said at the end of the first week when the fever had subsided. I had not eaten in several days. Drank sips of guava juice. They went to pick your pocket on their way home. The thief continued. One last one for the evening. But it was soaked with blood. It took four of us to carry you here. Luckily it was not far. I do not know how you made it to where you did.

My nose was not broken but three of my ribs had been cracked and both of my eyes blackened and difficult to open. I had bruises on my arms from my elbows to my wrists. Scratches on my face and chest and neck. Vargas had broken the skin on my arm where he had bit me and I now could not move this arm. The dentist gave me some medicine for the pain.

When the fever was gone the dentist made me climb out of the bed so that he could change the sheets. They smelled of sweat and blood and urine. The concrete floor was cold on my bare knees. My palms flat against it. The cracks curious ridges at my fingertips that I could not open my eyes yet to see. My elbows weak from hunger and limbs shivering. The thin mattress would have to be replaced. I slept more. Deep but now without dreaming.

At the end of the second week when I could walk some I sat in the garden with the dentist in the warm sun. The light was the most beautiful and difficult thing to see. I felt sweat begin on my skin.

Is he dead? I asked.

Yes. Jorge replied.

Are you certain?

Javier says yes.

Are they looking for me?

No. Cantana has handled the police.

It is hard to breathe. I said holding my side. My lungs feel heavy.

I coughed because my breaths were shallow and then it only hurt more. My head was hazy from all the sleeping I had done.

I do not remember much. I said. Only that he insulted someone close to me.

You do not have to explain. Javier has told me of your love. Jorge must have noticed the look of concern on my face because he said. We thought you were going to die. Your fever was very great.

If someone insulted Javier in this way. Would you kill them?

If I had your strength? Maybe.

We were quiet. The sun on the rooftops of the city was full. There were several clouds in the blue sky to the east over the sea thin and long.

I did not mean to murder him.

Later that night Javier sat beside my bed in the wood chair. He was in good spirits.

Jorge told me you sat in the garden this afternoon.

Yes.

I am happy to see that you are up and moving my friend. You had us very worried.

How is the poet?

He and Guillermo are fine. They understand what has occurred and they even think this will be good for your relationship with Cantana.

For their plans.

Yes. The thief responded.

Do they know why I killed Vargas?

No. No one does. But this is not uncommon among dog fighters.

Jorge tells me that Cantana handled the police.

Yes. Do not worry. Most of the businessmen and others just wish they could have been there to bet on it. The thief smiled. How are your ribs?

Very sore. I said as I eased down into the pillows on my bed.

What happened?

Javier sat beside the bed. I felt him wanting me to explain but I knew that Jorge would tell him soon enough and this was fine with me. I did not want to talk about her then.

I thought that this was no longer with me. I answered instead to ease the silence between us. You know that this is not how I am. It is not how I want to be.

But what you did.

It was wrong.

Many disagree.

Many have never had their hands around the neck of a man until the muscles give. The thief nodded after I said this. I want you to tell the poet that you saw me. Tell him I was walking in the hills and that I stopped you and asked for the time.

For the time? The thief smiled.

Tell him. Tell him I was picking flowers. And if he calls me a fool tell him that I said he would say this. And then tell him that I will be to see him soon enough.

Are you sure my friend?

Positive.

During the days at the compound I listened to the cleaning woman sweep the tiles around the blind mother of the dentist sitting in the courtyard. She sat in silence. Her world the courtyard. I wondered how she pictured this in her mind. How she pictured herself. I wondered that if to be blind was to live in a dream. The lines around the mouth of the dentists mother were deep from years of silence. When I asked him why she was so quiet he answered that she had always been this way.

Some are as terrified of their words as the sound of their own voice and the effect it will have on others. He said. She worries that she will be misunderstood.

I told the dentist that I understood. I suppose that like myself the words his mother kept behind her brow were tongues of lightning. Her hands were still in her lap. Her head tilted slightly to the sounds of palm fronds pressing air around their edges as little birds chased one another from limb to limb. Tiny seeds ringing sharply off the tiles below. Some days I sat in a chair in the cool of the back room studying her. Listening for what she was listening to. Imaging how beautiful it was to hear the world and from the sounds compose images of it for myself. But then her chin came down to her chest and she dozed and I realized that it was me listening carefully. That

I did not see how life is much more simple than I allowed myself to think.

I felt much better. My arms were sore from lack of use and the bite on my arm was a yellow bruise that the dentist worried might be infected. Sitting in the garden I kept my palms flat over my knees. I had no desire to make any more fists. The thought of fighting dogs made me sick to my stomach even when I pictured her there with me. The dentist worked pulling teeth but also he spent time with me in the back room.

Where are the young men? I asked him once.

You need the quiet. He said. They will return.

I do not think it will be safe for me to stay here much longer. I told him.

No. He clucked his tongue and wagged his finger at me.

I am a threat to you and your mother.

You are a friend dog fighter. Do not bother yourself over this.

I saw terrible things in my fever.

You were talking more than I have ever heard you talk before.

What did I say?

It was difficult to understand. You spoke to her very much though.

I looked to the tiles that made the floor and smiled to myself.

You have no reason to be embarrassed. The dentist said. You should hear the things I say to Javier. I wish I had fever for an excuse. We both laughed a short laugh at this and then Jorge said. Love makes us cling to our words dog fighter.

I cannot think of a way to be with this woman. I said then.

You are in a dangerous situation my friend. Cantana thinks very highly of you now. But if he were to find out that you desired his mistress he would use this as power over you. You cannot trust this man. No matter how generous he may seem. Remember. The rich have much they are willing to lose to gain in the end.

I sat on my bed admiring the creaks of the windmills beginning slowly to turn with the coming of the evening wind. In the distance the cathedral was full of shadows as the sun was heavy on the side of the mountains to the west. Dark birds circled the towers. Across the way a man came onto a roof. He ducked under clothes drying on a line and then made his way carefully over the fragile tiles. He came to a radio antenna and turned it. Someone called to him from below. He held his hands to the antenna and then let go. As if his hands affected the radio. On his way back down the man stopped and looked around himself. He seemed pleased with what he saw before returning below.

One day not long after this I was reading one of the poems the poet had given me in English. I was practicing the words.

Las góndolas sin remos. De las ideas cruzan. El agua tenebrosa. De tus iris quemados.

It felt good to say the words again. For me English is a challenge and a secret. That day I enjoyed recognizing words I knew and what they meant and how they were similar to words in Spanish that I knew. I will not lie and say that I understood the meaning of many of these poems but with time I came to small realizations. And I think that would be enough for the poets who wrote them. That I spent the time with the work and gave some thought to it even if I did not realize it as a whole. The words made me anxious to see my friend the poet again.

———

When the knocking came I was dozing with a book on my chest. It came to me hard and loud. I hurried down to the courtyard holding my side. I heard Jorge pleading with him to go before I saw Ramón standing in front of the blind mother waving his hands. The mother followed the voices in the air around her confused. Ramón laughing to himself.

Ramón! I yelled and it hurt to raise my voice.

Look at you! The slender dog fighter stepped back and opened his arms. His eyes glassy and wild. It was not like him to be unshaven. His shirt unbuttoned and fingernail scratches on his chest down from his neck. He was drunk. Look at you walking like an old man. He said to me. Vargas would be happy to know that at least he hurt you some.

Ramóns words were sharp. I did not know how to respond.

What do you want? I asked.

What if I just wanted to check on you? To see how my friend is healing.

I would not believe you.

Go to the back room! Jorge hissed at us.

Ramón motioned as if to hit Jorge but Jorge did not move. Ramón laughed at this. His balance unsteady.

Go! Jorge hissed again.

I looked to the dentist with apology in my eyes. Before following me to the back room Ramón snapped his fingers at the side of the mothers head.

We buried the fugitive today. He said to me.

I looked at him confused.

Can you believe it took us this long to get the money for the burial? You did something awful to him. I barely recognized his ugly face.

I was quiet. Ramón ran his finger over the Victrola and then began looking through the records.

He smelled worse than he did when he was alive. Ramón laughed. I did not know that was possible.

Where is he? I asked.

The cemetery. We took turns shoveling dirt to save on the cost. Then we stood over his grave trying to think of nice things to say but none of us could. And so then we started laughing. No one in the cantinas wanted to pay for his funeral. And each time we had enough money we drank it.

Who?

Elías and me and some of the businessmen who could stand him.

Why are you telling me this? I asked Ramón.

You are not curious about what you have done?

I did not know that you and Vargas were such good friends.

No. We were not. But he was not as bad as they said.

I heard that he spit at the feet of Cantanas mistress. That he licked her ear and called her a whore.

Ramón looked up from the records smiling.

I come here thinking I will get to share with you all the good secrets only to find out you know them all already. My friend the maricones you live with here have sharp ears. Ears to the walls and streets? Did they tell you who saved you from the police?

What do you want Ramón?

Again with this what do I want. Ramón joked. He straightened some when he realized that I was serious. Cantana is anxious to thank you my friend. To shake your hand and say job well done.

And you are his messenger?

We are friends.

Cantana has no friends.

He said he would give me some money if I did.

Ramón smiled. Held up a record to the light and checked the cover for dust. I wanted him to leave. I knew that he made Jorge nervous and I did not know if I had the strength for another fight. I knew only one thing I could do to make him leave.

Do you still dream of the teeth Ramón?

He leaned toward me then.

I am the better fighter. He hissed. I may die by the teeth but I will have fought all my fights against them. This is more than your strength can ever do. And besides. He brought his shoulders back. Raised his chin. The women prefer me.

As Ramón walked through the courtyard to leave he paused by the blind mother and bent to whisper in her ear. As he spoke he looked me in the eyes and smiled again. The blind womans hands went to her mouth. She stood as he left and walked in circles shrieking. The dentist and cleaning woman ran to her side. She yelled words we did not understand. Finally they coaxed her to her room where for the rest of the day she mumbled prayers until exhausted she slept.

The next morning I went to the poet at his stall in the market. I was anxious to see this to some end. When the children saw me they wrapped themselves around my legs playfully. I did my best not to grimace in pain. Not to let them see how weak I had become.

We cannot talk here. The poet said to me. Let us go for a walk.

We walked slowly to the malecón and then north toward the hotel.

I thought you left our city for good my friend. The poet said. His gray hair wild. His face tired but eyes restless.

I would have said good bye.

I figured you had more important things.

Like what?

Hiding from the police. Ghosts of dead husbands and fugitives haunting you.

He patted my shoulder and smiled.

It is good to see you. I said sitting down on one of the benches.

And you? He smiled. How are you?

I have some broken ribs. But otherwise I am healing fine.

What an incredible fight it must have been. Do you know what people would have paid to see such a fight?

Not as much as I would have paid not to be a part of it.

Have you seen Cantana since?

I would not visit Cantana without visiting you first.

We were not sure.

No. I have not seen him. Javier. And Ramón. But that is all.

When did you see Ramón?

Yesterday. He came to tell me that Cantana wants to meet.

When?

This afternoon. Do you think this is a bad idea?

No. If he wanted you dead he would have let the police have you. This is good for us. The poet lit a cigarette. Wiping ash from the front of his shirt. I heard you chauffeured the limousine.

I was driving us. Not just him.

The small pickpocket told me.

Was he able to take the businessmans money?

Of course. The poet boasted.

And?

Not as much as he hoped for.

The smell of the water in the bay made me want to swim. The wind warm. The bay calm and inviting. The boys in their canoes called to me for a race. I waved back without thinking and it hurt my side.

We have missed your company at the salon. The poet said. The boys there want to hear of your fight. There had been some talk of slitting the fugitives throat in his sleep. None of them liked him very much.

How is Guillermo? I asked.

Old. Angry. Drunk.

And Guillermo? I smiled.

I am fine too. Like I said. We miss you.

At the end of the malecón the skinny cats sunbathed on rocks. Glass bottle mouths showed like tiny dark eyes when the waves receded. Across the way at the hotel the men were working. The scaffolding was tremendous. The crane placed at the center of the hotel now lifted materials from the outside to compose the building from within. Some of the lower walls had been built in. Openings for windows yet to be filled. I pointed to a corner where a new tractor slowly plodded. The poet squinted.

A ship came in with them several days ago. He said. Cantana must have contacted the Americans the night of the fires.

He wasted no time.

He cannot afford to.

And the young men? Have they been busy?

Only rumors. The poet smiled.

We stood quietly. Some cats had wandered up before us on the rocks and lay licking their paws before bringing them down over the ends of their scarred noses. The voice of the construction on the hotel was wordless but it came to us over the field as a voice the same. Even and defined. Its own. I missed the voice. It was one that I had been used to. I spent my days walking and thinking to myself so much since I had begun fighting dogs. I thought that maybe I should have just stayed with the work. That I was doing well enough without fighting dogs. But it had been worth it to encounter her.

When I worked there. I said to the poet. At night after all the men had gone I slept on the top floor. I woke in the morning with the sun on the sea and the rooftops and it was the most beautiful and difficult thing.

I have no desire to go to the top of that thing. The poet said simply.

I was not inviting you.

Yes you were.

I looked away from him.

Let us go. The poet reached up and rested his hand on my shoulder. We have much to do before you meet Cantana.

That afternoon Cantana sat alone at a table in the plaza where I had met him before. He held a cigarillo in his gloved right hand. Several children sat at a table next to him sipping Mexican hot chocolate from cups larger than their hands. They ate cut melon with wet fingers. Their smiles very large in the reflection of the businessmans sunglasses.

My friend. Cantana stood and opened his arms as I came near to his table. How are you feeling?

Better. I said. I am sorry I have not been to see you sooner but I felt well only recently. He stopped my explanation by waving his hand and offering me a seat. Ramón told me all that you have done for me. I want to thank you.

It was nothing. Have you eaten?

No. But I am fine.

Nonsense. Look how skinny you have gotten. Will you be able to fight?

Of course. I smiled but I do not think he was convinced. I had not thought about the fighting yet. The moon was only days from being full.

I do not believe you. Cantana said.

He then ordered one of each item on the menu. When the waiter brought the plates of food the children continued using their hands to eat. When their small bellies were full and bloated they played with the food on the plates as the waiter watched in disgust. Cantana laughed. He did not have to pick up after the children. And once he was gone it was the waiter that would have to deal with the children all day bothering his customers and stealing from their plates.

During the meal Cantana ate little but smoked throughout. Talking of the hotel and progress made there. I was relieved that he spoke nothing of the fugitive. That Vargas spit at her feet and called her a whore was unsaid between us. When I mentioned Ramón Cantana only lit a cigarillo and waved the subject away with his hand. This gesture of his never ceased to bother me.

I sent for you because I want to take a drive.

Of course. I said. To where?

Mendozas. He has something I think you might like to see. We will go the day after the fight. I trust you to drive me.

Knowing that this was the opportunity the old men were waiting for I told him I would be happy to drive. I worried that in my agreeing I was giving my secret away. But Cantanas face displayed nothing.

Ramón will join us. He only said.

You think Ramón will want to visit Mendoza? I asked.

Why not?

The teeth.

He has beaten them every time. Besides he and Mendoza are friends.

I knew this was not true. I wondered why Cantana wanted

Ramón to be with us. I was not comfortable with this especially feeling so weak.

After I sat with Cantana for a while more Elías came to the table from a place I did not see him or expect him but realized then that he had not been far the entire time. We shook hands and then he whispered in Cantanas ear.

I must be going dog fighter. He explained. Business. Always business. I will see you at the fighting?

Yes.

I will have plenty of money on you as usual.

I will not let you down.

Bueno. Guillermo said when I told him of the drive to Mendozas. Several young men stood by the entrance to the salon. They looked to us wondering what was said. You will kill him and then you will kill Mendoza. The veteran continued.

And Ramón? I asked.

If he gets in the way. The poet said.

I do not think he will stand by while I kill Cantana. I said. Mendoza will not either.

Do not worry about Ramón then. Guillermo said to me. We will think of something. But that is when you are to do it. When you are at Mendozas.

What about the Americans? I asked.

We have plans for them of our own. Guillermo winked.

Find out what you can. The poet said. If Cantana mentions them and it makes sense not to kill him then do not. But only if he mentions them.

Make sure this works for us. Guillermo interrupted.

———

On the night of my sixth fight it was only to be myself and Ramón who fought. None of the men brought in on the ferry from Topolobampo for work on the hotel were willing to fight. With word of the attacks on the hotel fewer men were willing to come and work. Guillermo and the poet were winning their war from the shadows. Now they only had to wait for me to end it all with Cantanas murder.

They are anxious to see you out there dog fighter. Ramón said when we sat together in the small room on the rooftop. They expect to see scars on you from your fight with Vargas. To see how he left you.

I said nothing to Ramón. The mother of the dentist had refused to repeat what he had said to her and for this I could not forgive him.

There was much excitement through the crack around the door. Shadows of men passing through the light. There were only two sticks to draw at the bottom of the stairs. I had a good chance of drawing Mendoza. But Ramón and I both knew this would not happen. I felt weak though. Even a month later the fight with the fugitive had taken much from me. My ribs had not yet healed. But when I came into the ring she was beautiful and worth the chance. While they wrapped the heavy rug around my arm I was not afraid to look her in the eyes even if Cantana was to notice. But he was speaking with another businessman. They were both smiling very much. Their teeth white and clean in the last of the light of the day.

After my fight I did not return to the small room but instead stood with the yelling men. Cantana nodded to me across the ring while the ragmen took the heavy rug from my arm wet with the saliva of the dog. The blood thin on the metal claws taken from my hand. They wiped down my chest. I will be the one to murder you tomorrow I nodded to Cantana in return. Her eyes jewels.

Ramón came into the ring to a great commotion of whistles and yells. Men placing cigarettes into their mouths to squint from the smoke and clap. Even the young men taking bets turned to watch him enter. Ramón was always the favorite. When Mendoza brought the dog into the ring Ramón stepped from the ragmen to taunt it. To pretend as if he was going to pull back the dogs lips with his fingertips to check the filed ends of its teeth. The yelling men fell onto one another laughing. Ramón stood swiping his claws through the smoky air and then using the sharp metal ends to pretend to pick at something caught in his own teeth. He even turned to a ragman to have him look to see if they were clean. The yelling men laughed more. Mendoza watched this calmly from behind the fence of the ring holding the leash while Ramón laughed. Behind this laughing was much fear.

They come to me in my sleep. Ramón had confided in me. He confided this in me and I had used it against him to make him leave the compound. And then to have his revenge against me he had whispered into the ear of the dentists mother. But for the moment that it took for him to walk to her I had sat on a couch in the cool of the back room and felt a great satisfaction for using my words. For speaking my words to intimidate and beat another man without my fists.

This is the stronger fight. My father told me when my grandfather died. The more difficult and beautiful fight.

The poet once joked that God is two old men on a bench in the plaza mayor.

They play the cards that are our lives laid out on the wood of the bench between them. He said. The wind that deafens our ears each evening is them placing the cards. The air swept out beneath this. These old men deal us our fate.

Lost in the faces of the yelling men placing their bets I noticed Javier. He circled the ring without being noticed by the businessmen or yelling men. He did not know that I watched him. But he did not look for me either. He was there for other reasons. I followed him over the strong shoulders and raised necks to where a ragman knelt cleaning where I had killed my dog. Javier hissed at the ragman through the fence and the ragman looked up through his scraggly hair into the eyes of the thief. Javier spoke. Smiling almost. All this while Ramón was joking with the dog. Entertaining his audience. The ragman in front of Javier looked down at his bloody cloth when Javier spoke. Then he stopped when he saw the paper pesos folded longwise pointing at his nose like the end of a knife. The ragman snatched the money from the thief and fell back. Javier stood. He took one step back and there he stood at an angle so that he could hold his place in the shoving crowd and instantly leap to the fence.

The ragmen left the ring so that only Ramón and the teeth were across from one another. Mendoza held the leash taut through the fence. When he released the leash it went into the ring with the dog instead of staying behind in hand. It was nothing. An accident. Carelessness. But it never happened in the fighting of dogs. And when Ramón saw the flash of the colored leash it must have held his thoughts because he stepped back but did not think to put up his arm. He went toward the corner were Javier had been and slipped on the blood and fell to the floor of the ring. His shoulders pressed into the fence. The yelling men rushed forward. Javier with them. Knife in hand. When Ramón reached over his shoulder in confusion to place his hand over the wound where Javier had stabbed him it was enough to allow the dog to lock its jaws around the handsome dog fighters throat. It was as if Javier had never been there. The yelling men fell silent. Only the muffled tearing of the teeth into the muscles of the dog fighters throat could be heard. Mendoza did not stop the dog. All the men fell silent.

Cantana stood and he alone began the applause.

To the death of a great dog fighter! He yelled.

The yelling men dropped their cigarettes to the floor to applaud. Whistles and yells over the rooftops. The mistresses turned to see the dog gnawing at Ramóns throat. Their delicate chins trembled.

From where I stood my attention was caught by one businessman who leaned back behind the soft shoulders of his own mistress to give a quick whistle to another businessman sitting on the other side of her. They both leaned back but to keep their balance they kept their hands clapping in front of them outstretched like children making shark jaws. Like children chasing me through the market taking great chunks out of my thighs. The businessmen smiled at each other. Satisfied with his death.

I did not sleep that night. Cantana decided we were to wait until after the funeral for our drive to Mendozas. I spent the time sitting in the café across from her window. Some hours after her lamp came on each morning the old woman with silver hair came into the café. Then the old man would ask how the señorita was doing and this old woman would answer.

Singing. Always singing.

EIGHT

I slept little the night before meeting Cantana in the plaza mayor. I left from the dentists early to stretch my back after lying so long in my small bed held awake by voices of the quiet city. I went to the small square to wait for the light of her window and in the fading dark there I sat thinking of how we would talk this over one day lying in bed together. I would tell her of the hours I passed waiting for the lamp in her window. She would run her hand down my face and kiss my cheek.

You fool. She would smile. Why not just knock on the door?

Then it was not so easy as this. Or I did not think it could be.

I walked to the malecón as the sun was white just above the bay. The moon pale and opposite this descending slow into the mountains that hide Canción from the world. Around the hotel to the north posts of the scaffolding glowed like bones in that early light. In the evenings when the winds went through those empty rooms and hallways music rose from the lungs of some terrible howling instrument. But there was no wind now. The sea layered evenly beyond. The reflection of the hotel very large and clear. The sun rose as I walked the beach and my eyes were affected very much by the brilliance of the light. Even when I turned from this the white of the buildings along the malecón also stung. I walked with my back to the hotel and my eyelids closed guiding myself by the sound of the waves pulling rows of sand. Debating why Cantana needed to die.

At the docks a young boy threw heavy ropes onto the deck of a fishing boat leaving for the day. Tiny silver fish glittered like falling coins through the water around the boat as diesel smoke came over the boy rubbing his eyes still swollen from sleep. Already old women sat on the stones arguing while they sewed nets. Some wore string necklaces with shells and a single pearl on them. These treasures their sons the canoe boys long ago searched coral for. Their own treasures the days in Canción a necklace of endless suns.

School is for the children of businessmen. These boys laughed with some pride when I raced them swimming. Remember rich boys eyes cannot take the sting of the salt water.

The distraction of walking through the many songs of Canción was good for my thinking that morning. I was nervous with thoughts of never seeing her again. When I walked into the plaza mayor an old man swept near the gazebo. This man was something my time in Canción gave me to expect. Always the birds were as many as leaves around him. In the trees and hopping on the stones. I sat on a bench between two other benches and watched the old man sweep into some shade where he paused to rest. In the shade he pressed a hand-kerchief to his forehead. The sun just full above the bay. Dabbing sweat from the creases of his dark skin. Hanging from a limb in a tree a piece of colored tissue dangled stiffly above the old man. Left over from some festival. He tried with the end of his broom to get at the tissue but it was dry now as snakeskin and just from his reach. He went in this way without luck. Then he stopped and returned to his sweeping.

He went about his day while around him more and more men and women came into the plaza. They greeted one another with nods or brief words. Patted him on the shoulder or offered their hands. There were the sounds of window shutters unlocked and creaking open. Of floors swept and tables set with cloths they beat the dust from with palm brooms like drums. But this was his little secret. This game he played with the tissue to amuse himself. He knew it would last until the next rain.

In the café that opened before the others on the large square a waiter took delicate sips from a cup of coffee. He salted and then ate pieces of papaya on a plate a younger waiter had come and set out for himself to enjoy. When the young waiter returned the other waiter sang to himself but loud enough so that the young waiter would notice his having stolen the food. When the young waiter noticed this the waiter laughed and a man from a bakery who knocked with his elbow on the door of the café next to this also laughed. With his back to the door the man from the bakery held a woven basket to his chest filled with rolls small and warm that were to be hard by the end of the day. Then they were to be given to the children to feed the birds. Maybe even to feed themselves. The two men laughed at the young waiter until he smiled to himself also and went in for more of the fruit.

Later the mariachi bands arrived. Or blind men dressed in rags their faces shaded by wide sombreros strumming guitars held by rope over their shoulders led from table to table by small children with dirty palms open for coins.

Watching these people prepare for their day I was distracted from my thoughts about murdering Cantana. Watching the shutters open and waiters take down heavy chairs I understood that the old men were correct in wanting to protect Canción from the hotel. But my reason for wanting the businessman dead was much easier to understand.

These people. The poet had said. They work for themselves and also for each other. I sit at my stall in the market typing letters. For myself and for those who need them. Not for anyone who does not live in our hidden city. The same money exchanging the same hands. The hotel will change this. Cantana thinks that all of us are made of soft wax. Easy to mold. That we will work at pretending to be as it was before the hotel ruined this city. All for the cameras of the tourists. But some of us are willing to sacrifice. To lead by example.

But the money will be not so bad for the children. I said.

Cantana has no interest in the children of Canción. The poet said. He knows that you have a good heart my friend. And he is using this against you.

The old men would give their lives to protect the small songs of these people. Songs they wanted heard. But they needed my voice as well. What my strength and size allowed me fighting dogs before the businessmen the old men did not have. So I sat on the bench between two other benches and waited for Cantana. Waited to take his voice from the song the old men wanted sung in only their voices alone. And for this she would be my reward. Our voices our own song.

The night of Ramóns death her eyes told me there was not much time. When I saw Cantana place his hand in the small of her back I wanted to feel the bones of his fingers break between my teeth. She was not at the funeral the next morning. Those who did not want to give money for the burying of the fugitive were those first to come forward for Ramón. The one they admired when he stole their women. A game they played among themselves. Those most proud whose women Ramón did not know. Of course Cantana contributed the most. But only he and several other businessmen came to the hillside cemetery to honor the dog fighter in the hot sun. Cantana rode with the coffin in his own limousine. The other businessmen in their own cars. The rest of us walked barefoot or in huaraches in the dust of their tires. Men who attended the fights for the fighting of dogs and not for the games the businessmen played behind the backs of their crying mistresses. Men who respected the fighting of dogs not for the money to be made on the winning and losing but for the tradition of the fighting itself. I did not want to attend the funeral but the old men insisted.

Pretend Ramón was your friend. The poet folded his newspaper. Cantana will suspect you if you do not attend and this will ruin our plans for him.

I walked but at the end of the procession. The fat priest sweated through his robes stopping the procession to rest. When we came to the cemetery hill Cantana invited him to sit in the limousine. The priest accepted. Elías driving the coffin. With the priest in the limousine the two altar boys fell back alongside the workingmen to ask for cigarettes. At the top of the hill the sun glared into our eyes when the businessmen stepped from their automobiles wearing black dress shoes. I turned and went back down the hill before the fat priest could gather his breath enough to speak well of Ramón. I did not care to hear the priests words.

I am sure Cantana noticed when I left early but when the black limousine drove finally into the plaza the next morning he said nothing. Light shone down through the trees onto the fender of the limousine. The fender had been polished the day before for Ramóns funeral but had dulled some now with dust from the road that led to the cemetery. Cantana wore his sunglasses. He drove alone. I was glad to see this because I did not want to have to kill more men than was necessary just to kill Cantana. With a cigarillo in his gloved right hand he tapped the horn of the limousine with the other. Birds shadows flickered on gray stones through the green leaves. I stood and wiped the sweat from my hands on my pants as I walked to the limousine hoping he did not see this.

Qué pasa? He smiled shutting off the car.

Nada. Y tú?

Nothing good.

We smiled over these words. They had been favorites of Ramóns. They suited the smile the mistresses desired him for. Cantana looked over the large square and though I could not see his eyes I knew where he was in his thoughts.

I am glad you are here to drive. Cantana said then. I was up late last night celebrating the life of our dead friend.

I could not wait to kill this man. He offered his hand and I took it in my own. The bones of his fingers splintered in my palm.

Be his friend. Guillermo said.

No. He will not believe you. The poet said. Be quiet like you are. But not so quiet that you are not his friend.

I will be how I have to be to kill him. I answered the old men.

I looked for something dangerous that he might have brought with him. His coat was folded over the back of his seat. I looked for the heaviness of a gun in his pockets. On the floor at the back of the limousine I noticed the neck of a bottle of clear glass. But it was not within reach of the front seat. I found no weapons he could use against me.

Let us go then. Cantana put his hand on my shoulder before walking to the passenger side. We have a long day.

When I drove us from the plaza the old man with his broom rested in the shade again to try for the tissue. But still it was just from his reach. Cantana saw him. He leaned from the window with a cigarillo in his teeth and said good morning to the old man and the old man waved the handle of his broom to Cantana as if they were old friends.

On our way from Canción to Mendozas I thought Cantana preferred to drive by his hotel. This and I did not want him to think I was in some rush. I kept both my hands on the steering wheel but not so much that the knuckles became white to show how much I wanted to kill him. When my hands became slippery from the sweat I rested one on the windowsill to test the air and then the other on my pant leg. It was a secret I kept. The man next to me was to die in these hands.

Such a beautiful day. Cantana said more to himself than to me as we drove from the large square over uneven stones and then hard packed streets. Always such beautiful days in Canción.

But when I asked if he preferred to turn toward the malecón he said.

First we need to meet an old friend of my fathers.

So I turned onto a narrow street in the direction of the cathedral as he told me to. I followed the directions he gave. Made the turns. All of this to deceive him. But when he asked.

Who did you do last night dog fighter?

I answered.

Nothing.

And he laughed at me until I heard what he had said and I knew then that he was asking me this to suggest even that he had been with her that night while I was alone in my small room unable to sleep waiting to drive him to Mendozas where I would kill him. My knuckles turned white around the steering wheel.

With Cantana. The poet had said. We can expect nothing but more labor for our pains.

Think of how he holds her in his arms. I imagined my grandfather say. The way her cheeks feel to his lips. Squeezing her thighs in his hand.

When we entered Guillermos shop the young men were hunched over their workbenches and engines.

Where are you hiding the drunk? Cantana yelled. Startling them.

Their faces and silence showed the surprise they had when seeing the businessman Cantana. El Tapado. And then me alongside him. Afraid their pause would reveal my secret I looked them each quickly in the eyes. But you are used to people being startled by your presence when you are of a great size as I am or of much power as Cantana was. You can see them wondering why you are before them. Worrying what you will do to them.

He is in the back. One young man waved a wrench in his hand.

Call him out. Cantana said. Even if you have to roll the old fool across the floor beating him with his own cane.

Guillermo had been sleeping. The lids of his eyes were red. Half closed. He cleaned his glasses on his robe as he muttered to himself and felt his way into the room over the workbenches. The thin skin of his old fingers just missing the ends of sharp tools. His undershirt dirty with food and alcohol.

You look as if you used the bottle for a pillow old man. Cantana laughed.

Junior! Guillermo yelled. Putting on his glasses.

The two men hugged. Guillermo did not look at me over Cantanas shoulder.

I brought this for you. Cantana handed the veteran the clear glass bottle from the limousine. Now there was nothing in the limousine that I would have to use for a weapon. Only my hands.

Very nice. The veteran turned the bottle. The golden alcohol brilliant but distorted through the tiny bubbles in the clear glass. He set the bottle on the workbench and clapped together his hands. Flaco! Guillermo snapped to one of the young men. Go to the café for eggs and tortillas and coffee.

No no. Cantana rested his gloved hand on the veterans shoulder. The old mans face large and full of grease and tiny holes in the reflection of the businessmans sunglasses. We do not have time for food this morning old man.

We?

Me and my friend here.

Cantana put his hand in the small of my back as I had seen him do to her. He pushed me before the veteran with a smile.

Guillermo studied me. His eyes narrow and tired from many years of sleeping drunk. In his look I wondered if he recognized me. He made me doubt that I had ever known him. The old men were good actors if they were anything. They had been excellent in deceiving me as friends. But Cantana. To be able to deceive him was a great talent. It was good that I did not have to do this for much time. After Cantana's mentioning her and then touching me in that way I wanted to watch his eyes bulge. Feel the veins of his neck under my thumbs.

I know you dog fighter. Guillermo offered his hand. You are a very good fighter. Very dangerous. I have much respect for your work. The veteran stepped back to judge me more carefully. But I never bet on you. Always on the dogs. The dogs do not think why they kill. They kill for survival. Not for money. I respect this more. He smiled. Then he turned to Cantana. So?

I need something for Mendoza. Cantana answered.

Anything.

Dynamite.

But your soft hands? Guillermo chided the businessman.

The dog fighter here will carry it. Both Cantana and the veteran laughed at this. The young men smiled to themselves hunched over their work pretending not to listen but stealing glimpses of the mysterious businessman.

How much? Guillermo asked.

I do not know? Enough.

How much?

Enough to blow up a whale maybe.

Flaco! Guillermo snapped. The young man set down his wrench and wiped his greasy hands on a towel hanging from his belt. Go into the back. See what you can find.

The skinny young man hurried to the back. Metal shavings gathered in the grease on the workbenches and floor. The engines like sleeping metal animals on the benches.

How is your father? Guillermo asked Cantana while we waited.

Still dead. Cantana smiled. His teeth even and whole.

Guillermo dug into the pocket of his dirty robe and took from it a silver coin. Cantana waited for the rattling coin to still on the workbench where Guillermo set it there between them before picking it up and biting the coin.

One of these days. Guillermo smiled. Wagging his finger at the businessman. Your father will rise from the dead and you will be the one handing over the coins.

Cantana smiled.

You have been telling me this lie since when I was a boy old man. But I have always saved the coins.

And your mother? Guillermo asked. His voice serious now.

She is fine. Cantana bowed his head. I had not seen this respect in the veteran before. I wondered how he knew Cantanas father. If the poet did.

The skinny young man struggled from the back of the shop

under the weight of a large wood crate almost slipping on the metal shavings and grease on the rubber soles of his huaraches. He set the dynamite on the counter in a dusty thud.

Cuidado! Guillermo slapped the young man against the back of his head.

Guillermo opened the lid of the crate himself. Pried it back with a hammer and flat bar. Seven slender sticks. Spiderwebs over them thick with dust and smelling sharp. Damp even.

You should not need all of them. Guillermo said. Lifting one and turning it in his hands. But take the entire case to be certain.

Bueno. Cantana said. Running his gloved finger down the dusty edge of one. Cigarillo in the same hand. Then he reached into his pocket and said. What do I owe you?

Place a kiss on the cheek of your mother for me.

Señor. Cantana removed a simple gold money clip from a large fold of paper pesos. I insist.

Listen to me. Back there these do nothing but collect dust. Place a kiss on your mothers cheek for me.

I will. Cantana returned the money to his pocket. You have always spoiled me old man.

If I had a son your father would do the same.

I would do the same.

When the old man and Cantana finished talking I went for the box but Cantana set his hand on my arm and lifted it himself. He carried it to the limousine and I opened the door. Guillermo and I said nothing to one another as the businessman and I left. When Cantana sat in the front with me he wiped dust from the buttons of his shirt while I started the limousine. Licking the end of his gloved finger before rubbing each one clean.

Okay. He sighed as if there was much on his mind. Let us go to Mendozas.

Most of the fishing boats had gone for the day when we came down the malecón. The boys in their canoes at the mouth of the bay. Beyond the coral sharks.

In the past. The poet had told me. Before the men and boys dove for pearls a shark charmer would mumble over them first. Stand on the docks in the early morning and make much money with their magic. Convincing the divers they were invincible to the teeth. Fools.

The old women had dragged the ends of their nets into the shade. The rest heaped drying in the sun.

We drove on.

Such a beautiful day. Cantana inhaled deeply. Holding the fresh sea air in his chest before exhaling loudly.

I wondered if Cantana knew that I would take from his face his sunglasses so I did not have to see the reflection of my face looking into his when I wrapped my hands around his throat. I could think of nothing but of this killing.

Stand in front of a man. My grandfather told me as a boy. Look him directly in the eyes and nod. Do not listen to what he says to you but instead imagine not the consequences but how you will kill this man with your own hands. And know then that he has no thoughts of how he wastes his last words. It is some incredible feeling this power over another.

At the outskirts of Canción we passed a vacant lot. There was much concrete and trash. Two skinny children poked at something in the ruins of a stone wall with a rusted harpoon. A boy and his sister maybe. They watched the limousine. Their clothes stained and feet bare. Cantana shook his head.

Someday this will all be beautiful. He said. The malecón with more palms and flowers and white stones. And more lampposts to walk under at night. Imagine the light on the water.

I held my hand out in the passing air to concentrate. But I also listened to the businessman.

Canción. He said. The way it is now. It cannot last. You change with the world or the world will change you in ways you do not want to change. Trust me dog fighter. We are at the end of a dream here. Soon we will wake up suddenly and all will be different. The world will have changed it in ways we do not want. And then we will have much difficulty remembering how it could have been. But there are ways to save it.

The hotel? I said.

Exactamente. This will be for the better of Canción.

I looked over the water of the sea. The reflection of the sun on the glass of the windshield dusty but still bright in my eyes. I did not disagree with Cantana then and he was quiet. I drove from the city on a dirt road from the north of Canción. Some miles out we turned west toward a pass in the mountains. Many points in the narrow road had been washed out from the sudden rains. Floods that came down the steep hills. We passed an area where most of a mountainside had fallen in the rains. Another that had been burned by fire.

Lightning. Cantana pointed to the blackened slope. The fire burns with the wind until the wind burns it back on itself. The smoke from these fires gives the most beautiful sunsets. The tourists lucky enough to experience this will love Canción even more.

By noon bones of some large animal glowed from within the shade of bleached wood ribs of a wagon left to ruin in the dry sun. Cantana spoke little the farther we traveled. I said nothing. The sky above the color of the Bay of Canción. The steep mountains spotted with cacti and gray boulders. Small thorny shrubs. We passed a lizard sunning himself on a large boulder the road curved around. He did not move when we approached but stuck out his tongue to test the air. Cantana laughed. I drove on with his directions. The air hot and dry but salty some from the sea also. I felt it on my arms. In my skin. The wind peeled back the tobacco wrap of Cantanas cigarillo as the end reddened.

I helped Mendoza build this house we are going to visit. Cantana said some minutes later. We met each other working for the bootlegger in Texas. We were your age maybe. I soaked my hands in the salt water each night they were so raw from lifting stones. I swore I would never do that work again. Like you and the work on the hotel. You would rather fight dogs verdad? Cantana grinned.

I nodded.

I used the money I had to buy land in Canción. Tierra. The word alone empties your chest of breath. Stirs men to war. My father used to say this often. Take some advice dog fighter. Cantana set his bare hand on my shoulder. You fight one. Two more fights. Then buy yourself some land in Canción. Find some nice girl. He laughed. Raise me some more dog fighters.

I drove slowly over the sharp rocks embedded in the uneven road to avoid a flat tire. Ahead we came to a mound of stones. A grave. We had been more than an hour in the limousine from Canción by then. I slowed the car to look over the stones. I thought of the wagon we had passed before.

I cannot even imagine life then. Cantana said. Traveling distances between places you did not know how far apart they were. Leaving behind what you could not carry. Cantana shook his head. I have no patience for that life.

I drove on. Remembering how my forearms had tingled the night I killed the husband in Northern California. Vargas in Canción. Some miles after the grave we came down through the pass. Ahead I noticed a stand of low date palms over the top of a small knoll. The Pacific Ocean spread out massively beyond this. A colder shade of blue than the Sea of Cortés. Whitecapped waves. At the top of the knoll Mendozas stone house lay below this. The remaining length of the road filled with obsidian shards.

Stop here. Cantana tossed his cigarillo. The embers scattering brightly among the charcoal colored rocks. We will walk the rest of the way.

Before allowing me to lift the crate of dynamite from the limousine Cantana took from his jacket a length of dark blue ribbon. With his smooth fingers he tied a neat bow around the crate.

Bueno! He clapped and threw his hands back. He will like that just fine.

As we walked down the knoll I was excited to see the palms and the house and the dog pens to the side because they only brought me closer to what would have to be done. I was nervous also. Cantana walked in front of me careful of his steps. His hair combed. Trying to find the reflection of his eyes on the insides of his sunglasses I thought about taking a rock to the back of his head right then. His steps placed delicately in his dress shoes. Uncertain over the rocks. The road opened below into a flat yard. From this a path then led even farther down past the stone house to high sand dunes and beyond that the ocean as far as my eyes allowed. The wind strong without the bay we had in Canción for it to calm over. Heavy with salt. Several dark vultures circled high over the beach. I could hear the waves but I could not see them over the dunes. I could not see what held the vultures interest. I would have thrown the heavy crate of dynamite into the small of Cantanas back and then crushed his head with a stone when he crumpled back on himself but I did not know yet if Mendoza was alone. And where he kept his guns.

Mendoza! Cantana yelled. Mendoza!

A group of dogs we could not see stirred and barked in their pens. There must have been dozens of them in the low sheds. At the end of this row of pens stood a ring fenced in. One like those we fought in on the rooftop. An American made pickup was parked at the center of the yard. The back of the truck was made into several small pens with fencing and wire for the dogs to travel in. Chickens pecked open cigarette ends that were swept by the wind against the house.

On the opposite side of the house from the pens sat a small wood shed. Mendoza stepped from the door of this shed and into the shade of a tree just beyond the yard. A bloody rag over his shoulder. He waved us toward him before returning to the shed. I was grateful to see that he was alone. I decided to wait until they were together. To make sure Mendoza would not have a gun. A knife I could handle fine. I began to feel warm.

My friend. Cantana said when we stepped into the cool of the shed. Your road needs some work. When the tractors are done at the hotel I will bring them over here.

It will only wear it down more. Mendoza said. We need the rocks for traction when the rains come. I file the stones down so they are not so sharp.

When Mendoza turned to face us he stepped to the side of what he was working at. He wiped his hands on the towel and then offered his hand to Cantana. Behind this I saw the dog with its head held in a vice. A bar at the back of its mouth held fast with rope to keep the jaws open and the teeth exposed. A large belt wrapped around the waist of the dog to hold him in place. The dog growled some when we entered. Saliva dripped from its purple lips onto the dirt of the floor in flat dark pools. Its gums bleeding. Its tail wagging. Ropes holding the neck and legs had been looped and tied tightly to hooks in the walls and over cordón beams in the ceiling. Mendoza stepped over these to set the towel down. Several of the front teeth had been sharpened to a fine but not delicate point. On a workbench along this I noticed a handful of different sized files. Flecks of white tooth caught in the damp grooves. Mendoza and Cantana shook hands warmly. Then Mendoza turned to me. I still held the heavy crate against my chest. Staring at the dog I forgot why I had come.

He will be very happy that you have brought this. Mendoza said to Cantana. He has been down on the beach for two days now digging. Mendoza took the crate from me. How are you? He asked me.

Fine. I whispered almost. And you?

Busy. He indicated the dog behind him with its large head in the vice. Its eyes and tongue and tail the only thing moving. But good.

Is he down there now? Cantana asked and I came to as if from a dream.

Yes.

There was another then. One more that I would have to kill. I could not decide if I should kill these men together now or wait until I had judged the strength and size of the third man. Also I wanted to make sure there were no dogs out of their pens. I knew they would defend Mendoza and I did not have the claws or the heavy rug around my forearm to fight them. I had never fought the sharpened teeth. In all my time in Canción they had gone to Ramón.

Let us go and see his work. Cantana clapped his hands. I want to see this catch of his.

We followed Mendoza from the shed and down the narrow path toward the sand dunes. Grains thin in the wind along their delicate crests. I squinted my eyes. Scolded myself for not taking a file from the shed. A hammer. We left the dog with the bar pushed back in its mouth. Its tongue feeling around the rope at the corner of its molars. Whimpering.

Cantana and I walked looking down at our steps while Mendoza looked comfortably out over the horizon.

How do you keep the dog from gagging? The businessman asked Mendoza.

I do not put the bar so far back in their mouths. The dog trainer answered. When I first started this they would vomit on my boots. Pants. Todos.

I always thought that smell was your cheap cologne. The businessman chided his friend.

We saw the third man when we came to the top of the dunes. The he they had spoken of in the shed was a boy. The ten or eleven year old son of Mendoza. He sat on a boulder at the edge of the beach looking over the reflection of the sun on the sea. Throwing stones into the waves some distance away. The sounds of where we placed our steps hidden beneath the crashing waves. To the side of the boulder where he sat the boy had dug a large pit. He had left the shovel at the base of a great pile of sand to the side. I could not see what was at the bottom of the large pit because of this pile he had made. The vultures circled above. My heart went into my stomach at the sight of this boy. I would have to decide.

Ernesto! Mendoza called over the waves. Uncle Cantana has brought you a present.

The boy turned and leaped from the boulder and came running

toward us. Cantana laughed a short laugh the laugh of a child himself again when he saw the boy smile. In the shade of the boulder the hipbones of a large old dog struggled to stand in the sand. He struggled and then decided better. His tongue hanging in the heat. Cantana gestured to Mendoza to hand him the crate. Never taking his sunglasses from the direction of the boy. Then the businessman knelt one knee in the sand and set the crate over his thigh. The boy stopped before him. Their eyes at the same level.

What do you say? Mendoza asked his son.

What is it?

Ernesto!

Thank you Uncle Cantana.

It is nothing.

Then the boy tore at the bow. The men smiled. Cantana set the crate in the sand and the boy wrenched back the slats using the ends of his small fingers.

You are going to get a sliver under your fingernail. Mendoza warned his son. Run for a hammer and bar.

But the boy chose not to listen. Instead he bit his lower lip and pried until he fell back into the sand when the slats came off in his hands. The men laughed. The boy sat forward and looked into the crate. The sticks of dynamite lay still and quiet and dangerous. The boy lifted one delicately.

Cuidado. Cantana said softly. Do you have what else we need? He asked Mendoza without looking from the boy.

In the shed. Ernesto go up and bring it down.

The boy sprinted up the path.

Come see what he has. Mendoza said.

Cantana and I followed Mendoza toward the pit the boy had dug. The dog in the shade of the boulder was harmless lying in the shade.

Ernesto looped chain around the tail to move it. Mendoza said to us. Then around the jaw and over the top of its head.

At the bottom of the pit a large whale curled with its mouth into its tail. It had died in the Pacific and washed onto the beach bloated and stinking. Curled now so splintered ends of its ribs pierced through the tough skin like baby teeth in the sun against the red muscle and blood. Cantana whistled in disbelief.

Dios mío. He struggled to light a cigarillo in the wind. Mendoza cupped his hands around the flame for his old friend. I never thought Mendoza to be a father of a son. This man who sharpened teeth. Thank you. Cantana said.

Can you believe he dug this by himself? Mendoza continued with much pride. Using the burros he moved the tail. And then the head. The tail and then the head again. Only little distances at a time.

He is very patient. Cantana said just below the sound of the sea.

I promised him we would help him cover it.

Dog fighter? Cantana looked to me,

I nodded.

I would do anything for my godson. Cantana clasped the mans shoulder.

Mendoza smiled at this. He gestured with his fingers for a taste of the businessmans cigarillo. Beyond this the sun lingered brilliantly on the crests of the waves. Filled the deep troughs with a turquoise colored shade. The skin of the whale was torn and scarred. Dried barnacles spotted its sides and tiny crabs moved awkwardly on claws in the water that had seeped through the sand into the large pit. The water made the dead whales blubber soft and loose where the chains had worked into it deeply. The smell was so strong I asked for one of Cantanas cigarillos.

How can he stand the smell? Cantana asked.

He says he does not even notice.

The wind had dried a light salt over the brow of the large ink colored eye that now saw nothing but still reflected light. This eyeball peppered with sand. A cluster of flies blown by the wind. The men stood with their backs to me. Unaware that I was sent to kill them. Mendoza handed the cigarillo back to Cantana and then pointed to a vulture with a crushed skull on the other side of the pile of sand.

He chased that down.

Ernesto? Cantana laughed.

No. The dog.

This one that can barely lift himself from the sand?

He pretended he was dead. Mendoza smiled with great pride. He did not blink the entire day. We stood above and watched the vulture hop up to him. He went to poke the dog in the eye with his beak and then the dog put the birds entire head in his mouth and crushed the skull.

Throw him in with the whale. Cantana suggested.

No. This old fish gets a spot on this beach all to himself. Mendoza said. Besides. I think the dog would tear off my arm before he let me have that dead bird. Let him drag it around for a while until it begins to smell also. I will have the boy boil it and feed it to those in the pens.

The wet nose of the old dog had been sprinkled with sand. Dozing.

Did you ever fight him? I asked Mendoza but Cantana answered for the trainer.

I once witnessed this dog kill a man after the man broke both of his back legs. The businessman then turned to Mendoza. Does he still do the trick?

No.

Are you certain? Cantana nudged the trainer.

Do not tease him. Mendoza answered sharply.

You need to show the dog fighter the trick.

No.

The dog. Cantana held up his hand before his mouth to lean and whisper more to me but Mendoza interrupted.

Not anymore he does not.

But then the boy with his chin pressed to the detonation box and arms full of wire came down the rocky path. He did not need to look at his bare feet he knew the path so well.

Papá. The boy called Mendoza. The dog is still in the harness.

Mendoza had gone to urinate by the boulder where the old dog lay.

He is fine.

Cantana knelt by the side of the pit. He whispered to the boy.

Does the old one still do the trick?

Papá says no.

Maybe later we will ask him. Okay?

The boy slid down into the pit until standing on the bulk of the whale his head was just level with the beach. The boy held a large knife in his hand.

Before the sun goes down. Cantana smiled.

And then with the knife the boy made deeps cuts into the whales side for the dynamite. His hands and bare feet slippery from the blood. The sand sticking to his legs. Cantana and Mendoza cut the wire and handed them to me to braid. The boy fixed the wire to the three sticks and then buried them within the great body of the whale up to his armpit. In one great cut above the eye so one stick rested against the skull. While I shoveled sand over the tail Mendoza ran the cable a safe distance down the beach. The boy looked up at me to help him from the large pit. If I broke his neck the grown men would be more fierce than I wanted them. But if I left the boy in the pit with the whale and killed Cantana first then Mendoza would not be so difficult. The boy could watch. If he escaped from the large pit he would be too scared to run. Or I could chase him down.

Do not forget the knife. Cantana pointed.

Ernesto gathered his knife in one hand and then held out his arm for me to take the wrist of. Mendoza was still some distance away stretching the cable. Cantanas neck very near to my hands. The boy looked up to me. In his dark eyes I saw myself grab the neck of Cantana. His tongue lolled and his sunglasses fell to the end of his nose and sand sank to his burning eyes sharp as glass shards. The decision as delicate as the memory we have to judge them on. But room enough in the world to hold them all. The deaths and births and murders the same. Even without us making them the world does not end with each one not done or done.

There was too much of my grandfathers voice in this killing. Too much of the poets betrayal and Guillermos passion. None of my own decisions were made until I reached out for the boys wrist and pulled him from the large pit. I tousled his hair. Because that is what you do to keep them from thinking something is wrong.

I decided to wait to kill Cantana until during the return to Canción. The boy did not need to see me become my grandfathers voice before him. That would die with me. And so we spent the next hours burying the whale under a mound of sand. All of us working together. Even the businessman Cantana with his soft hands using a shovel. And when we finished we lured the old dog growling using the dead vulture from his shade in the boulder down the beach. There Mendoza fixed the ends of the wires in the box and the boy put all his weight on the handle and the explosion was tremendous. A cloud of sand lifted into the sky and heavy steaks of whale meat splashed in the water.

We never needed to bury it! Cantana yelled laughing.

Mendoza and the boy were laughing also. I could not stop smiling.

The boy ran to the blackened pit. A large portion of the whale still lay at the bottom of an even larger pit now. The boy danced laughing around the open grave.

Mira. Cantana smiled his smile. Look at the boy.

By not killing the boy or killing in front of him I had decided on my own. And this was more than the voice of my grandfather or the poet had ever given me in all their advice and stories.

Before we left Mendozas Cantana sat at a table in the small stone house and called the boy to his side. He whispered into the boys ear. Then the boy turned to his father standing near the stove preparing food for his dogs after we had eaten and asked.

Can we please show the dog fighter the trick?

Mendoza looked over to Cantana who only smiled at the ceiling. Whistling. Mendoza took a towel from his shoulder and wiped his hands. He squatted before his son.

Will you feed the boys on your own tonight? He asked in a serious voice.

Yes.

Before dark?

Yes. The boys eyes smiled more.

And tomorrow?

Yes.

By yourself?

I promise.

Bring him in.

The boy ran from the room. Cantana gave a short laugh. Smacked the table with his palm flat.

If only you had a son of your own and no wife. Mendoza shook his head at his friend. Both men smiling. Oh how I would torture you.

Look at that boys eyes. The businessman said to his friend. This is no torture.

The boy returned to the room struggling to pull the heavy dog by the scruff of its neck. The old dog wheezed some. Mendoza sat in a chair by the table. He sat facing it. The boy pushed the end of the dog to sit so that he faced Mendoza some feet away.

Bring me the matches. Mendoza instructed the boy. Cantana shifted in his seat like a child. Constantly smiling. Standing on his toes the boy took down a greasy box of matches from a shelf above the stove. Now show him. Mendoza said.

The boy rattled the box in front of the dog and its tail began to wag some flat against the hard packed floor. Whispering some in the sand. Its ears perked and saliva showed at the corners of its mouth. The skin around the eyes heavy with age. Eyes dim but alive now some also. The boy handed the box to his father and stood back as Mendoza leaned toward the dog and said in a voice that was very much pretend.

Excuse me señor. Do you have a light?

The old dogs bark filled the room. He stopped when Mendoza took a single matchstick along the box and in one movement made it a flame arcing toward the dog who opened his jaws and caught it in his mouth. There was a short hiss of the fire on the tongue and then a hard snap of his sharpened teeth on teeth.

Cantana and the boy clapped wildly.

Bravo. Cantana yelled. One more time!

Mendoza threw another lit match into the air for the dog to catch in his mouth. I also clapped. The dogs tail wagging. The saliva in small dark pools on the floor reflecting the dim light of the lanterns hanging from the beams in the room. The same light in all our eyes. Cantana and the boy cheered. Our voices encouraging the old dog to eat fire.

Night had just begun when we drove from Mendozas. The sun barely lowered behind the mountains. The headlights of the limousine emptied the dark before us. I could not stop thinking of the cloud of sand from the explosion. The eyes of that boy when he looked up to me from the hole with the knife and blood on his hands. The old men can find someone else to kill the boys father. I thought. By then I would be with her in my arms and thinking of nothing else.

We were some miles from Mendozas when I decided to pull to the side of the road to end this.

To protect Canción. They told me. Your name will be in the voices of this city as long as there is a city to carry them.

I could not wait any longer. I did not care if it was wrong. I had not cared for the voices for some time now. Only for her. Cantana had been napping with a cigarillo lit in his gloved hand out the window. The shoveling had made him tired. He had no idea what was before him.

I have to piss. I told Cantana when he stretched and yawned after I stopped the limousine.

I will join you.

The only sound in that darkness was that of our feet on the gravel. Some bugs knocking into the headlights. The engine tinked. We stood alongside one another waiting to piss. Cantana farted.

I appreciate you driving dog fighter. He said. You are a good man. Good for our small city. One day when you quit fighting dogs I will make you mayor.

From the light of the car in the side of my eyes I saw that Cantana still wore his sunglasses. I decided then to be careful not to break them so that I could present them to Guillermo and the poet to show them that the businessman was dead. I urinated.

That was something today. Cantana continued.

It was. I answered. Concentrating on my own thoughts. Pressing hard to finish so that I could keep the blood from inside the limousine.

She loves you you know? Cantana said. Buttoning his pants.

What?

My niece. The one you are always making eyes at at the fighting. I said she loves you.

I had no words.

Do you love her?

When still I did not answer the businessman laughed a short hard laugh.

This is what I thought.

I shook myself without thinking to and then buttoned my pants. I said nothing. I could feel Cantana smiling in that dark.

I want you to marry her. He said. To work for me here in Canción.

I do not believe you. I said finally.

You have always been so suspicious of me. Why?

I do not like that you always wear the sunglasses. I said.

You have your strength to hide behind and I have these. But I will make you an offer. You bring to me Guillermo and his old friend the poet and I will give you my nieces hand in marriage.

I do not know what you mean. I said.

Yes you do my friend. I had to be sure but both you and

Guillermo betrayed yourselves to me today. Pretending not to know one another. And while I am disappointed in you I know that you are a young man and have been misled. But my offer stands.

I do not trust you.

I should be the one not to trust you my friend. Have I ever given you anything but my word?

I said nothing.

Answer me.

No.

They want you to kill me today verdad? The businessman stepped toward me. Answer me young man.

Yes.

If I do not return to Canción alive I have told Elías to kill her. But my offer stands. Do not answer me now. There will be a dinner party at my house at the end of this week. I have guests coming from the United States.

But she is your mistress?

Unlike the other businessmen of Canción I am faithful to my wife. She is my niece. She has only been with us in Canción for several months. She is a very intelligent young woman. Very stubborn. I knew she would be perfect for the fighting and so she pretends to be my mistress. She keeps the money and I win in front of the other businessmen.

I do not believe you.

Then kill me dog fighter. Do what these old men are holding you to. And then when you return to Canción tonight alone know that the woman you love will be dead. But if you take my offer then I would like you to be my guest at the dinner party. To sit at my table. And that night I would like to know if I should announce your wedding. Do not decide now my friend. Think on this some.

Cantana lit a cigarillo. The flame reflected in his sunglasses as he raised the match to his face. Cupped by his bare hand the flame flickered in the wind. Cantana tossed the match to the side of the road.

Will you come?

If I was not to kill him then I was to join him.

Yes. I answered.

Good. He said without looking to me while walking to the limousine. I am going to nap some more. Wake me when we return to Canción.

NINE

It was April. The beginning of Holy Week. I had been in Canción for a little under nine months. In shadows at the back of
the cathedral I chose the last pew. Whispers of an old woman in
black hunched over her rosary at the altar filled that enormous
space. The woman knelt before a small statue of the Virgin Mary
surrounded by fresh flowers and numerous coins. Candle wax covered the bare cracked plaster feet of the statue and the smell of
incense burning in a brass dish beside her reached even to me faintly
metallic descending on the constant words of prayer sharp and clear
from the darkest shadows of the ceiling.

The stone walls of the cathedral were without windows but
shafts of sunlight came down over the wooden pews from several
narrow openings. The rest of the cathedral was shadow though and
this and the stone floor and walls kept the large space cool during
the heat of the day. Many candles flickered at a prayer altar to the
side of the Virgin. Large columns lined the central aisle of the cathedral and along the northern wall wine colored wood confessionals
sat empty. Shadows darkened up from these back into shadows of
the arched ceiling even darker more and only when the massive
wood doors at the main entrance to the cathedral opened was there

light enough to reveal chandeliers that were lowered and lit for mass.

The poet was correct. The Resurrection of Jesus on the towering brick wall above and behind the altar was beautiful. In the dim candlelight and shadow a handsome young man He stepped toward the empty pews swathed in flowing white burial cloths. His chest naked and the wound in His side exposed. He held His bleeding palms at His hips upturned so to accept those sitting before Him. Staring at the Resurrection I sat trying to empty my thoughts of what this gesture meant. I had done much walking in Canción but after Cantana presented his offer I needed someplace to sit and concentrate. I did not climb the steps of the cathedral to pray or for some answer but only for someplace to rest from the decision itself. I knew that no one would think to find me there.

The repetition of the old womans words were indistinct until I concentrated on each one. I slouched some in that last pew listening to her words while inspecting the Resurrection. I was quiet so not to be disrespectful of the woman. Jesus in His burial cloths loomed over the altar. His lips set comfortably in His silence. A hint of a knowing smile placed at the corner of His eyes. His step down from the wall in that welcoming gesture troubled me most. He stepped toward the pews but invited with His hands also. I did not feel I would have to walk all the way to Him or that He was going to walk all the way to me. The candlelight of the prayer altar and those few candles at the feet of the Virgin met curiously in shadows below the Resurrection. With the gentle breeze swirling in through the narrow openings the shimmering burial cloths seemed to billow and relax. The flames of the candles danced with shadows.

The rows of wood pews were more and more smooth as I approached the altar. The old womans cadence did not break when I climbed the steps. When I stood at the feet of Jesus I noticed then that the Resurrection was composed of thousands of tiny pieces of cracked tile and glass and mirror. I reached up and touched the shimmering pieces of the pierced feet. From the back of the cathedral the young mans skin had been absent of the many colors. I understood that light reflecting in the glass and mirror had deceived me. Made me think the cloths were flowing. But it was that shards of green glass had been set next to tiles of purple and red. And while the clay colored tiles were the most I did not believe how absent of color the mans skin was from the back of the cathedral. I did not understand how this could be. Running my fingers over the tiles of the mosaic I noticed the silence of the woman. She had gone. I turned and looked over the empty cathedral wondering which pews Guillermo and the poet slept in when they had first arrived in Canción.

The day before. When Cantana and I returned from Mendozas I lay on my bed at the dentists waiting for the soft knock of the silent thief. I decided to say good bye to them both. To warn Javier that I was leaving. Staring at the ceiling as shadows slowly crossed I listened for the smallest sounds on the street. I closed my eyes. A cool breeze stole through the window of the small room and soon I imagined myself lying beside the creek in Northern California. I walked among the prune orchards. Frost weighing on brittle yellowing leaves. A sharp moon in the clear night sky lighted down from the saw blade sil- houette of a redwood lined ridge. Through a field of knee high grass I followed a worn path down to the creek. Leaning against a fallen log I watched moonlight dance blue flames across the shallow moving water. Across little black stones until the flames became a string of blue bulbs on the creeks dark surface. I looked ahead into the stand of willow where she came from the shadows of parting green limbs on a low shiny black stage bathed in blue dawn light. Her hair tied back. The red dress. She held her hands before her inviting me to dance.

I woke late in the night. I must have slept through the soft knock. There was no sound from the back room. No light from under the door seeping into the courtyard. I gathered my things into a new canvas bag I had bought several days before. I folded the many sheets of paper covered in pencil smudged poems. The suit I rolled neatly. Before I went I left some money for the dentist on the bed. I wanted to leave some note of thanks but could not find the words I felt were right. I snuck down the inside stairwell and placed my palm flat against the door pushing as I pulled to close it silently behind me. Heading north I followed an alley that ran parallel to the street of Guillermos shop and the salon. It would be several hours before the sun rose over the trees of her square. I was not tired.

It was afternoon when Javier crossed the square with his hands in his pockets to where I sat in the café. He sat in the chair beside mine. Both of us facing her window.

It is a beautiful afternoon. Javier said after a moment.

It is. I answered.

Usually I am just now waking. With my work I stay up very late. I see the sun rise more than I see it set. But there are some days when I wake early in the morning. But usually on those days I am woken by someone. With my work if it is possible I do not like to be awake at that hour.

I understand. I said. The thief and I still had not taken our eyes from her window. I sipped from my coffee and then asked. Were you woken this morning?

I was. He said plainly. Some young men came to visit me. They wanted to know where a friend of mine was.

What did you tell them?

That I did not know.

Did they leave you alone then?

No. They suggested I go and find this friend of ours.

Ours?

Ours.

Señor? The old waiter interrupted Javier.

Café por favor. When the old man had shuffled to the back of the café Javier continued. These friends they told me a story. Apparently my friend was supposed to do something for them but did not. Have you heard this?

There was a boy. I said then in a serious voice. Mendozas son.

There was no chance on the return to Canción?

She is his niece. I said then.

Who? The thief asked.

I raised my chin toward her window.

Everyone thinks she is his mistress. I told him. Otherwise they would not think it right of him to bring her to the fighting.

The old man returned with Javiers coffee.

Thank you señor. The thief said. Once the old man had returned to the counter to read his newspaper Javier brought his chair close to mine. After I left our friends I went to visit this friend of mine that they are looking for. I did know where he was but I told them nothing. I have come to tell him this. This and that he should leave Canción immediately. But this friend of mine was already gone from where I thought he was. The thief continued. You see he left without saying good bye.

We are each given only one good bye. And I am not yet dead.

A line of the poets? Javier asked.

No. I winked. Something of my own.

For the next few days I slept on the concrete floor of the abandoned mine in the hills and sat late into the night in the back pew of the cathedral. Narrowly missing the great crowds for all the masses that week. In the cathedral I convinced myself I was concentrating on the decision. But when I rose from the bench each dawn and walked quickly to her square after waiting for her lamp I could not convince myself that I was not hiding.

In that quiet I hoped the poet would find me. He should have known from our walks that this is where I would be. Each time the massive doors opened my eyes burned some with the light. The ropes from the large chandeliers were tied at a taut angle to hooks in the walls. But the poet never came. Maybe because he knew that is where I would be and to come to me without a weapon or a group of the young men would betray his friendship with Guillermo. Guillermo was not as intelligent as the poet but the poet also did not have the passion Guillermo had. Together they were balanced though. Together they could oppose Cantana from the shadows.

Still I wanted the poets advice.

On Thursday the day of the dinner party in the afternoon I swam to the mouth of the bay and washed on the rocks below where the canoe boys had jumped. In the market that morning I bought a comb and a bar of soap and shaved without a mirror running the ends of my fingers over and over the skin of my face feeling for the last bristles. The tiniest imperfections. In the market I had not gone near to where the poet had his stall but when I found the small pickpocket I gave him a note to give to the poet.

What if he is not there? The small pickpocket asked.

Then go to the salon. I said.

I do not like that other man.

Neither do I. But this is important.

How important? The small pickpocket smiled holding the note behind his back.

If you do not get this to him now. I bent over so that my eyes were level with his. I will break off your arm and beat you over the head with the bloody stump.

And then will you buy me some candy? The boy did not move.

Yes. I smiled. Now run.

On the beach at the south end of the city where I could be alone and unseen I dried standing naked in the wind. I unrolled my suit from my canvas bag and put maybe too much cologne on. I had never worn something like this before and to smell myself in it now and then was very different from how I was used to being. I wondered if I would be able to smell her perfume through it. I considered swimming again to bathe but it was already evening.

Elías stood before the door to Cantanas. He was without his revolver.

I am glad you have come. He said to me then. I did not want to have to kill you. Ramón said that you would come to work for Cantana one day but I did not believe him.

How much did you lose?

Not much. The doorman smiled but looked away from my eyes. Lucky for me I never had to pay him.

Elías held open a small metal door set in two thick wood ones. On the backside of these doors were large iron hinges and several locks that Elías turned as well as a board that lay in a cradle lengthwise across the smaller door to keep it from being pushed in. I stood in this shaded entrance looking up a cobblestone driveway into a spacious courtyard where the limousine had been parked.

Did you bring any weapons? He asked me then.

No.

May I check?

I raised my arms for the doorman.

You have gotten skinny. Elías said. This will not be very good for you in the fighting of dogs my friend.

I am done fighting dogs. I said. That is why I am here.

The doorman nodded. Then as if to reassure me of my decision he said in a soft voice he used I think to convince himself often.

Cantana is a good man to work for my friend. You will see.

The chrome fender of the limousine shone after dust had been washed from the black frame since our drive to Mendozas. Only when Elías and I passed the limousine did I notice a smudge in a lower corner of the windshield. Arched passageways filled with shadows supported a balcony that ran around the inside of the second floor of the compound. The walls were painted a dark yellow and were beautifully offset by a black iron railing with fine swirling details that lined this balcony. Several doors on each of the four sides of the second floor of the courtyard were left open for music and voices to pass through. Above one of these doors stood a young man with a rifle walking on the roof. I followed him until he came to another young man dressed the same in dark clothes also holding a rifle. I was not surprised to see them. In front of each of the doors different colored bougainvillea grew in terra cotta pots set in holders along the railing. The vines of these flowering plants had been trained along the shadowed archways of the first floor. I stood for a moment at the center of this until Elías laughed at my amazement and said.

Follow me.

The inside of the compound was dark and cool. With dark wood walls and a wide staircase. Along a hallway of the second floor we walked silently over an intricate rug. One that in any other house would be hung on the wall. I followed the doorman toward music and voices. I heard a womans laugh behind two doors with smoky windows down the hall. I put my hand to my hair to arrange it without looking. I was more nervous to see her than Cantana.

Elías opened the doors into a large sunken room with a dance floor at the center. A long rectangular banquet table was beautifully set along the back wall where windows opened to a wide view of the Bay of Canción. When my eyes adjusted to the light Cantana was already upon me with his hands up and arms open. A dozen very well dressed and handsome businessmen and their beautiful mistresses decorated the room. One of the mistresses licked her thumb and rubbed lipstick from the shirt collar of a businessman. Those who were dancing stopped and stood across from one another smiling. Cantana was not wearing his sunglasses and his eyes for as much as I had imagined them red and glowing were unremarkable. As he came to me over his shoulder I found her holding a wineglass delicately by the stem standing at the edge of the dance floor talking with several other women. Our eyes met and she smiled. The music to some song had just ended and the musicians were tuning their instruments to begin something new.

My friend. Cantana said as I walked down the two low stairs to shake hands with him. He clasped my shoulder with his gloved hand. I am glad to see that you have come. Then he leaned forward and said. By coming here you have made your decision clear to me?

Yes. I answered.

Good. Then come meet our friends.

With her eyes on me I felt awkward in my suit and uncomfortable dress shoes. My cologne suddenly very strong. My ears felt very warm. Cantana led me through the room from businessman to businessman. I shook hands but wiped my own on my pants to take the sweat from them so that those in the room would not recognize how nervous I was. As we stepped from one businessman to another my eyes met hers through the shoulders and arms and laughing and conversation between us. Cantana introduced me to the businessmen as a friend and although most knew who I was he was careful to never once introduce me as a dog fighter. We were nearing where she stood. Many of the businessmen I had seen at the fights before but never met. Their faces and names still a blur with her in the room. Soft spoken old men with quick eyes. Their skinny mistresses. It took all my concentration to pull my eyes from her to seem courteous when meeting these men.

Finally Cantana led me to the side of the American investor. The American was a tall man almost as tall as myself and with broad shoulders and a healthy frame. His face was very tan and his eyes the clear blue of the bay. He spoke fluent Spanish and the businessmen he spoke with all seemed very fond of him. Only to this man did Cantana mention that I fought dogs and this he said in a whisper.

Well. I look forward to seeing this someday.

No no. Cantana spoke up. He is done with that now. He has come to work for us.

Even better. The American shook my hand.

I could feel her watching while I shook hands with this man. The musicians began a new song. A delicate melody for the mistresses to accept the soft hands of the businessmen. Cantana took my upper arm in his hand and gently led me to her. The women she stood with fell back like unfolding petals of some beautiful flower.

My friend. Cantana said to me reaching for her hand. I would like to introduce you to my lovely niece.

I took her small hand in my own and short of breath I said.

The pleasure is mine.

I held her hand a moment longer than was necessary and Cantana laughed a short laugh at this before clasping me on the shoulder and then calling to everyone for attention.

Let us sit and eat. Cantana said. I did not want to let go of her hand and I felt that she was reluctant to release mine but Cantana ushered us to the table. Lovers who would rather be left to themselves than eat for their own good.

At the banquet table thirteen of us sat man mistress man until Cantana sat at the head of the table but to the right of the American. I sat at the other end of the table. She sat next to Cantana opposite the American. The fading sunlight played in the imperfections of a mother of pearl clasp that held her dark hair above her ears and showed the gentle curve of her neck. Her eyes a softer green than I had seen before. Not jewels. The red dress she wore was the same as the one I had seen her wearing the night of my first fight. My only distraction from her eyes was the businessmen at the end of the table where I sat intently asking about the fighting while their quiet mistresses made eyes at me when I answered. Cantana and the American spoke to no one but each other and those around them except for her seemed to be listening very closely to their conversation. I ate awkwardly with the expensive silverware and felt embarrassed when I looked up chewing to find her eyes on mine smiling. It was strange that Mendoza was not at the table but then he was a trainer and not one of the businessmen. I drank little wine to keep my thoughts clear as to how it was that I was going to kill Cantana and the American. I did not want to do this in front of her but I knew that it had to be done tonight.

At the end of the meal the men sat smoking. Sipping expensive whiskey the American had brought with him specially. Cantanas face seemed empty without the sunglasses. His cheeks red with the warmth of the alcohol and food. I hoped that he and the American were very full because it would take the fight out of them. When the table was cleared Cantana stood and made a short toast. He was careful with his words and I thought he was very drunk.

To the success of the hotel! He said raising his glass. And the many more projects in the future of Canción.

While the businessman spoke she looked from my eyes up to Cantana and then back to me and then with the back of her hand she knocked over her glass so that red wine spilled over the businessmans place setting and some onto the front of his white shirt. Cantana took a short but quick step back from the table. His chin pressed to his chest. The abrupt movement unusual for his calm behavior. I prepared myself to kill him there when he raised his voice at her but he did not. She put her hand to her mouth and smiled the smile of a child. A fine actress herself. The businessman laughed as one of those serving dinner ran to his side with towels to clean the mess.

No no. He said. I am fine.

At his side she took her hand from her mouth and said something to Cantana that I could not hear and he smiled back and took her hand in his own. Then he raised his glass again as we raised ours.

To the success of the hotel! Cantana said and when her eyes met mine she winked. Now if we could only get the sun to set over the bay instead of over the mountains. That would be something!

To this everyone applauded and laughed.

The music picked up again. Several of the businessmen danced with their mistresses but most complained they were too full. One businessman chided another for threatening to steal his mistress for himself as he danced with both women. Resting his swollen cheeks on each of their shoulders one at a time smiling with his eyes closed. I sat with my hands in my lap quiet when Cantana rose from his seat and came down to my own. The red stain on his shirt. The beauty of her gesture. With his hand on my shoulder he said.

I think now my friend you should ask my niece to dance.

I stood and took a step from my chair. Cantana straightened the corners of my coat and smoothed the wrinkles in the arms. Those who sat around us looked up at this grinning. I looked to her and in her smile she knew how awkward I felt but determined also to be near to her.

Would you like to dance? I asked her with my hand out for her to accept.

Very much. She answered.

Those already on the dance floor made room for us. The song was very nice. Very delicate and slow but with a melody rising steadily. She smelled of cocoa butter and I breathed this deeply into my lungs and it filled my chest with warmth. When she tilted her head back to look up to my face the soft ends of her long hair played gently over my fingers cupping the small of her back.

Look at them! Cantana called. The most beautiful woman in all of Mexico dancing with our greatest dog fighter. We should make them breed.

The men and women looked to one another around us. The American raised his glass. She arched her neck gracefully to the side so that I could lean to hear her whisper into my ear.

You dance very well. She said.

I have never done this before in my life. I answered.

Well you do it very well.

I blame you. I said.

She smiled at these words and this for me meant everything.

The song was too short. But it was enough for me to realize how much more she was to me now. Entirely her own and nothing of my imagination. I had been a fool to make her something to me from so far all this time. With her it was as it had been with the mosaic in the cathedral. I did not know her even when I danced with her. I would not know her until I came to know all of her pieces. The words her voices would make me.

Cantanas voice broke our stare. Do you mind if I borrow our friend here for a moment? He asked her.

Of course. She said. As long as you promise to return him to me when you are finished.

Look at the size of this man. Cantana laughed. Who am I to stop what he does?

The American joined Cantana and me as we walked through the smoky doors of the room. Candles flames flickering in silver holders curved up from the wine colored walls dimly illuminating the narrow hallway. The intricately woven rug softening the steps of our heavy soles on the hardwood floor. I noticed Elías at the bottom of the staircase. He smiled up at me and began to climb the stairs. Over my shoulder I heard him head in the opposite direction of us toward the sunken room. When we came to the door at the end of the long hallway Cantana brought from the pocket of his pants a set of keys. I stared at the back of his and the Americans head. This was the moment. I would break their necks. There would be no blood. In the courtyard a dog barked.

When I stepped into the room one of the two men that I had seen on the roof hit me in the face with the butt of the rifle stock. I fell to the floor. My jaw broken. When I looked up the other man kicked me in the ribs. They broke easily.

Enough! Cantana ordered. That is enough.

With my hand on my jaw I let my forehead rest against the cool of the floor. The pain was very strong all down my neck and my ears rang. I could not swallow my own saliva. When I raised my head from the floor I saw that Guillermo and the poet were on their knees to the side of the businessmans desk. Their faces beaten and their hands tied behind their backs. The poet kept his head cocked to the side to prevent blood from dripping down from his broken nose.

Stand up. Cantana said to me then. His voice severe. He was not drunk at all. Get off the floor and stand up.

The American sat in an expensive wood chair turned from where it faced the front of the businessmans desk. The room was without windows. A lamp with a colorful stained glass shade was the only light in the room. This sat on a small table at the end of a dark patent leather couch. Cantana poured himself and the American a drink from a crystal decanter set on a cabinet behind his desk. The pain throbbing throughout the muscles of my face. My eyes watered. Cantana came around to sit on the front edge of the desk facing me. I could feel the two men aiming their rifles at my chest. Elías had gone into the room to get her I thought. The businessman set his hand on a piece of paper on the desk. It was the note that I had given the small pickpocket in the market. I worried about the small thief but I knew Cantana would not kill or have killed a young boy. The businessman picked up the paper and looked it over shaking his head.

You have betrayed me dog fighter. Cantanas teeth stained red from the wine. The stain on his shirt blood. I made you an offer honestly and then you come into my house and accept it but only after sending this note to your friends.

Cantana handed the note to the American. He read it over and then laid the paper flat on the desk.

I am very disappointed in you. Cantana continued. I offered you a tremendous opportunity here. But you have deceived me. Gone behind my back and warned these two men. Cantana reached to his side and held up the sheet of paper. You wrote this? That you were coming here to kill me?

I said nothing.

Cantana nodded to one of the men with the rifles. He kicked me in the stomach. I was prepared though so it did not hurt too much. Still the broken ribs made it difficult to breathe.

I know you wrote it. Cantana continued. I have my ways of knowing but what I do not understand is why? Why after I said she is yours?

I do not believe you.

What reason have I given you to doubt me? These men. Your friends here. They force you to join them and still you return to them when it is I who has what you desire most? You must tell me why? I have been thinking this over very much but I cannot decide why you would be such a. Cantana searched for the word when the poet spoke for him.

Fool.

Yes. Fool! Cantana laughed. Thank you. He said to the poet.

Guillermo laughed and this immediately distracted Cantana.

What is so funny old man?

I was only thinking. The veteran said.

Thinking about what?

How ashamed your father would be of you.

Ashamed?

Disappointed.

My father would have you killed for what you have done to me. Sending this fool to murder me. Cantana spit the word at the old man.

Because like yourself he could not do it himself. Guillermo spoke again. Yes he could hold a boys hand over fire but more than that he had no stomach for the violence.

Cantana laughed.

Maybe so. He said. But you will not be so fortunate as I was. Cantana made a fist of his gloved hand in front of the old mans face. I love the violence. Just like the dog fighter here. He turned to me then. She can never be yours now. You realize this?

I felt the poets eyes on me. I said nothing. Without moving my eyes I had been searching the room for something I could use as a weapon. But there was nothing and the two men with the rifles were too far away. If I made it to one the other would have the chance to shoot me. I wondered if I could still fight after being shot. If the pain would stop me.

I am going to give you a last chance though. Cantana said then. Let us say to be with her in the future. Guillermo here is dead. I do not know this other man but if he is a friend of Guillermo and a friend of yours then I do not want to know him. I think for me he is probably better dead than alive. But this also is not for me to decide. He has not betrayed me personally. So I will give you a chance to save him. And her. You can save her as well. But if you do not take my offer I will do two things. First I will kill both of these old men and then I will burn down the house that she lives in. I will tie her to the bed and let her die in this fire and then I will blame this fire on the old men and their army of young men.

Cowards. The American said as he shifted in his chair. Slouched some and raised his foot to rest on his knee. His socks of expensive silk.

Yes. Cantana agreed. Cowards fighting from shadows. But for her? Your love. I will say these cowards wanted me to die in that fire but that I was not there and my beautiful niece died as a result of these selfish men. Everyone in Canción will know of this and the hotel will have more support than ever. But you can save them dog fighter. Cantana urged. I will give you this last chance and although you have betrayed me twice before I will give you my word on this. I will keep my word if you agree to it. What do you think?

Do not listen to him! The poet yelled at me.

Hombre. Cantana turned to the poet. This young man has the opportunity to save your life. You should listen carefully.

Your word is nothing.

What is your name?

I am the poet.

The poet?

Yes.

Of what?

Canción.

I thought I was the poet of Canción.

You are a pimp.

Well. If your young friend here chooses to save your life then maybe we will see who is the poet and who is the pimp. Cantana turned to me. Do you accept?

What is the offer? I asked.

Very good. The businessman said. It is very wise of you to find out what you are getting into before agreeing to it. Cantana lit a cigarillo. One last dog fight. He said with smoke spilling over his lips. If you kill the dog you live and I let you go. But your friend the poet here and my niece? They die. But. If you die fighting the dog. A most noble death for a dog fighter. They live and then you still my friend have the opportunity to see her in heaven.

What makes you so sure I will not kill the dog and then kill you?

You could. But for the cost of her death? Has your love for her meant nothing all this time? Is her death to you something that can be avenged with my own? I do not think so. You have to look at this from where I am sitting. You have betrayed me twice now. You are dead either way. But I am giving you the opportunity to die in a noble way. A way that will prove your love. I am willing to make a great sacrifice. Are you?

If you die by the dog you will be committing suicide. The poet said. There is no way to heaven with this death.

Do you believe in God dog fighter? Cantana asked me. Because now is the time to pray that there is a God. And that He is a forgiving God. One that will allow you to be with your love someday. Because I. Here on earth. I will not allow this.

Do not believe him. The veteran interrupted. He was wheezing now. Coughing. I noticed small coins of blood on the floor in front of him. The American sat back in his seat. Crossed his foot to the other side. He had followed the conversation carefully with his eyes. I could no longer sense the two men with the rifles behind me.

No no. Cantana said. Do not believe me. Believe Guillermo there. You see the opportunity I am offering you works for me also. It helps solve my problems.

When I kill the dog I will become your problem. I said.

No. Cantana waved his gloved hand before me. The smoke heavy between us. I will have you killed before you ever get near to me. And besides dog fighter. I believe my niece has affected you very much. That your love for her has taken this will from you. I believe your love for my niece is true. That it is something I will never have for myself. I envy that. But I am not above destroying it. I give you my word.

At this the businessman removed the glove and held his right hand before me. The hand was scarred from some terrible burn.

The tissue red and smooth. Cantana was correct. There was no decision to be made.

Where is this dog? I asked accepting his hand.

Good. Cantana stood and then he said to me. You have a good heart dog fighter.

What do you know about the heart? I asked him but he only lowered his eyes to the floor and shook his head slightly smiling.

When we returned to the sunken room she was gone. Elías must have taken her. At the center of the dance floor where I had held her close to me Ernesto the son of Mendoza stood throwing matches to the old dog sitting on his haunches snapping down on the flame to the applause of the businessmen and their mistresses sitting in chairs at the far end of the room. The musicians had gone and Mendoza sat watching his son proudly.

When we came into the room Mendoza stood and walked to the dog with a rope leash in his hand. The boy went to his fathers seat where one of the businessmen tousled his hair. The boy accepted a kiss on the cheek from one of the mistresses. Cantana and the American took their seats as a single ragman carrying the glove and heavy rug shuffled over to where I stood across from the old dog.

No. I said to ragman. Not for this fight.

I looked across the ring at Cantana while the ragman turned his back to me to tease the old dog. The businessman sat without a mistress. Strange looking without his sunglasses. I did not take my eyes from his when the ragman stepped aside from the snarling dog. I did not take my eyes from his when Mendoza yelled.

Bastante!

And I did not take my eyes from his until the dog leaped and brought me to the ground under his weight. This old dog now surprisingly strong and quick his claws tearing through my shirt and into my chest. I leaned back my head to better expose my neck and I felt the pressure when the dog bit on but there was very little pain. So close to the dog I heard his jaw lock. My breathing difficult but not stopped. No blood came from where the teeth had pierced my neck because there were no teeth. The old dog tore at my neck with nothing but his gums. Cantana had Mendoza remove the teeth before the fight. I lay there waiting for the dog to kill me. I pressed down and up on its jaws to choke me but this was not enough. I brought up its claws to cut into the soft of my neck but the dog only wanted to tear at my throat with the teeth he no longer had.

The anger in me then was very great. The frustration even more. The decision to die had taken no time to make. It was the first thing in my life that I was certain of.

I threw the dog off of me and when he charged again I put up my arm as if the heavy rug were there to bite onto. When his jaws locked around my arm I felt his jawbone through the soft gums. I hit him in the head with my fist I was so angry. Hit him again like an angry child frustrated with his parents. Again and again until the dog released my arm and I stood over it kicking and beating it whimpering. I was alone in that room. Hitting and kicking the dog until I straddled it and began to pound its head into the wood floor. And when this did nothing I dragged it by the ears to where the low steps were and beat the dogs head against this edge until blood came from its ears and its tongue flopped loosely over its toothless gums. Smacking flat against the top of my hand each time I lifted the now lifeless head before slamming it back down.

When I felt the dogs bowels warm and wet along my leg I fell forward onto my arms. My forearms hot and sweaty against the cool of the wood floor. I buried my forehead in the nook of my elbow and there I smelled her. The cocoa butter smell from her there on my arm. I began to cry. Hard and quick cries that came deep from within my stomach. I lay like this for some time. My own voice thick in my head. The sound of shuffling feet leaving the room. The dog pulled out from beneath me and then I felt a hand grip my hair and lift my head. When I opened my eyes I saw Cantana in that blur.

The best part? The businessman smiled. I am the only one here who had money on you to kill the dog.

When I swung around to hit him he leaped back and then before my vision went black I saw Elías out of the corner of my eye. The revolver in his hand. His eyes pinched at the corners and his teeth biting down hard on his lower lip in fierce concentration.

I woke several times that night barely able to see my eyes were so swollen. Elías and another man had beaten me unconscious. My ribs cracked and my left arm somehow broken. I felt the cool of the night air pass over my body as we drove. I smelled the cigarette smoke of one of the men driving. At some point they threw water on me to wake and when I did they punched me in the face until I played dead. Lying there listening to their laughter until again I slept without dreaming.

I was very fortunate though. Cantana must have instructed them to leave me by the spring. He knew I would not return for him. That without her there was no reason to return to Canción. I lay on the ground following the shade of a small bush throughout the day for several days sipping water from my cupped hand and chewing on the petals and stems of wildflowers nearby. For three days I was there before a truck came with men who had been working on the roads. When they came I was disappointed to see them. I was disappointed in myself for allowing myself the flowers and water. She was dead. And so was the poet.

If Cantana was anything he was a man of his word.

This was many years ago when I fought dogs in Canción. I am an old man now living in a city I do not care for. I have lived a good life harming no one and helping others I think more than myself. No one here knows who I am and this is fine with me. This is better. No one knows what I have done. What decisions I have made and how they have affected the lives of others. I take some comfort in this. I feel that the world is forgiving me each day. Each day another bead on the rosary I do not say. Each day penance for my sins.

The poet once on one of our walks in the hills handed me a poem he had written in English.

This is for you he said to me. When you learn what it means write one to me. And write it then in English and it will be our secret. But I did not write this for the poet. I have forgiven him and he has I am sure forgiven me. God has nothing to do with this.

When my father was courting my mother he read to her from books of poetry. The poetry she enjoyed most was written in English. The words at first were foreign to her. My father inviting her into some mystery by sharing them. My mother died wanting me to become a man like my father but stronger. Is this not what all women want in the sons of men they love? She wanted this for me and not what the hissing whispers of my grandfather tried for. This is for my mother. But it is also a poem for my father. Something I think he will find in me much pride.

Each day I am in this city alone. Walking at night after a long day of labor but I am not tired. The windows are dark and the street-lamps bright in the limbs of the trees. Each of these days and nights I am only closer to her. Always I think of my death. How I would like to invite it to come soon but then fear that inviting this will only keep me from her. Only God keeps me alive for being ungrateful for this gift. I am like the poet sitting outside the cathedral in the shade of the knoll. He waits for me and I wait for Him. I like to think of myself in this way.

But always I am thinking of her. We are in rooms together with the windows open. She is with the water on in the shower washing the smell of cocoa butter all over her body and singing but not careful with her voice while I am in the other room with a small cool wind on my naked body smiling at the ceiling. My arms behind my head lying on a bed that soon we will make love together on. For that I am still here. This daydream. For her lovely voice singing that

I can hear but never heard. I imagine us in my small room together with her singing with the water running and me on the bed yelling to the ceiling how much I love her. But she pretends not to hear me through her singing with the water and it only makes me smile and yell I love her more. And then she sings and I smile more because we have each other and this is a small game we play as lovers.

The author wishes to acknowledge the excerpts from "El Legarto Viejo" (The Old Lizard) by Federico Garcia Lorca (page 232) and the following poems by Emily Dickinson: "That Love is all there is" (page 91), "God is indeed a jealous God" (page 98), "Not to discover weakness" (page 164), "Crumbling is not an instant's Act" (page 192).